Is he s...
or am I just being paranoia...

The youth seemed earnest and guileless enough, so she chose to think that all this skulking around and dissembling was simply getting to her. Straightforward by nature, she had never been much for espionage or intrigue; left to her own devices, she preferred a more direct approach to any situation.

Alas, that was not possible in this instance.

"That won't be necessary, Lieutenant. I know the way."

"It's no problem, Captain. I'm going that way myself."

Una repressed a few choice Illyrian curse words. Was all of Kirk's crew so inconveniently helpful? She glanced up and down the corridor, weighing her options. The last thing she wanted was for Kirk to hear that she had been loitering outside his quarters for no good reason. What if he or Spock started to put two and two together and guessed what she was actually after?

That just wouldn't do.

"Very well. After you, Lieutenant . . . ?"

"Riley, sir. Lieutenant Kevin Riley, at your service."

She let him step ahead of her, leading the way, before dropping him to the deck with a karate chop to the side of his neck. The strike wasn't quite as efficient as a Vulcan nerve pinch, but it got the job done. The lieutenant lay crumpled at her feet.

"My apologies, Mister Riley, but you were in the wrong place at the wrong time."

STAR TREK®

THE ORIGINAL SERIES

LEGACIES: BOOK 1

CAPTAIN TO CAPTAIN

Greg Cox

Based on *Star Trek*
created by Gene Roddenberry

POCKET BOOKS

New York   London   Toronto   Sydney   New Delhi

Pocket Books
An Imprint of Simon & Schuster, Inc.
1230 Avenue of the Americas
New York, NY 10020

This book is a work of fiction. Any references to historical events, real people, or real places are used fictitiously. Other names, characters, places, and events are products of the author's imagination, and any resemblance to actual events or places or persons, living or dead, is entirely coincidental.

First Pocket Books paperback edition July 2016

POCKET and colophon are registered trademarks of Simon & Schuster, Inc.

For information about special discounts for bulk purchases, please contact Simon & Schuster Special Sales at 1-866-506-1949 or business@simonandschuster.com.

The Simon & Schuster Speakers Bureau can bring authors to your live event. For more information or to book an event, contact the Simon & Schuster Speakers Bureau at 1-866-248-3049 or visit our website at www.simonspeakers.com.

Manufactured in the United States of America

10 9 8 7 6 5 4 3 2 1

ISBN 978-1-5011-2529-4
ISBN 978-1-5011-2530-0 (ebook)

Dedicated to my mom,
who never really understood this crazy sci-fi stuff,
but who was always very supportive of my interests anyway:
driving me to comic book stores
and science fiction conventions,
and, later on, showing off my books to all her friends.

We miss you, Mom.

Historian's Note

The events in this story take place during different missions of the *Starship Enterprise*. In 2245 the *Enterprise* was launched from the San Francisco Yards under the command of Robert April. After a major refit was finished in 2264, command of the starship passed to James Kirk. The events that occur during Kirk's mission take place several months after the *Enterprise* crew's journey to the diplomatic conference on Babel ("Journey to Babel").

2267

One

Captain's log, Stardate 3950.1

The Enterprise *is en route for some much-needed shore leave on Chippewa Prime. In the meantime, we find ourselves expecting a visit from a most distinguished guest, whom Mister Spock knows far better than I . . .*

Tractor beams guided the sleek courier ship into the *Enterprise*'s spacious hangar deck. Half the size of a shuttlecraft, the *Shimizu* was small but fast, designed for emergency deliveries of medical supplies, key diplomatic personnel, or anything else that urgently needed to be someplace yesterday, short of any actual time travel. Its aerodynamic contours enclosed the twin warp nacelles into a pair of triangular wings, the better to allow for planetary landings and atmospheric maneuvers. A white enamel glaze protected its streamlined hull. As Kirk understood it, the decommissioned Starfleet vessel was now more or less at the disposal of their newly arriving visitor, which testified to her illustrious career in Starfleet as well as to the high regard in which she was held.

"Right on schedule," Kirk observed. "I always heard that she was known for her punctuality."

"You heard correctly, Captain," Spock said. "In my experience, she is admirably precise in all matters."

Along with Doctor McCoy, Kirk and Spock viewed the *Shimizu*'s arrival from the observation deck overlooking the landing bay. The men were decked out in their best dress uniforms, complete with medals, decorations, and metallic gold piping. McCoy tugged on his uniform's stiff collar, no doubt wishing he was in his regular blue duty tunic instead.

"So tell me, Spock," the doctor asked, "are you looking forward to chewing the fat with your old crewmate?"

"As a Vulcan, I find that to be a singularly distasteful idiom, but, if you must know, I am indeed pleased at the prospect of renewing our acquaintance." Spock appeared perfectly at ease in his formal attire, which suited his reserved manner and bearing. "She has an exceptional mind, and is much less inclined to indulge in gratuitous emotional displays than certain other Starfleet personnel I could name."

McCoy huffed in mock indignation. "Who are you calling 'gratuitous,' you insufferable, green-blooded—"

"Now, now, gentlemen," Kirk interrupted, chuckling. "Company's calling, so let's be on our best behavior."

"All right," McCoy muttered, "but he started it."

"Excuse me, Captain." Yeoman Lisa Bates joined them on the observation deck. She was a slim, athletic redhead whose coppery tresses were piled high in a stylish beehive. Having recently taken over as Kirk's personal yeoman, after previously serving aboard the *Constellation*, she had so far proven herself organized and attentive to a fault. She held out a data slate and stylus. "Do you have a moment to sign off on the latest requisitions from the galley?"

The *Shimizu* was still touching down on the hangar

deck, so Kirk accepted the proffered items from Bates. A quick glance at the paperwork revealed nothing out of the ordinary, so he approved the requisitions and handed them back to Bates, who lingered on the deck, seemingly in no hurry to depart.

"Is there anything else, Yeoman?" Kirk asked.

"No, sir," she said a trifle sheepishly. "It's just that, well . . ."

Kirk thought he knew what this was about. "Would you like to stay and meet our guest, Yeoman?"

Her youthful face lighted up. "Yes, Captain, with your permission, of course. Her career and accomplishments have always been an inspiration to me."

"As well they should be," Kirk said, amused. *Nothing wrong with a little hero worship,* he decided, *particularly when directed at a worthy target.* "Very well, Yeoman. Feel free to stick around."

"Thank you, Captain. I appreciate it."

Down on the hangar deck, the *Shimizu* had come to rest, while the hangar's clamshell space doors were closing, sealing off the bay from the vacuum outside. This rendezvous was taking place in deep space, light-years away from the nearest system. The *Enterprise*'s own shuttlecraft were currently parked one level below in the maintenance hangar in order to accommodate the visiting courier. Kirk watched from above as the *Shimizu* powered down.

He walked over to a comm unit on the wall and pressed the speaker button.

"Kirk to bridge. The *Shimizu* is safely aboard. Resume course for Chippewa Prime. Warp five."

The *Enterprise* had naturally dropped out of warp to receive the smaller spacecraft, but now they could get back up to a decent cruising speed. Honored guest or not, his crew were no doubt looking forward to their shore leave, which they had more than earned, especially after all that excitement on the way to the Babel Conference several months back. Kirk's hand drifted toward his ribs, where that Orion assassin had stabbed him. His wound had healed nicely, but he still winced at the memory.

"*Aye, Captain,*" Lieutenant Commander Montgomery Scott replied from the bridge. "*We'll be back under way in two shakes of a lamb's tail, sir.*" His robust Aberdeen accent came through the comm system loud and clear. "*Will ye be needing me to hold down the fort much longer? I shudder to think what mischief my engines might be getting up to in my absence.*"

Kirk smiled. He knew that, given a choice, Scotty would rather be toiling in engineering than occupying the captain's chair on the bridge.

"Just a tad longer, Mister Scott. We still have our renowned visitor to attend to." He glanced down at the *Shimizu*, one level below. The courier had yet to disgorge its passenger. "Kirk out."

"*Landing bay re-pressurized,*" the ship's computer announced via a concealed speaker. "*Access allowed.*"

"That's our cue," Kirk announced. He turned toward his companions. "Gentlemen, Yeoman, let's not keep our guest waiting."

They descended by turbolift to the hangar deck, stepping out into the spacious bay even as the *Shimizu*'s starboard hatch opened and a short set of steps extended onto the deck. The welcoming committee fell into position, with Kirk in the forefront, as their visitor emerged from the craft.

She was a tall, handsome woman who looked to be in her mid-forties, with long black hair that as yet showed no sign of gray. Shrewd blue eyes surveyed her surroundings, while her cool demeanor was almost Vulcan in its inscrutability. Unlike Kirk and the others, she was dressed for comfort, not ceremony, and, in contrast to the current trend in Starfleet uniforms, had opted for crisply pressed black trousers instead of a skirt. The captain's bars on the sleeve of her gold tunic testified to her rank. A simple black carryall hung from a strap over her shoulder.

"Welcome aboard, Captain," Kirk greeted her. "Or should I say welcome back?"

"The former will suffice." She glanced around the bay, perhaps comparing it with her memories. Her neutral tone offered little clue as to what was going through her mind. "But I appreciate the sentiment."

Her roaming gaze lighted on Spock.

"Mister Spock. Now I do feel rather more at home." A slight smile softened her expression. "Good to see that the *Enterprise* still has a highly capable first officer."

"I can only succeed you," he replied, "not surpass you."

The woman once known as "Number One" approached the others as the hatchway automatically closed behind her. Kirk understood that she was the only passenger, having piloted the *Shimizu* herself.

"No need for flattery, Commander. We both know that I am hardly susceptible to such blandishments."

"No flattery intended," Spock said. "Your record, both on the *Enterprise* and subsequently, speaks for itself."

"And quite eloquently," Kirk added.

The captain was sincere in his praise. Although not well-acquainted with their visitor, having previously only met her in passing at various high-level Starfleet conferences, he was quite familiar with her impressive history, which dated back to the very earliest voyages of the *Starship Enterprise*. After serving with distinction under both Captains Robert April and Christopher Pike, she had eventually been awarded command of her own ship, the *U.S.S. Yorktown*, which was currently undergoing a major refit after several years of deep-space exploration. Starfleet scuttlebutt was that she would be promoted to commodore soon and perhaps reassigned to Starfleet Command in San Francisco. Kirk wondered how she felt about that possibility after having trod the decks of a starship for at least two decades. For himself, Kirk was in no hurry to be elevated to a desk job, not when there was still so much of the galaxy left to explore.

"It seems I'm outnumbered," she said dryly. "So I suppose I have no choice but to accept your compliments in the spirit in which they are intended."

"A highly logical conclusion," Kirk said. "No wonder you and Spock worked so well together."

"He was an excellent science officer," she recalled, "despite his relative youth and inexperience at first."

Spock raised an eyebrow. "Both of which defects were significantly remedied during the time we served together."

"I should hope so," she replied.

McCoy snickered in the background, clearly enjoying this.

"Hard to imagine Spock as a green young officer," the doctor said, interjecting himself into the conversation. "Well, aside from the green part, that is." He nudged Kirk with his elbow. "Where are you manners, Jim? Introduce me to the lady."

"You don't need to prompt me, Doctor. I was just getting to that." He stepped to one side and gestured toward the impatient physician. "My chief medical officer, Doctor Leonard McCoy." He turned to indicate their guest. "Doctor, Captain Una of the *U.S.S. Yorktown*."

That was not her real name, Kirk knew, but her actual Illyrian sobriquet was supposed to be all but impossible for outsiders to pronounce, so she had adopted the name "Una" at least as far back as her Academy days. A prodigy raised in an independent colony in the Illyrian system that prized personal excellence above all else, she had always been first in her class when it came to academics, athletics, intellect, and accomplishments, so she had been known as "Number One"—or "Una"—even before she rose to the rank of first officer under Pike.

Or so Spock had explained to Kirk.

"Seriously," McCoy persisted, "you'll have to tell me all about what Spock was like in his younger days."

"Much more mature than some ship's surgeons," Spock said.

"Company, remember?" Kirk chided them. He gave Una an apologetic shrug. "You'll have to forgive my friends. They only seem to be on the opposite sides of a neutral zone."

She took the jocularity in stride. "I've survived ion storms and Orion pirate fleets, Captain. A bit of banter between shipmates does not faze me." Her tone grew more serious, however, as she drew nearer to Spock. "But I would appreciate an opportunity to speak in private with you at some point, Spock, about . . . a mutual friend."

Kirk guessed that she was referring to their former captain, Christopher Pike. Only a year had passed since Spock had temporarily hijacked the *Enterprise* to provide one last service for Pike, delivering him to a better future on the forbidden world of Talos IV. The details of that incident remained highly classified, with Pike listed only as "missing" in the public records. Kirk wondered how much Una knew—or suspected—about what had really transpired.

Was that truly the motive behind this impromptu visit? Una had contacted the *Enterprise* only a few days ago, requesting permission to drop in. As far as Kirk knew, there was no official purpose to the visit.

"Of course," Spock said. "I am at your disposal."

"I'll hold you to that, at a more suitable moment." Her tone lightened as she turned to address the others as well. "For now, however, we don't want to bore Captain Kirk and Doctor McCoy with our old war stories."

"There will be plenty of time for reminiscing," Kirk agreed, "once we get you settled in. And you can also count on a guided tour of the ship in the near future." He beamed proudly. "I think you'll be impressed with how the old girl is looking these days."

"I'm certain I will be," she said. "I've heard nothing but good things about your chief engineer, who is supposed to be something of a miracle worker."

"I'll be sure to convey that to Mister Scott," Kirk said. "But you must be tired after your long journey and would prefer not to linger on the hangar deck all day." It was early morning by the ship's time, but Una was surely still on her own clock. "Allow us to escort you to your VIP suite, which I'm positive you'll find quite comfortable. Nothing but the best for one of the *Enterprise*'s most notable alumni."

"Thank you, Captain Kirk." She stifled a yawn. "I confess I would like a chance to stretch my legs. Even at warp seven, it was a bit of a trip from Memory Alpha."

Bates, who had been hanging back, reluctant to intrude on the discussion, came forward. "Can I help you with your bag, Captain?"

Kirk belatedly introduced the younger woman. "My yeoman, Lisa Bates." He briefly considered mentioning that Bates was a great admirer of Una, but decided to spare Bates the embarrassment. "At your service."

"Thank you, Yeoman," Una said, "but I can manage."

"Are you sure, Captain? It's no bother."

"Stand down, Yeoman," Kirk said lightly. "It seems Captain Una has matters in hand."

Bates retreated, looking slightly abashed. "Aye, sir."

Kirk made a mental note to give Bates a gentle talk on the difference between being helpful and being *too* helpful. Not that he wanted to come down too hard on the over-eager yeoman, who was still learning the ropes. Nor did he want to discourage her initiative, even if sometimes she seemed to be trying a little too hard to be invaluable.

She's no Janice Rand, he thought. *But give her time.*

"The rest of your luggage will naturally be delivered to your guest quarters shortly," Spock stated. "And your ship looked after by our hangar operations crew."

"I'm traveling fairly light," Una said, still toting her carryall bag. "But I'm sure my meager accoutrements are in good hands."

"Then let's be on our way." Kirk stepped aside to let Una pass. "After you, Captain."

Escorting Una off the hangar deck, the party strolled down an adjoining corridor toward a nearby turbolift, passing busy crew members going about their business, some of whom paused briefly to check out the captain and his party. Kirk led the way, while Spock and McCoy flanked Una, who knew the route well from her own familiarity with the *Yorktown,* even though the *Enterprise* had undergone a major refit since her days as first officer. Bates tagged along behind them, keeping her head down.

"So what brings you back to your old stomping grounds?" McCoy asked Una. "Nostalgia?"

"In large part," she confessed. "I'm between assignments while the *Yorktown* is being refitted, and my own chief medical officer practically threatened to have me court-martialed unless I took some much-postponed leave. I was doing some research at the Federation libraries on Memory Alpha, for a pet project of mine, when I noticed that the *Enterprise* was going to be passing through this sector, making a rendezvous feasible." She shrugged. "It seemed a shame to waste such a fortuitous opportunity, when I already had some time on my hands."

Kirk wondered again if there wasn't more to it than that. Fortuitous or not, she had still traveled at least twelve hours through deep space to intercept the *Enterprise*. Could this indeed be more about Pike and his whereabouts than any sentimental trip down memory lane? Una had served as his Number One for more than a decade; she had to be concerned as to what had become of him. He couldn't blame her if she wanted answers. Then again, maybe she really did just want to visit her old ship one last time before being anchored to a commodore's desk.

He couldn't blame her for that either.

"So this is purely a social call?" he asked. "Not that any of us are objecting, mind you."

"More or less," she said. "I hope I'm not imposing."

"Not in the least," Kirk said. The *Enterprise* had only needed to make a slight detour to rendezvous with the *Shimizu*. "We're delighted to have you."

A turbolift carried them to Level 4 of the saucer section, where a short walk led them to the guest quarters maintained for visiting dignitaries. They paused outside the door to the VIP suite.

"Here we are," Kirk said. "I imagine you'd like a chance to rest and freshen up after your long trip."

"A fair assessment," she said. "I *am* feeling somewhat fatigued and, in any event, I've detained you long enough. You surely have more important duties to attend to."

Kirk started to protest, but she held up a hand to ward off any polite demurrals.

"Please. As one Starfleet captain to another, I know how precious your time is." The door slid open, offering a glimpse of the stateroom beyond, which included both a living/work area as well as bath and sleeping compartments. "See to your ship, Kirk. I can take it from here."

"All right," he said. "On one condition: that you call me Jim."

"Fair enough . . . Jim." She deposited her carryall in the foyer of the suite, just past the doorway. "And my friends call me Una."

She shifted her gaze from Kirk to Spock.

"Or sometimes Number One."

Two

"Is now a good time?" Una asked Spock.

The reception, which was being held in the main rec room, had been under way for some time. Officers and enlisted personnel mingled freely, sipping brightly colored drinks while sampling a buffet of exotic hors d'oeuvres from the ship's galley, including Antosian puff pastries, Rigelian caviar, Illyrian mango slices, and bite-sized cucumber sandwiches. Given that the crew was already overdue for shore leave, Spock judged the festivities good for morale, which he had gradually come to realize was a significant issue with respect to humans and other more emotional species. The party was, of course, being held in honor of Captain Una, who certainly merited such hospitality.

"To have that private conversation you mentioned before?"

"Precisely," she replied.

Spock glanced around. Captain Kirk, who had been doing an impeccable job of feting his fellow captain, had been called away to the bridge, leaving Spock to play host. Doctor McCoy and the other senior officers were also otherwise engaged. McCoy had made his excuses to check on a patient in sickbay who was recovering from Cygnian measles, while Scott, Sulu, and Uhura were presently socializing by the punchbowl;

Spock's keen hearing informed him that the men were attempting to cajole Uhura into treating them to a song. The communications officer, whose musical gifts were considerable, was politely demurring, but sounded willing to be persuaded. Other crew members joined in the effort, which suggested that this might indeed be an opportune moment to converse privately with Una.

"If you wish, Captain."

It required a degree of effort not to address her as "Number One." Old habits, it seemed, truly did die hard.

"Good," she said. "It's been a pleasure socializing with your captain and crewmates, but I have been waiting for the opportunity to talk with you one-on-one."

"I am at your disposal."

They retreated to a quiet corner of the room, away from the upcoming musical entertainment, and claimed an unoccupied table littered with discarded plates and glasses. Spock noted that she too had abstained from the dubious benefits of alcohol, preferring a glass of pure Altair water instead. She cleared a place for her drink as they sat down opposite each other.

"Is this private enough to suit you?" he inquired.

She surveyed their surroundings. "It will do, unless this turns into a discussion of some length."

"I cannot accurately predict its duration without knowing the topic."

"Naturally," she agreed. Lowering her voice, she got to the point with characteristic efficiency. "I have questions about Captain Pike."

"I anticipated as much."

Number One had been arguably closer to Pike than

Spock had been during the 11.53 years they had all served together on the *Enterprise*. There had even been occasional rumors of a romantic attraction between the captain and his first officer, although Spock had always dismissed such talk as frivolous human gossip and irrelevant in any case; certainly, he had never personally observed any lapse in professionalism where their working relationship was concerned. Nevertheless, he well understood the deep loyalty that Pike had earned from his crew. That same loyalty had compelled Spock to risk his own life and career for Pike's sake.

"I heard about his accident, of course," she said. "But I was in the Beta Quadrant, on a protracted peacekeeping mission, when the tragedy occurred, so I was unable to immediately go to see him in the hospital." Sorrow cracked her stoic façade to a degree; her voice grew hoarse with emotion. "And, in all honesty, I was uncertain if he would even want me to see him in . . . the state he was in. Not that it could have possibly lessened my regard for him in any way, but I was conscious of his pride and dignity. Perhaps too much so."

Ice-blue eyes grew moist and she needed a moment to compose herself. She took a sip from her water glass.

"His condition was . . . disturbing," Spock conceded, recalling the debilitated state he had found Pike in following the captain's near-fatal accident aboard a Starfleet training ship. His body ravaged by a massive overdose of delta rays, Pike's still-vibrant mind had been trapped inside a scarred, paralyzed husk, barely capable of communicating even with the aid of electronic devices. Pike's nervous system had been so severely damaged by the radiation that even the most advanced prosthetic interfaces had been of little use. Spock was not ashamed to admit that Pike's grievous condition had touched even his tightly reined emotions. "It troubled me as well."

"So I gathered." She eyed him intently. "I know that you and Kirk visited him at a medical facility on Starbase 11, but what happened after that is classified. The available record holds only that Chris—Captain Pike—somehow went missing after being taken aboard the *Enterprise* for reasons unknown. And despite my own inquiries, both official and otherwise, I have been unable to determine any more than that."

Spock hesitated, torn between the temptation to tell her the whole truth and his duty to protect Starfleet's secrets. If anyone deserved to know what had truly become of Christopher Pike, it was this woman, who had been at his right hand through more than a decade of dangers and discoveries, and yet . . .

"As you say, the matter is classified."

"I understand that, and I have no desire to place you in an uncomfortable position, so just answer me one question, yes or no." She braced herself for the answer, before he could even accede to her request. "He's with Vina now, isn't he?"

There was no hint of jealousy in her voice, only an urgent need for the truth that Spock could not in good conscience deny.

He nodded.

"Thank you, Spock." Her tense posture relaxed, as though a weight had been lifted from her shoulders. She smiled sadly, while wiping away a single tear. "That's all I needed to know."

Clearly, she had already surmised the truth, requiring only that he confirm her supposition. A thought occurred to him and he had to wonder: Had she not been detained in the Beta Quadrant and unable to get to Pike first, might she have resorted to the same drastic measures he had taken to secure a happier outcome for their former captain? Her resolve and her loyalty to Pike were as steadfast as his own, if not more so.

This was pure speculation, of course. Logically, there was no way of knowing what *might* have occurred under different circumstances, but Spock felt strangely certain that, had he not commandeered the *Enterprise* on Pike's behalf, the *Yorktown* might well have made an unauthorized voyage to Talos IV.

"Let me ask you one question as well," he said. "Was this inquiry the actual motive behind your visit to the *Enterprise*?"

"Guilty as charged, Mister Spock. Why else?"

━━━━━━━

She regretted lying to Spock, although she'd had no choice but to do so. The deception still troubled her the following morning as she prepared to attain her *true* objective, while alone with her thoughts in the VIP suite Captain Kirk had generously provided. Repaying Spock's honesty with a falsehood stung her conscience.

Let's hope he can forgive me someday, she thought, *after what's to come.*

Not that she had entirely misled Spock at the reception; she had merely told him half of the truth. She had genuinely needed to confirm her suspicions regarding the whereabouts of Christopher Pike, but that had not been the only measure of closure she was in dire search of. There was even older business that she needed to attend to, while she still had the chance. And that was not a matter that she could safely share with Spock . . . or anyone.

Her guest quarters aboard the *Enterprise* were as comfortable as promised and, more importantly, suited her needs perfectly. Among its amenities was a desk with a computer access terminal, which she made ready use of.

"Computer. Specify location of Captain James T. Kirk."

"Captain Kirk is presently on the bridge," the computer responded. Despite the seriousness of her mission, Una was amused to hear a rather robotic version of her own voice answer her; apparently no one had altered the voice parameters since she and Spock had installed them, using her own voice as a baseline, several years ago.

"And First Officer Spock?"

"Commander Spock is also on the bridge."

She winced a little at the computer's cold, mechanical tone. *I don't really sound like that, do I?*

Still, she had confirmed that Kirk and Spock were both exactly where they ought to be at the moment. Given that it was approximately ten hundred hours, well into the alpha shift, this was to be expected, but she had wanted to verify that regardless. She could not afford to take any chances, not after waiting and planning this for so long.

It's time, she thought. *At last.*

She had been tempted to make her move last night, right after excusing herself from the reception, but prudence had won out over impatience. This endeavor was eighteen years in the making; a few more hours would not have made any difference, no matter how anxious she'd been to get on with it.

It was no coincidence that she had just happened to cross the *Enterprise*'s path at this particular juncture. Every step of this operation had been carefully planned, leaving nothing to chance, and now she had reached the point of no return.

Time to cross the Rubicon, she thought.

Stepping away from the computer, she took one last look around the guest quarters to make sure that she had not forgotten anything that might betray her larger design. Attired in her everyday uniform, she exited the suite. As she had no intention of ever returning, she took her carryall bag with her. She had everything she needed for the expedition ahead, aside from one last item.

Fortunately, she knew just where to find it.

As she made her way through the *Enterprise*'s bustling corridors, she couldn't help comparing her present surroundings to her own vivid memories of this very same ship. The colors were cheerier, with bright red doors and trimmings as opposed to the uniform blue-gray look of years gone by, and the halls more crowded than she remembered. Under Pike and April, the *Enterprise* had carried a crew of approximately two hundred. Now, like the *Yorktown*, it housed more than twice that number—none of whom had any idea what she was truly up to.

It was better that way, for their sakes.

To her relief, her presence in the halls attracted only minimal attention. Stray crew members acknowledged her respectfully, but nobody questioned her or offered unwanted assistance. She was a visiting Starfleet captain after all; why wouldn't she have the run of the ship? As expected, people assumed that she was simply going about her own business.

A turbolift took her down one deck to where the senior officers were quartered. She walked briskly but with feigned casualness to the door of Kirk's personal quarters. There was not much foot traffic around her at this time of day; still, she waited patiently until the coast was clear before knocking once on the door, just to be safe. Kirk was on the bridge, but Una wanted to make sure that helpful young yeoman wasn't busy fluffing the captain's pillows or whatever. Una's own yeoman, back on the *Yorktown*, knew better than to mess about in her quarters unless specifically requested to do so, but Kirk might be laxer about his privacy; in Una's experience, every captain and yeoman arrived at their own working relationship, depending on the captain's command style and preferences.

In any event, her knock went unanswered, so Una judged it safe to proceed. She retrieved a customized communicator from her belt; among its special modifications was a cybernetic skeleton key of her own devising. She was about to enter Kirk's quarters when an unexpected voice interrupted her.

"Excuse me, Captain."

Turning away from the door, she found that the voice belonged to a boyish young lieutenant who had just come trotting around the corner on an errand. Focused on the task ahead, she had carelessly failed to hear him approach. She mentally kicked herself for the lapse, which might have spoiled everything.

"If you're looking for Captain Kirk, I believe he's on the bridge."

She maintained a poker face while discreetly hiding the communicator behind her back. Despite her stoic demeanor, she was sweating inside.

"Of course. I should have realized." She mustered a casual shrug. "I guess I'm still not entirely on this ship's clock yet . . . and am still suffering from a slight case of warp lag."

"I can escort you to the bridge if you like," he volunteered.

Is he suspicious, she fretted, *or am I just being paranoid?*

The youth seemed earnest and guileless enough, so she chose to think that all this skulking around and dissembling was simply getting to her. Straightforward by nature, she had never been much for espionage or intrigue; left to her own devices, she preferred a more direct approach to any situation.

Alas, that was not possible in this instance.

"That won't be necessary, Lieutenant. I know the way."

"It's no problem, Captain. I'm going that way myself."

Una repressed a few choice Illyrian curse words. Was all of Kirk's crew so inconveniently helpful? She glanced up and down the corridor, weighing her options. The last thing she wanted was for Kirk to hear that she had been loitering outside his quarters for no good reason. What if he or Spock put two and two together and guessed what she was actually after?

That just wouldn't do.

"Very well. After you, Lieutenant . . . ?"

"Riley, sir. Lieutenant Kevin Riley, at your service."

She let him step ahead of her, leading the way, before dropping him to the deck with a karate chop to the side of his neck. The strike wasn't quite as efficient as a Vulcan nerve pinch, but it got the job done. The lieutenant lay crumpled at her feet.

"My apologies, Mister Riley, but you were in the wrong place at the wrong time."

Moving quickly, before any other crew members stumbled onto the scene, she used the skeleton key function on her communicator to crack the lock sealing Kirk's chambers. The gray door slid open automatically, and she hastily dragged Riley's limp body inside before dropping it gently back onto the floor. She sighed in relief as the door slid shut behind them, concealing the incriminating tableau from view.

So much for second thoughts, she reflected. *There's definitely no turning back now.*

Not that there had ever really been any possibility of her changing course at this late date. In a very real sense, these events had been set in motion nearly two decades ago on an all-but-forgotten planet many light-years away, two captains of the *Enterprise* ago . . . .

Stepping away from the unfortunate crewman, she glanced about Kirk's quarters, which, aside from a few personal touches, resembled her own back on the *Yorktown.* Potted ferns combatted the antiseptic feel of the sturdy metal bulkheads. Sculptures and knickknacks from a variety of worlds added character to the suite, which bore little resemblance to the captain's quarters back in Pike's day, as she remembered it from the last time she served aboard this ship. Pike's circular stateroom had actually been larger and more spacious than Kirk's quarters, a luxury that had been lost when the *Enterprise* had been refitted to accommodate a much larger crew. Kirk's stateroom consisted of three wedge-shaped chambers divided by partitions. The layout was familiar to her, but she knew that Kirk's quarters held one secret that was unique to the *Enterprise,* not to be found on any other Starfleet vessel.

But where was it hidden?

If this was still Pike's *Enterprise,* she would have known exactly where to look, but the subsequent refit complicated matters, forcing her to get creative. Rescuing a tricorder from her bag, she walked slowly through Kirk's quarters, methodically scanning for a certain item whose singular nature and composition were literally unlike anything else in the universe. Despite her legendary composure, she felt her nerves fraying as she searched the stateroom. Her heart was racing and she had to remind herself to breathe. Every moment that passed without her finding her prize added to her anxiety. Worst-case scenarios forced themselves into her mind.

What if it was not here anymore, after all these years? What if it had been accidentally destroyed during a heated space battle or near-disaster? The *Enterprise* had been through a lot under Kirk's command, including run-ins with both the Klingons *and* the Romulans. What if this entire plan was doomed before it even began?

No, she thought adamantly. *That would be too cruel.*

Forgoing the shower facilities for now, she worked

her way through the bed alcove and had moved on to the adjoining work area when an electronic chirp rewarded her efforts. She followed the signal to a decorative trapezoidal panel installed on the wall across from Kirk's desk and computer station. A triumphant smile lifted the corners of her lips.

Found you.

A more in-depth scan confirmed the existence of a secret compartment behind the panel, cleverly hidden so that it could be not be found unless someone was actually looking for it. She had to congratulate Kirk, and probably Spock, on their ingenuity. It was an excellent hiding place, easily as good as the one she had devised for April so many years ago, which she and Pike had subsequently guarded before, finally, passing the secret—and the responsibility—on to Kirk when he took command of the *Enterprise*. She assumed that it was the 2264 refit that had forced Kirk to find a slightly new cache for the item in question.

For close to two decades, the *Enterprise* had held a secret unknown even to Starfleet, passed down from captain to captain, first officer to first officer, until the present day. And during all that time the secret had remained securely hidden within the ship's very walls.

Until today.

With a twinge of guilt, she exchanged the tricorder for a phaser and set the weapon on its highest setting. A red-hot beam cut into the bulkhead around the bronze panel, causing vaporized metal to steam away from its edges. Cracking the locking mechanism would have been a more elegant solution, but she suspected that the encryption involved was considerably more formidable than the lock on a door, especially if Mister Spock had been involved in programming the codes. She had devised the original security system, but that had been a long time ago, so she could hardly expect the combination to remain the same—and she didn't have time to match wits with Spock.

Hence, the phaser, even if it did make her feel like an Orion looter.

Even still, the operation took longer than she expected, as the bulkhead resisted the high-intensity phaser beam. Perspiration glued the back of her tunic to her spine as the beam cut through the metal with agonizing slowness. Had Kirk and Spock reinforced the shielding around the hidden compartment? It certainly seemed as much, given the difficulty it was posing for her.

Damn, she thought. *I should have anticipated this.*

She worried about the unconscious lieutenant lying on the floor nearby. In theory, he would be out for forty-five minutes or so, and wake with nothing more than a sore neck and a mild headache, but she kept her ears open for any sound of him stirring. In a pinch, she could always stun him with her phaser, but she hoped to avoid that. She was imposing on Kirk's hospitality enough without zapping one of his crewmen.

And young Riley deserved better, too.

But what if he was expected on duty somewhere? He had said he was en route to the bridge before she waylaid him. How long did she have before his absence was detected?

Time was not on her side.

Precious moments dragged by as she cut around the

panel. A smaller aperture would have been faster, but she couldn't risk damaging the contents of the compartment by accident. Vaporized metal hissed and crackled, the acrid fumes assaulting her nose and mouth before she finally completed the process. The charred edges of the panel were still hot to the touch, but, putting aside the phaser, she grabbed onto them with both hands, wresting the panel loose to reveal the hidden compartment—and its occupant. Her breath caught in her throat as she laid eyes on it for the first time in too many years.

The Transfer Key was a flat, rectangular tablet-sized device only slightly larger than Una's palm. A blank viewscreen, framed by a blue border, occupied one face of the device, while an assortment of recessed buttons and switches ran along its edge. Painful memories flooded her mind as she contemplated the Key. It still amazed her that so compact a device could have caused so much heartbreak so many years ago. Old wounds, carried deep in her soul, bled afresh.

I'm so sorry, Tim . . . for you and the others.

The guilty memories stung, but also renewed her determination to keep to the course she had set out on, in hopes of finally making things right.

If that was still possible after all this time.

It has to be, she thought, snapping out of her reverie. *Or this is all for nothing.*

She lowered the heavy panel to the floor, much more gently than she had dropped poor Riley. It landed with a dull thump, but Una barely heard it. She only had eyes for the Key.

Reaching out, she claimed her prize.

Three

It was a quiet morning on the bridge, which was probably just as well, Kirk reflected, considering how late some of his crew had been celebrating last night. Sulu struck the captain as slightly hungover this morning, as opposed to his usual chipper self, while Uhura's voice seemed a tad hoarse from an excess of Venusian karaoke. And, honestly, Kirk could've used a few more hours of sleep as he nursed his second cup of coffee of the morning, thoughtfully provided by the ever attentive Yeoman Bates. Only Spock seemed none the worse for wear from the festivities, routinely manning his science station as effortlessly as ever.

Figures, Kirk thought.

He leaned back in his chair, sipping his coffee. The viewscreen before him offered nothing but distant stars streaking past as the *Enterprise* warped through the vast empty reaches of deep space. The final frontier could be dangerous at times, full of hazards both known and unknown, but it could also be serene as well, offering smooth sailing through an endless sea that was often far more still and placid than anything found at the bottom of a gravity well. Kirk reminded himself to appreciate such moments, before they inevitably encountered choppier waters once more.

"Clear skies today, it seems," he said. "Not a storm in sight."

"Tell that to my head," Sulu moaned. "It feels like a Horta is trying to burrow its way out of my skull."

"A word to the wise, Helmsman. Never try to outdrink our chief engineer, particularly if there's scotch involved."

"Lesson learned, Captain," Sulu said. "Trust me."

Kirk chose to take Sulu's aching head as evidence that last night's reception had been a success, and he hoped that Captain Una had enjoyed herself as well. Tonight's plans were less elaborate, involving a private dinner with the senior officers, but Kirk felt confident that an enjoyable time would be had by all. He was not entirely sure how long Una would be visiting, but he intended to extend her the ship's full hospitality for the duration of her stay. It was the least he could do, considering her personal history with the *Enterprise*.

"Would you like a refill on your coffee, Captain?"

Bates entered the command well, bearing a fresh pot of java.

"Why not?" Kirk said. "And while you're at it—"

He was about to suggest that she offer Sulu a cup as well when a silent alarm, which he had never expected to see, flashed abruptly on the microtape viewer built into the armrest of his chair. Kirk blinked in surprise; it took him a moment to register what he was seeing.

The Key, he realized. *Someone's found the Key.*

"Captain?" Bates asked. "Is everything all right?"

He assumed a less startled expression. "I'm fine." He waved away her and her coffeepot. "On second thought, I'll pass on the coffee, thank you. That will be all, Yeoman."

"Are you sure—" she began, then caught herself. "Aye, Captain."

Kirk barely noticed her retreat from the command well as his mind raced in response to this unprecedented development. His eyes sought out Spock, who had surely just received the same silent alert. Spock turned toward Kirk, his expression grave. They exchanged concerned looks that were hopefully lost on everyone else on the bridge.

This can't be right, Kirk thought. *It must be a technical glitch or malfunction. No one on this ship even knows about the Key, except for me and Spock and . . .*

He jabbed the comm button on his right armrest.

"Kirk to Captain Una, please respond."

There was no answer from her quarters, although he knew that there was any number of places she could be at the moment, from the ship's gymnasium to the officers' mess. He switched the comm setting in order to address the entire ship.

"Captain Kirk to Captain Una. Please respond immediately."

By now, all eyes had turned toward him. Puzzled faces betrayed the bridge crew's confusion as they tried to figure out what was up—and why Una had not responded yet. Kirk knew the feeling. He was worrying about that himself.

"Captain?" Uhura asked, her curiosity mirrored on the faces of Sulu and Bates and the others. Kirk was suddenly grateful that McCoy was in sickbay. Not even Bones could be let in on this secret.

"As you were, Lieutenant," Kirk said to Uhura.

"Aye, sir," she said uncertainly.

Bones would not have let the matter drop so easily, Kirk

thought as Spock slipped past Bates to join Kirk in the command well. He lowered his voice.

"Captain, perhaps more active measures are required to locate Captain Una."

"You may be right, but . . ."

Kirk hesitated, reluctant to dispatch a security team in search of Una. In part that was because such a drastic response would only invite more scrutiny regarding a matter that had long been a closely guarded secret, but also because it went against his gut to assume the worst of a fellow Starfleet captain, let alone a decorated veteran like Captain Una. It was almost impossible to imagine such a distinguished officer going rogue.

But nothing about this situation went by the rules.

"Security," he barked into the comm. "Locate Captain Una and bring her to the bridge."

Spock frowned as he returned to his station. Vulcan or not, he had to be bothered by Una's increasingly suspect silence, as well as the steps being taken to detain her. It would be highly embarrassing if this was a simple coincidence or misunderstanding, but Kirk found himself hoping fervently that that was the case.

"*Captain?*" a perplexed voice said from the comm speaker on Kirk's chair. "*This is Lieutenant Bresler in hangar control. Captain Una is leaving in her ship.*"

Kirk jumped to his feet. "On whose orders?"

"*Hers, sir.*"

Bresler sounded embarrassed, as though suddenly suspecting that he had erred somehow, but Kirk could not fault the man for following Una's orders. When a high-ranking officer asks to depart in her own ship, few crew members would think twice before complying.

"Don't let her leave!" Kirk ordered. "Close the hangar doors."

"We'll try, Captain, but she's already fired up her engines!"

She'd made good time getting from his quarters to the hangar deck, Kirk noted, but Spock had said she was efficient. An express turbolift would cover the distance quickly enough, if she moved briskly and knew exactly where she was heading.

"She had this all planned," Kirk guessed. "Right from the beginning."

"So it appears," Spock said, "if our suspicions are correct."

Kirk's doubts on that score were fading by the minute. *That alarm was no glitch.*

"On-screen," Kirk ordered. "Let me see what's happening."

"Acknowledged," Spock said. "Switching to internal sensors."

The image on the main viewer shifted from the star-flecked space ahead to an interior view of the hangar deck. The bay's massive space doors were beginning to slide shut again, per Kirk's command, but the *Shimizu* showed no sign of powering down. Twin nacelles, embedded in its wings, glowed azure as the small, sleek spacecraft lifted off from the deck. Its landing gear folded back against its hull.

"She is making her escape," Spock said.

"Tell me something I don't know!" Kirk snapped,

more brusquely than intended. "Uhura, hail the *Shimizu*. Get me Captain Una."

"Already on it," she said, anticipating his command. "*Enterprise* to *Shimizu*, respond at once."

As before, Una failed to respond.

"Captain," Spock said. "If we close the doors entirely, or even raise the shields, we risk significant damage to both vessels, unless the *Shimizu* remains where it is, which does not appear to be Captain Una's intention."

No, it does not, Kirk thought as the *Shimizu* tilted to port by forty-five degrees, the better to pass through the narrowing gap between the closing space doors. A sudden burst of acceleration, defying every prescribed safety protocol, propelled the courier craft out of the landing bay into the vacuum of space, leaving Kirk staring in frustration at an empty hangar. The *Shimizu* had well and truly flown the coop.

Taking the Key with it.

"Aft view!" he ordered. "Now!"

The empty space behind the *Enterprise* took over the viewscreen, just in time for Kirk to see the *Shimizu* zipping away at what looked like full impulse at least. The tiny ship was already shrinking into the distance, even as the *Enterprise* sped in the opposite direction at warp five. Exiting a starship that was cruising at warp speed was also hardly standard protocol, but Captain Una was clearly making her own rules at this point.

"Full reverse!" Kirk ordered. "And lock tractor beams on that ship. Don't let it get away!"

"Aye, sir!" Sulu no longer sounded remotely hungover. "Full reverse."

The abrupt shift in direction tested the *Enterprise*'s inertial dampers, nearly throwing Kirk from his chair. Bates seized a safety rail to steady herself, while a loose data slate clattered onto the deck. The coffee sloshed in Kirk's cup, threatening to spill over. He expected an indignant protest from engineering at any moment.

Sorry, Scotty.

"Employing tractor beams," Ensign Chekov reported from the navigation station to the right of Sulu. A thick Russian accent tinged his voice, along with what sounded like a growing sense of frustration. He muttered darkly under his breath as, on-screen, the *Shimizu* continued to flee the *Enterprise,* only barely within visual range.

Kirk frowned. "Is there a problem, Mister Chekov?"

"I'm trying, sir, but I'm having difficulty getting a lock on the other vessel. It's raised its shields, which are interfering with the tractor beam in a way I've never encountered before." He worked the controls stubbornly, but did not seem happy with the results. "It's as though the deflectors are making the *Shimizu* more . . . slippery."

"Captain Una's handiwork, I assume," Kirk said.

"Her brilliance and ingenuity are considerable," Spock said, "as I can personally attest to."

Kirk scowled. "Too bad those stellar qualities are working against us now."

"I quite agree, Captain. That is most . . . unfortunate."

Kirk wondered again how hard this was on Spock, but before he could ask Spock what his old crewmate could possibly be about, Uhura interrupted urgently.

"Captain! The *Shimizu* is finally answering my hails."

About time, Kirk thought. "Put her through."

Una's head and shoulders appeared on the screen. As ever, she appeared calm and immaculate.

"My sincere apologies for abusing your hospitality, Kirk," she said from the helm of the *Shimizu*. *"Perhaps someday, if all goes well, I can explain, but not today."*

Kirk tried to reason with her. "Think about what you're doing here. You're throwing away your career, your reputation. You may even be risking a court-martial. And for what?"

The Transfer Key?

"Closure, Kirk," she replied. *"Closure and . . . responsibility."*

Spock peered into the scope at his station. "She's powering her warp engine, Captain."

"Shall I lock weapons, sir?" Chekov swallowed hard. A photon torpedo at this range would risk destroying the smaller spacecraft, and phasers were not much safer. "Torpedoes loaded."

"Hold your fire," Kirk said. He was not about to open fire on a vessel piloted by another Starfleet captain, merely on suspicion of her having stolen a secret that Starfleet didn't even know about. He walked toward the viewscreen, as though reducing the distance between himself and Una.

"Talk to me," he said to her. "Before this goes too far."

She shook her head.

"I've waited too long already. I'm asking you, Kirk, captain to captain. Don't try to follow me."

Spock looked up from his scanner. "She is going to warp, Captain."

Una's image vanished from view as she abruptly cut

off the transmission. On-screen the *Shimizu* began to pull away from the *Enterprise,* shrinking farther into the distance. Within seconds, it had vanished from visual range.

"Captain?" Sulu asked. "Your orders?"

It occurred to Kirk that Sulu had to be just as baffled by this sudden turn of events as the rest of the bridge crew. Aside from Spock, none of them had the slightest clue as to why the *Enterprise* was suddenly in pursuit of Captain Una and her ship.

And I'm in no position to tell them, Kirk thought. *I can only count on them to follow my orders without question.*

"Follow that ship, Mister Sulu."

"Aye, sir." Sulu shrugged and did as instructed. "Coming about and commencing pursuit."

No longer flying in reverse, the *Enterprise* executed a tight U-turn that sent them chasing after the *Shimizu* at high speed. Kirk peered grimly at the screen before him. Una had asked him not to follow her, but Kirk couldn't do that, not until he knew what she was up to and what was at stake. Pike had passed the Key on to Kirk, and that was not a responsibility Kirk took lightly.

He looked to Spock, wanting answers.

"What is this all about, Spock? Why is she doing this?"

Spock turned away from his control panel. His voice and visage were even more guarded than usual. "I am reluctant to speculate . . . under the present circumstances."

His caution was logical. Kirk was all too aware of the many curious ears surrounding them. They could hardly talk freely here on the bridge.

"Captain," Uhura said. "Security is reporting that Lieutenant Riley has been found unconscious in your quarters." Her stunned expression suggested that she could barely believe the news she was conveying. "It appears that he was assaulted by Captain Una, sir."

Kirk's temper flared. To hell with Una's storied history and reputation. Nobody attacked a member of his crew, not even one of Starfleet's finest.

"Estimated time to interception?" he asked.

"Hard to say, Captain," Chekov said. "We're tracking her ion trail, but she's a fast ship. We could be in for a bit of a chase."

"Understood," Kirk said, judging that he had time enough to vacate the bridge briefly. "Mister Spock. My quarters . . . now."

Turning away from the viewscreen, he headed for the turbolift, where Spock quickly met him. There was something they needed to check right away, even though Kirk already knew in his heart what they were going to find.

"Mister Sulu, you have the conn. Alert me the minute the *Shimizu* comes back within visual range."

"Aye, sir." Sulu turned the helm over to a relief officer and took his place in the captain's chair. Despite last night's celebrations, he looked ready and able to handle the situation, even if he still was operating in the dark. "Captain, can I ask what this is all about?"

Kirk knew Sulu was speaking for the entire bridge crew. The captain deeply regretted what he had to say next.

"No, Mister Sulu. I'm afraid you cannot."

Four

"It is as we feared," Spock said.

The breached compartment in Kirk's quarters confirmed the captain's suspicions. The hidden vault had been broken into, and the Key was gone.

"I don't understand it," Kirk said. "Why now after all these years?"

Pike had personally entrusted Kirk with the secret, just as April had entrusted the secret to Pike years before. Only their respective first officers had been told about the Key, just in case a captain suffered an untimely demise. Aside from a brief period during the refit, when Pike had held on to the Key until Kirk was named the new captain, the one-of-a-kind alien device had been hidden safely away inside the *Enterprise*, unknown to history and Starfleet. April had made that decision nearly two decades ago and Kirk had never seen fit to question it. Up to an hour ago, he would have assumed Captain Una felt the same way, but now the Key had gone missing and the *Shimizu* was fleeing the scene of the crime.

"I cannot explain it." Spock contemplated the empty vault, which he had helped Kirk install a few years ago. "I can only assume she has her reasons."

"Like you did when you stole the *Enterprise* to help Pike?"

Kirk had long since forgiven Spock that betrayal,

given that Spock's intentions had been noble and had yielded a happier ending for Chris Pike. Kirk was simply trying to grasp what might have motivated Una to steal the Key.

If the allusion to his past transgression troubled Spock, the stoic Vulcan gave no indication of it.

"Perhaps," he said. "The individual I knew, and served beside for more than a decade, was not motivated by self-interest or venality, nor was she driven by irrational impulses. To the contrary, her personal discipline and integrity would do a Vulcan proud."

"High praise, coming from you," Kirk said, "and you certainly know her better than I. But I don't have the luxury of giving her the benefit of the doubt. I can't just sit back while a Starfleet captain steals a dangerous piece of alien technology and heads off on her own."

Spock nodded. "Regretfully, I must concur."

"I trust I can count on your full cooperation in apprehending her, despite your history with Captain Una?"

Spock did not take offense at the question, which Kirk had felt compelled to ask.

"You are my captain. Past allegiances will not compromise that."

"Like they did with Pike?" Kirk pressed.

"Those were . . . exceptional . . . circumstances."

And these aren't? Kirk thought, but held his tongue. Spock had more than proven his loyalty to the ship and its captain, both before and after the Talos IV incident. *If he says that old bonds won't get in the way of his duty, that's good enough for me.*

"All right," he said. "She has the Key. Where is she taking it, assuming we don't catch up with her first?"

"I have a theory, but it requires further proof." Spock exited the bedroom and activated a comm unit on the wall of the work area. "Spock to the bridge. Are we still tracking the *Shimizu*?"

"Affirmative, Mister Spock," Sulu's voice responded. *"She's a speedy one all right, but we're still picking up her warp emissions."*

"Acknowledged," Spock said. "Please transmit the *Shimizu*'s current course and heading to the computer access terminal in the captain's quarters."

"Will do, Mister Spock." There was only a momentary pause from the bridge. *"Coming through now."*

"Thank you, Mister Sulu. Spock out."

He stepped away from the comm unit and approached Kirk's desk. "With your permission, Captain?"

Kirk nodded. He circled around to watch as Spock activated the terminal.

"Computer, display course and heading of vessel *Shimizu*, registered to Starfleet Captain Una."

"Working," the computer responded.

A star map appeared on the monitor. The *Shimizu*'s present course was indicated by a flashing red line, while *Enterprise*'s pursuit was represented by a blue line that was steadily overtaking the red line. Kirk was encouraged to see that Una's lead appeared to be shrinking steadily.

"Project future route of *Shimizu* based on its current heading," Spock instructed, "assuming no significant deviations."

"Working."

The map on the screen shrunk to accommodate a much larger portion of the quadrant. A dotted yellow line depicted the *Shimizu's* possible flight path, extending to largely unexplored sectors at the outer fringes of Federation space.

Spock's brow furrowed. A hint of a frown betrayed his concern.

"I suspected as much," he said. "The *Shimizu's* heading places it on course for the Korinar Sector."

Kirk leaned forward to take a closer look at the screen. He lacked Spock's computer-like mind, but he could read a star map well enough, and what he saw was not reassuring.

"That's disputed territory, claimed by both the Federation and the Klingon Empire."

"Correct," Spock stated, "which makes Captain Una's current actions all the more troubling."

"You can say that again," Kirk agreed.

It was less than a year since the Federation and the Empire had nearly gone to war. If not for the unexpected intervention of the Organians, the *Enterprise* might well be flying into battle now—or perhaps already have become a casualty of war. The current cease-fire was a tense and fragile one, marred by occasional provocations on the part of the Klingons, but it had held so far. Kirk was aware that a major conference to finalize the Organian peace accords was already in the works and that much depended on that conference going smoothly. The last thing anyone needed was Captain Una endangering the peace by entering the disputed region for unknown purposes.

"That clinches it," Kirk said. "The possibility of a Starfleet captain—and the Key—falling into the hands of the Klingons must be prevented at all costs, especially with the peace talks coming up."

"An accurate assessment of our situation," Spock stated. "No matter Captain Una's motives, she cannot be allowed to jeopardize the Federation's relations with the Klingon Empire, nor can we risk the Key falling into the wrong hands. The consequences of such an unfortunate development could be . . . catastrophic."

"I remember the story," Kirk said grimly. "The last time the Transfer Key was used—"

The door to Kirk's quarters whooshed open, and McCoy barged into the suite. He stormed over to where Kirk and Spock were standing.

"What the devil is going on?" he demanded. "I've got a groggy lieutenant in my sickbay, claiming that he was bushwhacked by Captain Una, and now I hear we're chasing her across the quadrant as though she's an escaped felon. Did we accidentally cross into another mirror universe when I wasn't looking?"

Kirk reached forward and turned off the computer screen. *This is going to be tricky,* he thought; the cantankerous doctor wanted answers and wasn't going to be happy at being left in the dark. And an unhappy McCoy could be a stubborn one. Backing down was not in his nature.

"It's a complicated situation, Bones, which I'm not really at liberty to discuss."

"Don't give me that," McCoy said impatiently. "I'm a doctor. I know how to keep a secret." He turned toward

Spock. "Please don't tell me we're heading back to Talos IV."

"That is unlikely, Doctor," Spock assured him. "Our present course is leading us in an entirely different direction."

"Thank heaven for small favors, but, in that case, where exactly *are* we heading? And what's the story with Captain Una? Why did she attack Riley and then make a run for it?" He threw his hands up in exasperation. "None of this makes any sense!"

Tell me about it, Kirk thought. Part of him was tempted to let McCoy in on the secret of the Key. The longer this insanity went on, the harder it was going to be to keep the whole story under wraps. Thanks to Captain Una, the cat was in danger of getting out of the bag.

"I'm sorry, Bones, but—"

A whistle from the comm panel provided a welcome interruption. Kirk turned away from McCoy, leaving the frustrated doctor hanging, to answer the hail.

"Kirk here."

"We're gaining on the Shimizu," Sulu reported. "It *should be coming within visual range any minute now."*

"Understood," Kirk said. "We're on our way."

He marched briskly toward the door. "Sorry, Bones. Duty calls." He nodded at Spock. "Mister Spock, you're with me."

McCoy followed them out into the corridor and toward the turbolift.

"Hang on," he said. "I'm coming with you. Don't even think that you can duck my questions for long."

If only, Kirk thought.

———

Sulu returned to his regular place at the helm as Kirk took back the bridge. Spock sat down at the science station, while McCoy, lacking an assigned post on the bridge, joined Kirk in his usual position in the command well. He leaned against a cherry-red safety rail, as though settling in for however long it took to get to the bottom of things. As a rule, Kirk didn't object to McCoy visiting the bridge, but at the moment the command well felt a bit crowded. McCoy's unanswered questions and obvious discontent seemed to share the space with them.

"Shouldn't you be in sickbay, Doctor?" Kirk asked.

"Why?" McCoy answered. "Are you expecting casualties?"

I hope not, Kirk thought. In theory, the *Shimizu* was unarmed, but Kirk wasn't taking any chances. Una had already proven full of surprises and capable of violence if crossed. "How is Riley doing?"

"A sore neck and a bruised ego," McCoy said, "and I think the latter smarts worse than the former." He shrugged. "Unfortunately, I don't have a prescription for that."

Kirk was relieved to hear that Riley's injuries were minor, although he still held them against Una. A young officer's wounded pride was no big deal, but how far was Una willing to go—and how far would he have to go to stop her? Despite everything, he didn't want Una to end up as a casualty either. He wanted her in the brig, not sickbay.

Nor did he want her scattered to atoms by a photon torpedo.

"How much longer?" he asked.

"Coming within visual range." Chekov eyed his tactical sensors. "In approximately three, two, one . . ."

Sure enough, the *Shimizu* reappeared upon the main viewer. It was only a speck, barely distinguishable from the stars glittering light-years ahead, but Kirk felt his pulse quicken at the sight. Captain Una had not given them the slip just yet.

"Increase speed," Kirk ordered. "Warp seven point five."

"Aye, sir." Sulu winced slightly, aware that they were pushing the *Enterprise*'s engines, but he carried out the order. "Warp seven point five."

The *Shimizu* slowly grew larger on the screen as the *Enterprise* closed the gap between them. Kirk's heart sank as he recognized that the greater challenge was still before him. Catching up with Una was the easy part; stopping her without attacking the *Shimizu* might prove much more difficult, if not impossible. He prayed it wouldn't come to that.

"Hail the *Shimizu*," Kirk instructed Uhura. "Inform her that we *will* open fire if she does not halt her escape."

Uhura nodded grimly. "Aye, sir."

Don't make me to do this, Una, Kirk thought. *For both our sakes.*

He wasn't looking forward to explaining to Starfleet why he had fired on another Starfleet captain in order to stop her from absconding with a dangerous piece of alien tech that had never made it into the official records. Kirk imagined that Commodore April would testify on his behalf if needed; the *Enterprise*'s former captain was serving as an ambassador-at-large for the Federation these days, but he would surely take responsibility for hiding the Key from Starfleet in the first place, although Kirk hated the idea of putting his esteemed predecessor in that position. *The Key was in my care,* Kirk thought. *This is on me.*

"Captain Una is responding to our hail," Uhura reported.

"Good," Kirk said. "Let's hear what she has to say."

McCoy snorted. "I know I'm all ears. Maybe I can finally figure out what in blazes we're doing here."

That's what I'm afraid of, Kirk thought. *What if Una spills the beans right in front of Bones and the others?*

Una's face took over the screen once more. "*I asked you not to follow me, Kirk.*"

She sounded more disappointed than surprised.

"You know I had to."

He wanted to elaborate, but found himself hampered by the fact that he couldn't speak openly about the Key here on the bridge, which he could hardly leave in the midst of a crisis. Even as he spoke, Yeoman Bates was hovering right outside the command well, watching wide-eyed as this unlikely confrontation unfolded. Chances were, she was already transcribing the encounter for Kirk's convenience. How was he supposed to talk Una down when he had to watch his every word?

"*I suppose it's too late to ask you to reconsider?*"

"I'm afraid so," he replied. "We have reason to believe that you are on course for the Korinar Sector, which you must know is claimed by both the Federation and the Klingons. Entering that space now, only weeks before the upcoming treaty talks, is reckless in the extreme . . . and risks bringing us back to the brink of war."

He hoped that would be explanation enough for the crew, at least with regards as to why they were in pursuit of the *Shimizu*. With luck, the full story behind Una's actions could be kept on a need-to-know basis.

Or was that just wishful thinking?

"The Klingons' dubious claims to the region complicate matters," Una conceded, *"but I'm confident that I can slip in and out of the sector without being detected. I doubt, however, that the same can be said of the* Enterprise. *A small, inconspicuous spacecraft like the* Shimizu *is far less likely to attract the Klingons' attention than a* Constitution-*class starship."*

"You're probably right," Kirk said, "but I'm not about to let you test that theory. You need to stop and surrender your vessel before this goes too far."

"We are past the point of no return, Kirk. I have to finish what I started, no matter what."

Kirk noted that she was being deliberately vague as well, no doubt equally aware of the curious ears listening to them. He supposed he should be grateful for that, but he couldn't quite muster the feeling. They wouldn't be in this mess if she hadn't run off with the Key in the first place.

"We're coming within firing range, sir," Chekov reported, keeping his voice low. Taut body language betrayed his discomfort. He licked his lips nervously. "Torpedoes ready and loaded."

"Jim," McCoy said. "Tell me we're not actually thinking about firing. Good God, we were having drinks with this woman just last night."

"I know, Doctor. I know."

Kirk was just as appalled as McCoy at the prospect of firing on the *Shimizu*. Photon torpedoes were not delicate instruments. Even if they tried to surgically target the ship and not its pilot, there was no guarantee that Captain Una would survive the attack. A hull breach, a radiation leak, or even a warp-core explosion were all very real possibilities if the *Enterprise* unleashed its firepower in sufficient force to overcome the *Shimizu's* shields. But to keep Una—and the Key—from crossing into Klingon territory, he might have to take that chance.

If Una forced his hand.

"Hold your fire, Ensign. For now."

Spock shot him a worried look, no doubt equally concerned for Una's safety, if not more so. He had insisted earlier that Una surely had a good reason for pursuing this course of action, based on his past knowledge of her character.

Kirk wished he could be so sure.

"You're taking an enormous risk," he told her. "What if, despite your caution, you fall into Klingon hands? You'd be putting Starfleet—and the Federation—in a very difficult position."

"*Not if Starfleet disavows all knowledge of my actions, which would be nothing less than the truth, since I am genuinely acting entirely of my own volition here, Kirk. That's why I didn't want to involve you and Spock . . . or the* Yorktown. *This is on me alone.*"

Was that why she hadn't simply asked for the Key? So that no blame would attach to anyone else?

"You realize, of course, that you could end up in a Klingon prison camp? Or worse?"

"*That's a risk I'm prepared to take,*" she said. "*And that's why I'm asking you one more time to call off your pursuit. It's better for everyone if the* Enterprise *is not involved any further.*"

"Your argument would be more convincing if I actually knew what you're attempting to accomplish."

"*Again, it's better that you don't know.*"

"That's not good enough," Kirk said, losing patience. "And it's not your decision to make." He chose his words carefully. "What you . . . acquired . . . from my ship was my responsibility now. You had no right to proceed without my permission."

"*Granted, but I wished to spare you that choice, and I couldn't take the chance that you would deny my request.*"

Which implied that he might have wanted to if he'd actually known what she had in mind. Kirk did not find that reassuring. Whatever Una was up to, it was something she had expected him to object to. Perhaps with good reason?

"*Consider yourself relieved of the responsibility, Kirk. This is on my head now. Una out.*"

Her face vanished from the screen as she cut off the transmission.

"Captain," Spock said. "I have been scanning the configuration of the *Shimizu's* shields. They appear to have been programmed to repeatedly and rapidly cycle through a series of field harmonics, along with corresponding modulations to the graviton polarities, in order to increase their 'slipperiness' as Mister Chekov said. But I believe I have discerned a pattern to the frequency shifts, and should be able to adjust our own tactical responses accordingly."

Kirk cut through the scientific details. "And the bottom line is . . . ?"

"I believe I may be able to lock a tractor beam on the *Shimizu* if we can get close enough for a sufficient duration. To be more precise, a distance of approximately one point seven kilometers for a period of at least two point six minutes."

Kirk felt a surge of hope. Locking onto the *Shimizu* with a tractor beam was vastly preferable to blowing it out of the sky. Maybe there was still a way to end this crisis without harm to anything except, perhaps, Captain Una's sterling reputation.

"Do it," he ordered. "Mister Chekov, transfer tractor controls to the science station." He gazed resolutely at the ship on the screen, whose sleek contours could now be made out. "Mister Sulu, bring us closer to the *Shimizu*."

"Aye, sir!"

The *Enterprise* accelerated toward the other ship, which suddenly banked to the left and vanished from sight.

"Sulu," Kirk prompted.

"I'm on it," the helmsman said. The *Enterprise* changed course to match the *Shimizu*'s evasive maneuver, and Kirk waited tensely for Una's ship to reappear on the screen.

And waited . . .

"I don't understand," Chekov said. "Where is she?"

"Behind us," Spock announced, staring at his sensor

readings. "She dropped out of warp as soon as she was out of our way, so that we shot past her at warp speed."

Clever, Kirk thought, admiring her ingenuity despite everything. He recalled that she'd been Pike's helmsman as well as his first officer. *She's got more experience than Spock and I put together, so I can't afford to underestimate her. Who knows what tricks she's picked up over the years?*

"Back around, Mister Sulu!" he ordered. "Keep after her!"

"Aye, sir!"

Turning the bow of the ship upward, Sulu executed a partial loop that sent the *Enterprise* zooming back the way they'd come. Kirk thanked Starfleet engineering for the artificial gravity that kept up and down firmly in place no matter how the ship was oriented in space. Otherwise, Sulu's barnstorming maneuvers might have felt like an old-fashioned roller-coaster ride, and they'd all be crashing into the ceiling.

"The *Shimizu*?" Kirk asked. "Have we lost her?"

"Not yet." Spock peered into his scope. "I still have her on my sensors."

Good, Kirk thought. Una had bought herself a little extra time with her creative piloting, but what did she truly hope to accomplish by such moves? They were still hours away from the Korinar Sector, so how much of a head start could she hope to gain?

"Is she still on course for the disputed region?" he asked.

"Negative," Spock stated. "She is veering toward a nearby solar system."

"What system?" Kirk demanded. "An inhabited one?"

Could Una be attempting to rendezvous with accomplices, or perhaps seeking sanctuary on some unknown world? Kirk wasn't aware of any major civilizations in this region, but Starfleet had hardly charted every Class-M planet in the quadrant. The galaxy remained full of strange new worlds waiting to be discovered.

"Negative," Spock reported. "Sensors indicate that the system is a stellar graveyard with a solitary white dwarf at its center. Any inner planets were surely destroyed when the star swelled into its red-giant stage billions of years ago, long before it collapsed under its own weight. Only a few outer planets remain, held in place by the white star's gravity. A gas giant and an assortment of smaller planets, planetoids, moons, and asteroids."

A white dwarf was the last stop on many a star's life-cycle: the cooling, super-dense remains of a once-vibrant sun. Like a grave marker in space.

"A dead system," Kirk said. "What could she be after there?"

"Cover?" Spock suggested. "Even a sparse system offers more opportunities to hide and duck behind than open space. She may be counting on the *Shimizu*'s smaller size and increased maneuverability to help her elude our weapons and tractor beams."

Like darting from cover to cover during a firefight, Kirk thought. *Una's not making this easy on us.*

"Approaching system," Chekov reported. On the viewscreen, the white dwarf was barely visible in the distance. Roughly the size of Earth, the incredibly dense stellar remnant still had the mass of a much larger star. "Look! There's the *Shimizu*."

Kirk caught a glimpse of the fleeing spacecraft before it disappeared behind an ice planet at the outer fringes of the system.

"Slow to impulse," Kirk ordered, "and stay on her tail."

Barreling into a solar system, even a lifeless one, at warp speed was a recipe for disaster, so they had no choice but to slow down, especially if they were going to play cat-and-mouse with the *Shimizu* across the system. But the smaller craft couldn't go back to warp either, not without leaving the shelter of the system's varied moons and planets.

"Maybe we can cut her off at the pass," Sulu suggested.

"Whatever works," Kirk said. A highly fluid situation like this one, where the variables were constantly changing, was no time to micromanage his crew. Kirk found he often got better results by trusting his people to do their jobs to the best of their abilities. "At your discretion, Helmsman."

"Aye, aye, Captain." A cocky grin indicated that Sulu appreciated the vote of confidence. "Hold on tight."

Instead of pursuing the *Shimizu* around to the other side of the planet, whose very atmosphere was likely frozen due to its distance from its collapsed sun, the *Enterprise* sped forward, hoping to intercept the courier when it came out from behind the cover of the lifeless world. Kirk didn't like losing sight of the *Shimizu*, even for a moment, but if they could get in front of the other ship, it would be worth the risk. He was in no mood to play tag with the *Shimizu* for heaven knew how long.

"Ready on that tractor beam, Mister Spock."

"Affirmative, Captain," he replied. "Standing by."

At least she can't be planning to touch down on the planet, Kirk thought. The *Shimizu* was designed for planetary landings since, like a shuttlecraft, it wasn't equipped with its own transporters, but the desolate ice world before them offered nothing in the way of habitation or shelter, which made him wonder if there was any reason that Una had ventured into this particular system. Had she chosen it at random, on the spur of the moment, or was she up to something?

Knowing Una, he suspected the latter.

"Here she comes!" Chekov blurted as the *Shimizu* shot out from behind the planet less than a few kilometers away from the *Enterprise.*

"Now, Spock!" Kirk said.

The science officer shook his head. "Not possible. I need another minute to synchronize our polarities."

But Una seemed uninclined to grant them that minute. Taking full advantage of the three-dimensional nature of spaceflight, the *Shimizu* dived sharply at a forty-five-degree angle to put more distance between herself and the *Enterprise* before swerving abruptly to port, forcing Sulu to match heading and speed without warning. Yeoman Bates stumbled, losing her balance. Lieutenant Charlene Masters, who was posted at the engineering station, called out to Kirk.

"Captain, these maneuvers are placing a severe strain on the inertial dampers, not to mention the subspace field coils. Our engines weren't built to keep up with that high-speed courier."

"Understood," Kirk answered, trusting Scotty to hold things together in engineering long enough for them to snare the *Shimizu* and bring this maddening chase to a close. He tapped his foot impatiently against the deck. "Sulu?"

"I'm trying, Captain, but it's like chasing an old-time jet fighter with a jumbo jet," Sulu said, betraying his passion for aviation history. "There's no question that we can outlast her in the long run, but she's definitely making us work for it."

Kirk could wish that Una was less intrepid.

"She's switched course again," Chekov reported. "Heading for the gas giant."

The viewer confirmed the young Russian's announcement. Moving like a bat out of hell, and darting about just as unpredictably, the *Shimizu* plunged into orbit around the immense ball of gas, which dwarfed both ships by several orders of magnitude. Swirling brown and yellow clouds, each large enough to swallow several Earth-sized planets, mottled the giant's churning atmosphere as the swift, small spacecraft weaved in and out of the planet's numerous moons and debris rings. The distances between the obstacles were still vast by most standards, but required careful navigation nonetheless.

Kirk had to admire Una's fancy flying at the same time that her stubborn efforts to evade the *Enterprise* grated on his nerves. Still hot on the *Shimizu*'s tail, the *Enterprise* came in closer to the gas giant, which practically filled the viewscreen until Spock helpfully reduced the magnification by several degrees.

"The tractor beam?" Kirk asked.

"The *Shimizu*'s evasive tactics are defeating my efforts," Spock confessed, "as the planet's myriad satellites are repeatedly obstructing our tractor beams." A note of grudging admiration entered his voice. "I recall her employing a similar strategy some years ago when our shuttlecraft was ambushed by an Orion slaver vessel while scouting an uncharted system in the Beta Quadrant. She managed to elude capture long enough for Captain Pike and the *Enterprise* to come to our assistance, forcing the Orions to retreat."

Kirk vaguely remembered reading about the incident in Pike's logs. "Number One" had received a commendation for keeping the shuttlecraft and its passengers safe from the Orions. Kirk was less impressed now that the trick was being used against him.

"But what does she hope to gain by stalling this time around?" he asked aloud. "She must know we'll go back to warp the minute she bolts from this system."

Chekov inspected his sensor readings. "You don't think she's expecting reinforcements, do you?"

"I doubt it," Kirk said. "She said she was working alone, and I'm inclined to believe her. But keep a lookout for any other vessels entering the system." He turned toward Uhura. "You too, Lieutenant."

"My ears are open," she promised. "Trust me, sir, you'll be the first to know if I hear strangers on their way."

Bates reentered the command well, joining Kirk and McCoy. She prudently kept one hand on a safety rail. "Should we try to force her out of the system?" she asked. "Or will that just prolong the chase?"

"Good question, Yeoman," Kirk replied. "She can't

keep ducking behind moons forever, and she's running out of cover."

Beyond the gas giant, nothing remained between it and the white dwarf except empty space occupied only by the drifting gas and dust left behind when the star shed most of its outer layers during its contraction. The expelled matter would have formed a planetary nebula, which had gradually dissipated over vast stretches of time, while any inner planets had been cremated millions of years earlier, during the star's final expansion before its collapse. Una could find no more cover in the dead zone surrounding the white dwarf; she had gone as deep as she could into the system.

"Keep a sharp watch," Kirk instructed Sulu. "Don't let her double back to the outer planets, or we'll be right back where we started."

"Understood, Captain," the helmsman said. "I've got better things to do than play hide-and-seek all day."

Don't we all, Kirk thought. He shifted restlessly in his chair, feeling certain that Captain Una had another trick in store for them. But what was she planning next?

"I could go in closer to the planet," Sulu volunteered.

"And play tag amidst its moons and gravity wells?" Kirk shook his head. "The *Shimizu* has the advantage on us there. We're better off waiting her out."

As it happened, they didn't have to wait long.

"Captain!" Chekov said. "She's making a break for it!"

Kirk experienced a fresh rush of adrenaline. "Out of the system?"

"No, sir." Puzzlement could be heard in Chekov's voice. "She's heading deeper into the system, toward the dead star."

Kirk reeled back in surprise. "What?"

For a horrifying moment, he feared that Una meant to destroy herself and the Key. Was that the closure she had alluded to earlier? But, no, that didn't make sense, he realized. If Una had simply wanted to go out in a blaze of glory, taking the Key with her, there were far easier ways to go about that than diving into the crushing gravity of a white dwarf.

"Has she lost her A-number-one mind?" McCoy exclaimed. "What is she thinking?"

"The hell if I know," Kirk said. "Follow her, Sulu, as close as we dare."

"Aye, Captain," Sulu responded. "Continuing pursuit."

This could still be our chance, Kirk thought. Now that she was clear of any planets or moons, perhaps they could finally catch up with her long enough for Spock to grab her with a tractor beam—and drag the *Shimizu* back into the *Enterprise*'s hangar deck.

"It's too late, Captain," Chekov said, audibly aghast. "She's going to warp!"

"Toward the star?" Kirk didn't understand. "That can't be—"

Spock figured it out faster than anyone else.

"Slingshot," he said, looking up from his own sensor readings. Even his perpetually calm voice sounded hushed by the revelation. "She means to achieve a slingshot effect."

Kirk couldn't believe his ears. The slingshot maneuver was an incredibly risky and frankly desperate stunt that involved flying a vessel at high speed dangerously close to a star and then breaking away at the last minute, so

that the star's intense gravitational field would accelerate the vessel away from the star with tremendous force.
Rarely attempted, and only in the direst of circumstances,
a slingshot effect could even break the time barrier and
propel a ship into the past or future.

"To travel through time?" Kirk asked.

"Possibly," Spock said. "Or she could simply be
attempting to attain a velocity that we cannot possibly
match without resorting to the same extreme measures."

And people think I'm reckless, Kirk thought. "Is it
possible? Can the *Shimizu* pull it off, using a white dwarf
of all things?"

"In theory, yes," Spock said. "Despite its size, the
dwarf star has sufficient mass to generate a gravitational
field comparable to a standard main-sequence star. In
which case, all else that is required is split-second timing,
precise calculations, and a mind capable of performing
the necessary computations."

"Which Una has," Kirk said, "in spades."

"Unquestionably," Spock stated, although a trace
of worry showed through his Vulcan reserve. "There is
virtually no margin for error, however, and Captain Una
will require a healthy degree of luck as well."

McCoy gave him an incredulous look. "I thought
Vulcans didn't believe in luck."

"When attempting a slingshot maneuver, Doctor, luck
is always a factor."

As we know from personal experience, Kirk thought.
The *Enterprise* had barely survived the maneuver last
year, when they'd used it to return to the present after
an unplanned trip to the twentieth century. As far as

Kirk knew, the *Enterprise* was the only Starfleet vessel to attempt the feat, let alone come through it in one piece. The harrowing stunt had nearly torn the ship apart.

"On screen," he ordered. "Full magnification."

Spock deftly operated his control panel. "Increasing magnification to full."

The *Shimizu* appeared on the viewer, accelerating away from the *Enterprise* at warp speed. The gleaming, compact spacecraft looked none the worse for wear after careening wildly through the solar system, but was it sturdy enough to survive what lay ahead? A breathless hush fell over the bridge as Una's ship dived into a tight orbit around the dense white dwarf, flying opposite the dead star's own rotation in order to achieve a reverse slingshot effect. For a seemingly endless moment, the *Shimizu* could be seen streaking against the cold, faint radiance of the white dwarf . . . and then it vanished from sight.

"She's gone!" Chekov exclaimed. "I've lost her!"

"Likewise," Spock said. "She has disappeared from even our long-range sensors."

"But to where?" Kirk asked anxiously. "The future? The past?"

Time travel was new to Starfleet, having been first achieved by *Enterprise* barely more than a year ago— and duplicated months later after a near-catastrophic run-in with a black star. There was already some talk of employing the technique to deliberately travel back in time to conduct historical research, but this was still unexplored territory that nobody really had a handle on just yet. Starfleet itself was divided on the subject, with some urging extreme caution where time travel was concerned and others equally vocal about pushing forward into the fourth dimension.

Kirk wondered where Captain Una sided on this issue.

"A moment, Captain," Spock said, "while I analyze our recordings of what just transpired."

"This just keeps getting crazier," McCoy complained. He leaned in toward Kirk and lowered his voice. "You ever going to fill me in on just what the devil has possessed her?"

Kirk sympathized with the doctor's confusion, but remained conscious of Bates standing nearby, not to mention Sulu and Chekov and the rest of the bridge crew, who had to be just as baffled as McCoy. There was no way to fully explain Una's actions—or his own—without speaking openly of the Key.

"Not now, Doctor," he said firmly.

"Well, then when—?" McCoy began, only to be silenced by a stern look from Kirk. Getting the message, he backed off for the moment. "Never mind. I can wait."

Thank heaven for small favors, Kirk thought. *I've got my hands full with a renegade captain. I don't need a curious doctor breathing down my neck too.*

Spock spoke up from the science station.

"I have completed my calculations. Judging from her recorded speed, her proximity to the white dwarf, the precise mass of the star, and the duration of the maneuver, I estimate that the *Shimizu* did not actually break the time barrier, but simply used the slingshot effect to exit the system at high speed and accelerate beyond our reach."

"Just enough to shake our tail," Kirk said, understanding. "And get a substantial head start on us."

"As I expect she planned all along." Spock swiveled his seat toward Kirk. "This particular white dwarf was detected by long-range instruments generations ago and is duly listed in all the relevant databases."

"So she would have known it was here," Kirk realized. "Along her escape route."

Spock nodded. "Without a doubt."

The *Enterprise* continued to approach the dead star, albeit at impulse. Its faint luminosity cast a spectral glow over the surrounding space. More dead than alive, it had still proven capable of aiding and abetting a fugitive.

Sulu looked back at Kirk. "Shall we follow her, sir?"

Kirk was tempted. He hated being outsmarted by Una, if not quite as much as he was troubled by the idea of her heading toward the Klingon Empire with the Key. But he had not forgotten just how close the *Enterprise* had come to destruction the last time they had attempted the slingshot maneuver. Maybe Una was willing to take that chance with her own life, but Kirk was not about to risk his ship—and over four hundred lives—just to keep the *Shimizu* from getting away.

"Negative," Kirk said. "Set a course for the Korinar Sector."

Una may have gained a head start, but this chase wasn't over yet, since he had a pretty good idea where she was ultimately going with that Key.

Back to where it all began, eighteen years ago . . .

2249

Five

Captain's log, 2 October 2249 CE
Even after four years exploring the final frontier, the universe still finds way to surprise us. While conducting a routine survey of the remote Libros system, we find ourselves confronted with a most perplexing mystery, as well as, possibly, a troubling moral dilemma. . . .

"Well, I'll be," Captain Robert April said. "This is unexpected."

The first captain of the *Space Ship Enterprise* contemplated the latest sensor readings from the planet below, which were displayed on the data slate in his hands. A wooly gray cardigan, worn over his gold turtleneck tunic, gave him a benign avuncular air, as did his gentle, fortyish features, wavy brown hair, and twinkling chestnut eyes. A distinct Coventry accent betrayed his roots back on Earth.

"You can say that again," First Officer Lorna Simon replied from the science station at starboard. Nearing retirement age, she was a short, round woman whose silver hair and shrewd eyes testified to a lifetime of experience. Her tough, no-nonsense attitude had helped see the *Enterprise* through any number of challenges. A blue tunic and black slacks fit her comfortably.

"Preliminary sensor scans indicate a large artificial complex on the planet's surface that was not there ten years ago . . . and shouldn't be there now."

Probably not, April thought. Earlier unmanned probes, surveying the system a decade ago, had reported a primitive, preindustrial culture on the planet, but now an advanced technological fortress seemed to have appeared out of nowhere.

"Conquest, colonization," Simon ticked off the possibilities. "That's the only explanation that makes sense. The energy readings I'm picking up from the citadel indicate technology ridiculously beyond the natives' last-reported stage of development."

"You're most likely right," April agreed. "But can we be certain that alien intervention is the *only* explanation? Punctuated development—where a sentient species suddenly takes a great leap forward after centuries, even millennia, of cultural and scientific stasis—is not unheard-of in this galaxy. Look at the way the H'Ramo jumped from a feudal civilization, composed of warring fiefdoms, to a democratic world government in barely more than a generation . . . or even the rapid-fire, cascading scientific advances on Earth from, say, the twentieth century on. Or the Vulcans' Great Awakening, for that matter."

Simon shook her head.

"I'm still not buying it. According to those old surveys, the inhabitants of Libros III were barely out of the stone age. Even if they underwent a renaissance to end all renaissances, there's no way they could have built that citadel in less than ten years . . . not unless they had help."

"If that complex even houses the indigenous population at all," April said. "For all we know, it could be an alien outpost . . . or military base."

Lorna shot him a look. "The Klingons?"

"I hope not," April said. "Our most recent intelligence is that the Empire has not expanded into this sector yet, but you know the Klingons. They're always pushing outward, even where they're not welcome."

Almost a century had passed since the Broken Bow incident, and relations between the Federation and the Klingon Empire had hardly improved since that tumultuous first contact. With the Federation expanding by means of diplomacy and exploration, and the Empire aggressively extending its borders through naked conquest and subterfuge, the two galactic superpowers seemed to be on a collision course, with occasional border skirmishes becoming more and more frequent. April himself had butted heads with the Klingons more than once, sometimes with dire results. There were those, even in Starfleet, who thought that war was inevitable, but April didn't want to believe that. An optimist at heart, he wanted to believe that the universe had room enough for everyone.

But maybe he was just being naïve.

"Are there any indications that the citadel is Klingon in origin?" he asked.

"Nope," Simon admitted. "Honestly, the energy signatures don't match the technology of any interstellar civilization I'm familiar with."

And that's saying something, April thought, given his first officer's lifetime of experience. "So we may have newcomers on our hands, strangers to us and strangers to Libros III, who appear to have already established a toehold on the planet."

He contemplated the lush green world on the main viewer. Cottony white clouds drifted above scattered seas and continents that gave it a pleasant resemblance to Earth. Libros was a Class-M planet that looked exceedingly hospitable; only the fact that it was already inhabited by sentient life-forms had kept it from being a target ripe for colonization. The Prime Directive was quite clear when it came to setting up shop on planets with their own indigenous peoples. But perhaps these newcomers were not concerned with such niceties?

"I wonder where in the galaxy our new friends hail from," he said.

"And how they got here," Lieutenant Una added from the nav station. The dark-haired young Illyrian looked up from the readouts on her control panel. "Tactical sensors do not detect the presence of any other vessels in this system, let alone in orbit or on the planet's surface. The *Enterprise* is the only spacecraft for light-years in every direction."

April took her word for it. Over the last few years, Una had more than lived up to her reputation as a prodigy, showing a natural aptitude for every post to which she'd been assigned. Una had graduated first in her class at the Academy, and one year ahead of schedule to boot. Despite her youth, April considered himself lucky to have snagged her for his crew and had recently promoted her to lieutenant. She was going places, that was for certain.

"That's easily enough accounted for, Una," he said, addressing her with his customary informality. "The ship—or ships—that transported them here may have already come and gone. Lord knows the Federation has plenty of isolated colonies and science stations that may only see a visiting starship every few years at most. Perhaps our newcomers were dropped off some time ago and left to fend for themselves." He rested his chin on his knuckles. "Which still begs the question of who they are and what exactly they're doing on Libros III."

"And what they're doing to the original inhabitants of the planet," Lorna Simon said grimly. "Orbital scans are picking up evidence of sizable agricultural projects, deforestation, maybe even some degree of biological terraforming. Entire forests and jungles have been razed. Rivers have been dammed and diverted. Mountains strip-mined." A frown deepened the well-earned creases on her face. "Have to wonder where our newcomers are finding the labor for such ambitious undertakings—and whether the native Librosians are going along with this willingly."

April heard what she was saying. "You fear the colonists are exploiting the locals?"

"Wouldn't be the first time in history," she replied. "Sad to say."

"Nor the last," he admitted. April was an optimist, but he was also a realist. When a more technologically advanced culture moved into territory occupied by a less developed people, the results were often tragic for the latter. "Particularly if that new territory has resources to exploit."

"That's how I read this," Simon said. "Judging from

the way the newcomers seem to be running roughshod over the planet's environment, we may have stumbled onto a full-scale planetary occupation that's been under way for as long as ten years now." She scowled at her readings. "I guess those people in the citadel don't have their version of the Prime Directive."

"But we do," April said. "Which puts us in a thorny situation."

"Sir?" Una gave him a concerned look. "Surely we can't just stand by and let a primitive species be oppressed, maybe even enslaved, by alien invaders. The Librosians deserve the right to determine their own future, without outside interference. That's what the Prime Directive is all about."

April recalled that the Illyrians, perhaps even more than most cultures, placed great stock on freedom and self-determination. As a people, they were known to choose death over servitude. Indeed, Una had once bluffed some Suliban terrorists by threatening to blow up an entire space station full of hostages, including herself.

Or had she been bluffing?

"I'm afraid it's more complicated than that," he said. "The Prime Directive is our regulation; to force it on others, like those mysterious newcomers down there, might itself be seen as a violation of the Prime Directive."

Una eyed him skeptically. "Sophistry, sir?"

"Not at all," he insisted. "Suppose that conquest or colonization is an integral part of the newcomers' culture or biology. Are we imposing our own beliefs on them if we interfere with their efforts on Libros III?"

Simon snorted. "Conquest comes naturally to the

Klingons. Doesn't mean we have to roll out the welcome mat for them."

"When they venture into our territory, threaten our people, certainly not," April agreed. "But we're currently far beyond the boundaries of the Federation. We have no jurisdiction over Libros III, while, for all we know, the newcomers may well consider that they have a legal claim on the planet, according to their own rules and customs."

The newcomers had effectively planted their flag. Maybe that was enough as far as they were concerned?

"But what of the Librosians, sir?" Una persisted. "Wasn't it their planet already? And isn't their natural development already being interfered with?"

"Ah, there's the rub to be sure." April's affable manner grew more somber. "Don't think me insensitive to your concerns, Una. History contains all too many horror stories of native populations and cultures being oppressed and even exterminated by foreign intruders. The last thing this poor galaxy needs is one more such tragedy, but the Prime Directive exists to prevent us from rushing in and playing God where we don't belong. We need to tread lightly here, at least until all the facts are in."

The problem with the Prime Directive, he reflected, was that it was still subject to interpretation. Perhaps someday, a few generations hence, there would be a substantial body of precedents for future Starfleet captains to draw upon when making their decisions, but at present the ink was barely dry on the Directive, which allowed for considerable leeway when it came to the actual business of encountering strange new worlds and civilizations. And perhaps that was just as well. In his experience, there was seldom a one-size-fits-all approach to every situation, and a certain degree of flexibility was not always a bad thing, even if that meant some hard choices sometimes.

"In that case, Captain," Una said, "perhaps what is required is more data."

April nodded. "Right you are, Lieutenant. A discreet scouting mission is definitely in order."

"Permission to lead the landing party, sir?" Una requested.

"That's the captain's call, Lieutenant," Simon said. "Don't get pushy."

"Now, now, Lorna," April replied, unbothered by Una's request. Unlike some younger, brasher captains, he didn't feel compelled to lead every landing mission. "Let's not discourage individual initiative." He regarded the young lieutenant thoughtfully; Una had yet to lead a landing party on her own, but was probably ready for that respon-sibility. "You clearly have strong feelings on this subject, Una. Be honest now: Are you going to be able to keep those feelings under control?"

She raised her chin high.

"I'm Illyrian, sir. Vulcans envy our self-control."

She doesn't lack confidence, that one, April thought, repressing a chuckle. *Then again, considering her stellar track record, why should she?*

"Careful, Una," he said gently. "There's a human saying, 'Pride goeth before the fall.'"

"Proverbs, 16:18," she cited. "And I believe the actual quote is 'Pride goeth before destruction, and a haughty spirit before a fall.'"

Touché, April thought. "Very well, Lieutenant. Organize a landing party and report to the transporter room. And I'd advise including Lieutenant Commander Martinez in the party. He's a good man to have along in these situations."

Raul Martinez was a smart, able-bodied officer who had already spearheaded several successful planetary missions. He had proven he could keep a cool head—and, if necessary, a low profile—on any number of occasions, some of them more than a little dicey. Like that nasty business on Sofya V, for instance. April had faith in Una, but it couldn't hurt having a more seasoned officer backing her up the first time she commanded a landing party.

If Una's ego was threatened by Martinez's inclusion, she gave no indication of it. She was *that* confident, perhaps.

"Thank you, Captain." She sprang to her feet and turned the nav station over to Ensign Stevens, who was on standby. "I won't let you down."

She marched briskly to the turbolift, which carried her away from the bridge. Simon sighed as she watched the eager young lieutenant depart.

"Why do I always think she's gunning for my job?"

"Give her time," April said. "Give her time."

Six

"Hey, Number One," Ensign Tim Shimizu greeted Una as she entered the transporter room. "You get roped into this expedition too?"

She had personally selected her friend for the landing party. The gangly, easygoing biologist had been her best friend since their Academy days and was one of the few crew members aboard the *Enterprise* who still addressed her by that nickname. A neatly trimmed goatee added character to his face, or so he insisted. He had been a year ahead of her when they'd first met in San Francisco, but she'd caught up with him soon enough. Unlike others, he'd never acted threatened or intimidated by her excellence or even by the fact that, as of recently, she now outranked him. She appreciated that more than she ever let on.

"I didn't get drafted," she replied. "I'm leading this mission. And we're on duty, so it's 'Lieutenant Una' if you don't mind."

He shrugged and flashed an infectious grin. "What can I say? You'll always be 'Number One' to me, although we both know you would have never made it to the top without me backing you up all the way."

"Keep telling yourself that, Shimizu."

The transporter room was abuzz with prelanding excitement. Word of the mysterious alien citadel had spread through the ship faster than a Rigelian fever, proving again that subspace radio was no match for scuttlebutt when transmitting news. Besides herself and Shimizu, the landing party consisted of Martinez and three security officers: Griffin, Le May, and Cambias. All had arrived fully equipped for the mission; Una inspected her own gear, making sure her communicator, tricorder, laser pistol, and universal translator all were in working order. A lightweight backpack held additional equipment, such as a first-aid kit and containers for soil samples and biological specimens. She clipped her weapon and communicator onto the backpack's straps. The tricorder was slung over her shoulder. A lightweight gray jacket was intended to provide protection from the elements.

Martinez approached her.

"Reporting for duty, Lieutenant. I understand you're taking lead on this expedition?"

In contrast to the captain, whose command style tended to the fatherly, Martinez had a reputation for being tough but fair. He was a serious, by-the-book officer who projected confidence and competence and expected nothing less from those serving beside him. Una respected that, as she admired his commanding presence and well-built, athletic physique. He was a born leader, whose authoritative manner Una hoped to emulate as she worked her way up the ranks to a command position. That he was also ruggedly good-looking was only slightly distracting.

Contrary to rumor, she was *not* made of duranium.

"That's correct, Lieutenant Commander. Glad to have you along."

Even though Martinez outranked her, April had put Una in charge. She didn't imagine that would be a problem. The commander was nothing if not a team player.

She stepped up onto the platform and cleared her throat.

"Your attention, please." All eyes turned toward her and she waited for any and all conversations to die down before addressing those assembled. "No doubt you've all heard the rumors about recent discoveries concerning Libros III, but allow me to give you the facts as we know them." She briefed the others in a concise and efficient fashion. "Stealth is a priority here. So far there's no indication that these newcomers have detected the *Enterprise*'s presence in orbit, and we'd prefer to keep it that way. The captain wants a better sense of the situation on the ground, and the players involved, before attempting to make contact with either the native Librosians or the newcomers. *If* he decides to make contact at all."

Tim Shimizu raised his hand. "Is that what we're calling the mystery aliens? The Newcomers?"

"For lack of a better term," Una said. "Remember, this is strictly a reconnaissance mission. If at all possible, we want to avoid bumping into either the Librosians or whoever built that citadel. Ideally, no one should even know we're on the planet. Understood?"

"Absolutely, Lieutenant," Martinez said.

A security officer—Lieutenant Griffin—spoke up. "What if we encounter hostiles?"

"Defend yourself if necessary," Una said, "but don't

start a war if you can help it. Everyone set their lasers on stun."

She had already done so, but double-checked her own sidearm in order to set a good example. Better safe than sorry.

"Everybody ready?" Una asked, fully expecting as much. "Then let's get a move on."

The party took their places on the transporter platform, with Una and Shimizu staking out positions beside each other. "So what do you think these Newcomers look like, anyway? I suppose it's too much to hope that they're refugees from a distant pleasure planet, preferably of the humanoid variety."

"Keep your mind on the mission, Ensign," Una said, not wanting to show any signs of favoritism, while repressing an urge to roll her eyes. Her friend's irrepressible comic streak had earned him a reprimand or two from Martinez over the years. "This isn't shore leave."

Shimizu looked only slightly abashed. "Sorry, Num—I mean, Lieutenant."

"Put us down approximately half a kilometer from the citadel," she instructed the transporter chief and her assistant, who were already stationed at the transporter control console. Beaming living beings through space was a complicated procedure that, ideally, employed two operators to ensure a safe and smooth transmit. "Close enough to be within walking distance, but far enough away to reduce the risk of our arrival being observed."

"Understood." Chief Celeste Darcel peered into the gooseneck viewer mounted over her control panel, which displayed targeting data from the ship's scanners.

She keyed in the selected coordinates. "You've got it, Lieutenant."

Una nodded. "Energize."

"Bon voyage," Darcel replied.

The familiar whine of the transporter, accompanied by a distinctive tingling sensation, sent a thrill of anticipation through Una, who, as always, relished the prospect of exploring a new and alien world. As far as she knew, the landing party would be the first visitors from the Federation to ever set foot on Libros III; that the enigmatic Newcomers had apparently beaten Starfleet to the planet did little to dampen her enthusiasm. She hoped she never got so old and jaded that beaming down to a new planet became routine. Moments like this were why she had joined Starfleet.

Dissolving into atoms, she experienced less than a heartbeat of bodiless transit before rematerializing . . . elsewhere.

The cool, sterile confines of the transporter room were abruptly replaced by a clearing deep in the heart of a tropical rain forest. Her new surroundings did not startle Una, who had been briefed to expect just such an environment, but the dramatic change was momentarily disorienting nonetheless. Dense green foliage and towering tree trunks replaced blue-gray metal bulkheads. Her boots sank into the muddy forest floor. Birdsong, shrill and erratic, supplanted the steady hum of the *Enterprise*'s engines. Bright golden sunlight poured down from a cloudless turquoise sky, causing Una to blink against the glare and raise a hand to shield her eyes. Compared to the controlled climate of the *Enterprise*, the air was hot and muggy. Una was tempted to shed her jacket, but remembered that rain forests were called that for a reason; it wasn't raining at the moment, but a sudden downpour was a definite possibility. The buzz and chitter of insects competed with the screeching birds. She swatted a tiny winged pest away from her face.

At least the gravity felt more or less the same, being typical of a Class-M world. Una took a moment to get her bearings, as did the rest of the landing party. She took a deep breath of the humid atmosphere, which carried a profusion of rich floral fragrances. She was reminded of a white-water rafting trip she had once taken down a jungle river on Nova Amazonia; that air had been just as damp and perfumed. Listening closely, Una thought she heard a stream gurgling somewhere to the north, deeper into the surrounding forest. Leafy ferns, shrubs, and seedlings grew along the fringes of the clearing, obscuring her view. The shady woods called out to her, offering escape from the blistering sun.

"Look sharp," Una said, surveying the landing site. "We don't seem to have any company, aside from some noisy wildlife, but stay alert." She glanced around, further orienting herself, before briskly getting down to business. "Which way to the citadel?"

Martinez consulted his tricorder. "Energy readings indicate that the outpost is due east, at approximately fifty-six degrees." He pointed in the proper direction. "That way."

"Thank you, Commander." She took point, leading the way. "Move out, people . . . quietly."

This proved easier said than done, as the team had to

shove their way through the heavy underbrush circling the clearing. Tangled vines and branches obstructed their progress, making Una wish that she had packed a machete along with her laser pistol. Spiky leaves and thorns proved the worth of her protective jacket and trousers. Fallen leaves and twigs crunched beneath her boots, more loudly than she would have liked; she could only hope that the noise would be swallowed up by the everyday cacophony of the jungle—and that there were no sentient beings close enough to hear the landing party trampling through the brush. She also kept a close eye out for any unhappy snakes, spiders, or slime devils; the ship's computer library had provided scant information on the planet's natural flora and fauna, so she was not going to assume that those long-ago probes had cataloged every life-form that might possibly be encountered on Libros III. This was still a largely unknown world.

"Too bad there's no time to collect any plant and soil samples," Shimizu said, gawking at the abundant flora. "A biologist could spend years cataloging this forest."

"Maybe later," Una commented, "after we've found out more about these Newcomers."

"Promises, promises."

A bent branch whipped past her and she reached out to block it before it could swipe Shimizu in the face. It smacked harmlessly against her palm instead.

"Thanks!" he said from directly behind her. "Have I mentioned before that your reflexes are scary-fast?"

"I prefer the adjective *superb*, but you're welcome." She ducked her head beneath another branch and parted two leafy green fronds in order to step between them.

Something scuttled over the toe of her boot before vanishing into a shrub. A dragonfly the size of a hawk fluttered past overhead. "Correct me if I'm wrong, but I think we can confirm that this planet is capable of supporting life."

"You think?" He tugged some clinging lianas out of his way. "We couldn't have beamed down onto a nice moonlit beach somewhere? I hear the southern shore is lovely this time of year."

"Just be thankful this isn't the rainy season," she replied. "Relatively speaking."

In truth, there was likely little variation in the seasons this close to the planet's equator. Una glanced up at the sky, noting the position of the sun. By her calculations, it was early morning in this corner of Libros III, even though it had been late afternoon on the *Enterprise*. She was grateful for the extra hours of daylight, which gave them more time to complete their mission.

At this rate, we're going to need them.

Emerging from a thicket, they found some relief, both from the sun and the foliage, as they made their way farther into the jungle. The evergreen canopy overhead, which looked to be at least forty-five meters above the forest floor, cast plenty of shade so that the way ahead was significantly less overgrown than at the fringe of the clearing. Clotted vines and shrubs gave way to a spongy carpet of fallen leaves, branches, lichens, and moss. Huge hardwood trees, some as tall as sixty meters, rose like columns from the ground, supported by thick buttress roots that threatened to trip unwary hikers. Filtered daylight dappled the rough, irregular bark protecting the tree trunks. Rotting logs, lying here and there, played nursemaid to fresh saplings, growing from the composting remains of their deceased forebears. A chorus of random squawks, chirps, and barks echoed from the upper reaches of the canopy, which sounded much more profusely populated than it was at ground level. Floral fragrances infused the air, blending with the rich loamy smell of the forest floor.

It took Una's eyes a moment to adjust to the gloom. She stepped carefully over a thick root that bulged from the ground like a throbbing vein. "Watch your step," she warned Shimizu. "We've got a bit of an obstacle course here."

"Will do," he said. "Whatever would I do without you?"

"Let's hope we never have to find out."

"Knock on wood," he said, rapping his knuckles against the nearest tree trunk. "Or bark or whatever."

The party wound their way through the trees and logs, occasionally wading through shallow streams and puddles. Their progress was less than linear, but tricorder readings kept them heading in the right direction, more or less. An actual path through the woods would have been convenient, Una reflected, but would have also increased their chances of accidentally encountering a native or Newcomer. It was probably just as well that their route appeared far from well-trodden.

"Wait!" she called out. "Do you hear that?"

Having already grown accustomed to the jungle's ordinary background chatter, her keen ears caught a different sound coming toward them from somewhere high above the treetops: a loud, steady buzz that sounded distinctly artificial.

Like the engine of an aircraft?

"Take cover!" Una ordered, which was arguably redundant given that the impenetrable canopy already shielded them from view. Still, Martinez and the others flattened themselves against the looming tree trunks in hopes of foiling any invisible scans or sensors. Una peered upward, hoping for a glimpse of the approaching aircraft, but that same verdant canopy frustrated her efforts. She could only hear the unseen vehicle pass overhead and then gradually fade away into the distance, flying off to who knew where.

"The Newcomers?" Martinez guessed.

"Undoubtedly," Una replied, "unless the native Librosians have progressed to mechanized aircraft in only a decade, or have acquired the technology from the Newcomers."

She winced at the latter possibility, which was about as egregious a breach of the Prime Directive as she could imagine.

Martinez glanced down at his tricorder. "Whatever it was, it was coming from the direction of the citadel."

Una nodded in acknowledgment. "How much farther?"

"Approximately three hundred meters," he said gruffly. "As the alien aircraft flies."

"Then let's pick up the pace," Una said. "I want to see where that craft came from."

Curiosity consumed her. Ordinarily, Una would enjoy a vigorous hike through the woods, but she was eager to reach their destination and learn more about the Newcomers and what they were doing here—and how that was affecting the native Librosians.

As the party marched on, a disturbing phenomenon presented itself. Incongruous gray fungi, in shades ranging from charcoal to slate, began to infiltrate the evergreen jungle. Mushrooms and molds sprouted from tree trunks and spread like weeds across the forest floor as well, displacing the underbrush. The distinctive fungus was infrequent at first, but increased in abundance as they drew ever nearer to the citadel. A noxious, mildewy odor emanated from shelf-like growths that overlapped each other like scales. Reflective mineral deposits caused the plump fruiting bodies to glitter oddly, like nothing else in the forest.

Una paused to examine a lumpish toadstool. "These growths don't appear as though they belong here. An invasive alien species?"

"That's my guess." Shimizu scanned the specimen with his own tricorder. "Preliminary readings indicate that these fungi are not native to the planet."

"I was afraid of that," Una said, scowling. "But is the contamination accidental or deliberate?"

Neither explanation appealed to her. Whether by carelessness or design, the Newcomers were already wreaking havoc on the planet's natural ecosystem, perhaps irrevocably. "More importantly, is it still possible to contain or reverse the damage?"

Shimizu glanced around at the spreading gray fungi. "If you ask me, it looks like it may be too late to close the barn door here."

"That's for the captain to decide," Martinez declared. "We're just here to get the lay of the land."

"I didn't realize this was that kind of expedition," Shimizu quipped, unable to resist that straight line. He wagged his eyebrows.

"You're not on shore leave, Ensign," Martinez said, stone-faced. "As I believe Lieutenant Una already reminded you."

"Understood, sir." He cast a sheepish look at Una. "Sorry, Lieutenant."

Una repressed an urge to shake her head—or her friend. Tim's playful nature was a big part of why she liked him, but he really needed to stop pressing his luck where Martinez was concerned. Not everybody appreciated his joking around, as previously demonstrated by that unamused stellar cartography professor back at the Academy, or the jealous boyfriend of that Risian dancing girl.

"How far to the citadel?" she asked, hoping to take the heat off Shimizu. "We should be coming within sight of it, correct?"

"Affirmative." Martinez consulted his tricorder to be certain. "It should be right up ahead, less than a hundred meters away."

"Good," Una said, lowering her voice. "Heads down, everyone, and no unnecessary chatter. The key word is *stealth*."

She crept forward cautiously.

"Remember, we want to see the Newcomers. We don't want them to see us."

Seven

A few more paces brought them to the edge of the forest. Thinning vegetation, both native and not, gave way to a rocky beach studded with massive boulders. Beyond the beach lay a huge lake or lagoon whose wide, flat surface was completely covered by a thick layer of algae whose flat gray color betrayed its alien origins. The invasive algae had spread over the lake and onto the shore, coating the rocks and pebbles at the water's edge. Large rock formations, some at least forty meters high, thrust up from the contaminated water but were dwarfed by the monumental edifice rising from the center of the lake like an artificial island. Peering out from behind a thick tree trunk, while the rest of the landing party also concealed themselves behind available trees and fronds and thickets, Una gazed in wonder at the object of their search.

The citadel looked like nothing else on the planet. Smooth, opalescent walls, which had already proved impervious to the *Enterprise*'s sensors, appeared equally opaque to the naked eye. A circular outer wall, approximately 60 meters in height and curving slightly inward at the top, guarded a central tower that climbed at least 130 meters above the defensive ring. The tower consisted of a vertical cylinder supporting a series of rotating saucers separated at regular intervals by upright lengths of the cylinder, like dividers on a post. The saucers tapered in size until you reached the top of the tower, which was crowned by a larger saucer overlooking the citadel and environs. An elaborate sensor array sprouted from the domed ceiling of the saucer like antennae. Una instinctively drew back to avoid being detected, while continuing to carefully examine the citadel.

Both the walls and the tower had a shiny, nacreous finish that reminded Una of polished sea shells; possibly a clue toward the Newcomers' nature or technology? Loud, rumbling sounds, as might be made by heavy machinery, could be heard even at a distance. Corresponding vibrations rippled the scum-covered surface of the lake. The musty odor of the algae wafted off the water, leaving a bad taste in Una's mouth and throat.

"Noisy," Shimizu said. "Just a lot of loud equipment, or is there heavy construction under way?"

"Hard to say." Una squinted at the citadel. "They could be expanding or reinforcing their outpost, or maybe that's just what the citadel always sounds like. They could have very different hearing apparatus from us."

"If they can hear at all," Martinez said. "A Class-M environment often means fairly standard biology as well, but, then again, the Newcomers are not from around here."

Una peered at the fortress through a pair of binoculars. "I'm not spying any individuals on the walls, but the architecture doesn't appear Klingon to me."

"Nor does it match up with any major spacefaring civilization known to the Federation." Martinez examined the readouts on his tricorder. "The construction materials are highly exotic, too, and not likely to be native to this planet or even this sector. To be honest, I can't even identify some of the materials involved. Whatever that citadel is made of, it didn't come from Libros III . . . or any world in our computer library."

"In other words, more mysteries." She looked over at Martinez. "Can we tell how many life-forms are present in the citadel?"

"Negative." He lowered his tricorder. "Our sensors can't penetrate those walls, at least not at this distance."

The lack of solid data frustrated Una. "Perhaps we should sneak closer?"

"That's your call, Lieutenant," Martinez said, frowning, "but—"

A familiar buzz, approaching the city from the south, caused the landing party to retreat back into the woods while still keeping their eyes on the citadel and the surrounding lake. They watched intently as the previously unseen aircraft passed over their heads and came into view.

A flying pod, perhaps slightly smaller than a Starfleet shuttlecraft, soared above them. Capsule-shaped, it sported two triangular wings that rose at forty-five-degree angles on its port and starboard sides. A polished iridescent hull glistened in the sunlight.

The pod glided over the lake toward the citadel. Watching from the cover of the forest, Una expected it to enter the city from above, but was surprised to see it dive into the lake instead, disappearing beneath the dull, colorless algae. The (obviously) amphibious craft had entered the water smoothly, making barely a splash.

"Huh?" Shimizu asked. "Where'd it go?"

"An underwater hangar?" Una speculated, putting down her binoculars. "I'm not seeing any visible gates or entrances above the waterline, at least not from this angle."

Her theory gained strength as a second craft, distinguished by a larger carrying capacity and a somewhat more weathered hull, shot from the lake and took to the air, accelerating in the direction from which the first craft had come. It buzzed above the jungle canopy as it sped away from them.

"I agree," Martinez said. "Looks like the only way in or out is underwater, which makes infiltrating that citadel a challenge, if we were so inclined. We can't beam directly into it if we can't see through those walls, so our only options are to try to scale the walls from the deck of a boat, coming back with a shuttlecraft . . . or making a swim for it."

Just then, another of the hawk-sized dragonflies appeared from the jungle behind them and flew out low over the lake. Without warning, a blood-red tentacle burst from the water and grabbed onto the dragonfly before dragging its prey back beneath the water. The attack was over in a heartbeat, so that Una only caught a glimpse of barbed suckers lining the underside of the tentacle before the monstrous limb vanished from sight.

Shimizu gulped. "I vote against swimming."

"I concur," Martinez said, schooling his own startled features. "In my opinion, it's too early to think about dropping by to say hello. This is just a preliminary scouting mission." His gaze shifted from the lake to the sky and back again. "At least they don't appear to have detected our presence yet, which is a big plus."

Perhaps, Una thought, but she was frustrated by how little hard data they had acquired about the Newcomers so far. She had promised the captain facts, but those remained in short supply. How was April supposed to make any decisions unless they found out more about the Newcomers and their motives?

As the team continued to observe the citadel, another pod exited the lake and climbed into the sky. Una couldn't tell if it was a third aircraft or the same one they'd seen before.

"Lots of coming and going," Shimizu noted. "Wonder what all the traffic is about."

Una mentally charted the pods' projected trajectories, extrapolating from their apparent headings. "Orbital scans detected evidence of large-scale agricultural efforts in that direction. I suspect the crafts are going back and forth between the citadel and that location."

"Makes sense to me." Martinez turned away from the citadel and its secrets. "While we're here, we should probably check out that site as well."

"Definitely," she agreed, remembering Commander Simon's fears regarding the possible exploitation of the native Librosians. She didn't want to return to the *Enterprise* without confirming or dispelling those concerns.

Shimizu glanced back the way they'd just traversed. "Too bad we didn't come by shuttlecraft," he said, clearly not looking forward to retracing their footsteps and then some. "How long of a hike are we talking about?"

Martinez was ready with the answer. "By my estimates, the other site is approximately six kilometers away. Through more of the forest, I'm afraid."

Shimizu sighed. "Terrific."

"I think we can skip that trek." Una flipped open her communicator. Its raised lid doubled as an antenna. "I ought to check in with the ship."

"Excuse me, Lieutenant," Petty Officer James Cambias said. The security officer regarded the citadel warily. "What if the Newcomers pick up your transmission?"

Una paused to give the matter due consideration. "Good question, Mister Cambias," she said after a moment's thought, "but I think we can risk it. If they didn't detect our transporter beam, and haven't reacted to the *Enterprise*'s arrival yet, I doubt if a single communicator signal will set off alarms. Plus, the captain is waiting to hear from us." She addressed Cambias and his fellow security officers. "Stay alert, just in case."

He nodded. "Aye, sir."

"Landing party to *Enterprise*," Una said, raising her communicator to her lips. "Reporting."

"*Signal received, landing party.*" She recognized the deep, gravelly voice of Spirit Claw Sanawey, the ship's chief communications officer. "*What is your status?*"

"We have observed the alien citadel from a prudent distance," Una stated, "and are now continuing our survey."

"*Acknowledged,*" Captain April replied directly. "*Thanks for checking in, Una. What's next on your itinerary?*"

"We've observed air traffic between the citadel and another site—" She glanced at Martinez, who handed her his tricorder with the relevant data on display. "—bearing fourteen degrees from our present location. Can you track that traffic to verify the precise location of the other site?"

"*We'll get right on that,*" April promised. "*In the meantime, have you made any new friends down there?*"

"No, sir. We're still exercising discretion on that front."

"*Glad to hear it.*"

She directed the tricorder at the communicator in her other hand. "Transmitting exterior scans of the citadel now."

"*Receiving data,*" Sanawey reported.

There was a brief delay before April resumed communication. "*All right, we've detected that air traffic you reported, which appears to connect sites all over the region. The nearest one is indeed approximately six kilometers from where you are now.*"

Una gave Martinez an appreciative nod.

"Acknowledged," she said. "Request point-to-point transfer to the site in question."

"*Permission granted,*" April replied. "*Find out what you can, Una.*"

"That's the plan, sir. Una out."

She put away her communicator and barely had time to hand the tricorder back to Martinez before she felt the familiar tingle of the transporter begin to reduce her to atoms once more. Dissolving, she considered the mechanics of the operation; in theory, they would actually be returning to the ship momentarily, in the form of six discrete matter streams, before being beamed back to the planet, albeit six kilometers to the south.

Let's hope this hop is worth the trip, she thought, *and yields more in the way of usable data.*

The transition from one part of the rain forest to another was less jarring than beaming down from the transporter room before. The general climate, time zone, and visuals remained the same, although she stumbled slightly as the transporter put her down on the slope of a wooded hillside; in the absence of another transporter station at the receiving end, the computer was programmed to pick out the most suitable landing spot available, but sometimes the target destination limited its options. Una quickly adjusted to the incline, finding better footing as she got her bearings.

The landing party had materialized on a hill overlooking what appeared to be a large, cultivated valley, approximately two hundred meters below. Descending rows of trees and underbrush obstructed her view, but she glimpsed activity and industry below. A smoky odor permeated the air, along with the recurring sound of timber crashing to the ground. She could also faintly hear a low, atonal warbling that she could not yet identify.

"Seriously?" Shimizu muttered a few paces away. He stood ankle-deep in a puddle of rainwater, shaking his head at his bad luck. "You don't think one of the transporter operators has it in for me, do you?"

"I wouldn't be at all surprised," Martinez said, in what was quite possibly a joke. "Heads up, people. Stick close and keep quiet."

They crept forward, clinging to the concealing shelter of the woods, to get a better look at the scene below. Una led the way again, anxious to discover the truth about what the Newcomers were up to.

What she beheld was just as dismal as she had feared.

Hectares of primeval forest had been cleared to make room for a sprawling agricultural operation that seemed designed to replace the indigenous greenery with ugly gray crops of alien origin. Water, diverted from a nearby river, irrigated vast fields of the invasive fungi that were apparently being grown as foodstuffs. The fields surrounded a central complex composed of silos, sheds, dormitories, greenhouses, a power plant of some sort, and a few structures Una couldn't positively identify. Unlike the exotic, opalescent walls of the citadel, the buildings below appeared constructed of materials wrested from Libros III: hewn wood, quarried stone, cement, and so on. Cooling mist sprayed from the eaves of the buildings onto the pathways below, providing a degree of relief from the sun. Three pods, of varying colors and sizes, were parked on a small airfield next to the main complex, with possibly more stored in an adjacent hangar. The fungus farm seemed primitive compared to the citadel—or the *Enterprise*, for that matter—but it was far more ambitious and sophisticated than anything reported by the unmanned probes a decade before.

And seemingly dependent on forced labor.

Scores of native Librosians could be seen toiling beneath the unrelenting sun. Most were engaged in clearing yet more forest, felling trees with metal axes and saws, and burning the surviving vegetation to enrich the soil and make room for more alien crops. Crude slash-and-burn farming, Una realized, such as nearly destroyed the Amazon rain forests on Earth centuries ago and which had also reduced the fabled jungles of Chelana II to arid wastelands over the course of generations, causing the extinction of numerous unique life-forms. Smoke rose from the torched fields, as well as stacks of excess timber. Other Librosians tended to the growing fungi, uprooting any native weeds and nurturing the alien crops at the expense of the planet's own ecology, while still more Librosians were engaged in a variety of menial tasks: performing simple maintenance on the buildings, toting bundles of supplies and equipment, and running fresh water to the parched loggers cutting down the forest.

All under the watchful gaze of the Newcomers.

There was no mistaking one species from another. Viewed from above, the Librosians matched their description in the Federation database, conforming to basic humanoid design, if somewhat smaller in stature than the galactic average. The tallest adults topped out at roughly one and a half meters in height. Longish arms swung low as they walked, in a vaguely simian manner. Largely nude, as was typical of tropical cultures, their unadorned skin was a dark tan, while jade-green hair matched the leafy canopy that had once sheltered them. Said hair had been cut short on both males and females, contrary to images recorded by the Federation probes years ago. A change in fashion, or a practicality imposed on them by the Newcomers in the interests in efficiency or uniformity?

Una suspected the latter.

It took her a moment to spot one of the Newcomers, who seemed few and far between compared to the teeming Librosian laborers. Then she noticed a strange alien being emerging from the base of a tall watchtower.

There you are, she thought. *Finally.*

Unlike the Librosians, the Newcomer was not remotely humanoid, looking more akin to gastropods. A smooth, nacreous environmental suit or exoskeleton shielded most of its form, but a damp, glistening head, complete with six pairs of sensory tentacles, sprouted from one end of its artificial shell, while a single rubbery foot propelled it forward by means of muscular contractions. A pair of jointed limbs, sheathed in metallic coils, protruded like arms from its upper body. Claspers, resembling a cross between fingers and filaments, could be seen at the end of the segmented metal extremities. It was unclear from this distance whether the limbs were entirely prosthetic or simply covered by protective sleeves and gloves.

"You gotta be kidding me," Shimizu whispered. "Armored slugs?"

"So it appears," Una said. Now that she knew what to look for, she spotted maybe a dozen other Newcomers overseeing the operations. They mostly kept in the shade and to the misted pathways, no doubt to avoid drying up. "And don't judge them by their appearances. One of my best friends is an arachnid, remember?"

"I know, I know," Shimizu said. "I like G'Sissol, too. But let's be honest here. Do these look like good guys to you?"

No, she thought. *They do not.*

Una was appalled by the scene below. She found it hard to believe that the forest-dwelling Librosians were willingly slaving away to despoil their own environment. Beyond the evident oppression of the planet's native inhabitants, she was troubled by the rampant deforestation and contamination of the rain forest. That same gray algae had already infested the diverted river and an irrigation system, while the alien fungi was obviously encroaching on the planet's natural ecology, possibly with dire results. The Newcomers seemed intent on reshaping Libros III to their own liking—and were forcing the poor Librosians to assist in the colonization of their own world.

Her throat tightened at the tragedy unfolding before her eyes, which grew uncharacteristically moist. She wiped away a solitary tear.

The gesture did not go unnoticed by Martinez. "Everything okay, Lieutenant?"

"I'm fine," she lied. "The smoke's just bothering my eyes, that's all."

"Mine too," he admitted.

Unsure what he meant by that, she hastily changed the subject. "The Newcomers appear to be making their mark on the planet and its ecology, almost as though they've embarked on a deliberate campaign of terraforming."

"You know, I've never really thought that was the right word," Shimizu said. "*Terra* refers to Earth, right? So if a non-terrestrial species is trying to re-create their own homeworld, should we actually call it terraforming? Why not vulcan-forming or andor-forming?"

She gave him a look. "Don't be a pedant."

Martinez surveyed the river valley. "I'm counting maybe a dozen Newcomers, tops, although it's possible that there are more inside the buildings."

"That strikes me as a rather small amount to oversee

such a large work force," Una observed. There were easily twenty times that many Librosians at work in the valley. "Even with their superior technology, I wonder how they manage to keep so many native Librosians under control."

"I'm guessing it's not pretty," Shimizu said, "and *not* because they're slugs."

"We still don't know for certain that we're looking at forced labor here," Martinez pointed out. "The Librosians could have been enticed or persuaded to cooperate with the Newcomers somehow."

Una regarded the teeming laborers breaking their backs beneath the hot sun. She couldn't make out their expressions, but she saw no evidence that the Librosians were going at their arduous chores with any sort of enthusiasm. Maybe she was simply projecting her own instinctive aversion to one species dominating another, but the activity below struck her as singularly joyless.

"Do you truly think that's the case, Mister Martinez?" she asked. "That the Librosians aren't being exploited?"

He shook his head. "No."

A rustling came from a stand of leafy ferns growing in a patch of sunlight a few meters to the right. A fallen log, sprouting fresh growth from its carcass, provided a natural blind of sorts. Glancing toward the noise, which she assumed to be coming from some manner of wildlife, Una was surprised to see a pair of emerald eyes peering out at the landing party from behind the ferns. She quickly clamped down on her expression to keep from betraying her reaction. As casually as she could manage, she sidled closer to Martinez.

"Don't look now," she whispered, "but we're not alone."

She furtively gestured toward the lurking stranger. Yawning, he nonchalantly glanced in that direction and nodded in acknowledgment. Una discreetly signaled the others to draw their sidearms. Duly alerted, the party formed a protective circle, just in case there were more watchers surrounding the team.

"So much for stealth." Shimizu glanced around nervously. "Now what?"

"Lasers on stun only," Martinez reminded others. Taking out his communicator with his free hand, he looked at Una. "Maybe a strategic beam-out is in order, Lieutenant."

Una kept one eye on the blind of ferns, whose mysterious inhabitant had gone completely still. "Not just yet," she replied. "I'd like to attempt to make contact. Our new friend might have some of the answers we're looking for."

Martinez nodded. "It's your mission, Lieutenant. But I recommend proceeding with caution."

"Duly noted."

She activated the universal translator in her pack, hoping that it would suffice in this instance. The translator's ingenious algorithms, which were getting more sophisticated every year and with each new alien species Starfleet encountered, had become increasingly good at overcoming language barriers in first-contact situations. In her experience, it worked with the majority of humanoid species, even those previously unknown to Starfleet.

"Hello?" she said as mildly as she could. Holstering her laser, and displaying palms to show she was unarmed, she slowly approached the blind, taking care not to make any sudden, aggressive movements. "It's all right. We just want to meet you."

The brush rustled again. Una debated what to do if the watcher fled from her. Should she try to grab them before they got away, or let them escape unhindered? The latter was probably the wisest course, although the former was a lot more tempting.

Enough questions, she thought. *I want answers.*

Her dilemma proved academic as a tiny, camouflaged figure emerged from hiding. Barely more than seventy-five centimeters tall, the watcher was obviously Librosian— and less than fully grown.

"How about that?" Shimizu sighed in relief. "It's just a kid."

A little boy, in fact, of indeterminate age. He approached them hesitantly, seemingly torn between fear and curiosity, like a skittish fawn that might bolt at any moment. Una froze in place so as not to spook the child, while the rest of the landing party scaled down from their alert posture. They lowered their weapons.

"It's okay," she said, using simple sentences that were easier to translate. "We're friends. No one will harm you."

The boy's cautious approach gave Una time to get a better look at a Librosian. He had the same jade-green hair as the laborers in the valley, but his was long and un-shorn, falling past his shoulders. Green and brown dyes streaked his exposed flesh, providing a greater degree of camouflage in the jungle. A skimpy loincloth, woven from vines and moss and interlacing strips of pliable bark, was his only garment. A polished seed casing hung on a string around his neck.

Certain deviations from the standard humanoid model were more apparent close up. Most notable were the opposable toes on his bare feet, the better for climbing trees and clinging to the branches. His arms were longer in proportion to his body than was the norm, more like those of a Terran orangutan or a Crellonese gymnast. The evolutionary quirks suggested that the Librosians were primarily an arboreal species, dwelling in the treetops, as theorized by the Federation researchers who had studied the data from the early probes, which made the Newcomers' deforestation campaign all the more heartbreaking.

The Librosians were literally being forced to destroy their own habitat.

Una pushed that distressing realization aside to focus on the little boy, who gaped at the landing party with wide-eyed fascination. She recognized the light behind those bright emerald eyes; it was the same boundless curiosity about the universe and its myriad life-forms that was at the heart of Starfleet.

"My name is Una," she said, pointing at herself. "Una."

The boy caught on with laudable speed.

"Gagre." He pointed at himself. "Gagre?"

Was that his own name, she wondered, or what the Librosians called themselves? She guessed the former.

"Gagre?" she addressed him, pointing.

A grin broke out across his face, displaying small, flat teeth that hinted at a mostly vegetarian diet. The absence of fangs was reassuring, despite her own earlier admonitions about not judging a species by its appearance or phylogeny.

"Una!" he chanted. "Una! Una! Una!"

"Looks like you've made a friend, Lieutenant," Martinez said. "Although I'm not sure how valuable he'll be as a source of information."

"Give me time," she said confidently. "The universal translator allowing."

Sometimes the device required a large enough sample of a new language or dialect before it could facilitate communications. So far all they had was one name.

"Am I the only one wondering where this kid's parents are?" Shimizu said. "They say you're not supposed to play with baby grizzlies."

"He's a boy, not a bear," Una began, only to eat her words as several adult Librosians dropped from the treetops, surrounding the landing party and brandishing primitive weapons crafted from the forest's natural abundance: wooden spears and throwing sticks, thorn-studded batons, stone hatchets, and simple slings. Breastplates of peeled bark served as armor. Strings of polished seeds and pits adorned both men and women. Camouflage patterns were dyed into their skin.

"*Shalayi copprag mo blaff!*" one of the warriors vocalized, before the universal translator kicked in. Although short in stature, he appeared wiry and in his prime. Unlike the others, he wore a carved wooden helmet studded with polished seed casings. A token of leadership, perhaps? "Stay away from our child!"

"It's all right." Una maintained a cool head and tone. "We mean you no harm."

She slowly backed away from the boy, encouraged by the fact that, despite their weapons, the adult Librosians had yet to attack. She noticed one particularly distraught woman among the group, who had to be restrained by the others from rushing forward to snatch Gagre. Anxiety was written over her face in a language that required no computer algorithms to interpret. "My baby!" she sobbed. "My baby!"

Backing away, Una whispered softly to Gagre, "I think your mother wants you."

The boy hesitated, perhaps fearing that he was in trouble.

"Go," Una urged him. "She's calling."

Her words gave him the push he needed. He headed over to his mother, who tearfully embraced him before retreating behind the other Librosians.

"No!" he protested, squirming. "I want to see."

Una thought she felt the tension lift slightly as the Librosians reclaimed the boy, but the landing party remained surrounded by the warriors, who maintained wary expressions and body language while holding their weapons ready. Not that Una could blame them for being apprehensive and suspicious. *We're the intruders here.*

"You see," she said. "The boy was merely curious. No harm was done."

"Perhaps," conceded the same warrior, who seemed to be the leader. He let the tip of his spear dip slightly. "Gagre has always been an inquisitive child, lacking in caution. A dangerous quality in these dark times, since the Newcomers arrived to enslave our people and corrupt our world."

Una assumed that the universal translator had substituted "Newcomer" for the equivalent Librosian words. She wondered what these people called themselves.

"We are grateful for your forbearance," she said, "and restraint."

"You carry no weapons," the leader observed. "We had the advantage."

Una realized that the Librosians had not recognized the party's laser pistols as weapons, which implied that they were unfamiliar with firearms. Which once again begged the question of how exactly the Newcomers had conquered them and kept them from rebelling. What kind of weapons did the slugs possess?

Martinez casually holstered his pistol. The rest of the party followed his lead, although he held back and let Una make first contact.

"My name is Una. What may we call you?"

"I am Onumes, and I speak for we who are still free." He examined the landing party quizzically. "You are not like the Newcomers. You look like people. Strange people, but people still. Men and women, who walk on two legs, and do not leave a sickening trail behind them as they spread their slime across the world."

It seemed the landing party's humanoid configuration, compared to the slug-like Newcomers, counted in their favor. *Probably just as well that we're wearing boots,* Una thought, *so they're not put off by our general lack of opposable toes.*

"But you are not Usildar."

"Usildar," Una echoed, trying out the unfamiliar name. "Is that what your people are called?"

"What else? We are the firstborn of our world, Usilde, which once was ours alone. Before the Newcomers came to steal it from us."

Una wanted to hear more about that, in a big way, but Onumes required his own answers first. "Who are you and from where do you come?"

"We belong to a tribe called the Federation," she said, "and our home is a distant land very far from here."

It was a truthful enough explanation, although she left out the part about the *Enterprise* traveling across the galaxy from entirely different planets. Una doubted that the Librosians—the Usildar, she corrected herself—had mapped or explored their entire planet yet. It was probably easier for them to believe that the Federation was simply somewhere far beyond the horizon.

"And what brings you to this forsaken land?" Onumes asked.

"Merely a desire to learn more about your people," Una said, "and the Newcomers as well."

Fury contorted Onumes's features. He spat angrily upon the ground.

"They are despoilers, and a plague upon Usilde! They force our brothers and sisters to take part in the ruination of our land . . . and employ their unholy sorcery to unmake those who dare to defy them."

So much for the idea that the Usildar were cooperating voluntarily with the Newcomers, Una thought. She supposed it was possible that Onumes was misrepresenting the situation somehow, but everything she was hearing confirmed what she had suspected from the beginning. The Newcomers were invaders and the Usildar their victims.

"But not you and your companions?" Una asked.

"We are free but few, almost beneath the Despoilers' notice. Sanctuary trees shelter and hide us, but for how much longer I cannot say. Every day the great forest shrinks and the unnatural contagion of the Newcomers grows. Even the very air we breathe grows ever more foul and bitter to the taste." Anger surrendered to sorrow as he shot a rueful look toward the transformed river valley. "Indeed, I fear that we tarry too long so near the enemy's domain. Better that we go to where we can speak in greater safety."

"Fair enough," Una said. "Where did you have in mind?"

Onumes lifted his gaze toward the overhanging branches. "Above, where we belong."

Naturally, she thought. Judging from their feet, the Usildar probably spent most of their lives in the treetops even before the Newcomers arrived; no surprise that they would feel more comfortable there now that they were in hiding from the invaders. She shrugged. *When in Usildar . . .*

Martinez peered up into the branches. "Umm, we may need some assistance there."

Onumes looked puzzled. Martinez attempted an explanation.

"Our people are not the climbers yours are."

"Speak for yourself, Commander," Una said. She had scaled cliffs and mountains and the occasional tree all over the quadrant, including one particularly impressive redwood on Skalhem IV. Approaching the base of a tree, she considered kicking off her boots, but decided against it. She was confident she could manage the ascent fully shod. "I'm game if you are."

"Our help is yours," Onumes volunteered, "if you will trust your care to our hands."

"You have given us no reason not to trust you," Una said without hesitation. "We will be grateful for your assistance." She swept her gaze over the rest of the landing party. "Hope nobody has a fear of heights."

Shimizu shifted uneasily. "Only when there's gravity involved."

"Just pretend you're in zero g," Una said. "Sounds like fun, actually."

"Don't get cocky, Lieutenant," Martinez said, but maybe with a hint of a smirk. "We're not all fearless, you know."

"I'm certain we'll be in good hands," Una said.

"Then let us be on our way," Onumes declared. Scrambling up the side of an impressively tall tree with remarkable ease, finding purchase in the weathered bark and climbing lianas, he reached down with one leg to offer a helping foot.

Una stepped forward. "I'll go first. The rest of you try to keep up."

"Don't worry about us," Martinez said. "We'll be right behind you."

Shimizu grinned at her. "Always have to be Number One, don't you?"

Absolutely, she thought. *I wouldn't know how to be anything else.*

She hurried over to the tree and reached boldly for Onumes's foot, which gripped her hand with surprising strength and pulled her up after him. Following their leader, the other Usildar also took to the trees, taking the rest of the landing party with them. What transpired next was both exhilarating and occasionally terrifying. The Usildar traversed the jungle canopy as easily and fearlessly as a Peleian magmaphile swam through molten lava, scampering gracefully across narrow branches dozens of meters above the ground, or swinging hand-by-hand or feet-by-feet from one gargantuan tree to another. Often, Una clung to Onumes's muscular back, but at times she was flung from one Usildar to another, like an old-fashioned trapeze artist. Even as confident as she was in the forest dwellers' ability to navigate their own environment, she couldn't help holding her breath whenever she found herself tumbling through the air far above the forest floor, with nothing but leaves and branches to break her fall should a Usildar fail to make their catch. Part of her wished that the planet's gravity was significantly weaker, even as she wouldn't have traded the experience for a fortune in dilithium crystals.

Just don't look down, she thought.

She gasped in relief as, at the far end of another death-defying transfer, a strong foot grabbed hold of her outstretched hand. She was half pulled, half carried up and across the canopy until all concerned came to rest high within a closely packed stand of trees that offered plenty of thick branches to sit upon at approximately the same altitude. Dense layers of foliage, both above and below, shielded the company from view, either from the ground or the air. Brightly colored blossoms sprouted amidst wide green leaves. Tangled creepers, wrapped around the tree trunks, offered welcome life-lines to hang on to. Despite the leafy green umbrella above them, it was much hotter and sunnier in the treetops than it had been down below; Una sweated beneath her jacket and uniform. She was going to want a sonic shower if and when she got back to the ship.

"This is far enough," Onumes announced. "We may speak safely here, if any place on Usilde is truly safe in these unhappy times."

The Usildar deposited the landing party on separate branches facing one another. An adult Usildar stayed close to each member of the party, watching over them carefully. Una wasn't sure if that was for the Usildar's own protection or their guests'. Mostly likely a bit of both, she guessed. Glancing around, she spotted Gagre and his mother watching the proceedings from a higher branch across the way. The female Usildar was holding on tightly to her squirming child, who probably wanted to get even closer to the action. Una winked at him and was rewarded with a mischievous grin.

Onumes moved from branch to branch, like a host mingling with his guests. He plucked a large scarlet blossom from a flowering air plant and offered it to Una.

"Drink," he instructed her. "Refresh yourself."

She accepted the flower, which appeared to be some alien variety of bromeliad, and saw that rainwater had collected at its center. Taking a sip, she found that the flower's nectar had pleasantly flavored the water, making it both sweet and tart at the same time. It was a delectable combination that was just what she needed, given the heat and activity. She could practically taste her electrolytes being replaced.

"Thank you," she said. "It's delicious."

The flowers were abundant enough to quench everyone's thirst, although Martinez recommended scanning the liquid with a tricorder before determining that it was safe. Onumes was taken aback by the precaution at first, but Una managed to convince him that they meant no disrespect. Shimizu and the others helped themselves as well, aside from one suspicious security officer, Griffin, who was apparently still worried about being drugged or poisoned. Shimizu downed his drink in one gulp and smacked his lips. "Things are looking up," he said, "in more ways than one."

Una surveyed the arboreal setting. "Is this your home?"

"Merely an apt meeting place." Onumes settled into a crook at a slightly elevated altitude befitting his authority, his back resting against the tree trunk. "Ours is a perilous existence. You will forgive us if we do not trust all our secrets to strangers we have only just met . . . and who resemble no people we have ever seen before."

"Understood," Una said. "I would do the same in your place. But tell me, what do you know of the Newcomers? When and how did they come to Usilde, and how did they manage to enslave so many of your people?"

"The Newcomers are not known in your land?" Onumes asked. "They have not yet taken possession of your home and your people?"

Una answered vaguely. "We have heard tales and rumors, but would hear the story from your own lips."

"But if your land is truly free of the Despoilers," Onumes said, "perhaps my own people could find refuge there, far from the foulness that is despoiling the great forest? To abandon our captive brothers and sisters would surely break my heart, but if it would mean a new and safer life for those under my care . . ."

The naked hope in his voice tugged at Una's heart, putting her in an awkward position. The last thing she wanted to do was give the Usildar false hope . . . unless Captain April could be persuaded to intervene on their behalf?

"Our land is very far from here," she hedged. "Farther perhaps than you can even imagine, and very different from your forest as well. You might find life there too strange to endure. And it may be that the Newcomers pose a threat to the Federation as well. Perhaps if you tell us more about them, we can better judge what might be done."

Onumes frowned, clearly disappointed by her non-committal response, but accepting of it for the present. Perhaps he recognized that it was premature to ask the strangers for refuge when both sides had barely begun to get to know each other.

"Very well," he said. "You shall hear our woeful tale, and then perhaps you will find it in your hearts to render what aid you can." He took a deep breath before launching into his narrative. "It was many cycles ago, the strong rains having come and gone nine times since that fateful day, when the Newcomers and their dreadful island suddenly came into being, appearing out of nowhere as though they had fallen from the sky . . . or risen up from the deep waters that now guard their stronghold."

"The citadel in the lake," Una said. "We've seen it."

Eager to hear more, she started to lean forward, then thought better of it. Her attentive chaperone took hold of her arm anyway.

"But how did the Newcomers arrive on Usilde in the first place? Did they come in vessels of some kind, perhaps from the sky?"

"No one saw them come," Onumes insisted. "One day the citadel, as you call it, was not there. The next day it was. Thunder and lightning heralded its coming, and it is said that strange, shimmering lights could be seen in the sky and waters that terrible night. I was only a youth at the time, but I will never forget the first time I gazed upon the Newcomers' misshapen forms." He sighed mournfully. "Little did I know what an unparalleled calamity had befallen our precious forest."

Una tried to make sense of the leader's story. Starships and aliens were obviously outside the Usildar's frame of reference, but she found it hard to believe that the Newcomers' towering citadel had suddenly sprung into existence overnight. Granted, she and the rest of the landing party would have also seemed to have appeared out of nowhere when they beamed down to the planet, but transporting an entire fortress across space? That was beyond the practical limits of any transporter technology she was familiar with. The energy demands alone defied feasibility, and that still begged the question of where the citadel could have been transported to Usilde *from*. A gargantuan starship big enough to carry an entire outpost in its transporter room? A mobile spacedock, perhaps capable of warp travel?

The mind boggled.

"Go on," she urged. "What happened next?"

"A nightmare . . . from which we have yet to wake. At first, the Newcomers kept to their citadel, so that only the thunderous noises coming from the island disturbed the forest, but all too soon they emerged to bring fear to Usilde and enslave my people."

"How?" Una asked. Captain April would want to know what kind of weapons the Newcomers had at their disposal. "You surely outnumber the Newcomers. What threats did they employ against you?"

Onumes bristled. "Are you suggesting that the Usildar are weak and easily cowed?"

"Not at all," she assured him hastily. "I'm sure your people did not submit readily to the invaders, who must be very powerful to have forced so many of your people into servitude. I merely seek to know what weapons and powers the Newcomers possess, so that my companions and I are not taken by surprise."

Her explanation appeared to mollify Onumes. "Yes, you should know of what dangers you face, should you encounter the Despoilers and their sorcery."

"What kind of sorcery?" she asked. "You said something earlier about them 'un-making' people. What exactly did you mean by that?"

"No less than what I said," Onumes replied. "There were indeed those among us who dared to defy the Newcomers and defend Usilde from their corrupting touch, but that was before the Despoilers revealed that they could make their enemies vanish in the blink of an eye, as though they never existed." He shuddered at the memory. "Brave men and women, even entire tribes and villages, were made to disappear . . . to teach us what became of those who opposed the will of the Newcomers." He threw up in his hands in despair. "How could we fight such sorcery? How could anyone?"

Una tried again to interpret Onumes's words. Was he talking about disintegration beams? Transporters? She wondered if the "vanished" Usildar had actually been transported to another location, such as the alien fortress itself.

"What about their citadel?" she asked. "Do you know what they're doing there?"

Onumes shook his head. "No Usildar has ever set foot on that dread island, or at least none who have tried have ever returned. It is said that a few unlucky Usildar have been taken to the citadel against their will, but they too are never seen again. What becomes of them within the Despoilers' lair is a mystery that I prefer not to think of."

Una couldn't help speculating anyway. What would the Newcomers want with any abducted Usildar? Lab specimens? House servants? Dinner? Una was reluctant to contemplate such horrific scenarios, but knew that, realistically, they could not be eliminated from consideration. She had seen enough of the universe to know that not every culture was as humane and enlightened as Illyria or the Federation. The outer reaches of space still held its fair share of darkness.

"We heard loud rumbling noises coming from the

citadel," Martinez said. "It sounds like they're pretty busy in there . . . at something."

Onumes nodded. "The citadel never sleeps. Although my people have learned to stay well clear of that accursed place, we have heard those noises too. Sometimes the ground itself shakes from whatever unspeakable evil is under way within the lair of the Despoilers. And there are those who say that the citadel is slowly growing and changing like a living thing."

"Do you believe that?" Una asked.

Onumes gestured at the jungle around them. "Why not? All things grow and take new forms with the passing of time. Even rocks and rivers are reshaped by nature and the primal forces contained within them. Why should the dread citadel not do the same, in twisted mockery of our own sacred sanctuary trees?"

Definitely something to look into, Una thought. If the aliens' citadel was indeed a work in progress, Captain April needed to be informed of that. "I don't know about you," she said, "but I really want to get a look inside that fortress."

"Me too!" chirped Gagre from overhead. "I want to see!"

"Shush!" his mother scolded him, clamping her hand over his mouth. "Do not say such things!"

Gagre tugged her hand away. "But it's true!" He called out to Una. "Have you seen their flying boats? They're incredible!"

"We've seen them," Una said. "Coming and going from the citadel."

"Is that how you came here?" the boy asked. "In a flying boat from far away?"

"Something like that," she conceded. "Although we have nothing to do with the Newcomers, I assure you."

Gagre's bright green eyes grew even wider, if that was possible. "What's that like, flying above the forest? Can you take me for a ride?"

"Enough!" The boy's mother slapped him. "We are Usildar. We do not fly."

Gagre wasn't convinced. "But—"

His mother raised a warning hand. "Hush!"

The boy grudgingly fell silent, but Una suspected that his unquenchable curiosity remained unabated. *Too bad that there's no Starfleet Academy on this planet,* she thought, *and that the Usildar are still millennia away from space travel. Gagre would be a natural.*

And even if his people were merely free to forge their own destiny, perhaps he could still become a great explorer here on Usilde, venturing to uncharted corners of his own planet like a Magellan or a Dona Cestrix. If only the Newcomers were not stealing the Usildar's future from them.

"My apologies for the disturbance," Onumes said. "Gagre's restless spirit will be his undoing someday, unless he learns to curb it."

"No harm done," Una said. "We were all young once. But is there anything else you can tell us about the Newcomers? Anything at all?"

Onumes hesitated before answering.

"They call themselves the Jatohr," he divulged, spitting out the name as though it tasted foul upon his tongue.

Startled gasps greeted the disclosure. "Although the word has become a curse among my people, and we do not speak it."

Una did not recognize the name, which she was fairly certain was not to be found in the *Enterprise*'s computer library.

"That name is unknown to us," she said. "But I thank you for sharing it. The more we know about the Newcomers, the better."

"But to what end?" Onumes demanded, losing patience. "Speak truthfully. Will your Federation grant us refuge . . . or defend us against our enemy?"

"I can't answer that," she said honestly. "Not yet at least. We are strangers here and still have much to learn about your situation."

"What more do you need to know?" Onumes sprang to his feet atop a swaying branch. His voice rose with his temper. "They enslave my people. They despoil our world. Their corruption spreads daily, turning our green world gray." Grabbing onto an even higher branch, he pointed an accusing toe at Una. "How can you not wish them gone from Usilde?"

Una saw his point, but watched what she said. "I hear your words and appreciate what is at stake. But, as you just lamented, the Newcomers are powerful in ways that make them deadly to oppose . . . unless we understand more about them and their 'sorcery.' And, to be honest, this is not my decision to make. I answer to our own leader, who must decide for us."

"And where is this leader of yours?" Onumes asked.

"Waiting to hear back from us," she said. "But,

knowing him, he's going to want to know more about the Newcomers—where they come from, what they want, how they 'unmake' their enemies—before he makes any decision."

Onumes pondered her answer. He lowered himself back onto his original perch. "And how do you mean to find such answers? For your oh-so-cautious leader?"

She looked to Martinez for guidance. "Perhaps a closer look at that labor camp in the valley," she suggested. "With all due stealth and discretion, of course."

"Your mission, your decision," he stressed. "But maybe a bit more snooping *is* in order, assuming the captain approves." He squinted up at the sunlight filtering through the canopy. "What time does it get dark around here?"

Eight

Nightfall brought little relief to the enslaved Usildar, who were still laboring in the valley well after sundown. Levitating globes cast a cool white incandescence over the central complex and adjoining fields, providing light enough for the captive workers to keep toiling miserably, although Una wanted to think that there had at least been a change of shift since the last time the landing party had spied on the sprawling labor camp. No interior lights escaped the windowless wooden dormitories, where she hoped some Usildar were getting a little much-needed rest. Trees were toppled at the receding edge of the endangered forest. Bonfires crackled, throwing sparks up into the smoky air.

Una and Shimizu crept around the fringes of the camp, taking care to stay outside the radiance cast by the floating globes, which proved to be the source of the odd, atonal warbling she had heard before. The globe's darkened upper hemispheres were opaque in order to direct all the light downward. Some of the lamps appeared more or less stationary, but others patrolled the grounds in patterns that resisted easy recognition. The overhead misters had turned off now that the relentless heat of day had passed and the temperature had dropped to a comfortable twenty degrees centigrade or so.

The telltale song of a globe, which reminded Una of a

classical theremin concert she'd once attended on Octaro II, alerted her and Shimizu to the approach of yet another prowling searchlight. They ducked behind a stack of piled logs barely in time to avoid being caught in the cold white glare. Huddling behind the timber pile, they waited for the sphere to move past them. Una noted an annoying subsonic thrum beneath the device's discordant melody. It made her teeth tingle.

"You don't think we're getting too close, do you?" Shimizu whispered.

Una shrugged. "That's the idea."

After checking in with the *Enterprise,* and explaining that they weren't quite done on the planet, the landing party had spread out to investigate the huge camp from a variety of angles and approaches. The plan was to rendezvous later at a designated spot back in the nocturnal forest. Una hoped to have obtained valuable new data regarding the Jatohr by then—and she wasn't going to get that by playing it safe.

"There's a difference between getting close and *too* close," Shimizu said. "Why do I feel like you're pushing our luck?"

"Trust me, I know what I'm doing," she insisted. "Don't I always?"

A floating lamp scooted away and she took advantage of the opportunity to dart between a rough-hewn timber shed and a towering silo. The shadows between the two outbuildings, she judged, offered concealment enough to slink deeper into the central complex without being detected. Shimizu scurried after her, joining her in the narrow alley.

"Okay, now we're definitely pushing our luck," he said.

She was vaguely offended by his lack of faith in her ability to keep out of sight. Hadn't she once managed to slip in and out of a Klingon listening post to recover stolen Starfleet intelligence? Not to mention that time she and Tim had broken curfew at the Academy without being caught. He ought to know by now that any risks she took were calculated ones. And that you should never underestimate an Illyrian.

"Do you want to dig up some good intel on the Jatohr or not?" she asked him. "I for one am not reporting back to the captain empty-handed."

Una particularly wanted to make some compelling discovery that would persuade April to intervene on the Usildar's behalf. It was clear to her that the Jatohr's rampant colonization efforts were an unfolding atrocity, to say nothing of being a blatant violation of the Usildar's planetary autonomy. And it wasn't as though the Jatohr were all that deeply entrenched on this world yet; despite the worrisome degree of environmental contamination, the invaders had arrived less than a decade before and remained largely confined to a single citadel. There was surely still time to reverse the incursion and give the Usildar their planet back if Starfleet—or maybe just the *Enterprise*—moved swiftly enough.

I know what course I would choose, she thought, *if I were captain.*

Clinging to the shadows, she and Shimizu worked their way around the silo to where it abutted a hangar at the edge of the landing field. She kept one eye on the airborne globe-lights as she peered around the corner of the hangar. Bales of unfamiliar equipment and supplies, contained within some kind of artificial webbing, were stacked along one wall. A silent pod, its wings tilted downward to serve as landing gear along with an additional support at its tail, was parked just up ahead. She scanned the materials with her tricorder, but detected nothing incriminating. She made a mental note to examine the readings more closely back on the ship.

"I still wonder if we should have tried disguising ourselves as Librosians," Shimizu whispered.

"Usildar," she corrected him. The notion of resorting to disguise had been discussed and rejected quickly at the outset of the scouting mission. "I don't think there's enough dye and body paint on the planet to make us pass for Usildar except maybe at a great distance, but feel free to strip down to a loincloth if you think it will help."

"I'm good," he said. "I guess it's unlikely that the Usildar have the run of the place anyway, given the whole slave-labor thing."

"Exactly," she agreed. "Despite the visible lack of tight security."

She noted again how few Jatohr overseers appeared to occupy the camp. This was a mixed blessing when it came to spying on them. On the one hand, it made it easier to skulk about undetected; on the other hand, it was hard to covertly study the invaders when they were so scarce on the ground. Frustration gnawed at her patience. Despite her best efforts, they still didn't know any more about the Jatohr than they had before sneaking into the camp. Not even how exactly they "unmade" dissidents.

The telltale buzz of an approaching pod caught her

ear. Spying on the paved airfield beyond the hangar, she saw a gleaming aircraft coming in for a landing. A pair of Jatohr emerged from the far end of the hangar to greet the new arrivals.

This is it, she realized. An opportunity to observe the Jatohr close-up and perhaps even eavesdrop on a conversation. She couldn't let this lucky break slip by. "Here's our chance," she said. "Watch my back."

She broke from the shadows, counting on the pod's landing to serve as a distraction. Shimizu called to her, his anxious voice drowned out by the loud buzz of the descending aircraft.

"Wait! Where are you going?"

"Hang on!" she said. "I'll be right back!"

She dived beneath the parked pod, scooting forward on her stomach to get closer to the meeting farther ahead. Reaching the nose of the aircraft, she hid between its landing struts and watched intently as the arriving pod touched down, its wings converting into landing struts. A hatchway slid open to disgorge a ramp onto the pavement. Two more Jatohr oozed down the ramp. A glistening trail of slime marked their passing. The natural secretion presumably eased their way over any rough or slippery surfaces.

Una examined the aliens at greater detail than she'd been able to do before. Their glossy oyster-white exoskeletons were more or less identical, but their exposed heads and feet displayed a wide variety of colorations and markings. Stripes, whorls, rings, speckles, and blotches helped distinguish one slug from another, as seemingly unique to each individual as a face or fingerprint. They were larger than the average humanoid, measuring more than two meters from their brow to the sole of their large foot. Despite their notable lack of legs, they surely towered over the captive Usildar. Their sturdy exoskeletons appeared to be made of overlapping layers of some hard, chitinous material, while their metallic forelimbs did indeed appear to be prosthetic "waldoes" of a sort.

Their faces were strikingly inhuman. Unlike Andorians, whose twin antennae supplemented their conventional countenances, the Jatohr had tentacles instead of standard eyes and noses and ears. The tallest pair of tentacles bore recognizable eyes at their tips. Una theorized that the two smaller pairs of tentacles picked up olfactory and auditory stimuli instead. A triangular mouth occupied the bottom of their "faces," extending nearly to their chins. There was no evidence of sexual differentiation anywhere on their bodies; Una recalled that most gastropods were hermaphrodites.

Wonder what kind of pronouns they use? Genderless ones, I imagine.

The Jatohr greeted one another. Checking to make certain that her universal translator was still activated, she strained her ears to listen in, but all she heard was a wet, phlegmy gurgling that was certainly not any language known to her. She waited impatiently for the translator to kick in, but it seemed just as flummoxed by the alien tongue as she was. Scowling, she held back a few choice Illyrian epithets that might have fried the device's delicate circuits.

Just my luck, she thought. *The Jatohr are certainly not making this easy for me.*

One of the aliens turned back toward the hangar. A harsh, genderless voice issued from a speaker embedded in the neckpiece of hir armor: "Work crew, come here. Begin unloading the cargo transport."

At first, Una thought that the universal translator had finally cracked the Jatohr's speech, but then a team of weary-looking Usildar emerged from the hangar and trudged toward the parked aircraft. She realized that the Jatohr had issued its command in the language of the Usildar, which the translator *could* handle, unlike the invaders' own incomprehensible tongue, so that she could understand the Jatohr when they were addressing their Usildar slaves, but not when they were conversing among themselves.

That's something, I suppose.

She registered the mechanized, artificial quality of the Jatohr's command. Perhaps their natural vocalizations did not lend themselves to humanoid speech? She pondered the implications of that even as she recorded more of the Jatohr's gurgles for further study and analysis. It was possible that the computers back on the ship could decipher it, and there were other resources she could consult as well. If Spirit Claw couldn't find a way to translate her recordings, nobody could.

Or maybe the translator just needs to chew on the Newcomers' lingo a bit longer, she thought hopefully. Ordinarily it worked almost instantaneously, but the Jatohr's language might be a tougher nut to crack.

Oblivious to her presence, the Jatohr gurgled at one another as they crossed the airfield diagonally toward the front entrance of the hangar, accompanied by Usildar bearers weighed down by cargo. Judging that she had obtained an adequate sample of the slugs' speech, Una decided that she should scoot back and rejoin Shimizu, who was probably having a warp-core meltdown by now. She started to back away furtively, only to catch an unexpected movement out of the corner of her eye.

Oh, no, she thought. *What's he doing here?*

Swinging down from the roof of the hangar, Gagre dropped deftly onto the bales piled against the building's east wall. Crouching among the stacked supplies, he gazed intently at the unguarded pod—and its open hatchway.

It was all too easy to guess the boy's intent. He was out to sneak aboard the aircraft in hopes of taking a ride aboard the tantalizing flying machine. Maybe he even wanted to hitch a ride to the mysterious citadel of the Newcomers to discover what wonders hid behind its opaque walls. Una understood the impulse, but was alarmed nonetheless. According to Onumes, no Usildar had ever returned from the citadel.

But now what was she supposed to do?

Mission or no mission, she had to save Gagre from his own reckless curiosity. His mother's anxious face surfaced from Una's memory, steeling the young lieutenant's resolve. She couldn't let the boy get aboard that pod, not if she ever wanted to live with herself again.

"Psst!" she hissed from beneath the other pod, trying to get Gagre's attention, but he was too intent on his target, and probably too far away, to hear her hushed entreaty. "Over here."

By now, the Jatohr and their heavily laden work crew

were halfway back to the hangar, with their backs to the newly arrived pod. Seeing his chance, Gagre crept out from the shelter of the bales and scurried toward the beckoning hatchway.

No!

His impatience forced Una's hand. There was no time to devise a clever strategy; she could only scramble out from beneath the parked pod and chase after Gagre, while hoping that, against all odds, they could both somehow avoid being spotted by the distracted Jatohr.

What was it that Shimizu had said earlier about her pushing her luck?

Not that she had any choice in this instance. Catching up with Gagre, she grabbed him from behind and clamped a hand over his mouth to keep him from crying out. Maybe she could still drag him back into the shadows before it was too late.

"It's me!" she whispered urgently. "Your friend Una!"

But she had underestimated the young Usildar's strength. Startled, he yanked her hand away from his mouth and starting kicking and squirming in her grasp. Wiry arms and legs flailed wildly.

"Let me go!" he wailed, far too loudly for Una's peace of mind. "I want to fly!"

As she feared, the disturbance did not escape the Jatohr's attention. The aliens wheeled about and made agitated noises. Globe-lights converged on the commotion, spotlighting Una and Gagre. The other Usildar made themselves scarce, no doubt fearful of being caught up in the incident and incurring the wrath of their overseers.

"Halt!" a Jatohr demanded in (translated) Usildar. "Stand and be questioned!"

Una spun Gagre around, away from the pod, and shoved him away from her.

"Run!" she ordered. "Back to your mother!"

The boy finally grasped that he was in danger. Frightened by the upset Jatohr, who were rushing toward the intruders, flailing their forelimbs, he fled in panic back the way he had come, bounding onto the bales of supplies, then shimmying up a drain pipe onto the roof of the hangar and disappearing from sight. Una watched him make his escape, then took off herself, racing across the airfield in the opposite direction in order to draw any pursuit away from the boy.

"Forget him!" she shouted. "I'm the one you want!"

She reasoned, correctly as it turned out, that the Jatohr would be more concerned with an unexplained alien in their midst than a fleeing native child. The Jatohr chased after her as she raced across the tarmac away from Gagre's forest home. They bellowed in both Usildar and their own unintelligible language.

"Stop! You cannot escape!"

Possibly not, she conceded, but she was certainly going to try. She had no desire to provide the Jatohr with a hostage or any more information about Starfleet's presence on and above Usilde. Sprinting as fast as she could, as though competing for yet another trophy, she deliberately avoided retracing her steps so as not to draw her pursuers back to Shimizu. She could only imagine what was going through her friend's mind as he saw their whole covert scouting operation blow up like a supernova. Una hoped he would be smart enough to stay hidden and not try to play hero.

Don't do anything stupid, Tim. I've screwed up enough for the both of us.

Abandoning the open airfield, she tried to lose herself amidst a warren of outbuildings on the other side of the landing site, but the levitating globe-lights stuck to her like Denevan bloodhounds, depriving her of the shadows. To make matters worse, the globes emitted a deep, booming siren that called out to her pursuers wherever she ran. Drawing her laser pistol, she blasted one particularly persistent globe, which crashed to the ground, spewing sparks, but her expert marksmanship was to no avail; more globes swooped in to replace the one she had shot down. Commands blared from loudspeakers in the globes.

"Attention: Unknown Creature. Stand and be questioned!"

So much for her exemplary stealth and infiltration skills; she couldn't have attracted more attention if she'd flown a shuttlecraft into the middle of the camp in broad daylight. The only positive was that she hadn't been fired upon yet, if the Jatohr even employed hand weapons, which was an open question that she was in no hurry to have answered.

Fuel barrels blocked her path and she hurdled over them like the champion she was. Her eidetic memory called up the layout of the camp, as viewed from the hillside earlier, while she tried to calculate the swiftest route back to the jungle. Glancing back over her shoulder, she saw that she had temporarily left the slow-moving

Jatohr behind, even if she couldn't say the same for their floating sentry globes. Their low-pitched, almost subsonic alarms unsettled her even more than they should have. She gritted her teeth, feeling a headache coming on.

This way, she concluded, rounding the corner of a storage facility and charting a course for the rows of long, rectangular dormitories at the eastern side of the central complex. As she recalled, only a wide strip of cleared land separated the ugly, utilitarian dorms from the adjacent forest. If she could make it past the buildings, she had a straight shot to the jungle, assuming the Jatohr let her get that far.

If only I could stop running long enough to contact the Enterprise . . . .

A narrow pathway ran between the parallel dormitories. Una sprinted down the center of the corridor, grateful for the rigorous exercise regimen that kept her in peak physical condition at all times. The globe-lights kept pace with her, their booming alarums no doubt disturbing the exhausted workers housed within the buildings. She felt a twinge of guilt for adding to their woes and vowed to make up for it if she ever got the chance.

"Halt!" the globes demanded. "You cannot escape."

We'll see about that, she thought, spotting the forest looming ahead, beyond the cleared terrain past the dormitories. Would the globes pursue her into the woods? Would the Jatohr? Even if they did, she figured she had a better chance of shaking them in the overgrown depths of the forest than on their home ground. The night-cloaked jungle beckoned to her, no more than fifty meters away. Hope, mixed with adrenaline, fueled her desperate flight. Reaching deep, she pulled out a fresh burst of speed. Her pounding boots ate up the distance between her and safety. She wasn't even breathing hard yet. *I'm going to make it.*

Three Jatohr appeared at the far end of the pathway, blocking her way. They raised their forelimbs in a menacing fashion. An amplified voice rang out.

"Surrender, creature. You can go no farther."

Skidding to a halt, she spun around to see two more Jatohr advancing on her from behind. They slithered forward, making a hasty retreat problematic.

"Stand and be questioned," a Jatohr repeated. "You have nowhere to go."

It was hard to dispute that assessment. She looked around for an escape route, but found herself penned in, with Jatohr ahead and behind, and the steep wooden walls of the dormitories to either side of her. Each dorm was four stories tall and lacked anything in the way of windows or adornment. Gazing up at them, she envied Gagre's opposable toes and innate climbing abilities. She *might* be able to scale the walls if she had time, but not before the Jatohr closed in on her or brought any weapons to bear.

She was trapped.

A closed doorway, midway along the length of one building, called out to her. Darting over to the entrance, she tried the door, only to find it locked. She pounded on the door with her fist, hoping that the roused workers might help her escape. Once she was inside, she could try to find a back way out.

"Help! Let me in!"

But the door remained firmly shut. She briefly cursed the Usildar inside, but then realized that the door was surely intended to keep the workers locked up, so that they couldn't try to slip away from the camp between shifts. Chances were, the poor souls warehoused inside the building couldn't admit her even if they wanted to.

Never mind, then.

She turned away from the door as the Jatohr converged on her. They formed a half circle around her, approximately two meters in radius, so that she was backed up against the building. Multiple globe-lights caught her in their search beams, nearly blinding her. She raised a hand to shield her eyes.

"The chase is over, creature," a Jatohr declared. "Surrender to our custody."

Una shook her head. "Sorry. That's against my orders."

She raised her laser pistol and fired a warning shot over the heads of her pursuers. A crimson beam struck one of the hovering globes, which exploded in a shower of sparks. She was reluctant to shoot first—and in a first-contact situation, no less—but the Jatohr weren't giving her any choice. She couldn't allow herself to be captured and interrogated; she had already compromised the mission enough. Lowering her weapon, she took aim at the Jatohr directly before her.

"Please allow me to depart peacefully. I don't want to hurt anyone."

She assumed that her translator would convert her words to Usildar at least, so that the Jatohr could understand her, but was unnerved when her captors gurgled energetically to one another, leaving her out of the loop. Their gastropod faces, so unlike her own, also made it hard to read their intentions.

"Please, speak to me to me in Usildar," she implored. "I can't understand your own language."

Ignoring her request, a Jatohr spat out a phlegmy command. Una held her fire, uncertain what was being said, and kept her eyes on the Jatohr, who had yet to brandish any recognizable weapons. Her finger remained poised on the trigger of her laser.

Too late she realized that she should have been keeping watch over the floating globes as well. While on guard against any hostile moves by the Jatohr, she was caught by surprise when one of the globes dived sharply and slammed into the back of her head. Not only did the impact stagger her, knocking her face-first onto the pavement, but an intense electric shock jolted her nervous system. She convulsed upon the ground, losing her grip on her pistol.

A cattle prod, she realized. *The damn globes are cattle prods, too.*

The globe retreated into the air, leaving her dazed and disarmed. Her head ringing, she could not fight back as the Jatohr yanked her onto her feet and confiscated her equipment. Cold metallic claspers closed on her wrists like manacles as she was walked roughly across the grounds by two brusque Jatohr escorts. She counted herself lucky that she wasn't being dragged by her feet instead.

"What now?" she asked. "Where are we going?"

"To be questioned," one of the guards stated. "Answers are mandatory."

A brief hike brought her back to the airfield. Not a good sign, she realized, fearing that she might be seeing the inside of the Newcomers' citadel sooner rather than later. A small crowd of Jatohr was assembled on the tarmac, talking among themselves. She guessed that she was the number one topic of discussion, no pun intended.

Her guards held her in place as another Jatohr approached her. Swirls of brown blotches, not unlike the distinctive epidermal markings of a Trill, mottled the slug's otherwise olive-colored flesh. Protruding eyestalks scrutinized Una.

"What are you?" the Newcomer demanded. "What are you doing here?"

The Prime Directive, not to mention the security of the *Enterprise* and its crew, weighed on Una's mind as she chose her words carefully.

"I mean you no harm. I was merely observing."

"But what are you? Where do you come from?"

She wondered if she could convince the Jatohr that she was merely some exotic breed of Usildar from a different corner of the planet. All humanoids probably looked roughly the same to them, and how thoroughly had they explored this entire world so far?

Maybe we should have disguised ourselves after all.

"I am simply a visitor to these parts."

The Jatohr examined her, noting her unusual clothing, while its companions inspected her gear, passing it back and forth between themselves. She winced at the loss of her tricorder, wanting it back almost more than her communicator and laser—all that data that she had recorded and hoped to deliver to the captain.

"Are there others like you? Speak truthfully, creature."

"My name is Una. Not *creature*."

Which wasn't entirely correct, but now was no time to get into the finer points of her complicated nomenclature.

"Answer the question, creature," the Jatohr said, ignoring her protest. "Are you alone or are there more of you?"

Una thought of the rest of the landing party, who were possibly still in the vicinity. The Jatohr weren't searching for them . . . yet.

"I'm alone," she lied. "One of a kind."

Her interrogator retreated to confer with hir colleagues. Once again, Una found herself at a loss to comprehend what was being said.

"Please, speak in Usildar. I can't understand you."

"We were not speaking to you, creature." The spotted Jatohr gestured toward a waiting pod and gurgled a command at the guards, who began to march her toward the aircraft. "You are being transported to our sanctuary. Offer no resistance."

"Sanctuary? You mean the citadel?"

"There is no difference," the Jatohr said. "Do not feign ignorance."

Apparently the decision had been made to take her to the citadel for further examination or interrogation, perhaps by a higher authority. Una was open to the idea of meeting with the Jatohr's leaders, but not on these terms. The fact that the aliens persisted in referring to her as a creature rather than an individual did not bode well. She could be looking at dissection rather than diplomacy.

"Wait!" She struggled against the guard's metal claspers. "Let's talk about this!"

"Come quietly, creature. Do not compel us to employ any more force than necessary."

The claspers tightened around her wrists, squeezing the bones together painfully. Grimacing, she abandoned her struggles rather than waste energy on futile displays of defiance. She took a deep breath to settle her nerves. She needed to keep a cool head about her, as she had been trained to do.

You're Number One, remember? You can do this.

Still, panic fluttered in her gut as she was dragged toward the open hatchway. Una wondered if she would ever see the *Enterprise*—or Illyria—again. For all she knew, she could end up spending the rest of her life in some alien menagerie.

"Not so fast!"

Tim Shimizu emerged from the shadows, stepping out onto the airfield. A crimson beam stunned one of the guards escorting Una toward the pod. Hir facial tentacles drooped limply as s/he toppled over onto the tarmac, letting go of her arm.

"Sorry about that," Shimizu said, "but you're not taking her anywhere."

Anxious Jatohr hurried to check on their fallen comrade. Clearly, they valued Jatohr life at least.

"He'll be fine," Shimizu said, despite the slug's lack of gender. "Just let my friend go."

But the other guard refused to let go of Una's wrist. A solitary globe-light dipped toward Shimizu.

"Watch out for the globes!" she called out. "They have an attack mode!"

"Got it!" He blasted the globe out of the sky, then turned his weapon back on the Jatohr. "Don't try that again. Just let us leave in peace."

The Jatohr had other ideas.

"That cannot be allowed," said the lead interrogator. "Surrender your weapon, creature, or you will be removed from this plane."

Una remembered the Usildar's claim that the Newcomers could make their enemies vanish into thin air. She still didn't really know what that entailed, but feared that she might be about to find out. *Watch yourself, Tim. We have no idea what these beings are capable of.*

"Not a chance," Shimizu replied to the Jatohr's ultimatum. "This laser is our ticket out of here."

"You are mistaken. Surrender your weapon," the interrogator repeated. "You will receive no further warnings."

Shimizu targeted the interrogator. "Right back at you."

A new voice intruded on the standoff.

"All right. That's enough," Martinez said loudly. He marched onto the scene, backed up by the rest of the landing party. His laser pistol was drawn, but pointed at the pavement. "Everyone, calm down. I'm sure we can still work things out as long as nobody does anything we'll regret later."

His words seemed intended for the Jatohr as well as Shimizu and the others. Una couldn't believe that he was risking the entire mission for her sake. She blamed herself for this disaster. If only she hadn't let her overconfidence get the better of her.

"Commander," she said, "you don't have to do this."

Martinez shrugged. "The cat's out of the bag. Our duty now is to keep this situation from escalating any further."

The Jatohr clustered together, facing the new arrivals. The aliens outnumbered the Starfleet team, but not by a large margin. There were barely more than twice as many Jatohr as crew members from the *Enterprise*.

"Identify yourselves, creatures."

A veteran of many previous first contacts, Martinez took being called a creature in stride. "I'm Lieutenant Commander Raul Martinez, representing the United Federation of Planets, a peaceful interstellar alliance that poses no threat to you and your civilization." He kept his weapon lowered at his side. "May I ask where your people hail from?"

The Jatohr conferred unintelligibly before responding. "What do you and your Federation want?"

Martinez nodded at Una, who was still being held captive several meters away. "For starters, you can return our companion to us as a gesture of good faith. I suspect that there has been an unfortunate misunderstanding here, but nothing that can't be resolved amicably."

Una didn't begrudge Martinez making this first contact, given the circumstances; he was certainly in a stronger position to negotiate terms at the moment. It troubled her that Martinez had to make nice with the invaders who were oppressing the Usildar, but, of course, he wouldn't be in this position if she hadn't carelessly let herself be captured. *But what else was I supposed to do?* she thought. *Let Gagre stow away aboard that aircraft?*

"Your request is denied," the Jatohr said. "This specimen requires further study, as does the remainder of your party. Discard your weapons and prepare for transport to our sanctuary immediately."

"No doing," Martinez said. "That doesn't work for us." He raised his laser pistol. "We don't want conflict with your people, but nobody is going anywhere unless I can guarantee the safety of every member of our party."

"We offer no guarantees, only a warning." The Jatohr's artificial voice conveyed nothing but confidence. "Cooperate or you will be removed permanently."

Martinez frowned. "What do you mean by that? I told you before, there's no need for threats."

"Not a threat. An ultimatum. Surrender your weapons."

Una watched the confrontation apprehensively. A sick feeling grew in the pit of her stomach, even though there was no visible reason to be worried. Aside from their floating stun-globes, the Jatohr appeared to be unarmed. So why were they acting like they held all the cards?

"Commander—" she began.

"Sit tight, Lieutenant." Martinez kept his pistol aimed squarely at the Jatohr spokesperson. Shimizu, Griffin, and the rest of the landing party were armed and ready as well. "One thing you should know about my people," he warned the Jatohr. "We're peaceful, as I said, but we don't take well to threats."

"That is unwise."

The Jatohr issued a decisive gurgle—and the landing party vanished.

It happened so instantaneously that it took Una a moment to process what she'd just witnessed. One moment the landing party was facing off against the Jatohr, then they simply blinked out of existence. Only a split-second, almost subliminal flash of white light marked their abrupt disappearance. Una suddenly found herself the only Starfleet officer in sight.

She gasped in shock.

"What? What did you do?"

"They have been removed," the Jatohr stated. "Do not invite the same fate."

She stared numbly at the empty stretch of tarmac where her landing party had been standing only moments ago. Guilt and horror struck her like a shockwave from an exploding star. Her legs buckled beneath her.

Tim . . . Martinez . . . the whole team . . . . they're all gone.

And it was all her fault.

Nine

"Please tell me. What did you do to my friends? I have to know."

The Jatohr pod soared above the forest, carrying Una toward the citadel, but she had not left the memory of her team's shocking disappearance behind. Confined to the cargo area at the rear of the aircraft along with stores of harvested mushrooms, her wrists bound by the same synthetic webbing used to bale the other cargo, she called out to the Jatohr pilot and passengers—who studiously ignored her.

"Answer me!" Una shouted. A metal grille separated her from the passenger compartment. "I'm talking to you!"

A Jatohr turned hir head toward her. Tentacles twitched irritably. She recognized hir as the slug Shimizu had stunned before. Dark brown blotches speckled hir slimy yellow hide. She didn't need to be able to read hir inscrutable countenance to guess that s/he held a grudge. "Silence, creature. Save your breath for our leaders. They will surely have many questions for you."

"But my companions," she persisted. "Did you kill them, transport them, or what? Are they still alive?"

"Forget them. You will not see them again."

"That's not an answer, damn you." She kicked against the metal grille with her foot. "Tell me what you did!"

The Jatohr turned away from her. "That is not for you to know. Now stay silent or you will be subdued."

A stun-globe, which had been loaded into the cargo area with her, hovered menacingly nearby.

They're hiding something, she guessed. Or perhaps they simply didn't want to share the secret of their ultimate weapon with an alien spy. She could appreciate that, she supposed, even if it left her in agony of suspense regarding her lost shipmates. Grief tore at her heart as she acknowledged that the Jatohr had probably spoken the truth.

She'd never see Tim or the others again.

Her throat tightened, but her Starfleet training and experience kept her from breaking down. She could mourn her lost comrades later, if and when she was safely back aboard the *Enterprise*; in the field, she needed to remain focused on the mission. This was still *her* landing party, even if she was all that was left of it. Blinking away a tear, Una steadied her breath and inspected her surroundings.

The pod was making good time toward the citadel. Although opaque when viewed from the outside, panoramic one-way viewports offered Una an excellent view of their progress, which could be tracked by the disturbing increase in environmental contamination as they neared the alien outpost. It was still night in this part of Usilde, but the pod's cruising lights picked up the noisome gray fungi infiltrating the once-verdant jungle. The sight still troubled Una, despite her own difficulties.

There's more at stake here than my fate or even the

landing party's, she reminded herself. *An entire world is being stolen.*

In no time at all, the citadel and surrounding lake came into view. Una braced herself as best she could, but was still slammed roughly into the metal grille as the pod dived toward the algae-covered lake, entering it as gracefully as a shuttlecraft making a smooth descent into a planetary atmosphere. Plunging beneath the surface, the amphibious craft cruised toward the underside of the citadel, which appeared to be rooted to the floor of the lake. Landing lights, directly ahead, outlined the entrance to an underwater hangar, whose doors dilated open like the iris of a mechanical eye.

Una peered from the rear of the ship, straining to see more of what lay ahead. Despite her dire circumstances, she felt a thrill of excitement at the prospect of actually entering the citadel and discovering its secrets. She was truly going where no Starfleet officer had gone before.

Here's hoping I survive the experience.

A flurry of movement, outside the pod, drew her attention and she turned her head just in time to glimpse, through a starboard viewport, a large, multi-armed creature swimming through the murky, abysmal waters. A cephalopod of some sort, like a terrestrial squid or cuttlefish, the creature was at least ten meters long from its pulpy, bulbous red head to its flared tailfin. Muscular arms or tentacles surrounded a glossy black beak that looked big enough to crack a human arm to pieces. Disk-shaped suckers lined the underside of the tentacles, while the suckers themselves were barbed with claw-like hooks, the better to latch onto prey. Una recalled a similar tentacle dragging that giant dragonfly to a watery demise before and was grateful that the sturdy hull of the pod was between her and the lake creature. Round yellow eyes, roughly fifteen centimeters in diameter, inspected the pod briefly before the creature jetted away by expelling water from its mantle. Una watched it disappear into the depths.

"Those predators in the lake," she asked, "are they native to this planet, or did you bring them with you from . . . wherever?"

She suspected the latter, given their proximity to the citadel. The lake creatures were probably another invasive life-form, like the fungi and algae. Both squids and slugs were mollusks after all, sharing a common evolutionary process of development. The predatory cephalopods might well be related to the Jatohr, at least as much as other mammals were related to some humanoids.

"Quiet," the testy Jatohr replied. "Speak only when questioned."

Una bit her tongue. It seemed that, as far as the Jatohr were concerned, first contact was a one-way street. There was a chance that their leaders would be more communicative, but what she'd seen so far offered little grounds for optimism in that respect. The Jatohr were making the Romulans seem welcoming.

The pod entered the hangar via a large moon pool that was ringed by a promenade. Surfacing, the amphibious craft eased up a ramp onto the deck, where a voluminous bubble of pressurized air kept the water confined to the pool. Pale blue strips glowed overhead to illuminate the spacious hangar, which already held several other pods of varying sizes. The pilot gurgled a command to the pod, which appeared to be voice-activated to a degree. As the aircraft powered down in response, the Jatohr crew exited the pod and came around to the back of the craft. A rear hatchway opened, releasing Una.

"Come with us," a guard ordered. "And be prompt about it."

She offered no resistance this time, being as anxious as anyone to see more of the citadel. The wet deck was more slippery than she would have liked, but she managed to maintain both her balance and her dignity as she was escorted toward an inner door, which dilated before them. Silvery slime trails marked the paths of her escorts before evaporating into the air. Exiting the landing bay by way of an airlock, she got her first look at the interior of the citadel.

It was surprisingly beautiful.

The bay opened onto a spacious receiving area whose elegant lines and polished surfaces implied a sophisticated culture with an appealing sense of aesthetics. Walls, floors, and ceilings boasted a glossy, iridescent sheen not unlike the interior of a sea shell. Curved corridors and sweeping ramp ways shunned harsh right angles, flowing smoothly into each other; Una noted a conspicuous lack of steps, stairs, or ladders, which was understandable, considering the Jatohr's slug-like locomotion. Taking it all in, she found that the basic design and architecture reminded her of a gargantuan nautilus shell she had once explored on Ravenna III, complete with spiraling ramps leading from chamber to chamber.

Makes sense, she thought. *It stands to reason that*

intelligent gastropods would model their shelters on shells.

The lighting was gentle and subdued, easy on the eyes, but the air was damp and cool and smelled like rotting compost. Also, a persistent rumbling in the background grated on Una's ears and would surely prove wearing over time; that the Jatohr endured it suggested that their auditory faculties varied from the human model, which followed logically from the fact that they had sensory tentacles instead of ears. She tried and failed to place the source of the deep, almost subsonic grinding; it seemed to come from everywhere and nowhere.

All in all, she had to give the Jatohr their due. They might be heartless imperialists with no respect for Usilde's indigenous people and biosphere, but she couldn't fault their taste in decor. She'd toured Illyrian palaces and museums that were less striking, if perhaps not quite as smelly.

Not all menaces flaunt their pernicious qualities, she reminded herself. *Kodos the Executioner was said to be a man of great refinement and culture.*

A crowd had gathered to greet the returning Jatohr—and perhaps gawk at the mysterious alien "creature" apprehended at the labor camp. The size of the crowd suggested to Una that news of her existence had preceded her to the citadel. Straining eyestalks turned toward Una, who took the opportunity to examine the Jatohr right back.

Like the overseers at the camp, the assembled slugs sported a variety of colorations and patterns on their exposed heads and feet. The adults all wore artificial carapaces, although those waiting within the citadel

appeared less heavily armored than those who had
ventured beyond its walls, while smaller individuals,
whom Una assumed to be children, were largely un-
clothed. She theorized that immature Jatohr were not
fitted with their "shells" until they reached their full
growth.

Observing the youngsters, she saw that the Jatohr
had tiny, almost vestigial forelimbs that they presumably
used to operate the larger, prosthetic limbs displayed by
the adults. The Jatohr appeared to have helped evolu-
tion along by building themselves better extremities,
not unlike the cybernetic stilt-walkers of the T'Wispian
marshes.

One small grouping of Jatohr, composed of a solitary
adult and a couple of youngsters, broke away from the
crowd to rush toward the arriving crew and captive. For
a moment, Una feared that they were attacking her for
some reason, but then the group flocked to her old friend,
the speckled Jatohr who had been stunned earlier. The
adult Jatohr gurgled in an agitated manner and palpated
"Speckles" with hir tactile tentacles, while the children
squeezed between them, making anxious noises of their
own. Speckles responded by stroking the other adult's
face in what Una took to be a reassuring manner. Their
claspers clasped.

It's Speckles's family, she guessed, *come to make sure
s/he's okay.* They must have heard that s/he had been attacked back at the camp and were eager to see with their
own eyestalks that their loved one had not been harmed.
Una found herself genuinely touched by the tender re-
union. The Jatohr obviously cared deeply for one another.

"It was just a stun beam," Una said apologetically. "It doesn't cause any permanent damage."

Speckles's mate only glared at her.

"Come along," a guard ordered, prodding her with a forelimb. "The Commander is waiting."

Leaving the onlookers behind, Una was led into a clear, domed turbolift that resembled the top half of a bisected bubble. Water pressure, no doubt pumped from the lake, caused the bubble to accelerate upward. As it cleared the submerged levels of the citadel and rose up the base's central tower, one-way viewports in the tower offered her an aerial view of the citadel.

The basic design resembled an old-fashioned wagon wheel. Radiating spokes connected the central hub to the outer walls. Tinted sunroofs covered the gaps between the spokes. Ramps and walkways ran along the tops and inner faces of the walls. Una recalled the Usildar's claim that the citadel had simply appeared, fully formed, out of nowhere. Now that she'd witnessed the landing party being instantaneously "unmade" just as the Usildar had spoken of, she was inclined to believe their testimony regarding the citadel's miraculous arrival as well, but that still left her wondering where the vast fortress had come from and how the Jatohr had transported it here.

Maybe I can finally get some answers.

The bubble brought her to the topmost saucer, which was immediately recognizable as some sort of command center. Large illuminated screens lined the curved walls, offering views of various Jatohr operations throughout the continent. Una spotted the labor camp in the valley, alongside images depicting deforestation, fungus farming, and mining elsewhere. She winced at the brazen environmental imperialism on display, although the Jatohr appeared untroubled by the images. They slimed about the command center, attending to various banks of equipment and control panels, like the bridge crew on the *Enterprise*.

The buzz of activity quieted as she was herded into the ops center. Multiple eyestalks turned toward her, scoping her out, while hushed gurgles greeted her arrival as she was led up a short ramp to a raised platform at the center of ops, where she was presented to two waiting Jatohr, standing at either side of a tabletop display panel. The smaller of the two started toward her, hir tentacles extending curiously, but a brusque, phlegmy imperative from the bigger one called the curious slug back, as though urging caution. The Jatohr vocalized energetically at one another, leaving Una in the dark once more.

"I can't understand what you're saying," she tried explaining again. "But I can translate the Usildar's language. Can you please use that so we can communicate?"

The cautious slug ignored her. Nearly two and a half meters tall, s/he was the largest Jatohr she had seen so far. Canary-yellow rings striped hir glistening orange head and foot. Bright scarlet orbs topped hir optical feelers. Hir segmented armor appeared more ornate than the average Jatohr's. Lustrous pearls, embedded in the breastplate, formed an elaborate design that could have been a name, a number, a crest, or some other symbol. A particularly thick layer of mucous gave the slug a shinier, more impressive sheen than hir underlings. Perhaps a sign of health or vigor? S/he kept on gurgling as though Una hadn't spoken at all.

Typical, she thought. She was getting used to that treatment from the Jatohr.

But the more inquisitive Jatohr surprised her by switching to Usildar.

"The specimen is right, Commander. We should do her the courtesy of speaking in a manner she can comprehend."

Smaller and dryer than the big striped slug, this Jatohr was inky black in hue aside from some rust-colored markings around hir mouth that coincidentally resembled a mustache and beard. Hir comparatively desiccated and wrinkly appearance conveyed a general sense of age or infirmity.

A venerable elder, perhaps, or senior advisor?

The Jatohr commander gurgled in reply, apparently unconvinced.

"Never mind courtesy then," the elder argued. "Let us consider efficiency and results instead. We will surely learn more from the specimen if we can actually converse with her."

Una found the term *specimen* disquieting, but agreed with the elder otherwise.

"Very well, Professor," the commander said. "But she is not just a specimen. She is an anomaly . . . and a likely threat to our security."

"I'm no threat," Una said, fudging the truth to a degree. "But I appreciate the courtesy. Thank you."

The commander made a derisive noise. Una's gratitude was clearly of no concern to hir.

"See, Commander," the elder said. "Now we're making progress." S/he turned to address Una. "Introductions are in order. This is our esteemed leader, Commander Woryan, and I am Eljor, hir chief scientific advisor."

Una was glad to have names for the players. That made things easier.

"You may call me Una," she volunteered. "Which, for the record, I prefer to 'creature' or 'specimen.'"

Woryan disregarded her remark. Instead s/he got right down to business.

"What are you and where do you come from?"

As before, Una was hesitant to reveal too much about the *Enterprise* or her presence on the planet, and all the more so now that the Jatohr had proved themselves to be both hostile and dangerous. The loss of the landing party ached like a fresh wound that might never heal.

"I'm more concerned with what happened to my companions back at your farming operation. I need to know: Are they dead?"

"They have been removed . . . permanently," Woryan said. "As you will be if you fail to answer our questions fully."

"Not so fast, Commander," the scientist protested. "You may underestimate how valuable this specimen is. This is a unique opportunity that could teach us much about our strange new universe."

Una's eyes widened. "New universe? What do you mean by—"

"We will ask the questions, creature," Woryan said, cutting her off. "All we require from you is answers. What are you and why are you here?"

"My name is Una," she insisted. "And I'm only a visitor here. An explorer, who is also seeking to learn more about the universe. That's all."

"She could be telling the truth, Commander." Eljor approached Una's escorts. "I understand that some equipment was confiscated from the specimen?"

The guards presented Una's backpack and gear to the scientist, who spread out the items atop the central command table. Una tried not to flinch as Eljor inspected her tricorder, laser pistol, and communicator. S/he seemed particularly interested in the latter, holding it up before hir eyestalks to examine it more closely.

"Intriguing," s/he observed. "Most intriguing."

Woryan appeared more interested in the laser pistol. "How so, Professor? Do these devices tell us anything useful about the alien?"

"Absolutely." Eljor indicated the communicator. "She is most certainly *not* native to this world. Equipment such as this is manifestly the product of a highly advanced technological civilization, which could not have escaped discovery by our aerial survey. That such a civilization could evade our notice for nearly ten solar revolutions is inconceivable." S/he addressed Una directly. "You are not from this planet, correct?"

Sighing, Una abandoned any thought of pretending to be an exotic breed of Usildar. She consoled herself with the knowledge that the Jatohr, being newcomers to Usilde as well, were obviously conversant with the notion of interplanetary travel. It wasn't as though she was revealing the existence of alien life to a primitive, pre-warp society.

"No, I am not," she admitted. "My companions and I were conducting our own survey of this planet when we noted your presence. Curiosity alone compelled us to investigate, nothing more."

That was not entirely true, but it seemed politic not to mention the exploitation of the Usildar—or the possibility of the *Enterprise* intervening on their behalf. She was in no position to take an adversarial posture at the moment, not when Woryan already regarded her as a potential threat.

"I see," Eljor said. "What is your planet of origin? Is it located in this system or much farther away?"

"My home is a planet called Illyria, hundreds of light-years from here." She judged that a far distant location would sound less menacing than a possibly hostile neighbor. "It's in another solar system altogether, on the other side of the galaxy."

"Fascinating," Eljor enthused. "Think of it, Commander. Worlds after worlds of new and different beings."

"Alarming is more like it." Woryan sounded displeased. "Do you not realize what this means? It is not just the primitive creatures on this world we have to contend with; it seems this entire realm is infested with such beings. We are outnumbered and coming under surveillance by an unknown number of alien creatures."

Una did not like the way the discussion was heading.

"We mean you no harm," she insisted. "If you are new to our . . . universe, we may be able to render assistance."

Although she again neglected to mention her desire to liberate the Usildar, her offer was sincere. Perhaps the Federation could help relocate the Jatohr to a more suitable Class-M planet where they would pose no threat to the Usildar. Assisting the Jatohr and freeing the Usildar were not necessarily incompatible goals.

But Woryan didn't seem to see it that way.

"You hear her?" the hostile commander said. "She calls it *her* universe. She regards us as interlopers."

"No!" Una protested. "That's not what I meant. I just—"

"Enough! No more polite dissembling." Woryan threatened Una with her own pistol. "I gather this device is a weapon. Provide me with relevant tactical information, or it will be used against you. How many of you are there? What are your numbers and positions? How did you reach this planet?"

Una balked, unwilling to point the Jatohr toward the *Enterprise*. "We don't want conflict. We're a peaceful people."

"Who come bearing weapons and infiltrating our installations," Woryan said accusingly. "Who attacked an innocent Jatohr!"

"Only in self-defense," Una said. "We were simply observing—"

Woryan fired the laser at Una's feet, eliciting startled gasps from the other Jatohr. A brilliant red beam scorched the floor in front of her boots, far too close for comfort. She jumped back instinctively, only to be blocked by the Jatohr guards behind her.

"Careful," she warned. "It looks like you switched the settings. It's not just set on stun like before."

"It is you who should take care, creature." Raising the pistol, Woryan targeted her head. "Speak quickly or—"

"Patience, Commander!" Eljor slimed between Woryan and Una, shielding her with hir body. "No need to risk damaging the specimen. A closer examination of her equipment will certainly provide much of the information you require."

Woryan kept the laser aimed at Una. "I'm listening, Professor."

"Take this device, for instance." Eljor flipped open the lid of Una's communicator. "A cursory examination suggests that it is a two-way receiver/transmitter, as indicated by the built-in antenna."

Curious digits toyed with the controls and were rewarded with an electronic chirp. Lieutenant Sanawey's deep, sepulchral voice issued from the communicator:

"*Enterprise* to landing party, please respond. Repeat, *Enterprise* to landing party. . . ."

Una cringed inside. She had set the communicator on mute earlier, so that a stray beep would not betray her presence during the scouting mission, but Eljor had figured out its function with distressing ease. While the other Jatohr reacted in surprise, the intrigued scientist spoke into the device.

"Hello? Who is speaking?"

Una could just imagine the confusion on the bridge. They had to have been worried already by the long silence from the landing party. A strange voice at the other end of the hail was probably the last thing anyone had expected. She was not surprised when Captain April's voice replaced the communication officer's. The captain would want to handle this personally.

"*Hello? This is Captain Robert April of the* United Space Ship Enterprise. *Whom am I addressing?*"

"Greetings, Captain. I am Professor Eljor, first scientist of the Jatohr. I am pleased to make your acquaint—"

"Hold your tongue!" Woryan snatched the communicator from Eljor's grasp and slammed shut its lid. "Reveal nothing until we know who and what we are dealing with. Do not let your reckless scientific curiosity endanger our security!"

"Have no fear, Commander. You may count on my discretion." Eljor's tentacles stretched longingly toward the communicator, but the scientist deferred to Woryan's prudence. S/he turned toward Una. "But you can clear up some of these mysteries for us. This '*Space Ship Enterprise*' . . . it is indeed a vessel for traveling through space? As opposed to between realities?"

The implications of the query staggered Una. "Wait. You mean you didn't travel through space to reach Usilde? You're actually from another universe?"

"Our history is not your concern!" Woryan said, shutting her down. Unsurprisingly, s/he seized on the tactical issues posed by the *Enterprise*'s existence. "Where is this ship? On the planet or in space above us?"

"Well," Una hedged, "I can't testify precisely as to its exact location, but—"

Eljor interrupted.

"Allow me time to trace the signal, Commander, and I believe I can answer that question conclusively. For now, however, the reference to a 'landing party' suggests that the *Enterprise* is most likely still in space, possibly in orbit around the planet."

Woryan reacted decisively to the scientist's theory. "Direct long-range sensors into space," s/he ordered the operations staff. "Find that ship!"

The other Jatohr immediately went into action at their control panels and workstations. Unfamiliar with their equipment, Una couldn't tell exactly what they were doing, but their brisk efficiency would have done a Starfleet bridge crew proud. It occurred to her that, not being space travelers, the Jatohr would have had little reason to be watching the skies—until now. A fresh pang of guilt stabbed her.

"I recommend that we concentrate our scans at approximately twenty thousand kilometers above the surface of the planet," Eljor said. "Mathematically, that altitude would offer the most stable orbit."

Correct, Una thought, impressed by the scientist's intellect. There seemed little chance that *Enterprise* could evade detection now that the Jatohr knew what to look for and where. Cloaking fields, alas, were still only in the realm of theory.

"Commander," a mottled technician called out from hir post. "We've located a sizable artificial satellite directly above us, precisely where the professor suggested. Approximately 290 meters in length, with a mass of nearly 190,000 tonnes."

Eljor looked at Una. "A geosynchronous orbit, I assume?"

"Correct." She saw no point in denying it. "While maintaining a discreet distance from the planet's surface."

"Show me," Woryan demanded. "I want visual confirmation . . . now!"

"Complying," the technician said. Prosthetic claspers manipulated the controls at hir station. "Visuals received."

The *Enterprise* appeared on multiple viewscreens, including the tabletop display. Its familiar contours called out to Una, making her wish she was back on the bridge and not a potential hostage or bargaining chip.

I'm sorry, Captain. This has all gone wrong.

Woryan wheeled toward Una. "Tell me more about that ship. What weapons does it possess? What defenses?"

"Sorry," Una said. "You're not getting that out of me. It's a security issue. I'm sure you understand."

This was not what Woryan wanted to hear. The Jatohr commander smacked Una across the face with hir metallic claspers. The blow rocked her, nearly knocking her off her feet. She tasted blood.

"Understand this!" the paranoid leader railed at her. "You are at our mercy, and you *will* provide whatever information we require."

"Not a chance." Una spit a mouthful of blood onto the floor. "I'm a Starfleet officer. You can kill me if you want, but I am *never* going to betray my ship. Are we clear on that?"

Woryan's inhuman face twisted in rage, but Eljor hastened to intervene.

"Commander, please. This brutality is beneath you. There are surely other ways to ensure our safety."

"We still possess the Transfer technology," a technician

said. "As long as we can remove our enemies at will, no one can oppose us."

"True," Woryan conceded, the reminder calming him to a degree. "As this creature's companions learned too late."

Una's heart sank. She still didn't know how exactly the Jatohr "unmade" their enemies, but could they really employ their mystery weapon against the *Enterprise* and its crew? What was the actual range of their "Transfer" weapon?

Woryan eyed the imposing spaceship on the screen. Una thought she was starting to get better at reading the Jatohr's facial expressions, and it seemed to her that Woryan's earlier alarm and agitation was giving way to something more calculating, perhaps even covetous. Hir claspers twitched, opening and closing repeatedly, as though the Jatohr wanted to reach out and snatch the *Enterprise* from the screen.

"Perhaps we can turn this unexpected development to our advantage," the commander said. "We can use that ship, both to complete our colonization of this world and to speed our expansion across this vast new cosmos."

Eljor looked troubled by hir leader's declaration. "In due time, of course, but let's not get ahead of ourselves. We are still transforming this planet. There will be time enough to reach for other worlds."

"Not so, Professor. You fail to grasp the larger picture. Now that we know that other creatures infest this universe, it becomes all the more imperative that we secure our place in it and ensure that the future belongs to the Jatohr alone." Hir tentacles strained toward the screen. "And claiming that ship is the first step on the road to that future."

Una felt sick to her stomach.

Bad enough that her first landing party had ended in disaster. Now the *Enterprise* was in danger too, and she was to blame!

Ten

"Captain, we're being hailed from the planet."

April sat up straight. Hours had passed since they had last heard from the landing party, who had requested permission to take a closer look at the labor camp down on the planet, and the only communication they'd received had been from an unidentified voice that, according to Sanawey, had appeared to come from somewhere within the alien citadel. To say that the situation was confounding would be an understatement.

"Lieutenant Una . . . or someone else?"

"I believe it is a Newcomer," Sanawey said grimly. "Using one of our frequencies."

April shared the communications chief's unease. That a Starfleet communicator had fallen into the hands of the aliens did not bode well for the landing party.

"Can we make visual contact?" he asked.

"Affirmative," Sanawey said. "If you prefer."

"Do it," April said. "Let's see who's knocking at our door."

"Aye, Captain. Universal translator engaged."

The planet, slowly revolving on the main viewer, was replaced by an alien countenance distinguished by three pairs of tentacles in lieu of a humanoid face. Striped orange skin glistened wetly. April took in the Newcomer's unusual appearance. Truth to tell, he'd encountered more attractive beings before, but he knew better than to judge a sentient life-form on the basis of their appearance. One of the kindest, most honest beings he'd ever met was a sentient cactus on Zebulus Major, while an Aetherian seraph looked positively angelic before it bared its fangs. Appearances could be misleading, in more ways than one.

"Attention: foreign vessel. This is the Jatohr. Respond at once."

April recalled the landing party's discovery that the Newcomers called themselves the Jatohr. The brusque communication sounded more like a command than a request, but he tried to keep an open mind regarding the colonists. They had every reason to be wary of an alien spacecraft appearing uninvited above their outpost.

"This is Captain April. Whom do I have the pleasure of addressing?"

"I am Commandeer Woryan of the Jatohr and this world is ours. Surrender your ship and crew or face the consequences."

The crew reacted visibly to the implied threat, but maintained discipline. This was hardly the first time a newly encountered alien species had initiated contact by rattling their sabers, even though April would have preferred to commence relations on a less belligerent note. Alas, it seemed the Jatohr were not much for pleasantries.

"Hold on there," April said. "This is the first meeting between our two peoples. Let us not begin with threats and ultimatums." He went straight to the matter foremost on his mind. "What has become of our landing party?"

"Those intruders have been captured or removed. You would be wise to comply with our demands."

"What do you mean by 'removed'?" April asked, puzzled and fearing the worst. "Let me talk to my people."

"You are in no position to make demands. Your ship belongs to us now. Surrender it at once."

April frowned. So far the Jatohr were making the Klingons seem agreeable. He hoped that the Jatohr wouldn't resort to employing their prisoners as hostages, which would place any surviving members of the landing party in mortal jeopardy. There was, sadly, no question what his response to any such ultimatum would have to be. He could by no means surrender a Federation spaceship to hostile alien invaders of unknown origin, even if that meant sacrificing the lives of good men and women under his command.

"Your demand is unreasonable," he said firmly. "We are more than willing to talk to you in order to resolve any differences amicably, but understand that we will not surrender our ship under any circumstances." His face and tone hardened, revealing the steel beneath his affable manner. "And know also that we are fully armed and will vigorously defend ourselves if called upon to do so."

"Captain," Lorna Simon reported from the science station. "We're being scanned from the planet."

"Raise shields," April ordered. "Any evidence of long-range weapon placements on the surface?"

"Negative," she said. "No sign of any Jatohr ships either. Not in space or launching from the planet."

"Condition yellow," the captain ordered nonetheless. Blinking annunciator lights brought the entire ship to a heightened state of readiness. April felt the level of tension on the bridge rise perceptibly as well. They were in choppy waters here.

"*You have been warned,*" Woryan declared. "*We will now demonstrate our superior power.*"

At the nav station, less than a meter away from April, Ensign Cheryl Stevens abruptly blinked out of existence. A fresh cup of tea crashed to the deck as Yeoman Bruce Goldberg vanished simultaneously. Fine china shattered, accompanied by gasps and exclamations all over the bridge. As well trained as the crew was, none of them were prepared to see two crew members disappear into thin air, with only a momentary flash of light to signal their departure.

Their captain was equally startled. "What the devil?" he blurted, before responding to the attack. "Increase power to shields! Red alert!"

A button on his armrest switched the cautionary yellow lights to flashing red alarms. An emergency klaxon sounded throughout the entire ship, although April swiftly silenced it on the bridge. Under ordinary circumstances, the navigator might have carried out the captain's command to raise shields, but an empty seat forced the helmsman to take control of the ship's tactical systems instead.

"Deflectors at maximum, sir," Lieutenant Carlos Florida reported. "And then some."

April tried to figure out how the Jatohr were targeting their victims. "Kill the visuals!" he ordered Sanawey. "Don't let them see us."

The Apache officer complied instantly. Woryan's off-putting visage disappeared from the screen, replaced by the previous view of the planet below.

April hoped that would be enough.

It wasn't.

Ensign Dylan Craig hurried to take over at the nav station, but disappeared before he could even sit down. Across the bridge, Lieutenant Ingrid Holstine vanished in a flash. The rest of the crew froze in place, uncertain who would be next. There seemed to be nowhere to run and no way to escape whatever invisible force was being directed at the ship. It was as though they were being picked off randomly by an unseen sniper. To their credit, April noted, not one crew member abandoned their post or attempted to flee the bridge.

"Stop this!" he shouted at the Jatohr. "You've made your point. No more."

An endless moment stretched to infinity as he waited tensely for more personnel to disappear, but the rest of the bridge crew remained in place. He remembered to breathe as Woryan's bodiless voice emanated from the speakers.

"*This was merely a demonstration. Surrender or see your entire crew removed.*"

April worried about the lost crew members, but forced himself to focus on the immediate threat. "I'd rethink that strategy if I were you. This ship can't operate without a full crew complement, and how precisely will you board the *Enterprise* if you reduce it to an empty ghost ship?"

To date, there was no indication that the Jatohr had shuttlecrafts waiting to launch or that they were capable of beaming aboard the *Enterprise* if they were so inclined. Granted, they were obviously able to "remove" people easily enough, even through the ship's shields, but April gambled that that was a different kettle of fish.

"*Perhaps we cannot remove your entire crew,*" Woryan acknowledged after a moment's pause. "*But how many of your people are you prepared to sacrifice. A third? A half? Do not think that we will allow you to spy on us with impunity, nor to depart so that you may return again to menace us.*"

"We are no menace," April insisted. "And, unlike you, we have taken no hostile action"

"*You are not Jatohr and you have a ship. This cannot be permitted. If we cannot police our own skies, we are not safe.*"

"Paranoid much?" Simon shook her head in disgust. "Xenophobes . . . they're the worst."

April knew how she felt. His sympathy for the oppressed Usildar was growing by the moment, although he had to concentrate on saving his ship and crew first, which meant proving to the Jatohr that they were no pushovers.

He signaled Sanawey to mute the sound from the bridge. "Anybody up for a little target practice?"

Simon peered into her full-spectrum scanner. "I'm picking up a large rock formation approximately seventy-five meters from the citadel." She turned and nodded at Florida. "Transmitting coordinates to tactical."

April reopened his line to the Jatohr.

"We are not a menace," he repeated forcefully, "but we are not victims either. You have demonstrated your power. So be it. Let us demonstrate ours." He signaled Florida. "Show them our teeth, Carlos."

"With pleasure, sir," the stocky youth said. "Firing lasers."

———

A tremor shook the citadel, distinct and different from the everyday rumbling of the sanctuary's ongoing renovations. Woryan gripped the display table to maintain hir balance, while, nearby, the captive biped staggered atop her spindly lower limbs. The Jatohr commander was comforted by this timely demonstration of the alien's inferiority, but was alarmed by the jolt regardless.

"What has happened?" Woryan demanded. "Are we under attack? Report!"

Surveillance Deputy Frajas responded promptly. "The sanctuary is undamaged, but an energy beam from orbit barely missed us!"

Woryan glared at the alien captive, while shouting at hir staff, "Show me!"

The image on the main viewer, still depicting the bridge of the alien vessel and its grotesque inhabitants, switched to a view of the lake and landscape surrounding the citadel. A crimson energy beam shot down from the sky to strike one of the imposing rock formations in the vicinity, which was instantly reduced to dust. The force of the blast churned up the lake and sent a shock wave across its surface. Powdered debris flew in all directions.

The devastation rattled Woryan both physically and otherwise. That fearsome beam had come far too close for comfort. If it had struck the sanctuary instead . . . !

"I knew your ship posed a mortal threat to my people!" The commander had switched to the Usildar's bes-
tial tongue to confront the creature who called herself an
Una. S/he shook hir claspers at the revolting being. "Your
'peaceful' captain nearly destroyed us all!"

"If Captain April wanted this citadel destroyed, it
would be a smoking crater," the Una insisted. "That wasn't
a miss. That was a warning shot."

Eljor backed her up. "I suspect she's telling the truth,
Commander. We demonstrated our offensive capabilities;
her captain replied in kind." Hir tentacles swayed
pensively. "Indeed, it could be argued that Captain April's
response was a notably measured one, given that we
permanently removed four members of his crew."

"Are you siding with these creatures, Professor?"
Woryan extended hir head and throat, increasing hir
height advantage over the shriveled scientist. "Have you
forgotten where your loyalties lie?"

"Not in the least, Commander. I have devoted my life
and work to the preservation of our people, as you well
know. I am merely noting that Una's interpretation of
events has the ring of truth. I would advise against test-
ing the *Enterprise*'s aim for the time being." S/he gurgled
wryly. "We can remove their people, but it seems they can
just as easily blast us to pieces. An interesting dilemma,
don't you think?"

"I do not have the luxury of finding this situation
'interesting,'" Woryan spat. "I only know that these
beings—and all their kind—are a menace that must be
eliminated at all costs!"

Defeating the strangers, and capturing their mighty

vessel, was nothing less than hir sacred duty, no matter what "warnings" issued from the coarse, inscrutable countenance of the alien captain, whose voice reverberated through the command chamber once more.

"Don't even thinking about retaliating," April warned the Jatohr, before any more crew members could be deleted from the bridge, "or we will turn our weapons directly on your citadel. And even if you remove my entire crew at once, the ship's computer has been programmed to completely destroy your entire outpost and all your installations before self-destructing."

That last part was an outright bluff, but April wanted to head off any possible reprisals before the Jatohr escalated the conflict. He wondered, however, if he *should* program the *Enterprise* to self-destruct in the event of an alien takeover.

Heaven help us if it comes to that.

He waited tensely for the Jatohr's response, as did every other soul on the bridge. Knowing that their shields were of no use against the Newcomers' baffling attacks, which struck without warning, left April feeling singularly vulnerable. Facing off against a Klingon battle cruiser was one thing; at least you could see disruptor blast or photon torpedo coming and attempt a defense. But how did you protect yourself from a force that seemingly came out nowhere, claiming its victims without a moment's notice?

Except, of course, by striking back with sufficient force.

"*Do not attempt to leave orbit,*" Woryan replied finally, "*or risk certain destruction.*"

"No one wants that," April replied. "A negotiated solution would be to our mutual—"

"The transmission has been cut off, Captain," Sanawey reported. "They're not listening."

"But they're not retaliating yet or demanding our immediate surrender anymore," April said. "It appears we've given them pause at least." He nodded at Florida. "Good shooting, Carlos."

"Thank you, sir. I just wish *they* would surrender . . . and give us our people back."

If they still exist to be returned, April thought. For all they knew, the vanished crew members had been disintegrated somehow, wiped irrevocably from existence, while the fate of the landing crew remained a mystery as well. "If only, Carlos. If only."

"So we have a stand-off," Simon said, succinctly assessing the situation.

Based on the concept of mutual assured destruction, April thought. *An ugly tactic from a tragic chapter in Earth's history. Let us hope that matters here don't end as badly as they did on Earth back during World War III.*

"All right, children," he said. "Talk to me."

He welcomed the input of his crew, even if the final decision was his and his alone. Talking out their options might lead to a way out of their current impasse.

"I hate to say it," Simon said, "but we could always try to make a fast getaway. Break orbit and put plenty of distance between us and the planet." She shrugged at her station. "Mind you, we have no idea what their weapons range is, so it could be a short trip."

"Speaking of which, what manner of attack are we dealing with here?" April asked aloud. "And how did it get past our shields?"

"Not a clue," Simon admitted. "Sensor logs recording nothing in the way of conventional weaponry or even a transporter beam."

"Sir?" Florida asked. "What do you think happened to Stevens and the others? Are they just gone . . . or gone for good, if you know what I mean?"

April sighed. "I wish I knew, Carlos."

"I don't believe they were vaporized," Simon said, offering a smidgen of hope. "Internal scanners aren't picking up residue or remains, not even on an atomic level." Stepping away from the science station, she obtained a tricorder from a storage compartment and used it to scan the empty seat where Ensign Stevens had been sitting before. "There's no trace of her. Not even a quantum echo."

"So what does that mean?" Florida asked.

"That she's not here, which means she might still be somewhere else." Simon lowered the tricorder. "Possibly."

"Then we won't write any eulogies just yet," April said. "Nor abandon hope for our lost comrades until we have a clearer understanding of their fate."

A backup crewman, Lieutenant Michelle Roberts, came forward to take Stevens's place at nav. She swallowed hard, but hesitated only a moment before assuming the post.

Brave woman, April thought.

"What is the word, sir?" Carlos asked. "Are we breaking orbit?"

April shook his head. "Not yet, I think."

As Simon had so astutely pointed out, the range of the Jatohr's mysterious weapon remained undetermined, making a successful retreat far from a foregone conclusion. Moreover, April was not ready to depart Usilde with matters as they were: the landing party held captive, the Usildar losing their planet to the invaders, and, perhaps most crucially, an unknown, aggressive alien race in possession of a terrifying super-weapon against which there was no ready defense. Nor had the actual origins of the Jatohr, or the full extent of their territorial ambitions, been discovered yet; what if their colonization efforts extended beyond Usilde? Far more than the safety of the *Enterprise* might be at stake. This could be a matter of Federation security.

"We have unfinished business here," he explained, "and questions that demand answers before we can depart in good conscience."

Simon returned to her post. "Can't argue with that. I'm in no hurry to abandon our people on the planet."

"In the meantime," April ordered, "I want regular updates sent to Starfleet Command, both by subspace bursts and periodic log buoys."

Starfleet wouldn't receive the projectile buoys right away, but they increased the odds that the information would not be lost if the *Enterprise* was. Given the potential danger posed by the Jatohr, April thought it vital that Starfleet and the Federation got word of what was happening on Usilde.

"Aye, aye, sir," Sanawey said, carrying out the orders. "Launching first buoy, containing all relevant log entries and sensor scans."

"Thank you, Claw. Keep the brass back home informed." April rested his chin on his knuckles, gazing pensively at the spinning green-and-blue planet on the viewer. "Now we simply have to find a way to defuse this crisis, before anyone else is lost."

Only one option presented itself.

"Contact the Jatohr on that same frequency," he ordered. "Tell them I want a face-to-face meeting . . . on their turf."

"Captain!" Simon protested. "You can't be serious."

"I've never been more so," he replied. "Make it happen."

And pray that my silver tongue is up to the task.

Eleven

"I have to say I don't like this."

Doctor Sarah April was not just the *Enterprise*'s chief medical officer, she was also the captain's wife. A slender woman in her forties, wearing her blue Starfleet scrubs, she had come straight from sickbay to the transporter room. Concern showed in her sea-green eyes. Her hair was the same auburn hue it had been when April had first met her back on Earth all those years ago, when he'd thought that she was easily the prettiest veterinarian he'd even seen. That was before he had sweet-talked her into signing aboard the *Enterprise*.

"Can't say I'm fond of the idea myself," he said, preparing to beam down to the citadel. He'd traded his favorite sweater for his best dress uniform, the better to make a positive first impression, although he wondered just how fully a race of paranoid gastropods grasped the nuances of humanoid apparel. "But it may be our best chance at breaking this bloody stalemate and turning this fraught first contact around."

"I know," she sighed. "And I know you feel you have to do this, for duty's sake."

He appreciated that she didn't try to talk him out of it. She was a Starfleet doctor after all, which meant that she accepted the inevitable risks of interstellar exploration as a necessary part of their mission. And, like him, she worked hard at not letting their personal relationship get in the way of their professional duties, which was not always easy at times like this.

"Just be careful," she added.

"When am I not?"

"Do you really want a list?" she said, smiling wryly. "To start with, there was that carefree jaunt into the Neutral Zone . . . "

He held up his hand to forestall a longer recitation of his crimes against caution. "Point taken, love, but I've always come home safe and sound, haven't I?"

"Only because you know I'd never let you hear the end of it if you didn't." Sarah clasped her hands together to keep from wringing them. "Seriously, Rob, are you certain you don't want to at least take a few security officers with you just to be on the safe side?"

He shook his head. "I'm going to be in the belly of the beast, surrounded by the Jatohr in their own fortress. I doubt that a little extra muscle would make any difference if matters take a turn for the worse, so why put two more lives at risk?" Worry over Una and her landing party played no little part in his decision. "And arriving with an armed entourage might send the wrong message, given that the intent is to convince the Jatohr that we come in peace."

"But what if they're like the Klingons," she asked, "and won't respect you unless you look ready to put up a fight?"

"Then I may be making a strategic error," he conceded, "but heaven help us if we start approaching every new species as though they were Klingons." That sounded like a recipe for constant galactic strife to him. "Besides, we've already presented a show of strength by giving them a taste of the *Enterprise*'s lasers."

"And suppose they try to 'disappear' you the same way they did those poor people on the bridge?"

"In which case I would be no safer than if I remained on the ship. And it's not as though I'm beaming down without any protection." He patted the standard-issue laser pistol at his hip. "But it's the *Enterprise*'s formidable firepower that is most likely to encourage the Jatohr to be on their best behavior during my visit. Or at least that's the idea."

Sarah gave up trying to talk him into an armed escort. "Well, clearly I'm not going to change your mind, so I'll have to trust that you know what you're doing. Just come back soon . . . and bring our people home."

"My top priority, I assure you."

Which was true enough, but he was all too aware that the situation on the planet was far more complicated than that. He feared privately that he might have to choose between protecting the Usildar and making peace with the Jatohr, which was not a moral dilemma he was eager to confront, particularly now that he'd seen firsthand how ruthless the Jatohr could be when it came to other species. Honoring the Prime Directive was one thing; electing to save his own people at the expense of an entire alien culture felt less like prudence and more like brutal self-interest.

First things first, he reminded himself. *We'll cross that bridge when it looms before us.*

He turned toward the transporter crew. "Are we ready to proceed?"

"Aye, sir," Celeste Darcel replied. "I've keyed in the coordinates sent to us by the Jatohr; there were some language issues, but math is math and we managed to sort it out. By my calculations, you'll be beaming right into that citadel of theirs."

Although committed to his course, April acknowledged a touch of trepidation. He was practically delivering himself to the Jatohr on a plate.

"Well, at least I won't be needing my hiking boots."

Undeterred by the presence of Darcel and her assistant, he gave Sarah an affectionate peck on the lips before stepping onto the platform.

"See you as soon as I'm able, love. Don't wait up." He nodded at Darcel. "Energize."

He took one last look at Sarah's brave features before the sparkling veil of the transporter effect came between them. The annular confinement beam whined in his ears. He felt his body tingle from the inside out and . . .

He arrived at his destination, which turned out to be a sophisticated-looking command center populated by several Jatohr, all of whom gaped at his sudden appearance in their midst. He imagined they didn't often have aliens materializing right before their eyestalks.

"Matter stream transmission across space!" a shiny black Jatohr enthused. "Remarkable!"

"And dangerous, Professor Eljor," a larger slug added sternly. "Do not overlook that!"

April recognized the second speaker as Commander Woryan, the Jatohr who had demanded the *Enterprise*'s surrender earlier. Did their reactions mean that the Jatohr did not possess transporter technology of their own?

Then how had they removed those crew members from the bridge?

His hopes of recovering those people diminished. *If they weren't simply snatched away by a transporter beam . . .*

"Surrender your weapon," Woryan demanded by way of a greeting. "Or your spy will pay the price."

April spotted Lieutenant Una being held off to one side. A pair of Jatohr guards flanked her, securing her arms with their claspers. He was glad to see the precocious young officer in one piece, but where was the rest of the landing party?

"Una." He glanced around the chamber. "Where are the others?"

Her doleful face and tone answered before she could. "They're . . . gone, sir."

"Gone?" He could guess what that meant, but felt compelled to ask, "Do you mean—"

"Your weapon!" Woryan interrupted. "Surrender it at once!"

"All right, all right." April slowly removed the pistol from his hip, taking care not to make any sudden moves that might provoke the Jatohr, and handed it over to a waiting underling. "There we go. No need to make a fuss."

Starfleet really needs to develop smaller, less conspicuous sidearms, he decided. *I should write a memo to that effect, if and when I get back to the ship.*

Una tried again to update him on the landing party. "They just vanished, sir. One minute they were there, then—"

"Quiet, creature!" Woryan slimed toward April. "You are not here to confer with your leader."

April suspected that Una was present only to serve as leverage. He didn't want her hurt and punished for no reason. "At ease, Lieutenant. I get the picture."

Martinez and the others had apparently been removed the same way those unlucky souls on the bridge had been, consigned to the same unknown fate. Finding out what had actually become of them was a question he still needed answered, the sooner the better, but he feared he was not going to like what he heard.

"Commander Woryan," he addressed the Jatohr leader, who was somewhat taller than April had anticipated. "Thank you for agreeing to meet with me."

"The pleasure is ours, Captain." The smaller, inkier slug slid forward. "Permit me to introduce myself. I am Eljor, the commander's scientific advisor. Needless to say, I have many questions about your people and your origins."

Pure intellectual curiosity, April wondered, *or is hir interest more strategic than scientific?* He resolved not to give away the store on this first encounter. *Loose lips and all that.*

"I'm pleased to make the acquaintance of you and your people. I regret that we find ourselves in an adversarial situation, but perhaps we have simply gotten off on the wrong foot." He realized belatedly that the Jatohr only had one foot apiece and regretted the turn of phrase. "I sincerely believe that we can resolve any misunderstandings between us, so that my people and yours can make peace with each other and avoid any further conflict."

But what of the Usildar? his conscience pricked him. *What of their destiny?*

"What misunderstandings?" Woryan challenged him. "You are not Jatohr and we caught your spies invading our domain and installations, even as your fearsome warship hangs above our heads."

Well, when you put it that way, April thought. Despite the loss of his own people, he tried to put himself in the Jatohr's shoes, if only to try to defuse this crisis before more tragedy ensued. "I apologize for not alerting you to our presence earlier. Our landing party was merely trying to avoid interfering with your affairs." He almost added "before we knew more about the situation," but caught himself in time lest he make their discretion sound merely provisional. "And the *Enterprise* is not a warship. We're explorers in search of knowledge. Any weapons we possess are for self-defense only."

"Defense against whom?" Woryan asked. "Your enemies?"

April parsed his answer carefully.

"The galaxy is a vast place, inhabited by many intelligent species and civilizations. Some, alas, are less friendly than others."

Woryan's facial tentacles shot up in alarm. Clearly agitated by April's revelation, the Jatohr commander conferred anxiously with hir subordinates in an unintelligible tongue that stumped even the universal translator. The captain shot a quizzical look at Una, who shrugged helplessly.

Eljor came forward, less visibly perturbed than hir comrades.

"You fascinate me, Captain. How many worlds have

you visited? How many different sentient species exist in this universe?"

"This universe? Do you mean galaxy?"

He'd assumed that the Jatohr were a spacefaring people as well, since they had obviously come to Usilde from another world, and yet they seemed stunned by the revelation that there were many other inhabited worlds and systems.

"Not just the galaxy, no. We are indeed newcomers to this realm."

April wondered if he had heard that correctly, or if maybe something was being garbled in translation. "You mean you're literally from another universe? Another reality?"

Eljor started to answer, only to be cut off by Woryan.

"Do not indulge the creature's curiosity, scientist. We have more important matters to attend to now that we know that our situation is even more precarious than we feared. It seems this realm is positively overrun with violent, warring creatures who will surely challenge our dominion over our new home. We cannot wait to expand our domain at our own pace. We must claim this *Enterprise* before it is too late!"

April thought he was beginning to grasp the bigger picture here. The Jatohr were pioneers, wary of a new strange reality they had barely begun to explore and all too conscious of the fact that they were surely outnumbered by this universe's native inhabitants. Small wonder that the jarring appearance of the landing party had thrown Woryan into a panic. Suddenly they were faced with evidence of an advanced technological civilization that possibly rivaled their own—and that wasn't going to be quite so easy to overpower as the hapless Usildar.

"But how did you get here?" April asked. "Where is your ship?"

"You are standing in it, creature," Woryan said. "And threatening it with your energy weapons!"

April blinked in surprise. "The citadel is your ship?"

"More like a sanctuary," Eljor clarified. "Capable of carrying us from one reality to another by means of—"

"But that is not enough now," Woryan said. "We need your ship—a spaceship—to defend ourselves from a universe of rivals. We cannot wait to make our own way off this planet. We must secure the stars to truly make this new universe our home."

This is just brilliant, April thought sarcastically. The more Woryan learned about the universe, the more paranoid and aggressive s/he became. Coupled with the Jatohr's enigmatic super-weapon, their preemptive approach to defense made for an extremely dangerous combination. And if they should get control of the *Enterprise* . . .

"I'm sorry. You're not getting my ship. That's non-negotiable. But if you're worried about the safety of your colony, perhaps our Federation can provide you with protection . . . or even a safer haven for your people."

The latter option would be the ideal outcome for all concerned. The Federation could help the Jatohr resettle on another world, and the Usildar could get their own planet back. Everyone could pursue their destinies in peace if only Woryan could be persuaded that conquest was not the only path to safety for the Jatohr.

Unfortunately, that didn't seem likely at the moment.

"We don't need your Federation. We will protect ourselves . . . with your ship. But you are correct: this is not a negotiation." Woryan loomed over April. "You *will* give us the *Enterprise*, and then you will tell us everything we need to know about your Federation and its rivals. Do not think that you have any choice in the matter."

"But every other species does not have to be your enemy," April insisted. "Our own Federation consists of myriad species from a multitude of worlds, all working together in harmon—"

"Creatures, not Jatohr." Woryan was unmoved by April's heartfelt words. "You are all nothing but creatures to be subdued—or removed—if the Jatohr are to thrive. We cannot sleep easy until this universe is ours."

"You've got it all wrong, Woryan." April kept trying to reason with the Jatohr commander, even though it was becoming clear that he was fighting a losing battle. "You can't keep your people safe that way. You'll just turn this entire universe against you."

"Do not waste your breath, creature. The words of an absurd, two-legged animal mean nothing to the Jatohr." Woryan gurgled to hir staff and April's image suddenly appeared on multiple viewscreens. A second later, his figure alone was converted to a photo-negative image as though he had been "selected" in some fashion. "You have seen the power of the transfer field at work. Order your ship to surrender or you will be removed as well."

The transfer field?

"Please, Commander," Eljor protested. "Do not remove him. There is so much more that can be learned from examining a live specimen: his kind's strengths, their weaknesses, their limitations . . ."

Scowling, Woryan gurgled another command. The photo-negative image of April went back to positive, although his figure remained upon the monitors. April took this to mean that he was no longer one button away from being removed.

"What about that one?" The impatient commander pointed at Una. "Perhaps he will be more cooperative if we threaten to remove the female."

"I would prefer to retain both specimens," Eljor stated, "for breeding purposes."

Una looked more appalled than when facing the prospect of vanishing into thin air. "Now wait one minute!"

I'll try not to take that indignant response personally, April thought drolly, despite the severity of the circumstances. *Although I imagine Sarah might have strong words on the subject herself.*

"What does one creature matter?" Woryan asked. "You will have your pick of specimens when we take possession of the ship."

"*If* we can take possession," Eljor said, "without destroying it or ourselves."

"You should listen to him, Woryan," April advised. "My first officer is under orders to destroy the ship rather than surrender it to you. And if you make her angry, I won't be held accountable for the consequences. She might just decide to crash the *Enterprise* straight into your sanctuary."

Woryan quivered in frustration. "But we need that

ship. There must be some way to seize control of it. He must tell us how!"

"I quite agree, Commander," Eljor said, "but we require *accurate* information. Threats or even torture will only encourage lies. He will tell us only what we want to hear or, worse yet, what he wants us to believe." The scientist examined April with hir tentacles. "Allow me to have the specimens conveyed to my laboratory, where I may employ more sophisticated—and reliable—methods to extract the data we seek."

"What sort of methods?" Woryan asked skeptically.

"Drugs, conditioning, perhaps even corrective brain surgery." Eljor sounded disturbingly confident to April. "Science, Commander. That is how we will 'persuade' Captain April to turn over his ship to us . . . and tell us everything we need to know to subdue the Federation."

Woryan mulled it over. "Are you certain you can get this creature to cooperate?"

"I guarantee it."

———

"No word from the captain yet?"

"Not yet, Doctor," Sanawey told Sarah on the bridge. "I'm sorry."

The communications officer was more patient than he needed to be, given that she had already asked him the same question several times now, but she couldn't help it. Knowing that Robert was on his own on a planet where an entire landing party had already gone missing was torture. She wasn't sure if she should be relieved or not that no medical emergencies currently required her attention in sickbay. A routine checkup or procedure or two might have helped her take her mind off the very real possibility that she might never see her husband again. But who was she kidding? Work or no work, she was not going to rest easy until Rob was back on the *Enterprise* where he belonged.

Where we belong.

"How long has it been?" she asked.

"Fifteen minutes and counting." Lorna Simon occupied the captain's chair in Robert's absence. She studied the ship's chronometer just below the astrogator in front of her. "Forty-five more minutes to go."

Sarah paced restlessly around the bridge. "We're not really going to leave him behind, are we? If he doesn't get back in time?"

"Those are the captain's orders." The first officer shifted uncomfortably in her borrowed seat. Her voice was sympathetic but firm. "If we don't hear from him within the hour, we're to flee the system at maximum warp and report back to Starfleet Command."

Sarah watched the minutes and seconds tick down on the chronometer, wishing she had the power to slow or reverse them somehow. But practical time travel was still just a pipe dream as far as Starfleet was concerned. Time only flowed in one direction, sometimes far too quickly.

Hurry back, Rob, she thought. *Please.*

Twelve

Eljor's laboratory was located several levels below the command chamber, in the citadel's central hub. A short ride on a bubble lift brought April and Una to the lab, where a quartet of Jatohr guards herded them into a cramped cell that made the brig back on the *Enterprise* seem like a VIP suite. Leaves, branches, and other forest litter carpeted the floor in lieu of a bed or cot, leading April to believe that a Usildar specimen or two had once been confined here. A clear barrier, made of transparent aluminum or some similar substance, dialed into place, sealing the captives inside. April tested the barrier. It didn't budge.

My diplomatic efforts, he concluded, *are not going as well as one might hope.*

"You there, creature!" one of the guards shouted at April. "Back away from the barrier!"

"It's quite all right, sentries," Eljor reassured the guard. "The cage is a sturdy one. The specimens are not going anywhere." The scientist turned hir back on the cage to dismiss the guards. "Thank you all for your assistance transferring the specimens, but you may return to your regular duties now."

The spacious lab seemed to occupy an entire level. Sophisticated equipment of indecipherable purpose crowded the facility, along with assorted work spaces, counters, examination tables, and terminals. The furnishings were built to accommodate Jatohr anatomy, naturally, which led to a conspicuous lack of anything resembling chairs or sofas. A humanoid skeleton, whose proportions indicated Usildar origins, was mounted in a transparent display column not far from April's cage. One of the scientist's earlier "specimens"? Maybe even the previous occupant of the cage?

April could've done without spying that grisly exhibit.

"Are you certain, Professor?" the guard asked. "Perhaps we should remain to keep watch over the creatures."

"That is hardly necessary," Eljor insisted. "The specimens are in no danger of escaping, and I can readily sound an alarm should the impossible occur." The impatient scientist opened Una's backpack, which contained an impressive collection of Starfleet materiel, and laid them out atop a scuffed, acid-pitted counter. "In the meantime, I require peace and privacy to do my work."

The guards lingered, unconvinced. "But, Professor, your own safety—"

"Is my own concern." Eljor pointed at the exit. "Now leave me to my labors. That is not a request."

It suddenly dawned on April that he could understand the Jatohr as they spoke among themselves, as opposed to hearing nothing but unintelligible gurgles earlier. He could only imagine that the universal translator had *finally* cracked the Newcomers' exceptionally alien tongue after running a sufficiently large sample through a wide variety of decryption programs. He mentally thanked whatever brilliant cyberneticist had gifted the translator with the ability to learn.

"As you wish." The guard deferred to the scientist's authority. "Do not hesitate to call on us if you require assistance controlling the animals."

"I will be certain to do so. You are to be commended for your diligence. I will be certain to convey my appreciation to the commander."

"Thank you, Professor!"

The guards departed the laboratory, leaving Eljor alone with the captives. April observed the exchange with interest, noting that the Jatohr scientist seemed to wield considerable clout. April appreciated the courtesy. Eljor struck him as possibly more rational than Woryan and more likely to listen to reason.

Aside from that talk about drugs and brain surgery, that is.

"Excuse me, Captain?" Una contemplated their cramped new accommodations. "About that 'breeding' business . . . With all due respect, I have no intention of being used to breed more laboratory specimens or slave labor. I would sooner die."

"No offense taken, Lieutenant," April quipped. "I'm a married man, after all." He fingered his wedding ring. "But let's hold off on any such drastic measures for now. Frankly, you're my only backup at the moment, and I'm counting on your help."

"Understood, sir." She sounded relieved to change the subject. "You can rely on me."

As Eljor saw the guards out and closed off hir lab,

Una quickly briefed April on what had happened to the landing party. The captain had plenty of questions, but put them aside as Eljor slimed toward the cage. April tensed in anticipation, stepping in front of Una protectively. A chill ran down his spine. Given a choice, he'd rather face a firing squad than have his brain experimented on. He'd seen a victim of a Klingon mind-sifter once. It hadn't been pretty.

"Listen," he began. "Before you go any further—"

"My apologies for your treatment so far," the scientist said. "I fear that my fellow Jatohr lack the imagination to see beings such as yourselves as sentient beings much like us. I had to think quickly to protect you from the commander's wrath."

April's spirits lifted. Hope replaced apprehension.

"What are you saying, that all that talk about breeding and brain surgery was just a ruse? To keep Woryan from eliminating us?"

"Or worse," Eljor said. "Forgive me if I alarmed or offended you. It was for your own good . . . and perhaps for ours as well."

Was that a trace of remorse in the Jatohr's artificial voice?

"We'll trust your judgment in that regard," April said. "Can you let us out of this cage now, as a gesture of good faith?"

"A reasonable request." Eljor produced a compact remote-control device and aimed it at the transparent barrier, only to reconsider before unlocking the cage. "On second thought, however, how can I be certain that you will not take action against me? Alas, you have good cause to see my kind as your enemy and to want to avenge your lost companions."

"I just came here to talk," April said.

"And I to learn," Una added, coming forward, "about you *and* the Usildar."

April wasn't sure he would've mentioned the Usildar at this juncture, but recalled that the idealistic young lieutenant had taken their plight to heart right from the beginning, which was not something he could truly hold against her. If anything, it spoke well for her character.

"And yet who could blame you," Eljor replied, "for striking back after the unconscionable way you and your people have suffered at our hands?" S/he lowered the remote. "Perhaps a few prudent safety measures are advisable, at least until we get to know each other better."

April bit back his frustration. They had come so close to getting out of the cage. But matters were definitely looking up, so he didn't want to push Eljor too far too fast. At present, the sympathetic Jatohr scientist was still their best hope for turning this situation around.

"All right," April said, "for the time being. I'm disappointed, but I can appreciate your caution. My own people have a saying: good walls make good neighbors."

"A cogent truth, concisely put," Eljor said. "But there we get to the crux of our current difficulties. Where we come from, we had no neighbors. To our knowledge, we were the only sentient life-forms in our universe. Little wonder then that my people are alarmed at the very idea of sharing this new cosmos with rival species. The Usildar posed little threat, due to their primitive ways and lack of technology, but an advanced civilization such as yours . . ."

"Is rather more intimidating?" April said, completing the thought.

"Sadly, yes." Eljor's tentacles drooped ruefully. "You must understand. The Jatohr are not a predatory species by nature. We are a compassionate, civilized people who treasure life and peace and prosperity."

"As long as it's Jatohr life," Una said bitterly. "The rest of us are just 'creatures' who don't really count as people."

"Precisely. To my great shame."

Guilt radiated from the scientist, perceptible despite hir inhuman form and body language. A triangular mouth twisted itself out of shape.

"You can't blame yourself," April said, "for the attitudes of the other Jatohr."

"Perhaps, but I must certainly blame myself for their actions, since I am responsible for bringing us here in the first place."

"You?" April was intrigued, wanting to know more. "Maybe you should explain."

"You should know the truth," Eljor agreed, "since it is your realm that is paying the price for my well-intentioned attempt to preserve my people from . . . a catastrophe in our own universe."

"What sort of catastrophe?" Una asked.

Eljor hesitated, as though loath to reveal too much. "That is . . . difficult to explain. Suffice to say, the sanctuary was created to save my people by transferring us from one reality to another by means of the transfer-field generator, a mechanism of my own invention. We are refugees, seeking a new life on an alien shore."

Finally, we're getting some real answers, April thought,

listening intently. "So it was this 'transfer-field generator' that brought your citadel to our universe?"

"You misunderstand." Eljor swept hir limbs to indicate the glossy oyster walls surrounding them. "The citadel *is* the transfer-field generator. Only a mechanism of such size is capable of amplifying the field to transfer an entire population, although the heart of the generator is a master control unit I named the Transfer Key." Hir limbs sagged toward the floor. "The Key is both my proudest accomplishment and my greatest crime. Once my people's salvation, it has been corrupted into an instrument of oppression."

"That's how you make people disappear," Una deduced. "You use the transfer field to banish them to a parallel universe."

"Correct," Eljor said. "Transferring this citadel required substantially more energy, of course, but the Key can also be used on a much less ambitious scale to target small groups or individuals, such as a rebellious Usildar tribe or your unfortunate companions."

"But how exactly do you target people?" Una asked. "I didn't see any obvious weapons employed when—" Her voice briefly caught in her throat. "When the landing party was 'removed' right in front of me."

April heard the anguish in her voice, leaking through her professional composure. She had lost the rest of her team only hours ago, he recalled; the pain and shock were obviously still with her. It couldn't be easy to be the last crew member standing after that tragedy—and on her first time leading a landing party no less. Chances were, she was carrying a hefty load of survivor's guilt.

He placed a comforting hand on her shoulder. "Steady there, Una."

"There are no weapons as such," Eljor explained. "Our security forces cannot remove people on their own. What transpires, when the need arises, is that they contact the master control room here in the sanctuary, where operators lock onto the target remotely. The only actual weapon is the transfer-field generator itself."

April thought he got the idea. "In other words, it's less like blasting someone with a laser and more like paging the transporter room and ordering the crew there to beam your opponents away, all from the safety of the *Enterprise*."

"I suppose so," Eljor said, "if I take your meaning correctly."

"But that begs the bigger question," April said. "Where did you send our people?"

Once again, the Jatohr scientist hesitated before answering. "To . . . the next realm."

"Which would be?" April pressed.

"Beyond your comprehension, I suspect. To describe it in terms you would understand is not something that can be quickly or easily accomplished at present."

April got the distinct impression that Eljor was not being entirely forthcoming with him, despite being a good deal more communicative than the rest of the Jatohr. Hir cryptic responses smacked of deliberate evasiveness.

Was s/he hiding something?

"But they're still alive?" Una asked urgently. "Somewhere?"

"Possibly, probably, but the fate of a few unlucky individuals pales in comparison to the larger crime being committed against this planet and its inhabitants."

"Like the Usildar?" April prompted.

"Just so," Eljor said. "Those poor primitives are the true victims of my hubris. Please believe me, it was never my intention to bring harm to another intelligent species. I sought only to save the Jatohr from extinction. But it is one thing, I assure you, to devote your genius to rescuing your people; it is quite another thing altogether to witness your life's work being employed to conquer and enslave others."

April could well believe that Eljor's conscience was bothered by what was happening on Usilde. Certainly s/he would not be the first scientist in history to be troubled by how their brainchildren were put to use.

Just look at Oppenheimer or N'Brullus.

There was just one thing April didn't understand. "How is it that you feel differently about these matters than Commander Woryan and the others?"

"Not to be immodest, but perhaps it is simply that, as a scientist, I am fundamentally more open-minded than the majority of my species, and thus more capable of imagining that other forms of life might be as worthy as our own. Certainly I could not have conceived of the transfer field, let alone brought it into being, unless I was able to think beyond certain preconceptions and conceive of an entirely new paradigm when it came to the very fabric of the space-time-ethereal continuum. In short, I've made a career of thinking the unthinkable."

"Like realizing that the world is round instead of

flat," April said, "or that subspace underlies conventional space."

"Or that the Jatohr is not the only species that matters," Una added.

"Indeed," Eljor said. "Or perhaps it is simply that I am more acutely aware of the Usildar's suffering because I bear the greater weight of responsibility."

"My people have another saying," April said. "The road to hell is paved with good intentions. We too have learned, from painful experience, that even the most benign of interventions can yield unexpected consequences, particularly when it comes to dealing with alien cultures and civilizations. That's why we have adopted what we call our Prime Directive, which prohibits us from deliberately interfering with the affairs of others. It's not always easy to follow, but it has served us well when it comes to avoiding tragedies such as what's happening here on Usilde."

"A wise policy," Eljor said. "Would that my people had adopted such a directive upon arriving in this realm. I fear that Commander Woryan and the others will not rest until they have reshaped this entire planet to their liking—and then, perhaps, your entire cosmos."

"Using the *Enterprise* to carry them from world to world?" April asked. "Is that why Woryan wants my ship?"

"Correct. The Transfer Key only allows us to cross from one reality to another, not to traverse space within your universe. To further colonize this realm, and sub-due its inhabitants, a different form of transport is required . . . such as your magnificent spaceship. Woryan cannot resist such a prize, not if s/he desires to promptly expand our dominion beyond this planet."

"Why Usilde?" Una asked. "Why arrive on this planet in particular?"

"Purely a matter of chance and quantum geography," Eljor explained. "As it happens, the curvature of space-time in both universes, along with various other contributing factors, such as brane energy differentials, cosmic string entanglements, and the prevailing multiversal currents, deposited us here on Usilde rather than elsewhere, to the misfortune of the Usildar and every other life-form on this world."

"Tough luck for them," Una said, "and anyone else you run into."

"Which is why I must stress that this world is only the beginning," Eljor warned. "Now that my people know that there are other, possibly competitive species roaming the stars, they will be intent on eliminating that threat."

Which could spell bad news for the Federation, April realized, not to mention the Klingons, the Romulans, the Orions, and countless unaligned and independent races, some of them yet to be discovered by Starfleet.

"So what do you want of us?" he asked. "How do we prevent this crisis from escalating?"

Eljor spoke slowly and deliberately, as though every word cost hir.

"I cannot permit the Jatohr to do to other worlds what we are doing to Usilde. This madness must end, and I need your help to make things right."

Eljor clicked a control on the remote and the cage door slid open, releasing April and Una, who wasted no time exiting the cell. Retrieving their equipment, s/he returned the laser pistols and communicators to hir former prisoners.

"I caution you not to communicate with your ship immediately," the scientist said. "Now that my people are monitoring the *Enterprise*, any transmissions on that frequency might be detected."

"We could try to vary the wavelength," Una suggested, "and establish an encrypted channel."

Eljor frowned on that idea. "I would not advise such an attempt. Do not underestimate my people's zeal where our security is concerned."

"Even still, perhaps it would be worth the risk." April considered Una, who had already been through enough, in his judgment. "We could contact the ship just long enough for them to beam you back to the *Enterprise*, while Eljor and I settle matters here."

Una shook her head. "With all due respect, sir, my mission isn't over. If there's even a chance we can bring back our people from wherever the Jatohr banished them, I'm not going anywhere." She dug in her proverbial heels. "And as you said earlier, you need someone to watch your back."

"Can't argue with that, I suppose," April said, respecting her decision. He suspected that he'd be just as adamant if he was in her shoes. He wished, however, that he could safely contact Lorna—and Sarah—back on the ship. The clock was ticking down to the moment when, per his orders, the *Enterprise* would attempt to escape the system. "Very well, Lieutenant. Count yourself in for the duration." He looked at Eljor. "How can we help you?"

"We need to reach the master control room, which is located directly below my laboratory, the better to allow me easy access to the Transfer Key and generator. The room is staffed by a crew of devoted operators who, despite my eminence, would never permit me to do what must be done. On my own, I am helpless because there are no other Jatohr that I can I trust to share my views, but perhaps with your assistance . . ."

April wanted more details. "What exactly do you intend to do?"

"Disable the transfer-field generator, thereby eliminating the primary threat to both your ship and the Usildar. Without my dreadful creation at their disposal, my people will be forced to make peace with the Usildar rather than simply eliminating them. Compromise will be easier than conquest."

I can work with that, April thought. Removing the transfer field from the equation would take the *Enterprise* out of danger and, possibly, shift the balance of power on the planet toward the Usildar, giving them back the freedom to chart their own course into the future. And as for the Jatohr . . . ideally, the Federation could find them a safe haven elsewhere in the quadrant.

Granted, that was easier said than done. Class-M planets were eagerly sought after by both the Federation and the Klingons, to name but two galactic powers. Finding an uninhabited world just for the Jatohr would be tricky, but perhaps they could be persuaded to share a world with some open-minded Federation colonists if they were promised a continent or two for privacy's sake. It wouldn't be a perfect solution, as far as the Prime

Directive was concerned, but it would be a good sight better than the current situation on Usilde—and far safer for all concerned.

"That's the best plan I've heard so far," he said. "But we need to move briskly, before matters escalate further."

He saw no need to mention the *Enterprise*'s upcoming departure. Mutual trust was all very well and good, but April was not inclined to test it. What Eljor didn't know couldn't hurt the ship's chances of making a strategic retreat. They just couldn't afford to dally if he and Una wanted to make it back to the ship in time.

"But before you disable the transfer device," Una asked, "will we be able to recover our lost crew members?"

"Possibly, if the opportunity allows," Eljor said, sounding evasive again. "But do not forget that there are much larger matters at stake here, involving the fate of this entire world and, in time, many more worlds to come."

It was obvious that rescuing the landing party and the other missing crew members was low on the scientist's list of priorities. Sadly, April saw hir point; while he shared Una's desire to rescue his crew from eternal exile to another universe, and fully understood why she was dead set on that goal, the captain had to consider the safety of the ship and the Federation first.

The clock was ticking in more ways than one. It was only a matter of time before Woryan demanded results from Eljor's experiments and found out about the scientist's shifting loyalties. If they were going to defang the Jatohr, they needed to do so with all deliberate speed, no matter what sacrifices were required.

"We'll do what we can for them, Una," April promised, "but stopping the Jatohr and saving the ship is job one. Are we on the same page here?"

"Aye, sir," she said gravely. "But I'm not going to forget them . . . ever."

I wouldn't expect you to, he thought. *But first things first.*

He turned back to Eljor.

"How do we get to that control room?"

Thirteen

A private ramp connected the laboratory to the master control room one level below.

"One of the perks of being the First Scientist," Eljor explained, "as well as the esteemed creator of the transfer-field generator." The Jatohr scientist led Una and the captain down a long spiral ramp that they indeed appeared to have to themselves. "It was deemed only fitting and sensible that I should always have ready access to the core of the generator."

"Rank has its privileges," April said, nodding. "And genius too, I suppose."

"Which my people may soon have cause to regret," Eljor said ruefully, "now that I must betray their trust in me . . . for all our sakes."

Una hurried down the ramp. She could well imagine that the conscience-stricken scientist had profoundly mixed feelings about what they were attempting, but, frankly, she was less concerned with Eljor's moral dilemma than with completing their mission and rescuing her lost comrades.

I'm coming for you, Tim. Hang on . . . wherever you are.

That persistent rumbling echoed all around them, grating on her nerves. "What's that irritating noise, anyway?" she asked.

"Merely ongoing renovations," Eljor said, continuing to slime down the ramp. "Elsewhere in the sanctuary."

"What kind of renovations?" April asked.

"Nothing that need concern us now."

A sealed doorway greeted them at the bottom of the ramp. Indecipherable alien runes were inscribed upon the door. Una found the Jatohr's written language just as baffling as their speech had been before the universal translator had finally gotten a handle on it. *Better late than never.*

"Beyond this portal lays the control room," Eljor said. "There should be no more than three operators in attendance, but you must strike quickly. Our activities will not go undetected for long."

It occurred to Una that Eljor was using them to do the dirty work of actually attacking his fellow Jatohr so that s/he could keep hir claspers clean in that regard.

She had no problem with that.

"Lasers on stun," April reminded her. "We're after that generator, not revenge."

"Understood, sir."

Eljor had brought no weapon, not even a stun-globe. S/he had assured them that they were unlikely to encounter any such globes in the control room; the floating security devices were primarily employed in the labor camps, to keep the Usildar under observation and control. The citadel was considered a secure location, and the Jatohr had no reason to fear that one of their own might attempt to seize control of the Transfer Key.

That's going to cost them, Una thought. *I hope.*

"May posterity forgive me," Eljor murmured. "Ready your weapons."

The scientist approached the doorway and gurgled a brief command. The gleaming door dilated open to admit hir.

"Now," Eljor said. "Be quick about it."

"You don't need to tell us that," April said. By his reckoning, more than thirty minutes had transpired since he had first beamed down to the planet, which meant he had less than half an hour to get back in touch with the *Enterprise* before the ship attempted a tactical retreat as ordered. *We need to get that generator shut down before then.*

The control room was circular and ringed with screens, like the bridge on the *Enterprise,* and laid out in tiers of concentric circles, like an old-fashioned wedding cake, with sloped ramps connecting the levels. A towering cylindrical apparatus dominated the center of the chamber, resting atop a sloped pedestal, while workstations ringed the central column facing outward toward the screens. Elevated catwalks ran along the upper levels. The air felt dryer than elsewhere in the citadel, possibly as a concession to the delicate equipment. The cylinder hummed and crackled noisily.

"Professor?" A trio of Jatohr technicians looked up at Eljor's arrival, then reacted in surprise to the sight of the two humanoids accompanying hir. Their eyestalks extended and they started to turn away from their stations. "What is this—"

April's laser stunned the nearest operator, even as Una shot past him to knock out the next one, but the third had time enough to gurgle sharply and jab at hir control panel with a metallic digit. A reverberating basso alarm, similar to the one that had pursued Una across the labor camp, sounded through the control room.

"Damn," the captain muttered. "Seal the door, Professor. We're going to have company."

"Without a doubt." Eljor, who had hung back by the doorway, gurgled a command and the door dialed shut behind them. S/he took a moment to manipulate an adjacent control panel. "There! I have reconfigured the security protocols to deny admission to any new visitors, but I fear that the door is not strong enough to withstand a prolonged—"

"Traitor!"

A *fourth* operator, who had been hidden from view on the opposite side of the central column, charged at the scientist with surprising speed. The metallic claspers at the end of hir right forelimb clicked together to form a sharp point, which s/he rammed into Eljor's back with enough force to pierce the other Jatohr's brittle carapace. Eljor gurgled in shock and pain as the point of hir attacker's arm burst from hir chest, spraying dark green blood on the sealed door. S/he slumped forward, sliding off the prosthetic arm impaling hir.

"No!" April exclaimed before turning his laser pistol on the hostile Jatohr. A crimson beam stunned the murderous slug into unconsciousness, but the damage to Eljor was done. The scientist was still alive, but watery olive blood spilled from both the front and the back of hir punctured armor. A distinctive metallic smell, along with its color, suggested that, like most mollusks (and

Vulcans, for that matter), the Jatohr had copper-based blood that employed hemocyanin instead of hemoglobin to transport oxygen through hir veins. Hir breathing was labored, making Una fear that the scientist's lung had been injured, along with who knew what other internal organs.

"It seems I was . . . mistaken about the number of operators on duty," Eljor said haltingly, gasping for breath. "The commander must have . . . assigned additional personnel during the present crisis . . ."

Una rushed to the wounded scientist's side. She was no xenobiologist; she had no idea what constituted a mortal injury to a two-meter-tall gastropod, but being speared through the trunk had to be serious. And s/he was losing a lot of blood.

"How badly are you hurt?" she asked. "What can we do?"

Eljor reeled unsteadily, struggling to stay upright.

"Just help me to the primary control column, so that I can finish this . . . and do what must be done."

April hurried to assist Una. Working together, they draped Eljor's arms over their shoulders and grabbed onto the injured slug's leaking trunk, heedless of the slick, sticky fluid flowing from hir wounds. They half supported, half dragged the bleeding scientist toward the control column. The wizened Jatohr was heavier than s/he looked, but hir natural mucous made dragging hir across the floor slightly easier. That the silvery slime was now streaked with green worried Una.

That can't be good, she thought.

Reaching the column, Eljor sagged against it.

"Thank you, my alien friends. My life is . . . seeping away. I could not have managed without you."

The low-pitched alarm kept booming. Isolating the source of the racket, April blasted the speaker with his laser pistol. Sparks flared from the device as it fell mercifully silent.

"Now maybe we can hear ourselves think," the captain said.

But the quiet was short-lived. Woryan's irate face took over several of the viewscreens lining the walls of the control room. Hir bellowing voice accosted the intruders.

"*Despicable creatures! I knew you were not to be trusted!*"

April lifted his chin to address one of the larger screens. "Trust is a two-way street, Commander, and you've offered precious little on your part. And for the record, my name is April. Robert Timothy April."

"*Your senseless appellation means nothing to me,*" Woryan ranted. "*Give us back our control room. You do not belong there!*"

"And you don't belong on Usilde," April shot back, "but that didn't seem to stop you from taking it."

Una lowered her voice to question Eljor. "Can your commander 'remove' us like the others?"

"Not while we remain in possession of this control room," the scientist assured her. Green dribbled from hir mouth, indicating possible internal bleeding. "But Woryan is unlikely to let us keep it for long."

Proving hir point, Una heard commotion outside the sealed entrance to the chamber. Jatohr voices shouted angrily, loud enough to be heard through the contracted door. Something pounded against the door with great impact. Dust fell from the ceiling.

"*You cannot defy us!*" Woryan declared from the wall screens. "*We will break down the door if we must!*"

"That is no idle threat," Eljor said to Una and April, "but you must not . . . let my people retake this chamber before . . . I am done." The scientist was quivering from head to foot, seemingly staying upright only through sheer force of will. S/he was having trouble keeping hir tentacles elevated as well. They swayed up and down erratically. "I need more time!"

Pistol in hand, April headed toward the door, leaving Una with the dying scientist. "I'll hold them off if I have to," he said. "Una, you stay with Eljor. Help hir finish this."

"Yes, sir."

The scientist's right arm remained draped over Una's strong shoulders, while the exhausted lieutenant struggled to keep her grip on Eljor's increasingly slippery, bloody trunk and exoskeleton. It had been hours, Una realized, since she'd eaten or rested, and even her exceptional constitution was nearing its limits. Propping the shaky Jatohr up, she examined the imposing mechanism at the heart of the transfer-field generator.

The central control column towered over them, stretching all the way to the ceiling, which was at least twenty-five meters overhead. The bottom quarter of the column, rising up from the pedestal, consisted of machinery, complete with gauges and controls and instrumentation whose functions were not readily apparent; Una made a mental note to scan the equipment with her tricorder if and when an opportunity arose.

Meanwhile, the bulk of the column consisted of a clear cylinder, roughly seventy centimeters across, that appeared to be an advanced holographic imaging tank, which was presently displaying, ominously enough, a three-dimensional view of the *Enterprise*'s bridge, seemingly unfolding in real time. Una registered the sight of First Officer Simon occupying the captain's chair while Doctor April paced restlessly within the command well. Both women looked exceedingly tense and worried.

Una knew how they felt.

"How are you doing this?" she asked. "Spying on us this way?"

Not even the *Enterprise*'s scanners were so sophisticated when it came to locking onto images from inside an alien spacecraft or outpost. Moreover, the *Enterprise* had not detected any high-powered surveillance satellites in orbit around Usilde earlier.

"Information, entanglement, cosmic strings connecting all things . . . " Eljor wheezed and coughed, as though choking on hir own fluids. "A universe is nothing but information if you know how to read it . . . "

Hir words trailed off into another ragged cough.

Una figured that was as much explanation as she was going to get right now. "Never mind," she said, wondering just how long the failing scientist had left. "Save your energy."

Heavy objects slammed repeatedly against the door from outside. A battering ram, Una wondered, or maybe a volley of sentry globes dive-bombing the door? Standing guard before the besieged entrance, April called out to them.

"Whatever you need to do, do it soon."

"You heard the captain," Una said to Eljor, hoping there was still a chance to rescue Tim and the others from their undeserved exile, preferably before the *Enterprise* fled the system without them. April had informed her of the approaching deadline back in the laboratory, so Una understood they had a good chance of getting stranded on Usilde—if Woryan's troops didn't dispose of them first. "Make it snappy."

"The urgency . . . has not escaped me." Eljor manipulated a small rectangular control panel embedded in the larger apparatus above the pedestal. Buttons and knobs of unknown function framed a small, data slate–sized viewscreen. "Allow me . . . a few more moments."

In the looming cylinder, the holographic view of the *Enterprise*'s bridge was replaced by a three-dimensional projection of the entire planet, rotating slowly in space. At the same time, the majority of the screens occupying the walls were taken over by scenes from all over the planet, including the labor camp in the contaminated river valley. The views subdivided into smaller and smaller windows, each highlighting a different Jatohr until it seemed as though every alien on the planet had been targeted. Eljor weakly croaked a verbal command, and every Jatohr on the screens was selected as a photo-negative image. Even Woryan, who continued to rail at them from a single large monitor, was now depicted in negative.

"Wait," Una said, not liking what she was seeing. "What are you doing?"

"That which is necessary," the scientist wheezed. "Forgive me, my beloved people."

S/he pressed a button on the control panel—and the Jatohr went away.

White light flashed from every screen, briefly washing out all the color in the control room, as every Jatohr in every window simultaneously blinked out of existence. Woryan's glowering visage vanished along with the others. The pounding at the door ceased abruptly, as did all shouting and commotion outside. The entire citadel seemed to fall silent, so that Una could hear nothing but her own pounding heartbeat and the obvious agony in Eljor's weak, wet voice.

"It's done," the Jatohr said. "They're gone . . . all of them."

Fourteen

April lowered his pistol. He gazed at the emptied screens in shock.

"Oh my God," he whispered, turning to look at Eljor. "What have you done?"

The scientist leaned heavily against the generator controls. S/he looked even worse than s/he had mere moments before. Hir wounds were still bleeding profusely, so that Eljor appeared to be literally drying up right before April's eyes. Hir voice was weak and halting.

"I undid my greatest mistake . . . and sent my people back . . . where we came from."

April tried to grasp the enormity of what had just occurred. "All of them?"

"All . . . from everywhere on the planet." A wet, congested sigh escaped hir damaged lung. "I am now the last Jatohr still living on Usilde, if not for very much longer . . ."

April glanced around at the control room. One by one, the screens were going blank as the generator powered down, although a subdued rumbling still came from elsewhere in the citadel. The holographic-imaging cylinder held nothing but an empty void. "You sent your people back, but not the citadel?"

"There was . . . no other choice," Eljor explained. "If I

banished the sanctuary as well, my people could simply use it to . . . return to this realm." Hir tentacles retracted into hir face so that only their tops could be seen, while hir head and throat were retracting as well. "And re-creating the Transfer Key is no easy task, not without my genius to guide them. It is unlikely that the Jatohr will ever threaten your universe again . . ."

"But I don't understand," April said, putting away his weapon. "You said you were only going to disable the transfer device, not use it to expel your entire species from the planet."

"A deception on my part," the scientist confessed. "Even without the Key, my people possessed . . . technology enough to subdue this planet. Only by removing the Jatohr entirely could the Usildar have a chance . . . to regain their world." Hir head sagged forward. "If it is not already too late . . ."

What did he mean by that? April wondered. *The environmental contamination that the landing party had reported before?*

"But you didn't need to do that," he insisted. "The Federation could have protected the Usildar and found a way for both your species to endure."

"Despite your Directive against interfering?" Hir sunken eyestalks met his gaze. "I could not ask you to violate your own laws . . . nor take the chance that they would prevent you from saving the Usildar from the evil I brought upon them . . ."

Una remained intent on her own prime directive. "But what about our people? You were going to bring them back!"

"There was no time," Eljor said, "and the reactor must never be reactivated . . . lest my people find a way back to this realm." Fumbling digits wrested the compact rectangular control panel from its slot in the larger apparatus. "Behold the Transfer Key. Without it, this sanctuary is but a shell . . ."

The Key looked innocuous enough, like some sort of portable scanner or data slate. April found it hard to accept that this small, unimpressive device, which was barely larger than the *Enterprise*'s chronometer back on the bridge, could be the primary component of the Jatohr's fearsome super-weapon.

"This little thing?" Una scoffed. "This is what allowed you to cross from universe to universe, and to enslave the Usildar, and to condemn good men and women to some forsaken alien reality? This so-called Key?"

"Do not be fooled by its size," Eljor said forcefully, despite hir declining strength. "In the multiverse, all dimensions are relative, and the difference between the infinite . . . and the infinitesimal . . . is merely a matter of perspective . . ."

A choking fit cut off hir lecture. S/he crumpled to the floor, landing in the puddle of sticky green blood and mucous. Hir dry, desiccated body had shriveled dramatically, as though there was more of hir spilled outside her skin than was left inside. Hir shattered carapace threatened to swallow up hir actual physical form. Trembling digits reached up to pass the Key to April.

"Take this. Guard it. Tell no one of it. Not even your own Federation."

April accepted the device, but balked at the dying scientist's injunction. "I'm not certain I can do that. I have a responsibility to report on what happened here."

"But what of your Prime Directive? Does not its wisdom apply to me as well . . . and to the Key I rashly brought to your universe? Do not let me go to oblivion knowing that I have . . . forever interfered with this realm." Hir wrinkled skin was flaking and falling off. Hir tremulous voice was barely more than a whisper. "Swear to me, in the spirit of the Prime Directive you so revere, that you will not . . . let my creation . . . pervert the course of future events."

The scientist's desperate, dying request was hard to deny. Even Una, who was doubtless still upset over Eljor's failure to rescue Martinez and the others, appeared moved by the Jatohr's fervent plea. April guessed that, after what had happened to her landing party, she understood too well what it was like to be haunted by a mistake you couldn't take back. He hoped she could forgive herself in time.

"I'll do what I can," he promised Eljor. "Rest easy, Professor."

Eljor sank away, practically melting into hir own spilled substance. Hir lips moved and Una had to strain to make out the scientist's final words.

"Never tell . . . never forget . . ."

"Never," Una whispered to herself. "Not as long as I live."

The last Jatohr fell still and silent. The once-brilliant scientist was now little more than a dried husk drowning in a spreading green puddle. Una scanned the remains with her tricorder but detected no life signs. She shook her head at April.

"Gone?" he asked anyway.

"Like the other Jatohr, if not quite in the same way."

"You don't sound too broken up about it, Lieutenant."

"I'm sorry, sir. You'll forgive me if I mourn our losses instead."

April gave her a searching look. "Fair enough, Una. I grieve for Martinez and the others as well. Their bravery and sacrifice will be remembered for as long as I'm captain of the *Enterprise* . . . and beyond."

He flipped open his communicator. "April to *Enterprise*."

Lorna Simon's voice responded almost immediately. *"Good to hear from you, Captain. We were starting to fear that you were going to miss our departure."*

A reasonable fear, April conceded, given that there had been less than ten minutes to spare. He and Una had called in practically down to the wire.

"Don't go anywhere just yet. The situation down here has been resolved, in a manner of speaking."

"Oh? And how is that?"

"It's a long, rather sad story." He contemplated Eljor's lifeless remains and the empty citadel all around him. The Jatohr's sanctuary had become a ghost town, just another failed colony like so many other deserted ruins throughout the galaxy, haunted by the doleful specters of lost hopes and dreams. "I'll give you the full particulars later, after Lieutenant Una and I beam back to the ship."

"Just you and Lieutenant Una, Captain?"

"I'm afraid so, Lorna." He paused before delivering the bad news. "There are . . . no other survivors."

Silence ate up the transmission as that harsh truth sank in. *"Damn. I'm sorry to hear that, Captain."*

"No more than I, Lorna. Believe me." He supposed that Martinez and the others could be listed as missing in action, as opposed to deceased, but that would be small consolation to their friends and families. As always, he knew that for every crew member the *Enterprise* lost during her voyages, many, many, more lives were irrevocably altered as well. He felt a sudden yearning for his own family. "Is Sarah there on the bridge?"

"I'm here, Rob," his wife's voice chimed in. He guessed that she was standing by the captain's chair, alongside Simon. *"When are you coming home?"*

"Soon," he promised. "We're almost done here. There's just . . . a few more matters we need to attend to."

"Acknowledged, Captain," Simon said. *"We can lock onto your communicators at any time. Let us know when you want us to beam you back here."*

"Stand by," he said. "April out."

He put away his communicator and inspected the Transfer Key. He regarded it pensively as he turned it over and over in his hands. It was surprisingly lightweight, considering that it carried the potential to wreak untold havoc on the galaxy.

"What are you going to do about that, sir?" Una asked. "And hir final request?"

"I don't know," he admitted. "Deep down inside, I fear that Eljor was right, that this Key is too dangerous to let loose in our universe. Suppose it fell into the hands of the

Klingons or the Orions or even someone like Kodos the Executioner. Imagine what Kodos could have done with this Key. How easily he could have 'removed' those he deemed unfit to survive."

Only a few years in the past, the tyrant's genocidal atrocities were still spoken of in horror throughout the Federation. The *Enterprise* had been one of the first starships to arrive on the scene in the wake of the massacre, bearing food and medical supplies that arrived too late for the half of the population that Kodos had ruthlessly put to death. The memory of that ghastly crime still haunted April, and served as a cautionary example of the evil that supposedly civilized beings were capable of, even in the twenty-third century.

One hand went to the pistol on the captain's hip. "Perhaps it would be better to simply destroy this bloody thing before it can cause any more heartache."

"Don't," Una urged him, "for science's sake, if nothing else. Even if you don't think the galaxy is ready for it just yet, perhaps the future will be."

Activating her tricorder, Una made a methodical circuit of the control room, recording as much data as the device could hold. She gave special attention to the central column, scanning it from every angle and along every spectrum.

"We may not fully understand this technology now," she stressed, "but that doesn't mean it might not prove invaluable to the Federation at some point. If you feel you must honor the late Professor Eljor's wishes, perhaps we can merely *conceal* the Key until . . . whenever."

"That might be best," April decided. In truth, the

scientist and explorer in him also resisted the idea of completely eliminating a genuine artifact from another universe, let alone one that held the secret to unlocking the multiverse, even if that artifact also unquestionably threatened to destabilize the balance of power throughout known space "We'll hide it then, from the galaxy and from the records, for posterity's sake."

He tucked the Key into Una's backpack, so that it would not attract any attention when they beamed back to the ship. He'd have to find a better hiding place for it later.

"Is that it?" Una slung her tricorder over her shoulder. "Are we done here?"

"Not quite. There's still one last task before us."

He gazed down at Eljor's grisly remains, drew his laser pistol, and twisted the setting on the weapon to maximum. He squeezed the trigger and an incandescent beam completely incinerated all that was left of the tragic scientist, leaving nothing but a blackened scorch mark on the floor.

"Now we can go." He put away the pistol and flipped open his communicator. "April to *Enterprise*. Bring us home."

The secret compartment was installed behind a bookshelf in the captain's spacious quarters aboard the *Enterprise*. April placed the Transfer Key into the hidden niche and watched grimly as an automated panel slid into place, hiding it from view.

"There we are," he said. "For better or for worse."

A small party—consisting entirely of the captain, his wife, the first officer, and Una—was gathered in April's quarters to witness the interment of the Key. As far as they knew, they were the only living beings in the universe who knew of the artifact's existence or its whereabouts.

It's better that way, Una thought. *At least for the present.*

"The compartment is built into a negative space behind the bulkhead," Una reminded the captain, "so it should go undetected unless anyone goes looking for it. And I've programmed the lock to open only to the code you selected."

She had done the installation herself in order to keep the secret contained to just the four people in this room. Ordinarily, there'd be no reason to include the ship's medical officer in the conspiracy, but given that these were her private quarters too . . .

"Thank you, Una." The captain regarded the panel uneasily. "I just hope we're doing the right thing, keeping this from Starfleet. I admit that it goes against my grain to take part in a cover-up."

As Una understood it, the "official" story more or less matched what had occurred on Usilde, aside from the game-changing revelation of the Jatohr's origins and the salient fact that the Key had been passed on to Captain April. According to the logs, the *Enterprise* had simply encountered a colony of hostile alien explorers, of unknown origin, that had inflicted casualties on the ship's crew by means of a mysterious weapon, before the Jatohr had retreated back to wherever they came from, abandoning their outpost on the planet. April had further recommended that the planet's native inhabitants be left alone to chart their destiny, in accordance with the Prime Directive.

At least some good came of our visit, Una thought. The Usildar were now free to reclaim their world, without any interference from the Jatohr or anyone else. *If only their salvation had not cost us nine of our own . . . including my best friend.*

"Then again," Sarah April said to her husband, "this isn't the first time you've omitted a detail or two from your logs for humanitarian reasons. Remember those Durganian refugees, hiding out on that moon, who wanted the whole galaxy to think they were dead? Or that time you fudged the logs so that no one would ever know what *really* happened to Lieutenant Emmett . . . or what he became."

"Granted," the captain said. "I suppose there are times that the whole truth can do more harm than good, even though that runs counter to my sworn duty to Starfleet."

"You ask me, you're making the right call," Simon said. "That infernal device has already caused enough trouble. Let's keep this to ourselves, at least until a new captain takes over the ship and has to be let in on the secret."

Given Simon's advanced age, she was unlikely to succeed April as captain of the *Enterprise*, and everyone knew it. Rumor had it she was planning to retire after the end of this five-year mission, meaning that the Key would shortly fall into other hands.

"That's the plan," April confirmed. "And that future

captain can share the secret with their own first officer, just in case."

Simon looked pointedly at Una. "If she doesn't know it already, that is."

Una took the prediction in stride.

"I appreciate the vote of confidence, Commander, but let's not get ahead of ourselves."

The future remained to be written.

2267

Eighteen years later

Fifteen

"Approaching border of disputed territory."

Unlike the computer on *Enterprise*, the *Shimizu*'s automated systems had a masculine voice. Captain Una had customized it that way so that she didn't feel like she was talking to herself. That the *Shimizu*'s voice also resembled its long-lost namesake was not a coincidence; it was a deliberate reminder of matters left undone.

Seated at the ship's controls, Una glanced at the black carryall riding shotgun beside her on the copilot's seat. The Transfer Key still rested inside the bag, waiting to be put to use for the first time in nearly two decades, assuming she could make it back to Usilde without encountering any unwanted interference.

"Scan for Klingon vessels," she instructed.

"Scanning," the computer said. *"Negative. No Klingon vessels detected."*

Una trusted the computer, but conducted her own sensor sweep anyway, which came up with the same reassuring results. Not that she could relax entirely; rumor had it that the Klingons were already negotiating with the Romulans for their new cloaking device. Starfleet Intelligence believed that cloaked Klingon warships were still years away, but it was always possible that those estimates were too conservative. For all she knew, there could be an entire fleet of cloaked battle cruisers just up ahead, in which case this might be a very short trip. If necessary, she was prepared to destroy her ship—and herself—to keep the Key from falling into Klingon hands.

"Scan also for unmanned border sensors," she added, "or listening posts."

"*Scanning.*"

The Korinar Sector, which included the Libros system, had not been claimed by the Klingons all those years ago, but times had sadly changed and the Empire had expanded since her early years aboard the *Enterprise* under Captain April. She was taking a calculated risk crossing into the disputed territory, but figured that the odds were in her favor. Borders or no borders, space was vast and this particular corner of the sector had no significant strategic value. Even the Klingons couldn't patrol every parsec of the border—or was that just wishful thinking on her part?

Such doubts were why she'd had to go rogue, instead of simply going to Kirk or Spock for the Key and enlisting their aid, so she'd be the only one caught defying orders by entering the disputed space and risking capture by the Klingons. Una couldn't ask anyone else to take the same gamble. This was her mess to clean up, no matter what.

"*Negative,*" the computer reported, after a longer, more comprehensive scan. "*No sensors or listening posts detected.*"

Unless, of course, they were cloaked, or in dormant mode, or disguised as space debris. Una knew that the sensors could not completely guarantee her safety, only alert her to the more obvious hazards. She was entering enemy territory.

But she'd come too far to turn back now.

The *Shimizu* accelerated, continuing on its course for the Libros system and a forbidden planet she had never forgotten.

"Entering disputed territory," the computer announced.

It was actually a bit anticlimactic. No Klingon warships burst from concealment. No strident alarms were picked up by her sensors. No belligerent hails demanded her immediate surrender.

Was she actually going to get away with this?

So far, so good, Una thought, letting out a sigh of relief. *Now let's make this quick.*

She had no intention of lingering in this sector. In and out, that was her plan, revisiting Usilde only long enough to finally take care of some old business—by rescuing Tim Shimizu and the others who had been lost so many years ago.

Eighteen years had passed, but she had never given up on those "missing" crew members. She'd spent years, and many sleepless nights, studying her tricorder readings from that fateful mission, trying to figure out how to reverse the transfer-field effect and bring the exiles back to this universe. This had proved far easier said than done, especially without the Key to study, and at times she had despaired of *ever* comprehending the otherworldly science behind the late Professor Eljor's singular creation. The transfer-field generator was not just revolutionary in its design and operation; it bore next to no resemblance to any technology she was familiar with, alien or otherwise. It truly was something from a completely different universe, frustrating her efforts to pry loose its secrets. She had been stumped, in fact, until recently.

But then the *Enterprise* came to her rescue.

Reviewing the classified logs and reports on Kirk's recent visit to a barbaric alternate universe had been the breakthrough she'd needed to push past the obstacles that had been blocking her. Not only had that bizarre transporter accident provided her with concrete data on the physics of how exactly beings from one universe could, under the right confluence of events, pass over to another, parallel reality, but Kirk's description of the "Tantalus Field" he had encountered in that universe bore a provocative resemblance to the transfer field the Jatohr had used to eliminate their enemies, suggesting a similar mode of operation.

Granted, any connection between the Tantalus Field and the Transfer Key remained highly speculative. Her current working theory was that, in that mirror universe, a different *Enterprise* had visited Usilde and an alternate version of Captain April had taken possession of an alternate Key, which had eventually fallen into the hands of an alternate Kirk, as reported by the Kirk of this universe. Or perhaps events had played out differently in that other reality, and the other Kirk had been the one to visit Usilde and discover the Key. In any event, the transporter data from that incident, as well as Kirk's observations regarding the Tantalus Field, had been the final pieces of the jigsaw puzzle she had been wrestling with for years. Una felt reasonably confident that she could operate the transfer-field generator well enough to rescue those lost men and women.

If they were still alive in that other realm after so many years.

And this was probably her last chance to make the attempt, before the Klingons cemented their hold on the sector, and before Starfleet promoted her into a desk job. She had to get this done now, before it was too late.

And before Kirk could stop her.

She wanted to think that the *Enterprise* had given up the chase after she'd lost them with that slingshot maneuver earlier, but suspected that was wishful thinking. From everything she knew of Kirk, he wasn't the kind of captain who would just let this go or choose to play it safe. He'd even crossed into the Romulan Neutral Zone last year, risking interplanetary war, because he deemed it necessary. She couldn't imagine that he would just let her get away with the Key.

"Estimated time to Libros system?" she asked the computer.

"*Approximately fifteen-point-nine-seven hours at current rate of speed.*"

Una hoped that would be time enough to reach Usilde and complete her mission before either Kirk or the Klingons could get in her way. She upped her speed, pushing the *Shimizu's* engine close to the red line.

I'm coming, Tim. I'm coming for all of you.

———

"*Entering Libros system.*"

The *Shimizu* slowed to impulse as it approached its

destination. Una's throat tightened as she gazed at Usilde through the front viewport, laying eyes on the planet for the first time in years. She had been so young and cocky then, so eager to lead her first landing party and overly confident in her abilities. That youthful arrogance had cost Tim and the others dearly, all because she had carelessly let herself be captured by the Jatohr.

I pushed my luck, but they paid the price.

At least she didn't have to worry about the Jatohr this time around; in theory, the "Newcomers" were all gone, sent back to whatever unimaginable realm they had originally come from, the same alien universe that the lost crew members had been exiled to as well. Not for the first time, she wondered what had become of her shipmates in that other reality or if any of them had even managed to survive all this time. It was very possible, she knew, that she was attempting to rescue people who were long dead, but Una had been living with that uncertainty for longer than she cared to think about. She needed to at least *try* to rescue any survivors, now that she finally had the means and knowledge to do so.

And if any of the Jatohr attempt to slip back into our universe . . . well, I'll deal with that too.

Slowing further, the *Shimizu* entered the atmosphere and descended toward the larger equatorial continent. From high above, the planet looked much as Una remembered it; she liked to think the Usildar were thriving now that the Jatohr were gone and that they'd been able to reclaim their world. It was tempting to check in on them, see what they'd accomplished since being liberated, but that was not what this mission was about. With any luck, she would come and go without encountering the Usildar at all, which was probably best for all concerned. After everything they'd been through earlier, the forest dwellers deserved to be left alone.

She zoomed in on the river valley where she had been captured years before. The sun was going down in that time zone, but her landing lights assisted her memory in relocating the site. Frankly, she would have preferred not to revisit the place where Tim and the rest of her landing party had been removed right before her eyes, but the logistics of her plan required a detour to the slave-labor camp to pick up a ride back to the citadel.

If all goes according to plan . . .

Getting back into the citadel presented a challenge. Unlike a *Constitution*-class starship, the *Shimizu* was not equipped with an onboard transporter station, so she couldn't simply beam down into the fortress. And, as she well recalled, the only way in or out of the citadel was via the underwater landing bays, which meant she needed one of those submersible pods and, ideally, its access codes. In theory, there would still be some abandoned pods at the landing field in the valley.

Here's hoping they're still operational, she thought.

If worse came to worst, she could always try to salvage some codes or equipment from any leftover pods. Although Una had scuba gear stored aboard the *Shimizu,* just in case, or could conceivably take the airtight courier into the lake, she was reluctant to try to force her way into the citadel for fear of damaging the transfer-field generator in the process. And as for swimming down to the underwater entrances . . . well, she had not forgotten the multi-armed predators lurking in those waters.

A working pod would make everything *much* easier.

Breaking through the cloud cover, the spacecraft came within view of the labor camp—or what was left of it. Darkness shrouded the valley, making it difficult to discern every detail, but what Una could see by the ship's landing lights indicated that the once-busy farming operation was now nothing more than ruins. She glimpsed the torched remains of buildings and rusting equipment. The surrounding rain forest had encroached on the deserted camp, attempting to reclaim it, but was being counter-infiltrated by the invasive gray fungus that was still spreading out of control, both in the ruins and beyond. Fresh stands of trees, which had grown up in the many years Una had been away, played unwilling host to jutting shelves of fruiting gray bodies climbing their trunks. The stumps of long-fallen giants, cut down by the Jatohr's bygone operations, were practically buried beneath ugly, slate-colored mushrooms and molds, while the related gray algae still contaminated the adjacent river as well as a few stagnant canals. The sour odor of the alien weeds was all too easy to imagine.

Una winced at the sight. The Jatohr might be long gone, but they had clearly left their slimy footprint on Usilde.

The *Shimizu* touched down on the old landing pad, not far from where everything had gone to hell years ago. Una powered down its engines and geared up for the mission, stowing the Transfer Key in a Starfleet-issue backpack, while bringing along a phaser and tricorder as well. She didn't anticipate needing a weapon, now that the Jatohr had departed, but there were still the Usildar and the local wildlife to consider, not to mention those creatures in the lake surrounding the citadel.

Better safe than sorry.

A peculiar sense of déjà vu afflicted her as she exited the *Shimizu,* sealing the hatchway behind her, and set foot on Usilde once more. The globe-lights that had once illuminated the facility had gone dark; she spotted a few lifeless spheres resting inertly on the ground here and there, like antique glass buoys washed up on a shore. So she had to resort to a palm-sized beacon to make her way across the abandoned landing field. Small animals of uncertain *genus* scurried away at her approach. The beacon's cool white beam exposed more evidence of the camp's ravaged state.

The old wooden dormitories and other timber buildings had been burned to the ground, while more metallic structures and equipment showed signs of deliberate vandalism as well. Una guessed that the Usildar had done their best to eradicate what remained of the Jatohr's occupation of the planet, but they were obviously fighting a losing battle against the stubbornly aggressive fungus contaminating their environment. Spongy gray mushrooms sprouted like weeds from the cracked tarmac and from the ashes of torched fields and buildings. Even the hot, humid air smelled more foul than she remembered; the sour, mildewy odor of the fungus invaded her mouth and nostrils, spoiling every breath. Her nose wrinkled in disgust. It was like walking through a badly ventilated organic compost facility—or enduring the bad breath of a Tennekian emissary.

Perhaps we should have offered the Usildar more assistance years ago, she thought, *when it came to reversing the damage done to their environment.*

But there had been the Prime Directive to consider, and, in all honesty, the captain and crew of the *Enterprise* had been anxious to put Usilde behind them. At the time it had seemed enough that they—or rather, Professor Eljor—had given the Usildar their world back, even if it wasn't entirely unscarred by the Jatohr's presence. Or so they had told themselves.

That might have been a mistake.

Una made her way across the fungi-choked tarmac toward a waiting pod, growing ever more dubious regarding her chances of finding the aircraft in working condition. Of more immediate concern than the contaminated ecosystem was the discouraging possibility that the Jatohr's pods had also come under attack by both time and the Usildar, in which case she was wasting precious time here and would have to find another way into the citadel. Preferably before Kirk came looking for her.

The beam from her beacon confirmed her fears: the nearest pod had been trashed. Scorch marks blackened its formerly iridescent hull, while the one-way viewports had been smashed in. Arcane runes were scratched across its cracked and dented surface; it was even money on whether they were hex signs intended to banish evil or merely angry obscenities. Creeping vines fought the ubiquitous gray fungus for possession of the derelict aircraft, clotting the shattered viewports. One downturned wing had buckled, possibly under the weight of rampaging Usildar, so that the parked pod listed to one side.

It was not going to be taking to the air ever again.

"Damn," Una muttered. She kicked a dead globe-light in frustration, but it only rolled a meter or so before it was halted by a clump of fruiting mushrooms. Una stared at the wrecked submersible in dismay. This complicated her plans in a big way.

She glanced over at the nearby hangar, which was also in ruins. It was possible that there was a more intact pod somewhere inside the hangar, but she doubted it; the Usildar seemed to have spared no effort in taking out their wrath on the former site of their oppression. Not that Una could blame them. She would have wanted to raze the place to the ground, too, if she'd been in their shoes.

Too bad they couldn't leave me one working pod, though.

Sighing, she drew nearer to the overgrown aircraft, looking for the best way inside, past tangled vines and fungi. She wasn't looking forward to climbing inside the wreck, but maybe her tricorder could still pick up the access codes to the citadel from whatever was left of its controls. Granted, she could always take the *Shimizu* down into the lake, but she still needed a way to get into the underwater landing bay. Even if the courier had been equipped with phasers, which it wasn't, she didn't want to have to blast her way in—unless she absolutely had to.

She started to climb onto a wing, only to be startled

by a large, spiky nut that struck the wing with a loud
smack. The nut ricocheted off the wing, barely missing
her face.

"What the—?"

"Step away from the unclean relic," a stern voice
commanded her. "To touch it is forbidden."

Una spun around to find several Usildar converging
on her, brandishing weapons. She recognized their lithe,
lanky bodies and simian proportions, as well as their
wary, fearful expressions. The forest dwellers clutched
an assortment of spears, clubs, maces, and slings. Their
arsenal had not improved noticeably since the last time
she'd encountered them, but remained crudely effective
nonetheless. Her hand went instinctively to the sidearm
on her hip, but she refrained from drawing it. Apparently
the *Shimizu*'s arrival had not gone unnoticed, and she
could hardly blame the Usildar for being suspicious of
alien visitors from the sky. She needed to assure them that
she meant no harm.

"I am not Jatohr," she called out. "I am not your
enemy!"

An older male Usildar stepped forward. Unsurprisingly, given the number of years that had transpired since
her last visit, he was not the same Usildar leader she'd met
before, but Una thought she saw a slight resemblance beneath the dyes and dust camouflaging his face. A carved
wooden helmet denoted his authority. He shook a spear
at her.

"You have trespassed on unholy ground—and forced
us to do the same! This is an evil place. None may venture here!"

"Please forgive me." Una moved away from the useless pod, lowering her palm beacon so that it did not shine in the Usildar's faces. "I did not know your laws, but have no wish to break them. I will depart if you wish."

The *Shimizu* was parked several meters away, with the Usildar between her and the ship. She hoped that they would allow her to leave unmolested. The Usildar were not her enemy. She didn't want this to get ugly.

So much for salvaging anything useful from these ruins, she thought. *Time to adjust my plans.*

The Usildar blocked her path to the ship.

"Please let me pass," she requested. "And I will leave you in peace."

Her hand drifted toward her phaser, hoping she wouldn't have to use it.

"You have already disturbed our peace," the leader protested, "and tempted disaster by tampering with the baneful relics of the Despoilers. This cannot be tolerated."

Una felt the situation going south. "I told you, I meant no harm—"

Something sharp and pointy struck her in the neck. She yelped in pain as another spiky nut dropped to the ground, bouncing off her boot. Her hand went to her throat and came away bloody. The puncture was not deep, but it stung like blazes. She shook her head at the Usildar, more in sorrow than in anger.

"You didn't need to do that."

The stinging subsided as a numbing sensation spread from the wound and throughout her body, and she realized she'd been drugged. The narcotic worked with remarkably efficiency; within heartbeats, she was

Sixteen

Cold water splashed against her face, rousing her.

Una awoke to an aching head and water dripping down her cheeks. Blinking and sputtering, she tried to wipe the wetness from her eyes, only to find her arms tied behind her back by what felt like knotted vines. Rough hands yanked her to her feet. Still groggy, she shook her head to clear it, which didn't exactly help the throbbing in her temples, as she rapidly took stock of her new surroundings.

She found herself standing atop a sizable tree stump, at least two meters in diameter and rising nearly a meter above the forest floor. The trees surrounding the stump were packed with Usildar, sitting on or dangling from a multitude of low-hanging branches. It was still night out, but a ring of torches driven into the ground around the stump held back the darkness. Scowling Usildar guards, along with the large number of forest dwellers watching from the trees, discouraged her from making a break for it. Unarmed and bound, she wouldn't get far.

"The accused stands ready," one of the guards announced. He tossed aside a large blossom that had probably held the rainwater used to wake her. "Let her face judgment for her crimes."

The accused? Una thought. *Judgment?*

That did not sound promising.

A quick self-inspection confirmed that her gear, including the pack containing the Key, had been taken from her. She spotted it lying at the foot of the stump, so near and yet so far away. She eyed the equipment longingly; as much as she wanted her phaser back, she was even more anxious to reacquire the Key. Without it, her entire mission was doomed, and a dangerous piece of alien technology would be loose in the universe. She needed to get the Key back, she realized, not to mention get herself out of whatever trouble she was in.

"Hello?" she said. "What's going on here?"

At least the effect of the drug appeared to have worn off. Aside from the headache, and an irritating itch where the spiky missile had poked her neck, she felt alert and functional once more. She wondered how long she had been out and how far she had been taken from the abandoned labor camp and the *Shimizu*. The nocturnal forest offered no clues as to her exact location. Her ship could be just past the trees or kilometers away.

"Prepare to be judged," the guard said, glowering, "but expect no mercy."

"But I was only—" she began.

"Save your words for the High Ranger," the guard interrupted. "He will decide your fate."

The noisy rattling of many hollow gourds, shaken by the hands and feet of the Usildar gathered in the trees, precluded any further discussion. Una gathered that she was on trial and that the hearing was getting under way.

Better than a summary execution, she decided. *Hopefully.*

The whistle of a flute heralded the arrival of the

Ranger, who swung down from the upper reaches of the canopy to occupy a perch overlooking the scene below. No surprise, he was the same Usildar who had confronted her back at the landing field. His saturnine countenance promised little in the way of sympathy. The camouflage dyed into his flesh failed to entirely conceal some old scarring on his face and arms, which suggested that he had been badly burned at some point in the past. Possibly during the Jatohr occupation?

She hoped that wouldn't prejudice him against her.

Una was reminded of a certain treetop conclave many years ago. Despite her own predicament, she was genuinely pleased to see that the Usildar were still populating the forests, regardless of the creeping legacy of the Jatohr, and that they appeared to be a free and living culture, no longer under the thumb of their former oppressors.

Perhaps the sacrifices of years past had been worth it after all?

The Ranger held up a carved wooden flute, and the ceremonial rattling ceased. He peered down at Una from above. His apparent age suggested that he was old enough to remember vividly the dark days of the Jatohr occupation.

"Stranger," he addressed her. "Have your wits returned to you?"

"More or less."

Recalling the last time she was taken captive on Usilde, she decided that she preferred "stranger" to "creature," as the Jatohr had once referred to her. At least the Usildar regarded her as a person, not a thing, and deserving of a trial of sorts. That was an improvement, she supposed. She scanned the arboreal audience viewing the trial, but failed to spot any familiar faces, let alone any friendly ones.

"May I ask who is judging me?"

"I am Banev, High Ranger of the Winding Waters tribe. And you stand condemned of treading on forbidden ground and disturbing the secrets of the bygone Despoilers."

Una wondered what mythology had grown up in the years since the Jatohr had vanished and how the Usildar had reacted to their sudden disappearance. From what she could tell, the forest dwellers retained a superstitious dread of their former conquerors and any sites or artifacts associated with them. If anything, they seemed even more suspicious and xenophobic than before.

"I meant no harm or disrespect," she said. "As you say, I am a stranger, ignorant of your laws. And I have nothing to do with the Jatohr."

That wasn't entirely true, of course, but she doubted that the Usildar would recognize the Transfer Key as a creation of the Jatohr. She kept one eye on her pack, wondering if it was to be used in evidence against her.

"But you are not Usildar," Banev accused her, sounding more like a prosecutor than a judge. "And you traffic in the unholy and the forbidden."

"I apologize," she said. "The error was mine. Let me go in peace and you will never see me again."

"And why should we trust you? How do we know that you will not reawaken the troubles of old?"

"That is not my intention," she insisted. "I promise you."

"I believe her," a new voice called out. A younger Jatohr dropped from the trees to stand before the stump. "She is not of the Despoilers. We need not fear her."

Her defender was a wiry youth, painted brown and green like his treemates. Handsome enough, if you liked long arms and opposable toes. Intelligent green eyes glanced at Una, briefly meeting her gaze. She saw neither dread nor suspicion in those eyes, which made for a pleasant change. It was good to have at least one Usildar on her side.

Let's hear it for youthful idealism, she thought, *and the courage to challenge your elders.*

Startled exclamations and hubbub greeted this new development. Banev blew on his flute to quiet the commotion, which quickly died down. He peered down at the youth, looking vaguely displeased.

"You would defend the stranger?"

"I would," the youth said. "You recall the days of seasons past. Strangers such as she, shaped much like us, visited Usilde once before, and their coming heralded the disappearance of the Jatohr, who vanished from our lands not long after. There are many who believe that it was those very same strangers who exorcised the Despoilers and gave us back our world."

"This is true," Una confirmed. "My companions and I visited you before and sought only to help free you from the Jatohr."

"That may be," Banev grudgingly conceded, "but then

why have you returned?" His emerald eyes widened in alarm. "Unless the Despoilers are returning as well?"

A shudder seemed to go through the tree-borne audience at that terrifying possibility. Banev had to whistle for order again, even as Una rushed to calm the frightened Usildar.

"No, no, nothing like that! The Jatohr are gone for good. I came only to honor the memory of companions who were lost here long ago, the last time we visited Usilde."

And to try to rescue them, she added silently. *If possible.*

"By disturbing that which should be left alone?" Banev shook his head. "We Usildar are wise enough to shun such places, lest we call back the evils of the past. The Despoilers have left us alone for a generation. We will not have strangers digging up the hardships of days past."

"Just let me go on my way then," Una pleaded. "You will be left alone as you wish."

"Go where? Back to the forbidden valley—or perhaps even to the haunted lair of the Despoilers, which slumbers restlessly above the gray waters?"

Una assumed he was speaking of the deserted Jatohr citadel, if it was in fact still deserted after all these years. She hoped that the Usildar had indeed shunned the citadel, so that it would be in better condition than the demolished labor camp. Biting her tongue, she resisted the temptation to ask what shape the fortress was in these days.

"The Jatohr are gone forever," her young defender declared. "We don't need to live in fear of them . . . or any innocent stranger who visits our forest."

Banev was unmoved by the youth's words. "Our laws are clear. To trifle with the works of the Despoilers is punishable by death."

Death?

Una registered that dire detail, but refused to let it rattle her. To be honest, she had rather suspected that matters were heading in that direction. The way the Usildar were acting, this was obviously a grave offense. She hadn't expected to get off with a slap on the wrist.

"But she did not know our laws!" the youth argued again. "Where is the justice in punishing her for a crime she did not know she was committing?"

"This is not about justice," Banev said bluntly. "This is about the protection of our people. We have been enslaved and watched our loved ones unmade before our eyes. Our world remains defiled by foul, unnatural growths. The very air still reeks of the Despoilers and their evil." His voice quaked with emotion. "We cannot allow outsiders— any outsiders—to ever trouble Usilde again!"

"My people would never do that," Una said. "We have laws too, and one of our highest is that we do not meddle in the affairs of others."

Banev's face hardened as he regained his composure. "Then you should have stayed where you belonged, by your own laws and ours. Here you are like the foul gray growths choking our rivers and forests: a foreign weed that must be stamped out and burned before it can do any more harm." He snapped his flute in two, as though signaling the end of the proceedings. "My judgment is made. At dawn, you will be taken back to the cursed valley where you were found. There you and all your otherworldly possessions will be burned and the ashes buried deep in that unclean soil, where they belong."

"No!" Una's self-appointed advocate protested. "She has done nothing to deserve this!"

"She came uninvited, flying through the night sky like the Despoilers once did. She violated our laws, bringing fear and uncertainty into our lives after years of peace." Banev scoffed at the passionate young Jatohr. "What has she *not* done . . . and what more might she still do if given a chance? We can take no chances with our people's safety. This is the only way to ensure our survival, both today and tomorrow."

Una could tell that the Ranger's mind was made up. The horrors of the past were rooted too deeply in his soul. He could not see past them.

"It's funny," she said. "The Jatohr felt the same way. They also believed that their security depended on treating any other intelligent being as a threat. They were mistaken, and so are you." Her voice softened as she addressed the young man who had defended her. "Thanks for sticking up for me. I appreciate it."

He turned mournful green eyes toward her.

"I am sorry," he said. "Forgive us our fear and suspicion."

"You have your reasons. I understand."

The death sentence was upsetting, though. Aside from her own peril, she hated the prospect of her mission ending like this, before she could save Tim and the others. She had come too far to end up burned alive before she could try to reactivate the transfer-field generator and bring her old comrades home.

Keep calm, she told herself, not letting anxiety cloud her thinking. *This isn't over yet.*

She had been in sticky situations before, and this was far from the first time she'd been condemned to death by unfriendly aliens. She was a Starfleet captain after all; she just had to keep her wits about her and wait for the right opportunity to turn the situation around, provided that opportunity arrived before sunrise.

Maybe I shouldn't have tried to do this on my own.

Seventeen

The trial concluded, the Usildar swiftly dispersed into the forest canopy, leaving Una alone with only Banev and a pair of guards to keep her company. Even her young defender retreated in defeat, apparently unwilling to witness what came next.

"Be brave," he urged her before taking to the trees. "And do not think too ill of us."

"I won't," she said. "And thank you again for speaking up for me."

Una was sorry to see him go. She was woefully short of allies at the moment.

"Young fool," Banev muttered, watching the youth depart. Avoiding eye contact with Una, he issued instructions to the guards from his judicial perch. "Bind her to the place of the judgment, so that she may not escape her fate. And watch her carefully through what remains of the night. I will return before dawn to see the sentence carried out."

"Yes, High Ranger," a guard replied. One of his front teeth was chipped, giving it a jagged look. "It will be done as you say."

Banev nodded grimly. "See that it is."

Una considered pleading her case one last time, before the Ranger went his way, but decided that it would be a waste of time and energy. The traumas of the past had scarred him in more ways than one. She might as well try arguing with one of the surrounding tree trunks—or the long-departed Commander Woryan.

Banev vanished into the canopy, leaving behind the broken ceremonial flute. Una was in no hurry to see him again, given his stated intention to preside over her execution. Glancing around, she looked for a way to alter that agenda. There were only two guards, but she was on their turf, unarmed, with her hands tied behind her back, which put her at a distinct disadvantage, despite her considerable hand-to-hand combat skills. Starfleet training could only aid her so far.

"Watch her while I secure more restraints," Jagged Tooth said to his comrade. He scurried off into the shadows beyond the torchlight. "I'll be right back."

"Make it quick," the second guard said. Gripping his spear, he glowered at Una with bloodshot eyes. "Don't try any tricks!"

"I wouldn't dream of it," she lied.

Una expected the first guard to fetch more vines, but instead he returned bearing a large purple melon the size of a cantaloupe and placed it on the stump between her boots. He raised an edged stone hatchet above the melon.

"Don't move," Jagged Tooth warned her.

The hatchet split the melon, spilling a sticky yellow sap over her boots. Una wasn't sure what to make of this. She tried to lift one foot only to find it effectively glued to the stump. She pulled harder, but was barely able to lift the sole of her boot more than a few centimeters above the spilled sap. Gooey strands tugged on her boot, refusing to release their grip.

"I said, don't move!"

He grabbed her ankle and yanked her raised foot back down into the sap, which quickly hardened like resin around both her feet, cementing them in place. Within moments, she was stuck fast to the stump and confronted with yet another challenge to overcome if she wanted to live past dawn and complete her mission.

This complicates matters.

It was possible that, with difficulty, she could manage to extract her feet from the trapped boots, but it was unlikely that the vigilant guards would allow her to do so. She peered up at the sky, which was barely visible through a gap in the canopy, and wondered how many hours she had until dawn. Usilde rotated on its axis every twenty-seven hours, she recalled, but there were also seasonal factors to consider, and she still wasn't certain how long she had been unconscious prior to the trial. Unfamiliar constellations, peeking out from behind the cloud cover, defeated her efforts to reckon the time, but she knew that, subjectively, the sun would be rising all too soon.

I might have to make my move later, she thought, *after they've unstuck me from this stump.*

Her standing position made sleep impossible and her legs were soon aching for a chair. She was considering asking the guards for something to sit on when a rustling in the trees put the guards on alert. Spears ready, they spun toward the rustling, relaxing only slightly when Una's youthful defender dropped from the branches, bearing a basket woven from strips of bark and a pair of stoppered gourds hanging from vines slung across his chest. He started toward the stump, only to be blocked by the guards, who raised their spears in warning.

"What do you want?" Bloodshot asked, scowling. "Have you not said enough tonight?"

"I bring a last meal for the condemned, as is only merciful." The youth, whose earlier defense of her had apparently not won him any friends, presented his offerings for the guards' inspection. "Why should she spend her last night hungry and thirsty?"

The guards dipped their spears somewhat. They regarded the basket and gourds with interest. Jagged Tooth licked his lips. "What have you there?"

"Fresh fruit and nutmeats, from my private store." The youth unslung a gourd and held it out to the guards. Something sloshed wetly inside it. "And strong drink to ease her final hours."

That got the guards' attention.

"A shame to waste such fare on one who will soon be nothing but ash," Bloodshot said. "You look to have brought a feast."

"And who can say if our food is to her taste," Jagged Tooth added. "It might be poison to her kind."

"She is already condemned to death, so where is the harm?" the youth said with a shrug. He handed over the basket and a gourd. "But, please, help yourselves. There is enough for all."

The hungry guards welcomed the repast. Putting aside their spears, they dug into the food and drink, biting into the juicy fruits and taking deep swigs from the unstopped gourd with such enthusiasm that Una began to doubt whether she was going to see any of the refreshments at all. Her stomach grumbled in protest, reminding her that she hadn't eaten since downing some Starfleet rations on the voyage to Usilde. Then again, she probably ought to abstain from the "strong drink" anyway.

I need to keep a clear head, she thought, *if I'm going to avoided being cremated before my time.*

Although a bite of food wouldn't hurt . . .

"Don't forget to save some for me," she said. "That's my last meal you're devouring."

"Wait your turn," Jagged Tooth said with mouth full. He washed down a handful of nutmeats with a gulp from the gourd. A smoky brown liquid dribbled down his chin. "You're already as good as dead."

He slurred his words, leading Una to speculate as to just how potent that brew was. Swaying unsteadily, the guard also appeared startled at how quickly the drink had gone to his head. Bleary eyes examined the gourd, and he sniffed its spout.

"This is stronger than I . . ."

The gourd slipped from his grip, much as Una had dropped her palm beacon after being drugged. Jagged Tooth's legs gave out beneath him and he collapsed onto the ground. He tried to stand up again, but without success.

"What's happening . . ."

His voice trailed off as he went limp and still.

"Sugol!" the other guard cried out, his tongue sounding equally impaired. He grabbed for his spear, but his body refused to cooperate. He toppled over, landing on the forest floor not far from his insensate companion. "Wake up," he groggily urged Jagged Tooth. "You have to wake . . . wake . . ."

His face hit the dirt, leaving both guards passed out on the ground. Heavy breathing, punctuated by snores, testified that they were still alive. Una put two and two together.

"You drugged them," she said, not exactly objecting.

"The forest holds solutions to many problems," the youth said. "Fear not. They will wake unharmed, but none too soon."

"Fine with me."

Using a sharpened stone, he sliced through the vines binding her wrists together, then unstopped the second gourd he'd brought with him and poured a clear, bubbly fluid over the hardened sap trapping her feet. The potion acted as a solvent, dissolving the resin-like substance so that she could pull her boots free. She wasted no time hopping off the stump and recovering her gear and pack. It felt good to be mobile again. She checked to make certain that the Key was still secure in her pack.

"Thanks so much," she said. "But why are you doing this? Not that I'm complaining, mind you."

"I am saving you from your own recklessness," he said, "as you once did for me."

The proverbial lightbulb went off above Una's head. She stared at the young man's face, peering past the dyed skin and time's changes to find the curious little boy she had befriended so long ago. Now that she thought of it, there was a familiar brightness in his eyes.

"Gagre?"

"You did not recognize me?" he asked. "I knew you at once, Una."

Nice to know that I'm not showing my age too much, she thought. "Well, it's been a long time and you've grown up a lot since then."

"Thanks to you," he said. "If not for you, I would have never returned from the walled fortress of the Despoilers or grown to manhood here in our forest." He shuddered at the thought, before turning worried eyes on her. "But tell me true: Does your return mean the Jatohr are coming back as well?"

She shook her head. "You don't need to worry about that. I'm simply looking for something I lost the last time I was here, that's all." She wondered how far Gagre was willing to go to aid her in her quest. "I need to get to the Jatohr's citadel. Can you help me?"

"The island of the Despoilers?" He backed away from her in dismay. Fear filled his emerald eyes. "You must not go there! Even now, it is haunted by their unclean presence. Some say they dwell there still, slumbering perhaps, or merely biding their time until they emerge again to plague us."

"What do you mean?" she asked. As far she knew, the citadel had been unoccupied for years now, ever since Eljor had banished the other Jatohr from this universe. "Haunted how?"

Gagre paused, as though reluctant to talk about it. "None may go near that accursed place, but all know that strange things go on there to this day. Thunder sounds from behind its walls, even when the sky is clear, while the ground trembles sometimes as though the fortress is stirring in its slumbers. It is . . . an unquiet place."

Una recalled the persistent background rumbling she'd heard in and around the citadel before. Professor Eljor had mentioned something about ongoing renovations or construction. She supposed it was possible that some automated systems had kept running all these years, even after the Jatohr were sent back to where they'd come from. How that might affect her mission remained to be determined; she would cross that bridge when she came to it.

"I still have to go there to recover what was lost," she said. "Can you show me the way?"

"You ask too much." He retreated further from her. "My debt is paid. I can go no further."

She remembered a time when Gagre would have been eager to join her on the adventure, but it seemed he had learned to temper his curiosity over the years, perhaps because of his close call in the camp that one time. Una appreciated his caution, but couldn't help mourning the bold little explorer she'd once known.

"Fair enough," she said. "You've already done more than I could have hoped for and saved me from going up in flames. Don't think I'm not grateful for that." She nodded at the unconscious guards. "But won't you be in trouble when they come to?"

"I'll drink what is left of the drugged spirits, so no trace of my trickery will remain." He shrugged. "It will seem as though you somehow bewitched us all."

"I hope so," she said. "But will your people really believe that?"

"Some may suspect, but there will be no proof. And my clan enjoys much respect and honor. Not enough to spare you from the Ranger's harsh judgment, I fear, but enough to shield me from any accusations of wrongdoing."

He sounded confident enough. Una figured that he had a better grasp of the local tribal politics than she did. If he thought that his family's connections and influence would keep him safe, that would have to be good enough for her.

Not that I have any better ideas.

"Thank you again," she said. "You may have rescued more lives than you know."

The guards stirred fitfully in their drugged state. Gagre gave them an anxious look, then turned his apprehensive gaze toward the cloudy night sky. Dawn appeared hours away yet, but he looked worried anyway.

"The night passes and others may come this way. You must go, and quickly, before we are discovered."

Una had to agree. She strapped on her pack and readied her phaser and tricorder. The latter, which contained the geographical coordinates for the citadel, would help keep her on the right track in the jungle. On consideration, she helped herself to Jagged Tooth's hatchet as well. An idea for how to get past the citadel's walls was already forming in her mind . . .

"All right," she said. "Just point me toward the citadel."

He shuddered again, but gestured reluctantly to the right.

"Please believe me, friend Una. You should stay far

away from that dread place. Only danger waits for you behind those monstrous walls."

Been there, done that, she thought. "Don't worry about me. I know what I'm doing."

"No," he said dolefully. "I don't think you do."

Eighteen

"Bad news, Captain." Uhura held her hand up to her earpiece. "I'm picking up chatter from a Klingon listening post a few systems away. They've detected our incursion into 'their' space."

Kirk could practically hear the quotation marks in her voice regarding the Klingons' questionable claim to this region, which the *Enterprise* had entered less than five hours ago. Frankly, he was surprised that it had taken the Klingons so long, even if the Libros system was somewhat off the beaten track.

I was afraid of this, he thought, *with good reason.*

"Their response?" he asked, already anticipating the answer.

"Three Klingon battle cruisers have been dispatched to engage us," Uhura said, frowning. "Sorry, Captain."

"Never apologize for being the bearer of bad news, Lieutenant." Kirk appreciated being kept informed. "What about the *Shimizu*? Any indication that the Klingons are aware of its presence in this territory?"

He was still working on the assumption that Captain Una was heading back to Usilde with the Key, as seemingly confirmed by the faint traces of a fading ion trail. According to Spock, the trail's decay indicated that the *Shimizu* had a roughly eight-hour head start on the *Enterprise* and had probably already reached Usilde.

"Negative," Uhura reported. "That seems to have escaped their notice, at least so far."

Kirk could believe it. As Una had argued earlier, it was one thing for a small, inconspicuous spacecraft to slip into the region, but a Federation starship was bound to attract a lot more attention—and provoke a more substantial response.

"Estimated time until the Klingons intercept us?"

"The Klingon commanders are vowing to crush us within three hours," Uhura said. "They claim to be heading our way at maximum warp, assuming this isn't deliberate misdirection on their part. They could know that I'm listening in."

"Or maybe they simply don't care," Kirk said. "Have they made any attempts to hail us?"

"No, sir," Uhura said. "They sound more eager to fight than talk."

"Imagine that," McCoy said sarcastically. The doctor had remained on the bridge, loitering in the command well in order to stay abreast of the crisis. "Who would have guessed it?"

"Anyone who has ever gotten on a Klingon's bad side," Kirk replied.

The captain was inclined to take the intercepted communications at face value. The Klingons were nothing if not territorial, even when they had no legitimate right to be. He couldn't imagine that they wouldn't want to confront the *Enterprise*—and defend "their" space—with extreme prejudice.

"They have a good side?" McCoy asked.

"Not that I've ever seen," Kirk admitted. "Granted,

they can be subtle and cunning if they have to be, but when it comes to enforcing their claim on this sector? They're going to bring out the heavy guns."

"I concur," Spock stated, studying the readings at his science station. "Which can only complicate the upcoming peace talks, if not derail them entirely. An armed confrontation with Klingon military forces is best avoided for any number of compelling reasons."

That's putting it mildly, Kirk thought. He was already going to have some explaining to do to the Federation's diplomatic corps if and when this affair was concluded. Not that this was the first time he'd rushed in where angels feared to tread. He'd butted heads with bureaucrats and ambassadors before.

"We're approaching the Libros system, sir." Sulu looked back over his shoulder at the captain. "Should I keep on course, or turn back?"

Kirk exchanged worried looks with Spock. The Klingons posed a serious threat, but so did the possibility of the Empire getting their hands on Una and the Key, which could not be discounted with those enemy battle cruisers already heading in this direction.

"We could still retreat back across the border," Spock stated, "and perhaps lure the Klingons away from this system and the *Shimizu.*"

But that would still leave Una and the Key in the wind, with no guarantee that her activities wouldn't attract the Klingons' attention eventually. Kirk weighed the pros and cons of leaving her to her own devices and concluded that he couldn't in good conscience do so.

There was too much at stake to leave matters in the hands of one rogue captain, even if she was one of Starfleet's finest.

"Not yet," he said. "We're here and we still have a few hours to recover Captain Una—and certain valuable Starfleet assets—before the Klingons show up." He nodded at the helmsman. "Stay on course, Mister Sulu."

"Aye, sir." Sulu turned back to his controls. "Proceeding to Libros III."

"Usilde," Kirk said pensively. "The planet's inhabitants call it Usilde."

Kirk had reviewed April's abbreviated log entries on that previous mission years ago. The official record held only that April and his crew had encountered some mysterious alien explorers on Usilde, who had retreated after a confrontation that had left nine crew members missing in action. April had also advised that Starfleet and other Federation vessels steer clear of the planet in the future out of respect for the Prime Directive and the independent cultural development of the Usildar. As far as Kirk knew, no Federation vessel had visited Usilde since.

Until now.

"So, now that we're here," McCoy said, "are you *finally* going to let us in on what in blazes is going on?"

Kirk assumed the rest of the crew shared his impatience and curiosity, even if they were too well disciplined to voice it. Given the mortal threat posed by the imminent Klingon battle cruisers, he knew he owed them some answers.

"When this becomes a medical matter, Doctor, you'll be the first to know," he said sharply. "But I understand that you all have questions."

He pressed a switch on the armrest of his chair to address the entire ship via the comm system.

"Attention, all crew. This is the captain speaking. No doubt you are wondering what we are doing here in this disputed region of space. Certain details are classified, but I can tell you this: Captain Una has absconded with a potentially dangerous piece of alien technology that was recovered from Libros III some eighteen years ago, when the *Enterprise* was under the command of Captain Robert April. We have reason to believe that she is pursuing her own agenda on the planet, but her objective is uncertain and her mission has not been sanctioned by Starfleet. Our goal is to recover Captain Una—and the aforementioned technology—before either can fall into the hands of the Klingon Empire. We hope to achieve that goal and return to our previous course with all due speed. Captain out."

Kirk ended the broadcast.

"Oh, is that all?" McCoy said. "Why didn't you just say so?"

Kirk let the doctor's attitude slide. "The rest, I'm afraid, is on a strictly need-to-know basis, and right now only Spock and I need to know." He looked pointedly at McCoy. "Is that understood?"

McCoy harrumphed, but backed down. "Clear as dilithium, Captain."

The frustrated physician would surely try to pry more details out of him in private later on, Kirk guessed, but that was the least of the captain's concerns right now.

Finding Una and the Key before the Klingons arrived was enough to worry about.

The parallels between the Transfer Key hidden in his stateroom and the Tantalus Field device his barbaric counterpart had deployed in that alternate universe had not escaped him, and he had often pondered the connection between the two. That other Kirk had used the Tantalus device to ruthlessly "disappear" his opponents in his pursuit of power. The mere possibility of a similar weapon falling into the hands of the Klingons was something to be averted at all costs.

"Approaching Libros . . . Usilde," Sulu reported, correcting himself. "Entering standard orbit."

Kirk examined the infamous planet as it appeared on the main viewer. This was the second time the *Enterprise* had gone into orbit around Usilde, even if there was no one left among the crew who remembered the previous visit. The cloudy Class-M planet looked hospitable enough, despite having claimed at least nine Starfleet officers years ago.

Although those people weren't actually trapped on Usilde, he recalled, *but in another reality accessible only by the Key.*

"Any sign of the *Shimizu*?" Kirk asked.

"Negative, Captain," Chekov replied, after consulting the tactical displays at the nav station. "There are no other vessels in orbit around the planet."

Spock looked up from the science station.

"Sensors detect the *Shimizu* on the planet's surface," he reported, "approximately six kilometers from . . . a particular habitation."

The Jatohr citadel, Kirk thought, *that Una and April escaped from years ago.*

"Understood, Mister Spock."

It wasn't hard to guess where Una was heading, or what her ultimate objective was. She was out to reactivate the transfer-field generator, by means of the Key, and rescue those lost castaways.

But was that even possible? After all these years?

He stabbed the comm switch again. "Kirk to engineering. Mister Scott, report to the bridge at once. I need you to take command while Mister Spock and I beam down to the planet's surface."

Scotty replied at once. *"Aye, Captain. I'll be right there."*

"Acknowledged. Kirk out."

He trusted the stolid engineer to take charge of the bridge in his absence and to get the *Enterprise* to safety if the Klingons showed up ahead of schedule. The *Enterprise* was formidable in its own right, but was unlikely to prevail over a trio of enemy battle cruisers, and then there were the diplomatic repercussions of a major battle on the brink of the peace talks. If worse came to worst, he and Spock were expendable.

Yeoman Bates came forward. "Request permission to join the landing party."

"There will be no landing party." Kirk still wanted to keep the secret of the Key contained if possible. "Just Mister Spock and myself."

"Now wait just one minute," McCoy protested. "Not that I'm in any big hurry to beam down to a planet I've never heard of, to find some gadget you can't talk about, but what if you need a doctor on this little expedition? Or Captain Una does?"

Kirk considered it. Lord knew he trusted McCoy as much as he trusted Spock, but this wasn't the doctor's mess to clean up. He and Spock bore sole responsibility here, after keeping the existence of the Key hidden from Starfleet. It didn't feel right to jeopardize McCoy—or anyone else—over a secret they never signed on to protect.

"Sorry, Bones, but this is between me and Una, captain to captain." He held up his hand to forestall any indignant objections. "And if we need you, you're only a transporter beam away."

"I suppose," McCoy conceded unhappily. "But how come he gets to go along," he added, gesturing at Spock, "if this is just between you captains?"

"Spock knows Una much better than I do," Kirk said, "having served with her for over a decade. He may be able to get through to her where I might not. Plus, he has a better understanding of how she thinks and reacts."

"Well, when you put it that way," McCoy muttered. "But I still don't like it."

"That comes as no surprise, Doctor." Spock left his station to join them. "But the captain is correct. I have more experience dealing with my former superior than any other individual on this ship. That personal experience may prove valuable if we hope to achieve a peaceful resolution to this situation."

Kirk knew that despite his dispassionate tone, Spock had to be hoping for just such an outcome. He didn't envy Spock having to treat an old friend and crewmate as a fugitive. Kirk had felt the same way when Spock had defied Starfleet to rescue Pike from a living hell, and when Gary Mitchell had been driven insane by cosmic forces. Accepting that Gary had become an enemy had been one of hardest trials of Kirk's early captaincy; he still missed the friend he once would have trusted with his life.

Let's hope Una's story ends less tragically.

The turbolift door opened and Montgomery Scott strode onto the bridge. "Reporting for duty, sir."

Kirk appreciated the speed with which Scotty had abandoned his precious engine room. "I commend your promptness, Mister Scott." He turned his chair over to the engineer. "You have the bridge."

"Aye, sir." Scott inspected the deceptively benign-looking planet on the viewscreen. "Any special instructions, Captain?"

"We have a fleet of Klingon battle cruisers heading our way," Kirk said. "With any luck, Spock and I will be back with Captain Una before they get here, but if things go amiss, I don't want you risking the *Enterprise* for our sakes. Get my ship to safety, Scotty."

Scott nodded grimly, absorbing the worrisome news and orders. "Understood, Captain, but I don't mind saying that I'd just as soon it not come to that."

Kirk had no intention of putting his crew in that position.

"You and me both, Mister Scott."

Nineteen

Una rushed through the pitch-black forest, pursued by an unknown number of Usildar intent on recapturing her. Strident shouts and frantic rustling disturbed the nocturnal jungle, shaking the treetops behind her while leaving no doubt that her escape had been discovered. Had Gagre managed to evade any blame, as he'd insisted he could? Una fervently hoped so, but that was out of her hands. She had to focus on keeping herself out of the Usildar's grasp, which meant striking the right balance between stealth and speed, while also coping with a notable lack of light to see by.

Sweat dripped down her face and beneath her uniform. She'd lost track of how long she'd been fleeing through brush and brambles and shadows as black as the hungriest singularity. The stygian forest both hid and hindered her. Fallen logs and bulging roots lurked in the night, causing her to stumble over them. Cool water dripped from overhanging leaves and blossoms. Looming tree trunks formed an irregular maze that was even harder to navigate in the dark. At times, she regretted losing her palm beacon, even though she knew, intellectually, that she wouldn't have dared use it for fear of the bright artificial light attracting unwanted attention and guiding her hunters straight to her. All things considered, she was better off creeping through the dark, even if that slowed her down to a worrying degree.

Good thing she'd always had exceptional night vision.

Phaser in hand, she pushed through a web of hanging lianas. The dense foliage brought back memories of her first arduous trek through these forests so long ago. She was nearly two decades older now, but she liked to think that she was still in better shape than green cadets half her age and could match her younger self in endurance and stamina.

Not that I'd turn down an easier route, she thought, *if one was available.*

Unfortunately, heading back to the *Shimizu* was not an option; that was surely the first place the Usildar had looked for her, which meant that she would have to do without certain supplies as well. Instead she made for the citadel on foot, relying on her tricorder to keep her on course. Pausing for a moment, she risked a glance at the device's illuminated display. According to readings, the citadel was still approximately half a kilometer to the northwest. She sighed inwardly.

Could be worse, she consoled herself. *At least it's not on the other side of the planet.*

She flinched as a twig snapped beneath her feet. The darkness definitely had its drawbacks when it came to keeping quiet, although she hoped the noise would be lost amidst the jungle's customary nighttime symphony. Wildlife hooted and howled overhead. Random stirrings in the canopy and below kept her nerves on edge. Despite the lack of light, she kept one eye on the leafy branches high above her, watching out for any arboreal ambushers, half expecting a hostile hand or foot to grab her without warning. The commotion behind her continued unabated and sounded as though it was getting closer by the moment.

Her finger hovered on the trigger of her phaser.

Her stomach grumbled and she wished she could take the time to break into the Starfleet rations tucked away in her pack. Any late-night snacks would have to wait until she was safely inside the Jatohr's empty citadel, provided she actually got that far.

"Over here! I found her!"

An armed Usildar dropped from the trees to land directly in front of her. The night masked his features, but Una could make out the raised spear clutched in his hands. A volatile mix of fear and anger roiled his voice.

"Go no farther! You cannot escape our justice!"

"Sorry," she replied. "I have other plans."

She didn't waste time arguing with him. A stun beam caught him by surprise, and it dawned on Una that, as far as she knew, the Usildar had never witnessed a phaser in action before. Her poleaxed victim had probably been more worried about the crude hatchet tucked into her belt.

Let's hear it for the element of surprise.

She hopped over the downed hunter's prone body, anxious to make tracks before his cries drew more hunters her way. The phaser improved her odds, but she was still outnumbered and out of her element. She couldn't let herself get overconfident.

Like last time . . .

Out of nowhere, a noose tightened around her neck,

choking her and yanking her off her feet so that her legs dangled in the air. Unseen arms or legs pulled her up with shocking strength and speed. Gasping for breath, Una tugged at the strangling vine with her free hand while firing blindly into the branches above. Phaser beams lit up the night, sizzling through the leafy understory.

A stunned gasp rewarded her desperate blasts. The noose around her neck slackened, allowing her to breathe again, even as she plummeted toward the forest floor many meters below, bouncing painfully off an unyielding branch on the way down. A prickly thicket helped cushion her landing, but the jarring impact still knocked the wind out of her and caused her to lose her grip on the phaser. She landed face-first, mercifully sparing the gear in her backpack, but making it rougher on her. Lying dazed atop a heap of flattened underbrush, Una thought she heard another body thud to the ground nearby.

She was civilized enough to wish the Usildar a soft landing.

But not *too* soft.

Bruised and battered, she was tempted to take an extra moment to recover, but she didn't have a second to spare. Brambles scratched her and tugged at her uniform as, wincing, she climbed to her knees and groped in the dark for her lost phaser, which had ended up somewhere in the endless brush.

"This way!" another voice cried out from the canopy, much too close for comfort. Branches shook beneath the weight of running and swinging bodies. "I saw a spear of red light blazing from below!"

Una sprang to her feet, reluctantly giving up on the

phaser. There was no time to rummage through the brush searching blindly for the weapon. More Usildar were closing in on her. She had to keep moving if she wanted to stay ahead of her hunters.

She drew the "borrowed" hatchet from her belt.

This will have to do, she thought.

Wielding the hatchet like a machete, she hacked her way through the brush ahead of her. Speed trumped subtlety now. She was racing for her life—and the future of those she had left behind years ago.

You had better appreciate this, Tim.

Adrenaline, first-rate Illyrian physical conditioning, and eighteen years of survivor's guilt kept her going, despite the scrapes and scratches and fatigue that were beginning to wear on her. Her ribs felt like a mugato had pounded on them. How long had she been running anyway? Was it just her imagination, or was the sky lightening high above the forest? The thick canopy still filtered out most of the available light, but it seemed to her that the sun was finally rising.

She wasn't certain if that was a good thing or not.

A thick stand of ferns blocked the gap between two immovable tree trunks. Una hacked at the fronds to clear a path and was suddenly confronted by a shadowy figure looming ominously before her. Startled, she spied the unmistakable outline of an enormous gastropod posed atop a single large foot. A sextet of tentacles rose like horns from the figure's inhuman head. Two forelimbs reached toward her.

A Jatohr?

Instinct got the better of her and she swung the

hatchet at the figure. To her surprise, the edged weapon dug into what felt like solid wood instead of flesh or armor. She tugged the hatchet free and stared at the still, silent figure in confusion.

What in this world?

A closer inspection revealed that what she had mistaken for a Jatohr was in fact a life-sized wooden effigy of the same, carved from a once-living tree rooted deeply in the ground. She wondered at its purpose, intrigued despite the urgency of her situation, until she looked past the effigy, where the rising sun allowed her to see that she had arrived at some sort of boundary marking the edge of the forest. Beyond the trees lay a swath of scorched, blackened soil at least a hundred meters across. Nothing grew or lived in that barren zone, not even the ubiquitous alien fungi, which she could glimpse sprouting in abundance on the opposite side of the dead zone, where, even farther in the distance, the citadel could be seen rising up from the gray lake, its high walls and tower reflecting the dawn's ruddy light. A familiar rumbling, which Una recognized even after so many years, indeed emanated from the distant fortress, stirring unpleasant memories and sensations. She knew she should be pleased to be within sight of her goal at last, but a chill ran down her spine in a way that was quite uncharacteristic for her. Una was not one to let her emotions overrule her training and professionalism, and yet her throat tightened at the sight of the citadel. Goosebumps erupted beneath her soiled, sweaty uniform.

I'm back for you, Tim. Or almost.

The dead zone stretched between her and a hilly landscape that appeared totally overrun with the invasive gray fungi. A row of wooden effigies, identical to the one she had just stumbled upon, marked the opposite end of the zone.

Like scarecrows, she guessed, guarding a no-man's-land between the forest and a forbidden region surrounding the citadel. The Usildar had presumably scorched the earth between the markers to create a buffer between themselves and the "haunted" vicinity of the Jatohr, not unlike, say, the Neutral Zone between the Federation and the Romulan Star Empire. And the grotesque wooden Jatohr were posted in warning, reminding the unwary to keep to their side of the zone, for beyond slept monsters.

Una peered cautiously past the effigy she had instinctively attacked, worried that there might also be sentries guarding the dead zone, but saw nothing resembling watchtowers or patrols. Thinking it over, she reasoned that such measures were surely unnecessary, since what Usildar in their right mind would want to get that close to the citadel anyway?

Only a Starfleet captain—and an obsessed one, at that—could be so crazy.

Una contemplated the barren wasteland ahead, which offered little in the way of cover or concealment. Breaking from the forest risked exposing herself to the tireless lynch mob pursuing her, but what alternative was there? The citadel—and its long-forgotten secrets—awaited her. And she no longer needed a tricorder to tell her which way to go.

No time like the present, she thought. *Why wait for the Usildar to catch up with me?*

Hurrying out from beneath the shadow of the forest canopy, she sprinted past the scarecrow into the dead zone. Almost immediately, a hue and cry erupted from the jungle behind her as treetop observers spotted her exiting the woods. Amidst the frenzied shouting, Banev's voice rang out commandingly:

"She goes to disturb the Despoilers! Stop her at all costs!"

That was by no means her intention, but explaining that was a lost cause. Not looking back, Una dashed across the charred earth, hoping that that the Usildar wouldn't follow her into the zone. Now that she was out from beneath the canopy, the morning sun made it easier to see. Her boot bumped against a soft, round object that bounced off her heel; to her dismay, she saw that the dead zone was littered with dark purple melons, of the same variety used to glue her to the stump earlier. The melons were strewn across the no-man's-land like land mines, no doubt intended to slow anyone attempting to come or go from the citadel. She came close to stepping on a second melon before veering to avoid it at the last minute. Getting sticky sap all over her boots was not on her agenda either.

Her life, and the lives of others, depended on not letting anything slow her down.

The treacherous melons turned the zone into an obstacle course, forcing her to zigzag around them when she wasn't leaping over them altogether to avoid slowing down. Una flashed back to her basic training at Starfleet, which had been child's play compared to the rigorous courses she'd run on Illyria in her youth, where she had always taken first place.

They'll have to do better than this to stop me.

The ground gave way beneath her and she realized instantly that she'd stumbled onto an old-fashioned pitfall, like a Piklite tiger trap. Razor-sharp reflexes came to her rescue, and she grabbed onto the edge of the pit before it was too late. Her body slammed into the side of the trap, but her free hand dug into the rocky soil, fighting gravity. Glancing down, she spied an ash-covered mat, woven from strips of bark, impaled on sharpened wooden spikes waiting to skewer her as well. The mat must have been stretched over the pit, hidden beneath a coating of dirt and ash.

It seemed the Usildar *really* didn't want anyone getting too close to the citadel.

Holding on with one hand, she placed the hatchet between her teeth to free her other hand. Grunting, she pulled herself up and out of the pit and back onto the solid ground, where she took the axe in hand again. She scrambled to her feet, slightly shaken by the close call. Her quest to save her old comrades had almost come to a grisly end.

A spear thudded into the ground beside her.

"After her!" Banev ordered. "Bring her down before she gets any farther!"

Glancing back, Una saw that her hunters had reached the edge of the forest. In the forefront of the pack, Banev was urging his people on, but the other Usildar appeared hesitant to venture into the dead zone. Entering the deserted labor camp had been worrisome enough, Una guessed, but to draw nearer to the rumbling citadel, from which no forest dweller had ever returned? Una wasn't surprised that other hunters were balking at their leader's commands.

"But, High Ranger," an anxious Usildar addressed Banev, "she passes beyond our lands, where we dare not follow!"

"And what evil might she awaken if she reaches the lair of the Despoilers?" He shoved the reluctant hunter forward and shook his fists at the others. "After her, all of you, while there is yet a chance to stop her!"

Unwilling to defy their leader, the hunters ventured cautiously after Una, wary of the sticky melons and hidden pitfalls. Spears, rocks, and other missiles hurled past Una, who ducked low and kept her head down to avoid being hit. The last thing she needed was to get winged by another drugged spiky nut. Her eyes scanned the blackened ground before her, watching out for another trap. Her heart pounded in her chest.

"Faster!" Banev shouted. "Don't let her get away!"

Eight meters ahead, a row of slug-like scarecrows marked the far end of the dead zone, which, despite the Usildar's efforts, was being slowly invaded by the ugly gray fungi beyond. The wooden effigies called out to Una, offering the possibility of sanctuary. Would the fearful hunters be willing to follow her past the final boundary into the forbidden realm of the Jatohr? Una was anxious to find out, if she could make it out of the zone.

Only a few more meters to go.

Mushrooms crunched beneath her racing feet, releasing a noxious odor. A projectile whistled past her ear, missing her by centimeters. A stone-tipped javelin slammed into one the Jatohr scarecrows, embedding itself deep into the effigy's chest. Heavy footsteps pounded behind Una, gaining on her. Another missile flew over her head.

"Hurry!" Banev ran after his warriors. "Your families and future may depend on it!"

The border was tantalizingly close, but so were the hunters and their weapons, which were definitely gaining on her. Una dived between the carved effigies, going into a roll before springing back to her feet beyond the boundary. Fruiting gray fungi carpeted the ground, which led to a low rise just up ahead. The pungent growths had also colonized a number of dead trees and logs, which were being slowly consumed by the spreading alien invasion. She was in Jatohr territory now and their pervasive legacy stretched between her and the citadel.

Shouts of fear and frustration erupted behind her. The racing footsteps slowed and fell silent. Peering back over her shoulder, Una observed that, as hoped, the hunters had halted at the edge of the zone, unwilling to go farther.

"What are you waiting for?" Banev railed at them, catching up with the other Usildar. "Keep after her!"

Thunder rumbled from the direction of the citadel, although the morning sky was clear and blue. Una appreciated its timing, while putting more distance between her and the dead zone. Scary noises from the "haunted" fortress might not be enough to discourage her pursuers much longer.

"No!" a female hunter said defiantly. "Let the stranger go to her doom. We will not share her fate.'"

The other Usildar murmured in agreement. "She is as good as dead," a younger forest dweller insisted. "We will never see her again."

"Fools! Cowards!" Banev snatched a thorn-studded mace from the grip of a recalcitrant warrior and loped out of the zone, leaving his followers behind. "I will save you despite yourselves!"

He pursued Una across the fungal field. She turned to face him, realizing that, unlike spears or spikes, this confrontation could not be avoided. Banev was determined to shield his people from bygone horrors, albeit at her expense. She had to admire that, along with his undeniable courage in daring to chase her beyond where every other Usildar feared to go. His bravery and dedication would have done a Starfleet captain proud.

Aside from that whole business about burning strangers.

"Listen to me, Banev." She felt obliged to make one last attempt to reason with him, although she knew in her heart that she was wasting her breath. "Or, better yet, listen to your own people. Just let me go and you'll never have to worry about me again."

"I will do nothing *but* worry," he countered, "as long as you are free to trespass upon forbidden ground, risking the return of yesterday's evil and suffering." Genuine fear, bordering on panic, raised his voice an octave. Desperate green eyes met hers. "Can you not see the danger you so rashly tempt?"

A flicker of doubt undermined her resolve. Perhaps

the Jatohr citadel—and the transfer-field generator—*was* best left alone?

That's what Eljor would have wanted.

But then she remembered Tim and Martinez and Griffin and Le May and Cambias being "removed" right before her eyes, banished to another reality for eighteen long years, and her jaw set in determination. She'd vowed never to forget them and she wasn't about to do so now, not when she was finally so close to bringing them home.

"It's worth the risk," she said. "Trust me."

"Never! Not when my people's future is at stake!"

Raising his thorny mace high, he charged at her. His simian arms gave him a longer reach, but she doubted that he had ever faced a foe like her. The mace came swinging down at her, but she expertly sidestepped the attack so that his own momentum carried him past her. Not wanting to employ lethal force, Una flipped her hatchet around and smacked him in the head with the flat of the blade. The blow dropped the fear-crazed Ranger as effectively as a phaser set on stun. She nudged him with the toe of her boot to make certain that he was out cold. She felt a twinge of sincere regret.

"Forgive me," she said to the unconscious Usildar. "I understand that you only wanted to protect your people. But there are people depending on me too."

And they had been waiting for far too long.

———

Past the next rise, the ground sloped down to the shore of the algae-encrusted gray lake. If anything, the alien pond scum looked even thicker and more entrenched than

Una remembered, while the rank odor was positively oppressive. Gas pockets beneath the surface bubbled and burst, releasing more foulness into the air. Curious, she unslung her tricorder and tested the air quality. She noted with concern an increase in nitrogen levels in the atmosphere. A negative side effect of the algae's growth, she wondered, or part of a deliberate, long-term attempt to reshape the planet's environment to suit the Jatohr? Recalling the other damage the Newcomers had inflicted on Usilde, she suspected the latter. If this went on, she realized, the Usildar would be unable to breathe their own air within a generation or two. All of their efforts to reclaim their planet would be in vain.

One more thing to worry about . . .

Across the lake, the slick, nacreous walls of the citadel appeared just as steep and impenetrable as before. The sun shone down on the island fortress, reminding Una that she had lost an entire night to her travails with the Usildar, costing her a significant portion of her head start on the *Enterprise.* If Kirk was indeed still on her trail, he'd be catching up to her any time now, if he hadn't already reached this system.

Una switched off her communicator, just to be safe. She didn't want the *Enterprise* locking onto her before she was ready.

And I need to get to that generator before Kirk can interfere.

Contemplating the deep, fetid waters between her and the citadel, and whatever predators might still be lurking beneath the surface, she regretted that her original plan to commandeer an abandoned Jatohr pod had not worked out. She would have to improvise instead, taking advantage of the materials at hand.

Fortunately, she'd already devised a plan.

Pieces of driftwood, coated with algae, could be found upon the beach. With the aid of the stolen hatchet, she lashed them together with vines to form a crude but usable raft. It wouldn't win any yachting contests, and wasn't as convenient as the inflatable life raft stowed away on the *Shimizu,* but it might serve to get her across the lake to the citadel, where the towering walls of the fortress required another creative solution.

Una shrugged off her pack and opened it. Tucked inside, along with the Key and some basic survival gear, was an intact purple melon she'd claimed back at the clearing when she first made her escape. Her plan was to crack it open when she reached the base of the wall and apply a measured quantity of the adhesive sap to her hands and boots so that she could scale the sheer walls as easily as a Suliban—as long as she moved quickly enough to avoid ending up stuck to the side of the wall like a barnacle.

It was a risky plan, but she couldn't think of a better one.

Granted, even if she did succeed in making it past the walls and using the Key to bring back Tim and the others, they would still have to make their way back to the *Shimizu* in order to escape the planet. But she figured that there had to be a working pod or two left in the city, and that, with whatever was left of the landing party at her side, they could deal with the Usildar long enough to reclaim her ship.

Assuming that there was still anybody left to rescue.

But she was getting ahead of herself. First she needed to get to the citadel. Any future challenges could wait.

Dragging the makeshift raft to the water's edge, she shoved off from the shore. The ubiquitous algae made the driftwood slick and slimy to the touch, but she overcame her disgust to climb aboard the rickety craft and, kneeling atop it, paddle toward the citadel. A single wooden oar propelled her forward, while memories of the monstrous cephalopod she'd glimpsed years before kept her on alert for any sign of movement beneath the scummy surface of the lake. She had no reason to expect that the lake creatures had vanished with the Jatohr, so she could only hope that any submerged beasts did not recognize her as prey or smell the blood from the various small cuts and scrapes she'd picked up during the chase through the woods. For once, her eidetic memory worked against her. She could all too vividly remember the beast's baleful yellow eyes, snapping beak, and clawed tentacles.

Remind me to bring an extra phaser next time.

Paddling rapidly, she made it two-thirds of the way across the lake before her fears were borne out. Ripples in the algae hinted at the presence of a sizable something swimming just beneath the surface, circling her warily as though uncertain of her nature. She oared faster, but the strenuous activity only seemed to draw the unseen creature in closer, so she paused and raised the oar defensively. Her tricorder remained slung over her shoulder, but she didn't need to scan for life-forms to know that she was in trouble. She shifted her grip on the oar, getting ready to use it as a weapon. She didn't want to harm the creature, but then again, it probably didn't belong on this planet.

Greedy arms, lined with suckers, burst through the lake scum to grab at her. Hooked claws jutted from the suckers, making them all the more dangerous. She swung at the arms with the oar, desperate to keep the vicious suckers from latching onto her. Wood smacked loudly against wet, glistening tentacles that whipped about like loose cables in zero gravity.

Something thumped forcefully against the bottom of the raft, upsetting it and nearly tossing Una overboard. A tentacle whipped over her head, and she swung at another arm with the oar. She found herself envying the creature's multiple limbs; she could have used a few extra arms herself at the moment.

Not to mention that phaser.

The monster surged up from below, capsizing the raft and spilling Una into the lake. She swallowed a mouthful of scum and water before spitting the rest out and swimming madly away. Looking back, she saw the raft between torn apart by eight furious arms. The squid's huge, bulbous head broke the surface and a vicious black beak, the size of old-fashioned starship grapplers, bit down on the floating oar, snapping it in two. A malevolent yellow eye swiveled in Una's direction.

It had spotted her.

Kicking and splashing, she swam toward the citadel, but its smooth walls offered her no ready way up and out of the water. Frantic fingers searched for a handhold but found no purchase. The sap-filled melon she'd hoped to employ was still stuck in her backpack, along with her other supplies, yet she doubted that the predatory cephalopod would give her a chance to get glued up. Bobbing in the water, dog-paddling to stay afloat, she turned away from the wall to see the alien squid jetting toward her. She drew the hatchet from her belt, determined to sell her life dearly, but having little confidence that such primitive tactics would suffice to keep her alive much longer. All indications were that her belated quest for redemption was about to end in the belly of the beast.

Sorry, Tim. I almost made it.

But Illyrians did not surrender. She would go down fighting if she had to.

"Number One!"

Spock's voice called out to her from above. Turning her gaze upward, away from the oncoming creature, she spied Kirk and Spock peering down at her from atop the wall. Kirk fired his phaser and a crimson beam shot past overhead to strike the monster, whose tentacles convulsed violently before the entire creature sank back to the murky depths, disappearing from view. Una wasn't sure if the beast had been stunned or simply repelled and, frankly, she didn't much care as long as it was no longer intent on making a meal of her. She was more concerned with what Kirk and Spock were doing here—and what this meant for her mission.

"Hold on, Captain," Kirk hollered down to her. "Help is on the way."

Spock hurled a Starfleet-issue emergency ladder down to her. She grabbed onto the lower rungs and hastily clambered out of the water. Spock utilized his superior

Vulcan strength to assist her ascent by pulling the ladder up and away from the lake below. Given the length of the irate cephalopod's tentacles, Una didn't entirely relax until she was well out of the creature's reach. Soggy and breathless, she let Kirk help her over the lip of the wall and onto an elevated walkway overlooking the sprawling complex below. Her tricorder remained slung over her shoulder, having survived her unplanned dip into the lake. She leaned against the parapet to catch her breath.

"Welcome back to the citadel," Kirk greeted her. "We've been expecting you."

Twenty

"My apologies, gentlemen. I fear you find me not at my best."

Despite nearly being eaten by a monster squid, Captain Una quickly regained her customary cool poise and assurance. She was in a bedraggled state, having clearly been through the wars since Kirk last laid eyes on her. She was soggy and dirty and beaten-up and, all in all, very far from her usual immaculate self, but you wouldn't know that from her crisp, professional attitude. Kirk had to admire her aplomb, if not her recent actions.

"Well, this is hardly a formal occasion," he remarked, "so I suppose we can make allowances."

Meeting atop the outer walls of a deserted alien out-post was indeed very different from a reception aboard the *Enterprise.* Kirk reflected ruefully on how badly matters had deteriorated since that pleasant social occasion only a day or so ago. Una regarded her rescuers warily. Tension hung thick in the air, along with a sour, unpleasant aroma that reminded Kirk of the noisome mushroom caves of Tennek VI.

"My thanks for your timely intervention," Una said. "May I ask how this came about?"

"It was not difficult to deduce your ultimate destination," Spock explained. He drew up the rescue ladder, which the *Enterprise* had beamed down only moments before in response to an urgent request from the landing party. "We simply transported down to the citadel to intercept you . . . although I gather you encountered some delays en route."

"You could say that," she said wryly. "A pity I lacked the option of beaming directly onto these walls as well. The disadvantages of not arriving via a *Constitution*-class starship."

"We were actually somewhat surprised to discover that we'd gotten here first," Kirk added. "Good thing all that ruckus on the mainland attracted our attention, so we were on the lookout when you ran into your multi-armed admirer down there." The levity left his voice as he confronted the renegade captain. "Seems like you've stirred up no end of trouble on this crusade of yours."

She didn't deny it. "Unavoidable, I'm afraid."

"That's for Starfleet Command to decide." Kirk held out his hand. "I'll take that Key back now, if you please."

She opened her mouth as though to protest, but apparently thought better of it. Her shrewd eyes darted from the phaser in Kirk's other hand to the one holstered at Spock's hip. Una appeared to be unarmed. Kirk wondered what had become of her own sidearm.

"You do seem to have me at a disadvantage." She grudgingly removed her sodden backpack and extracted the Key. Frowning, she handed it over to Kirk, who tucked it into his belt. "There you go, Captain. Back in your custody once more."

"And none too soon," Kirk said sternly. "You've led

us a merry chase, Captain, and placed my ship—and the upcoming Organian peace talks—in jeopardy, but this ends now. You're coming with us, back to the *Enterprise*."

Holstering his weapon, he flipped open his communicator. "Kirk to—"

"Kirk, wait!" Una protested, desperation cracking her stoic façade. "Let me finish what I started." She gestured toward the lofty tower rising up from citadel's central hub. "We're practically at the finish line. You can't expect me to turn back now, when I'm so close to completing my mission."

"To rescue those crew members you lost here?" Kirk asked. "By using the Key to reactivate the transfer-field generator?"

"Of course," she replied. "What else?"

The citadel's central tower loomed above them, only about fifty meters away. A walkway running across one of the fortress's radiating spokes connected the wall they were standing on to the tower. Water, most likely pumped up from the lake below, filled the gaps between the spokes. The ubiquitous gray algae rippled atop wedge-shaped pools.

"Nothing doing," Kirk said. "There's a fleet of Klingon battle cruisers heading this way, and I'd just as soon not be here when they arrive."

Her eyes widened at the mention of the Klingons, whose approach was clearly news to her, but Una remained fixated on her quest. "How long before the cruisers get here?"

"Approximately one hour, ten minutes," Spock supplied.

"Then we still have time," she insisted. "Please, Kirk. I'm asking you, captain to captain, for a chance to rescue nine Starfleet officers who have been trapped in another universe longer than they should have ever had to endure." Raw emotion energized her voice. "*I* left them behind eighteen years ago. The *Enterprise* left them behind. But now we have the opportunity to finally bring them home . . . and we may never have another chance, not if the Klingons cement their hold on this region."

Her words, and the passion behind them, gave Kirk pause. He knew too well the pain and regret of losing comrades and crew in the line of duty. Part of the burden of command was carrying the weight of the lives lost under your watch. What wouldn't he give for a second chance to save some of them, like those two hundred men and women back on the *Farragut*.

Or Gary Mitchell.

"Do you really think you can do this?" he asked.

"I do," Una said confidently. "If we can get to the master control room and plug the Key back into the transfer-field generator, I believe I can reverse the effect and bring those people back to our universe."

"But what guarantee do you have that they are still alive to be rescued?" Spock asked, logically enough. "It has been several years, after all."

"I'm quite aware of that, Mister Spock," Una said, perhaps a tad defensively. "But they're listed as 'missing,' not deceased, for a reason. And these are trained Starfleet officers we're talking about. If anyone could survive in an alien universe all this time, it's Lieutenant Martinez and the others. If there's even a chance we can rescue them, how can we let it slip by?"

She knows their names, Kirk observed. *Of course she would.*

Those lost officers weren't abstractions to her, listings on some old casualty reports from two *Enterprise* captains ago. These were people she had served beside on the very same starship that was now orbiting the planet: flesh-and-blood individuals with names and faces and people who cared about them. They served before Kirk's time, but they had once called *Enterprise* home, and he was the captain of the *Enterprise* now.

Which meant he had a duty here too.

"All right." Kirk put away his communicator. "You'll have your chance, as long as time allows. We have one hour to try to rescue those people. But if that time runs out, we're beaming back to the *Enterprise* and getting out of here, with or without those missing officers."

"Understood, Kirk," she said. "And thank you."

"Don't make me regret it."

The hot equatorial sun beat down on them as they hiked down a long ramp to the spoke leading to the central hub. An outdoor walkway, complete with guardrails, ran along the top of the spoke. Kirk noted the inconvenient lack of any open plazas or spaces large enough to land the *Shimizu* in or on. No wonder Una had been forced to park her ship some distance away and make her way through the forest to get to the citadel.

"I don't suppose you've already found a way into the hub?" she asked.

Kirk shook his head. "To be honest, I was kind of hoping that you had some plans along those lines."

"I did," she admitted, "but let's just say they went awry."

Apparently so, Kirk thought.

When he and Spock had first arrived at the citadel, there had been some concern that Una was already inside the hub and about her work. Beaming directly into the opaque structure without precise landing coordinates would have been suicidal; they could have easily ended up occupying the same space as a wall or piece of furniture. Transporting onto the outer walkway, which could be viewed from space if you increased the magnification enough, had been the smarter move, even if it had meant they'd had to cool their heels waiting to intercept Una on her way in or out of the citadel.

Not that she'd kept them waiting long.

The walkway led them to a sealed doorway blocking the way into the central tower. A circular porthole, installed in the door, offered a view of some sort of vestibule beyond, with an inner door on the opposite side of the chamber. Kirk didn't see any obvious knobs or latches they could use to open the door. He tried to pry the door open with his fingertips, but the seam was too smooth, giving him nothing to grab onto. He stepped back from the door, conceding defeat.

"Well, Spock," he asked. "Any suggestions?"

"Negative, Captain." He scanned the uncooperative door with his tricorder. "As noted, the alien material composing these walls is opaque to our sensors, making it difficult to locate the locking mechanism, let alone access it." He lowered the tricorder. "Ironic. It seems we possess the Key, but not a key."

Una inspected the porthole, which was perhaps fifty centimeters in diameter. "I believe I can squeeze through this if we can remove this transparent pane." She tapped the clear material with her knuckles, then held out her hand. "A phaser, if you please."

"I don't think so." Kirk was only willing to trust the other captain so far. He adjusted the setting on his own phaser. "I'll handle this if you don't mind."

"Suit yourself." Una stepped back to let Kirk work. If she was offended by his lack of trust, she gave no sign of it. "I regret having to damage the citadel, but I can't imagine that opening a single porthole will harm any essential systems."

Kirk judged that a safe bet. The intermittent rumbling coming from within the Jatohr's former sanctuary clearly indicated that some mechanisms were still in operation even after all these years, but a window was still just a window. It was not as though they were planning to blast blindly through the walls and hope that they didn't hit anything crucial.

Which would probably be the Klingons' approach, he thought.

Narrowing the phaser's output to a thin, high-intensity beam, Kirk cut around the edge of the circular porthole like an old-fashioned burglar or jewel thief. It occurred to him that this was basically the same technique Una had used to steal the Key from his quarters in the first place. Another irony to add to Spock's list.

To his relief, the beam successfully cut through the clear alien material, which felt more akin to amber than glass or transparent aluminum. Steam rose from the crack carved out by the phaser beam. The liberated disk fell inward, clattering onto the floor of the vestibule beyond. Kirk instinctively flinched at the noise before remembering that, in theory, the citadel had been deserted for years. No Jatohr remained to hear them breaking and entering.

Thank providence for small favors, he thought.

Kirk stepped aside to let Una approach the newly created opening. "Ladies first."

"You trust me to go through without you?" Una eyed him quizzically. "How do you know I won't try to leave you behind?"

"I think we can trust you that far, as long as we hang on to a certain item." He patted the Key in his belt.

"Very logical, Captain." A rare smile lifted her lips. "Perhaps Spock is rubbing off on you."

Kirk shrugged. "I like to think it's the other way around, at least sometimes."

"I respectfully disagree," Spock said. "I am, and will always be, impeccably Vulcan in my logic . . . despite the best efforts of Doctor McCoy."

"I'm sure he'd regard that description as a badge of honor, but now is not the time to invoke him in absentia." Kirk bent down and cupped his hands together. "Can I give you a leg up, Captain?"

"Thank you, Captain."

With the men's help, Una squeezed through the porthole and dropped onto the floor of the vestibule. Despite his statement to the contrary, Kirk experienced a moment of trepidation at letting Una get a head start on him again. He repressed a sigh of relief as, moments later, he heard a lock disengage, and the door dilated open to reveal Una waiting for them on the other side. She greeted them calmly, more like a colleague than a fugitive.

"There was a manual override on this side," she explained. "Let us be grateful that the Jatohr had practical emergency measures in place."

They followed her into the vestibule, where Spock took a moment to survey their surroundings.

"Curious," he observed. "This appears to be a functional airlock, which raises the question of why they would need airlocks on a planetary outpost whose atmosphere they were reportedly capable of breathing."

"Oh, they could definitely breathe outside," Una confirmed, "although I've reason to believe that they were in the process of 'improving' the atmosphere in ways beneficial to their species, if not to the Usildar." A touch of bitterness colored her voice. "As for the airlock, perhaps they were unsure what kind of atmosphere they would encounter when they transferred this entire citadel from their universe to Usilde. Or maybe they thought this section might end up beneath the waterline as some of the lower levels are."

"Both plausible theories," Kirk said, "but academic at the moment. We need to get to that control room." He glanced at Spock. "I assume I can count on you to keep track of the time?"

"We have approximately fifty minutes to complete Captain Una's mission, plus or minus a second or two."

"I won't need those extra seconds," Una declared. "Wait and see."

There was no manual override on the outside of the inner doors, so they had to repeat the maneuver with the phaser and a porthole to make their way out of the vestibule. The effort cost them valuable time that they could ill afford to lose. Despite Una's confidence, Kirk had his doubts on whether they would be able to pull this operation off in time to get the *Enterprise* out of harm's way.

He hoped he'd made the right call.

"There's something else you ought to know," Una said, taking advantage of the delay to brief Kirk and Spock on her recent adventures, including the disturbing discovery that the Jatohr's terraforming efforts had created an escalating environmental crisis on the planet. "Something needs to be done, if not today, then someday, before it's too late for the Usildar and the other indigenous life-forms on the planet."

"We'll see to it Starfleet is informed," Kirk promised. "What the Klingons might have to say about the matter is a question for another day."

Beyond the airlock, they found themselves in what appeared to be a hermetically sealed ghost town, empty and untouched for nearly two decades. Their footsteps echoed through long, curving corridors that were otherwise devoid of any life-forms, let alone a race of sentient gastropods from another reality. The persistent, vaguely mechanical rumbling in the background reminded Kirk of a classic science-fiction story from the twentieth century about an automated house that kept on running long after its inhabitants had been vaporized by an atomic blast. The deserted citadel seemed to be stuck in the same sort of melancholy half-life.

Leading the way, using her own tricorder to guide them, Una kept her gaze fixed strictly ahead, aside from brief glances down at her readouts, as though determined to ignore their mausoleum-like surroundings. Kirk had to wonder what she was feeling, returning to this place after so many years. Probably much the way he would feel if he returned to Tarsus IV, where he'd once been among the sole survivors of a genocidal massacre, or if he set foot once more on Tycho IV, where so many of his fellow crew members had died unnecessarily.

"This must be strange for you," he said to her, "and hard as well."

Una looked up from her tricorder while setting a brisk pace.

"I confess to a certain degree of déjà vu. The last time I was here, I was a cocky young lieutenant . . . and a prisoner." She sighed heavily. "Although I suppose I'm technically your prisoner at the moment and can expect more of the same in the future. I can't imagine that Starfleet is going to look kindly on this unauthorized escapade."

"That's up to the brass," Kirk said. "For now, let's just bring our people home, if we can, and get out."

"I quite agree," she said.

Her flawless memory, abetted by her original tricorder readings, guided them down a steep ramp that ended before a sealed doorway that had seen better days. Several deep dents in the door's surface suggested that somebody had tried to force their way in at some point. Inert crystal globes littered the floor like discarded cannonballs.

"This is the entrance to the control room," Una explained. "Professor Eljor sealed it off to keep the other Jatohr from interfering with hir plan. They were trying to batter the door down when they were . . . removed."

Kirk found himself wishing that those vanished Jatohr had done a slightly better job of busting through the door before they'd been sent back to where they belonged. "How do we get past this last barrier? I don't see any portholes."

"An excellent question, Captain." Una ran her hand over the door. "I'm reluctant to blast our way in this close to the core of the generator, for fear of damaging any vital systems."

Spock indicated the abused doorway. "That did not seem to concern the Jatohr who laid siege to the entrance."

"They were not using energy weapons," she pointed out, "and they were in a state of panic. Not to mention being much more familiar with the technology and engineering here than we are."

Kirk saw her point. Scotty would know how to break into main engineering without wrecking anything important, and had done so on occasion, albeit very cautiously, but they were intruders here, very much out of their element. Using their phasers to carve a way in might well be riskier than they knew. They had no real understanding of this alien technology, so anything was possible. In a worst-case scenario, a weapons discharge near the generator's core might even set off some kind of explosion or chain reaction.

"No phasers, then," he agreed. "Any other suggestions?"

"I have one," Una said, "but you might not like it."

"Let me be the judge of that," Kirk said. "What are you thinking?"

"The *Enterprise*'s transporters. I've been on the other side of this doorway and remember the exact layout of the control room. What's more, I've retained the precise coordinates from when the *Enterprise* beamed April and me out of the control room eighteen years ago. In theory, your ship's transporters should be able to beam us back inside."

Kirk frowned. "But we'd be beaming in blind. That was years ago, as you said. What if something has shifted or collapsed in that time? You hear that rumbling going on? Things are not entirely in stasis here. Automated systems are still in operation, possibly undergoing maintenance or repairs."

"Professor Eljor did mention something about ongoing structural renovations," she conceded. "Those might still be under way, running on automatic pilot, but I doubt that they would have refitted the master control room in any way. It should be exactly as we left it, which means that I know exactly what coordinates to provide the *Enterprise* with, compensating for upgrades in the transporter targeting protocols, of course."

"But can you be sure you have the coordinates right?" Kirk asked. "After all these years?"

She looked mildly offended by the question. "My memory is completely reliable, Captain, as is my ability to factor in any necessary adjustments. Just ask Mister Spock."

"I can vouch for the exceptional precision of her mind," Spock said. "If Captain Una says that we can safely beam into the control room using the adjusted coordinates from her previous visit, I am inclined to believe her."

"Thank you, Spock," she said. "I appreciate the vote of confidence."

"No thanks are necessary. I am merely reporting my own empirical observations regarding your abilities, which are also a matter of public record."

"You have my gratitude anyway." She turned toward Kirk. "Your thoughts, Captain?"

Ordinarily, Kirk would have thought the tactic too much of a gamble, even for him, but who was he to question two of the *Enterprise*'s finest first officers?

"If Spock is on board with this, that's good enough for me." He flipped open his communicator. "Kirk to *Enterprise*. Put me through to the transporter room."

As Scotty was currently commanding the bridge, Lieutenant John Kyle responded at once:

"Kyle here, Captain. Did that emergency ladder come in handy?"

"It was a lifesaver, Lieutenant, but I need a site-to-site transport to a location a few meters from where we're standing."

"A few meters, sir?"

"You heard me, Mister Kyle. There is a barrier obstructing us and we need to get past it. Captain Una is with us. Can you lock onto her communicator as well?"

"Just a moment, Captain," Una interrupted. She retrieved her own communicator and switched it back on. "Are you reading me, Lieutenant?"

"*Yes, Captain,*" Kyle replied. "*Loud and clear.*"

"Good." She keyed the data into her communicator. "I'm transmitting the coordinates to you now. Stand by."

"*Affirmative.*" A moment passed as Kyle received the data. "*Captain Kirk, I'm afraid we have a problem here. We can't do a preliminary scan of that location. You'd be beaming in blind.*"

"We're aware of that, Mister Kyle," Kirk said, "but are confident that the coordinates will land us in a safe place."

A hint of worry infiltrated Kyle's pronounced English accent. "*If you say so, sir.*"

"Perhaps I should go first," Una suggested, "simply to prove it's safe."

Kirk found her proposal worrying. Was she simply attempting to put their minds to rest, or was she actually not quite as confident about those coordinates as she purported to be?

"Belay that," Kirk said. "No offense, Captain, but I'm not inclined to let you have that control room to yourself, Key or no Key. I'm going with you."

"No offense taken, Kirk. I've given you little reason to trust me. But perhaps Mister Spock should wait and follow after us—in the unlikely event that I've miscalculated. There's no need to risk all three of us at once."

"A reasonable precaution," Spock said, "but it might be wiser if Captain Kirk waits while you and I go first."

Kirk wasn't having it. "You know me better than

that, Spock." He spoke into his communicator. "All right, Mister Kyle. Beam Captain Una and me to the specified coordinates."

"*Not Mister Spock?*" Kyle asked.

"Not yet, Lieutenant."

"*Acknowledged, sir. Energizing now.*"

The scintillating glow of twin transporter beams lit up the control room before twinkling away. Kirk was relieved to find himself standing in one piece on the other side of the door, as opposed to being painfully merged with a wall or computer terminal. Pausing to get his bearings, he took in the sight of a large circular chamber, lined with blank, dead viewscreens and dominated by a tall transparent cylinder that stretched all the way to the ceiling. A series of tiered levels led up to a control pedestal at the base of the column. A musty, stale atmosphere permeated the chamber, as though it had been hermetically sealed for a long, long time.

"Is this it?" he asked Una.

"The master control room," she confirmed. "Exactly as we left it years ago."

Her voice trailed off as she spied a large, oddly shaped scorch mark on the floor. An unreadable expression came over her face as she gazed at the charred floor tiles for a moment or two before looking away.

"Congratulations, Captain," Kirk said. "You made it here after all."

"Yes," she said in a hushed tone. "Finally."

Kirk decided not to leave poor Kyle in suspense

any longer. "Transport successful," he said into his communicator. He and Una cleared away to make room for another arrival. "You can beam over Mister Spock."

"Aye, Captain. Energizing."

A transitory column of energy deposited Spock in the control room as well. Like Kirk, he took a moment to inspect his new surroundings.

"Fascinating."

Overcoming nostalgia, Una proceeded directly to the central column, which sat atop a complicated control station resting on a large pedestal. Kirk and Spock followed her up a ramp to the controls, which were labeled in an incomprehensible alien script that might as well have been some obscure Aenar dialect as far as Kirk was concerned. None of the controls made any sense to him.

"Do you really think you can operate this?" he asked Una.

"I've spent close to two decades studying my recordings of the Jatohr's language and technology, aided by continuing advances in translation algorithms and your own experiences in transporting from one parallel universe to another." Una situated herself before the controls. "I may not be the revolutionary genius the late Professor Eljor was, but I think I've got the basics down."

Kirk felt time ticking away. The Klingons were only getting closer.

"Prove it."

She chuckled. "Try and stop me."

Don't tempt me, he thought. Despite Una's confidence,

they were messing with alien tech from a completely different reality. His own experiences in a certain barbaric mirror universe—and with that universe's Tantalus Field device—were enough to make him acutely aware of just how dangerous such tampering could be. He was by no means certain that he was making the right call here.

She held out her hand. "The Key?"

Taking a deep breath, Kirk handed it over. *In for a penny, in for a pound,* he thought. *Let's see if she can do this.*

An empty slot in the control panel matched the rectangular outline of the Key. Considering the towering apparatus before him, Kirk found it hard to accept that this one small component could be so crucial to the entire operation. Then again, he reflected, the *Enterprise's* colossal warp engines were worthless without a dilithium crystal small enough to fit into a coffee mug.

Una placed the Key back where it belonged. At once, the dormant control room began to awaken. Dead screens and display panels lit up, so that the chamber felt more like the engine room of a starship than a forgotten tomb. Unknown energies manifested inside the towering cylinder, forming seemingly random three-dimensional shapes and patterns. They hummed and crackled sporadically.

"Well, now you've done it," Kirk said. "I suppose that's a good sign."

"Hold your applause for a while longer," she advised. "I'm reactivating the generator, but I still have to locate my lost comrades and reverse the transfer effect that carried them away."

"Presumably without bringing the Jatohr back as well," Kirk said.

"The mechanism allowed the operator to select the subjects to be transferred. That should apply in reverse as well." She eyed the amorphous shapes inside the main cylinder. "And, needless to say, I will be watching carefully for anything resembling a restless gastropod."

Spock observed the procedure over her shoulder. "Do you require assistance?"

"No, thank you, Mister Spock. You and Captain Kirk have helped get me this far, but I can take it from here."

She closed her eyes momentarily, as though visualizing the operation in advance, or perhaps calling up memories of the last time she'd seen this equipment in use. She whispered something to herself, too faintly for Kirk to hear. Her eyes opened and her jaw set in determination.

"Here goes nothing," she said. "Cross your fingers."

She carefully manipulated the controls on the Key, and the entire chamber responded to her commands. The chaotic energies in the cylinder coalesced into a holographic view of an alien landscape that bore little resemblance to what Kirk had seen on Usilde so far. Instead of lush rain forests, bleached-white salt flats baked beneath two pitiless suns. Rocky, forbidding mountains loomed on the horizon, beyond a distant sprawl of hills. No sign of life, neither plant nor animal, could be spied anywhere in the desolate vista. Only dust and rock and heat.

"What are we looking at?" Kirk asked.

"The other universe," Una said, gazing intently at the

otherworldly scene. "By my calculations, this should be exactly where the missing officers were banished to years ago."

Kirk spied no trace of them. Not even their bones.

"I'm not seeing anyone," he said.

"I know, I know," she said curtly, clearly under stress. Working the controls, she called up more perspectives of the same vista on the myriad viewscreens surrounding them. Magnified scenes from a wide variety of angles supplemented the three-dimensional display in the holographic imaging cylinder, but yielded no evidence of the long-lost Starfleet personnel. "I'm trying to find them."

He and Spock exchanged concerned looks. A positive outcome was looking less likely by the moment.

"Are you certain you have the right location?" Kirk asked gently. "Another world is a big place, let alone another universe."

"This is the only place I know to look," she insisted. "The place they were sent all those years ago." Una's celebrated composure cracked as she vented her frustration. "They have to be here, damn it. They *have* to be!"

"But even if they have survived," Spock said, "there is no telling where they might have ended up after all this time. Indeed, the location on display appears to be distinctly barren and inhospitable. It is reasonable to suppose that they might have eventually been forced to relocate, willingly or unwillingly."

"More than reasonable." Kirk realized that Una's master plan had always been something of a long shot. "I suppose it was unrealistic to expect that they would just sit tight waiting to be rescued for nearly two decades"

"You think I never thought of that?" Una snapped. "But this was my only hope . . . my last hope."

Kirk's heart went out to her. He didn't entirely approve of her methods, but he couldn't fault her stubborn desire to do right by her lost comrades. Nobody but another Starfleet captain, perhaps, could understand what she was going through now. That her obsessive quest to save those people looked to be ending in failure was more than just a damned shame; it was a tragedy.

"You did your best," he offered by way of consolation. "Above and beyond the call of duty."

That was no exaggeration. She had risked her life, her reputation, even her career in Starfleet to save nine people from exile in an alien reality. Kirk could respect that choice and wished profoundly that those sacrifices had not been in the service of a lost cause.

"No," she insisted, refusing to give up. "I can find them. I know I can." Images flicked by on the screens, one after another. "I just need more time."

"That's the one thing I can't give you," Kirk said. "The Klingons will be here in—"

He glanced over at Spock, who supplied the precise data.

"Twenty-point-two minutes."

That was already calling it closer than Kirk liked. "You heard the man. We have to get back to the *Enterprise*."

She shook her head.

"You do. I don't have to."

Kirk disagreed. "We can't just leave you here, where the Klingons might find you . . . and the Key."

"You misunderstand me," she said. "I'm not proposing

that I stay here on Usilde. I'm volunteering to continue my search over there." She indicated the alien wasteland depicted inside the looming cylinder. "In the other universe."

Spock caught on. "You mean to use the Key to transfer yourself to the other reality."

"It's the only course left to me," she said. "The trail has gone cold here. I need to pick it up over there." She squared her shoulders. "If all goes as planned, I'll be far from here if and when the Klingons show up."

"But you're talking a one-way trip," Kirk protested. "Even if you do track down those people over there, after so many years, you'll be trapped there along with them. How do you expect to get back to our universe?"

She had it all figured out.

"That's where you come in, Kirk. If you take the Key with you when you leave, but return to Usilde, say, sixty days from now, you may find me and the others waiting for you, right where you left me."

He contemplated the desolate salt plains occupying the viewscreens. "In other words, the plan is for us to come back and pick you up at a designated rendezvous spot, after you've had time to locate and retrieve the others?"

"Precisely," she said.

"But what if you can't find them," he asked, "or we can't come back?"

The latter was a very real possibility, with the Klingons laying claim to the sector and the Organian peace talks coming up. There was a good chance that Usilde could end up on the wrong side of a newly drawn border.

"That's a risk I'm willing to take," Una said. "And it's not as though I have a lot to lose at this point, considering." She shrugged. "And, frankly, exploring an alien universe beats commanding a desk back at Starfleet HQ."

Kirk had to chuckle at that. "Spoken like a starship captain."

"Let me do this, Kirk," she pleaded. "I can't turn back now. I have to go forward . . . or I'll never be able to live with myself."

A chirp from his communicator intruded on the discussion. "Kirk here," he responded. "What is it?"

"*Bad news, Captain,*" Scotty's voice answered. "*The Klingons are here, ahead of schedule, the rude blackguards. They've just entered the system and are heading toward us like bats out of hell, if you'll pardon the expression. They'll be on us at any minute, sir.*"

So much for having time to spare.

"Raise shields immediately," Kirk ordered, "and get my ship out of here. Do *not* engage the Klingons, do you understand me? Head back to neutral territory at warp speed . . . and don't be afraid to step on the gas."

"*But, Captain,*" Scotty said. "*What about you and Mister Spock? And Captain Una?*"

A Klingon battle cruiser, Kirk knew, came equipped with disruptor cannons and photon torpedoes. And Starfleet Intelligence had it that the Empire was constantly working on expanding the range of their weapons.

"Raise those shields now, Mister Scott. That's an order." He lifted his gaze to the ceiling as though he could see the *Enterprise* in peril. "Don't worry about us. Spock and I will catch up with you in the *Shimizu* if we can."

He didn't bother to mention that the courier ship was kilometers away across hostile terrain. Scotty and the others didn't need to know that.

"And Captain Una, sir?"

There was no time to update Scotty on Una's audacious proposal. "Just get moving, Scotty, before the Federation's truce with the Klingons gets blasted to atoms."

"Aye, sir. Good luck to ye all. Scott out."

The transmission ended, leaving Kirk to hope that the *Enterprise* would be out of range in no time at all. Frustration churned in his gut; being stuck down on the planet while his ship was in jeopardy was a form of torture worse than any the Klingons could devise. He belonged on the bridge.

But there was no way around it. He had to trust in Scotty and the rest of the *Enterprise*'s highly capable crew while dealing with Una's proposition here in the alien control room.

"You sound like you've made your decision," she said. "Or did I hear you wrong?"

"No. You heard right." He looked Una squarely in her eyes. "This is your quest. If you want to take it to the end, I'm not going to stop you. And I'm pretty sure I wouldn't be doing you any favors by dragging you back to the Federation to face a court-martial." He nodded at the machinery before her. "Get on with it."

"Thank you, Kirk," she said. "I hope you never find yourself in similar circumstances, caught between your duty to your uniform . . . and your loyalty to your crew."

"Give me time." Kirk handed her his phaser. "You may need this where you're going."

She accepted the weapon with a smile. Along with the phaser, she was equipped with a tricorder and a pack of Starfleet survival gear. Kirk wished he could provide her with more.

"Thank goodness I managed to hang on to my boots," she said. "You have no idea how close I came to having to leave them behind a few times."

Kirk didn't ask her to explain. "I'll take your word for it."

She fitted the phaser to her hip and went to work. Her hands confidently manipulated the baffling alien controls, and her own image replaced the sun-blasted landscape in the cylinder and on the screens. No trace of trepidation registered on her elegant features, only a steadfast determination to follow this path wherever it led, even if that meant exiling herself to another universe.

"The Klingons are bound to detect this citadel now that the generator is up and running again," she warned them. "You're going to need to find the launch bay and commandeer one of the Jatohr pods to get away before the Klingons arrive."

She quickly and concisely provided them a description of the landing bay and its approximate location in relation to the control room. Kirk absorbed as much of the intel as he could and was confident that Spock had memorized the rest.

"Got it," he said. "But you need to get going if you're going to do this."

"That's not in question, Captain. Just don't forget to come back for me—for *us*—if you can."

"I'll do my best," he promised.

"That's all I ask, and more than I could have hoped for." She prepared to take her leave of them. "Good luck, Captain Kirk, Mister Spock."

Spock offered his former crewmate a Vulcan salute. "Live long and prosper, Number One."

"Don't doubt it," she replied. "I'll be back."

A twist of a knob caused her image to flip to a photo-negative image of herself on the various monitors. Her finger hesitated only for a moment above a solitary blue button on the Key's control panel. She took a deep breath and pressed it.

She vanished in a blink of light.

"I wish her success," Spock said quietly, "although I fear the odds are against her."

"Maybe," Kirk said, "but I wouldn't bet against her."

"Nor would I," Spock confessed.

Captain Una was gone, "removed" to another universe, but the eminent arrival of the Klingons remained a danger in this reality. Kirk knew that he and Spock were on borrowed time when it came to having the citadel to themselves.

"Grab the Key," he ordered Spock. "We need to get to those pods she told us about."

"My thoughts exactly." Spock deftly removed the Key from its slot in the control column. The machinery around them began to power down in an orderly fashion, with the central cylinder going dark, followed, one at a time, by the various viewscreens. The humming and crackling from the cylinder fell silent.

Spock handed the Key to Kirk, who secured it to his

belt. It felt good to have the device back in his custody again.

Now if I can just keep it away from the Klingons.

An explosion went off somewhere above them, causing dust and debris to rain down from the ceiling. Warning lights went off around the control room. An automated voice sounded stridently:

"Intruder alert! Intruder alert! The sanctuary has been breached!"

A jolt of adrenaline shot through Kirk's veins. It was easy to guess who the intruders in question were.

The Klingons had come calling.

Twenty-one

Alarms echoed through the master control room. Judging from the racket, the Klingons had been considerably less than subtle when it came to blasting their way into the citadel.

Imagine that, Kirk thought. "It appears we have company, Mister Spock."

"Beyond a doubt, Captain. I do not recommend that we linger to greet them."

"I wasn't planning to wheel out the welcome wagon." Kirk had no idea how long it would take the Klingons to reach the control room, but he wasn't about to stick around to find out. If they moved quickly enough, he and Spock might be able to slip out of the citadel without running into the new arrivals. "I think we're done here."

Exiting the sealed chamber was easier said than done, however. In all the excitement and drama, Kirk had forgotten about the locked doorway cutting the control room off from the rest of the citadel. He was starting to wish that he hadn't given Una his phaser when Spock calmly operated a control panel adjacent to the door, which dilated open to reveal the empty corridor beyond. Downed globes still littered the floor.

"Nicely done, Mister Spock," Kirk said. "I'm impressed as ever by your efficiency."

Spock shrugged. "Deducing how to open a locked door from the inside is hardly a praiseworthy accomplishment."

"But is appreciated nonetheless," Kirk said, relieved that the barrier no longer obstructed their escape. "About time something went our way."

They rushed out of the control room and took off down a tubular corridor, following Una's hasty directions to the underwater launch bay. To Kirk's dismay, he could hear a Klingon landing party heading their way, stomping and shouting like a *targ* in a china shop. They were making good time toward the control room; Kirk had to give them that. He assumed that their battle cruisers had detected the energy emissions from the citadel, just as April and his crew had years ago.

Perhaps Una should have left well enough alone?

Inconveniently, the advancing Klingons sounded as though they were directly between the fleeing Starfleet officers and the path Una had laid out for them. The Klingons' booming voices and heavy tread made it clear that, intentionally or not, they were on a collision course with Kirk and Spock.

"I suggest a strategic detour," Spock said in a low voice.

Kirk nodded. "I don't think we have much choice."

Ducking into a side tunnel to avoid running into the noisy Klingons, they found themselves in need of a less popular route to the pods. Branching corridors presented a dilemma; it would be all too easy to get lost in the sprawling complex. Kirk glanced around for clues as to which way to go, but the signage, such as it was, was all in

Jatohr. He looked in vain for a map of the "You are Here" variety.

Spock, on the other hand, was scanning various examples of Jatohr script with his tricorder. He squinted at the readings.

"Progress, Mister Spock?" Kirk asked

"The Jatohr's written language is indeed unique, lacking any common roots or cognates with most humanoid languages, but I am running these postings through a highly sophisticated translation program in order to achieve a crude approximation of their meaning." He lowered the tricorder and pointed to the right. "I believe that we need to proceed . . . that way."

Kirk peered down the tunnel, which curved out of his line of sight. There was no way to tell where it led.

"Are you sure of that, Spock?"

Spock arched an eyebrow, as though mildly bemused by the query.

"Never mind," Kirk said. "Forget I asked."

They moved swiftly but quietly around the curve, which led to a string of diverging tunnels and ramps descending toward the lowest levels of the hub. Encouraged by their success at eluding the Klingon landing parties, Kirk began to think ahead to their next moves: reach the launch bay, commandeer a pod, fly back to the *Shimizu,* and then somehow get past those battle cruisers to make a dash for a border . . . and the *Enterprise.*

That was going to be the *really* tricky part.

They were darting across an intersection where six different corridors crossed one another when a gruff, guttural voice yanked him roughly back to the present.

"Starfleet!"

Kirk whirled about to see several armed Klingon soldiers glaring at them. Bristling black beards and mustaches gave them a fierce appearance, compensating for their lack of facial ridges. Their familiar gold-and-black uniforms were much more aggressively militaristic than Kirk's and Spock's primary-colored Starfleet apparel. Startled by their unexpected discovery, it took the hostile soldiers a moment to open fire with their disruptor pistols.

"Take them!" a Klingon officer bellowed. "Dead or alive!"

Kirk and Spock dashed into the tunnel before them, just ahead of a barrage of sizzling emerald beams that scorched the pearlescent inner walls of the citadel. Rounding a curve as fast as they could, they fled from the Klingons, only to find themselves blocked by a fully contracted doorway. An annunciator light flashed urgently above the blocked passage. Kirk heard the Klingons chasing after them, shouting threats and egging one another on. Truce or no truce, it seemed to be open season on trespassing Starfleet personnel.

"After the spies!" the Klingons' leader shouted. "Show them no mercy!"

Kirk found the command redundant. Since when had the Klingons ever shown mercy to their foes? It was a wonder the word was even in their vocabulary.

"The door, Spock! Can you get it open?"

"I am endeavoring to do so, Captain, but certain emergency protocols appear to have gone into effect, sealing off key areas of the citadel . . . such as, for instance, the launch bay." Spock examined the locking mechanism as coolly as he might a particularly intriguing sensor reading at his science station back on the bridge of the *Enterprise*. "It may take me a moment to override the security system."

Vulcans were not prone to exaggeration, Kirk knew, so the delay had to be a necessary one. Kirk reached for his phaser only to remember again that he'd given it to Una.

"Lend me your phaser," he ordered. "I'll try to buy you that time."

Spock nodded and handed Kirk his weapon. Leaving the preoccupied science officer to his work, Kirk made sure the phaser was set on stun before firing around the curve of the corridor to discourage the oncoming Klingons. Furious shouts and epithets, along with the satisfying sound of a Klingon soldier planting his surly face onto the floor, testified to his aim. Falling back, the Klingons returned fire with a vengeance. Kirk ducked his head back barely in time to avoid having his ear singed by a crackling disruptor beam, which passed so close that he could feel the heat of the blast against his skin.

"Any time now, Spock."

Spock did not look away from his efforts to crack the lock on the door. "The need for haste is not lost on me, Captain." He aimed his communicator at the control panel. "Allow me to isolate the correct sonic frequency."

Kirk recalled that Spock had once managed to use a communicator to start an avalanche. Come to think of it, they had been pursued by Klingons then too.

"Whatever it takes, Spock, but quickly."

Kirk heard the Klingons advancing, albeit more cautiously. He risked firing another warning shot in their direction, before ducking back out of the line of fire. A ferocious burst of return fire sent his pulse racing and made him *very* glad that nobody had yet invented an energy weapon that fired around curves and corners.

"Starfleet!" a voiced called out harshly. "Surrender and you will not be harmed . . . much."

Now *they want to talk*, Kirk thought, although he knew better than to trust the Klingons to play nice. *But maybe I can stall them long enough for Spock to clear our path?*

"I'm listening," he shouted back. "What do you want?"

"Why, your worthless hides on trial for trespassing and espionage, naturally, and the Federation's abject apologies for this brazen incursion on our territory. Along with whatever information you possess about this fortress and its technology, which already has our scientists as excited as a hunter scenting fresh prey."

I'll bet, Kirk thought. "Oh, is that all you're asking for? Well, the thing is—"

A whirring noise alerted him that Spock had succeeded in unlocking the door, which dilated open. The emergency light above the portal blinked off. "After you, Captain."

Kirk had another idea. "Get through that door, Spock, and get ready to cover me."

Firing back at the Klingons, while dodging their own blasts, he waited until Spock was through the doorway before abandoning his position to follow after him. He hurled their only phaser to Spock.

"Catch!"

Requiring no further instruction, Spock snatched the phaser out of the air and immediately began laying down cover to shield Kirk's retreat. He fired past Kirk at the corridor beyond, holding off the Klingons, while Kirk dived through the doorway, rolling onto the floor beyond and back onto his feet.

"Nice catch, Mister Spock."

"That Vulcans have superior eye-hand coordination has been well documented," Spock replied, while knocking out an overly impetuous Klingon soldier with a well-aimed stun beam. "The odds against me failing to make the catch—"

"Are not worth citing at this moment." Kirk nodded at the door. "If you don't mind."

Spock triggered a manual switch on their side of the portal, while simultaneously firing through the aperture, and the door dialed shut. Frustrated howls, from the other side of the doorway, penetrated the barrier. Fists pounded against the unyielding door.

"They're getting away!" the Klingon officer railed at his men. "Blast through this door before we lose them!"

Disruptor fire loudly assailed the barrier from the other side. The hard, shell-like material began to glow ominously. Vapor rose from newborn cracks in the besieged door. An acrid burning smell offended Kirk's nostrils. The door began to sizzle and bubble.

"The Klingons have already demonstrated their ability to overcome the Jatohr's fortifications through brute force," Spock noted. "We must assume the barrier will not delay them for long."

"Then we had better get to that launch bay before they do. Lead the way, Mister Spock."

A smooth spiral ramp reminded Kirk that the Jatohr had possessed a slug-like mode of locomotion, ill-suited to steps or stairs. He and Spock sprinted down the ramp while the Klingons continued to blast away at the sealed doorway above. Kirk didn't like leaving the citadel—and the Jatohr's singular technology—in the Klingons' hands, but at least he had the Key, without which the Klingons would be unable to operate the transfer-field generator.

Or so he hoped.

The citadel's winding corridors remained a maze as far as Kirk was concerned, but Spock clearly knew where he was going. A final doorway, complete with an airlock, brought them into the launch bay, which consisted of a large moon pool surrounded by a doughnut-shaped deck. The rippling water in the pool cast shifting shadows on the smooth walls and ceiling. An empty pod, matching Una's description, rested on a ramp sliding into the pool.

"Close the door behind us," Kirk said, "before our new friends catch up with us."

"That was always my intention," Spock assured Kirk as he sealed off the portal. "The Klingons are certainly intent on our capture or deaths, but I see no reason to accommodate them." He stepped away from the door. "Nor to experience a Klingon mind-sifter again."

They hastily boarded the pod. The seats, if you could call them that, were hardly designed for humanoid bodies, but there was plenty of room for them in the cockpit. Kirk let Spock take the flight controls; he wasn't too proud to recognize that the brilliant Vulcan science officer could more readily decipher and master the unfamiliar controls.

"Let's hope we don't have to hot-wire this thing," Kirk said.

The archaic expression did not confound Spock. "Unlikely. By all accounts, the Jatohr had little reason to anticipate visitors and would not have needed security measures against unauthorized use."

He inspected the controls for only a moment before discerning how to activate the pod. The vehicle came to life and an automated voice addressed them with the aid of the universal translator. There was a time, Kirk understood, when the translator had struggled with the Jatohr's native tongue, but, thankfully, those days were years past.

"Commence launch procedures?"

"Affirmative," Spock instructed the pod. "Follow standard procedure."

The pod began to slide down the ramp into the waiting pool, even as a sudden explosion rocked the launch bay and the inner entrance of the air lock blew apart, spraying the interior of the bay with shrapnel. Twisted pieces of debris banged against the pod's opalescent hull, jolting the vehicle. Kirk recognized a photon grenade when he heard one. The Klingons were breaking out the heavy artillery.

"Spock," he prompted.

"Expedite launch procedures," Spock stressed. "Initiate immediate departure."

"Acknowledged," the pod replied. *"Rapid-release protocols in effect."*

Klingons poured through the breached doorway, preceded only barely by a cloud of dust and smoke. Through
the haze, they spotted the pod sliding into the water. Disruptor beams struck the pool, producing bursts of steam.
A photon grenade bounced off the top of the pod and
ricocheted into an upper bulkhead, where it went off with
a directed charge that blew open a hole in the bay's outer
wall, letting in the lake outside.

"Dive!" Kirk ordered. "Dive!"

The hull breach, added to the damage to the doorway,
fatally compromised the pressurized air bubble holding
the water out. Churning white water flooded the launch
bay, sweeping them off their feet and back into the
corridor outside, while submerging the pod completely.
The submersible vessel descended to the underwater
exit, which dilated open to let them pass into the murky
depths beyond.

"*Departure complete,*" the pod announced.

The pod shot out of the citadel at an accelerated rate,
throwing Kirk back into a padded backrest intended for
less-humanoid passengers. He shot a concerned look at
Spock.

"Please tell me you can fly this thing."

Spock experimented with the flight controls. "Forgive
me, Captain. This will require a modicum of trial and
error."

"More trial, less error," Kirk replied. "If that's all right
with you."

The pod yawed, rolled, and pitched beneath the
water while executing abrupt turns and loops in three
dimensions. Startled by the pod's erratic course, a multi-

armed monstrosity jetted away from the vehicle in panic. Kirk wondered if it was the same one he had repelled with his phaser earlier. The alien cephalopod was definitely having a bad day.

A sudden dive sent Kirk tumbling forward toward the front of the cockpit, and he grabbed onto an auxiliary console to keep from slamming his head into the windshield. As the pod descended at a precipitously steep angle, Kirk worried that they were about to slam into the bottom of the lake, a concern shared by the pod's onboard computer system, which blurted in alarm:

"Proximity alert! Collision imminent!"

Through the murky water, Kirk spied the rocky floor of the lake dead ahead. It seemed to be rushing up at them like the cratered surface of a killer asteroid.

"Pull up, Spock! Pull up!"

"Correcting course," Spock said calmly. "Brace yourself."

At the last minute, just as they were about to crash into the lake bottom, the pod tilted upward and climbed steeply toward the surface. Bursting from the rippling, scum-coated water, the pod took off into the bright blue sky and kept on climbing. The speed of its ascent blew any clinging algae from the pod's hull.

"I believe I am getting a feel for the controls, Captain."

Kirk was glad to hear it. "Just be thankful Doctor McCoy wasn't here for that takeoff. You'd never hear the end of it."

"That is undoubtedly correct."

The pod leveled off high above the sunlit rain forest, leaving the citadel behind. Once again, Kirk regretted ceding the alien fortress to the Klingons, but took comfort in the fact that he still had the Key—and that the Klingons didn't. How much they might learn from studying the Jatohr's equipment remained a concern, but that was a problem for another day. Right now he and Spock just needed to get off Usilde and back to the *Enterprise*.

If only he knew how his ship was faring.

Cruising above the jungle canopy, the pod headed south toward the *Shimizu*, whose location the *Enterprise* had detected earlier from orbit. Peering down at the endless verdant growth below, Kirk saw little in the way of landmarks.

"You sure we're heading in the right direction?"

Spock looked at him askance. "Captain, your continued lack of faith in my abilities is becoming most disconcerting. I assure you that we are approaching the proper coordinates."

"My apologies for doubting you, Mister Spock. I'm simply anxious to get the Key—and ourselves—back to the *Enterprise* as quickly and easily as possible."

"I share your concern, Captain, as well as your desire to return to the ship without further incident." He piloted the pod with ever-increasing skill and dexterity. "We should be coming up on the *Shimizu* momentarily."

True to his word, Spock soon brought them into view of an abandoned farming operation in a river valley that, even from a high altitude, appeared positively overrun by the invasive gray fungi and algae. Captain Una had not been exaggerating when she'd lamented the environmental contamination left behind by the Jatohr.

He reminded himself to inform Starfleet if he got the chance.

Although that may be the Klingons' problem now, if they choose to stick around.

The pod touched down on a weed-infested airfield, only a few meters away from the *Shimizu*. Kirk was relieved to see that the sleek cruiser appeared to have been undisturbed. Reclaiming the phaser from Spock, he cautiously disembarked from the pod while keeping a sharp eye out for either the native Usildar or any lurking Klingons. No immediate threats presented themselves.

"Looks like the coast is clear," Kirk said. "You picking up anything we need to worry about?"

"Negative." Spock scanned the surroundings for humanoid life-forms as he emerged from the pod behind Kirk. "I surmise that the Klingons may be preoccupied with the Jatohr citadel at the moment, as opposed to the surrounding area. It's very possible that they have not even detected the *Shimizu* yet."

"Sounds about right," Kirk agreed. "The fortress and its technology are a tempting prize, probably even more so than a couple of stray Starfleet officers." He glanced around the site; the oppressive odor of the fruiting fungi sickened the air. "I'm not seeing any Usildar around either."

"Nor I." Spock's eyes also scanned the surrounding ruins. "I would not be surprised if the increased activity at the citadel, up to and including the Klingons' assault on the fortress, has induced the Usildar to flee the region, at least for the time being."

"Given their history, I can't blame them for heading

for the hills," Kirk said. "And they're probably better off staying clear of the Klingons in any event."

"That would be advantageous," Spock agreed. "The Klingons are not known for their delicacy when dealing with indigenous peoples who lack the technology to defend themselves."

That was putting mildly, Kirk thought.

Unlocking its hatchway, they piled into the *Shimizu* and fired up its engines. Kirk took the helm this time. The cruiser was no enigmatic alien aircraft; it was a Starfleet vessel.

"I think I've had enough of your piloting, no offense."

Spock gave him a bemused look. "If I had feelings, they would be hurt."

"Somehow I doubt that."

Under Kirk's control, the *Shimizu* took off from the airfield and accelerated toward space. Within minutes, they had left the planet and its atmosphere behind. Kirk was relieved to put Usilde in his proverbial rearview mirror, even as he knew that he was merely saying adieu to the planet, not goodbye. He was honor bound to return to Usilde someday soon—for Captain Una's sake.

We'll be back, he promised her silently. *Count on it.*

But they were not out of the woods yet. No sooner had they exited the planet than they were hailed by the Klingons.

"Attention: Starfleet vessel! This is Captain Guras of the Klingon battle cruiser Ch'Tang. Surrender or be destroyed!"

Spock consulted a display panel. "Sensors confirm the presence of three Klingon battle cruisers in orbit around Usilde. One of them is breaking orbit to pursue us."

"And the others?" Kirk asked.

"Remaining in orbit around the planet. As I theorized earlier, the Klingons are likely more interested in seizing the Jatohr citadel at this juncture."

"And judge that a single battle cruiser is more than enough to deal with a ship the size of the *Shimizu*," Kirk said. "In any event, I suspect we've outstayed our welcome in this system."

"By a considerable margin," Spock agreed. "Raising shields."

The *Shimizu* was unarmed but fast, Kirk recalled. It was time to put that speed to the test. He cranked the impulse engine up to maximum, and the sleek courier ship rocketed away from the *Ch'Tang*, which accelerated to keep pace. An aft viewer showed the fearsome battle cruiser chasing after them. Its bulbous green command pod was connected by a narrow neck to a massive engineering hull, which emulated two downward-pointed wings. Many times the size of the *Shimizu*, the *Ch'Tang* was big enough to swallow its fleeing prey whole.

"*You will not escape us,*" Guras vowed. "*Surrender and you may live to see another day!*"

"In a Klingon penal colony or torture chamber?" Kirk replied. "We'll pass, thank you very much."

A jolt shook the cruiser. Kirk felt a drag on the ship's progress, retarding their speed.

"Klingon tractor beams attempting to lock onto us," Spock reported. "Despite his bluster, it appears that Guras would prefer to take us alive."

"He wants to know what we know about the citadel." Kirk pushed the impulse engine harder to compensate.

Power gauges crept toward the red zone. "Can we shake those tractor beams?"

"I believe so, thanks to Captain Una's singular modifications to the shields." He manipulated the deflector settings to augment her innovations. "The ever-shifting harmonics and polarities should interfere with the Klingons' efforts to lock onto us."

Kirk felt the courier slip free of the tractor beams. He hoped that Guras was finding the *Shimizu* just as slippery as Chekov had earlier. The irony of the situation, that they were using the same tricks Una had used to evade the *Enterprise*, did not escape Kirk.

This gave him an idea.

"Hang on," he warned Spock. "I'm going to try something."

With Usilde behind them, the *Shimizu* made a run for the fourth planet in the system—an icy, inhospitable chunk of rock—where Kirk feinted diving toward the planet's thin, wispy atmosphere.

"*Cease your craven flight,*" Guras ordered. "*You will find no sanctuary anywhere in this system. All these planets belong to the Klingon Empire.*"

But Kirk wasn't looking for a hideout, just a convenient spot to make a U-turn. Pulling out of the dive at the last minute, he circled around the planet, briefly putting it between the *Shimizu* and the *Ch'Tang*, before heading back and deeper into the system. The trick bought them a few minutes, but only a few. Making a half orbit around the planet, the stubborn battle cruiser reappeared in the courier's aft viewer.

"*No more games, Starfleet! You court destruction!*"

"I wouldn't do that if I were you," Kirk said, stalling. "We're carrying some valuable artifacts from that fortress on the planet. You really don't want to risk blowing them to atoms."

"Better to destroy them," Guras countered, *"than let Starfleet have them!"*

"I was afraid you were going to say that," Kirk said with a sigh. "Guess we have nothing more to talk about."

He terminated the transmission.

"The *Ch'Tang* is opening fire, Captain," Spock said. "Disruptor beams incoming."

Kirk attempted evasive maneuvers, but a disruptor blast grazed the *Shimizu*'s shields, causing the courier to tilt violently to starboard. A blinding blue flash lit up the cockpit as the shields deflected most if not all of the beam's destructive energy. Even a glancing blow from the *Ch'Tang*'s high-powered disruptor cannons had jarred Kirk to the bone. He tasted blood and realized that the jolt had caused him to bite down on his lip. Warning lights flashed across the control board.

"Shields down twenty percent, Captain," Spock stated. "I would not advise absorbing many more attacks of that magnitude."

"I don't intend to, Mister Spock."

Steering well clear of Usilde and the other two Klingon warships, Kirk aimed the *Shimizu* toward the very center of the solar system and the blazing yellow orb that reigned there. "Check your scanners, Spock. Do we have a straight shot to the sun?"

A flicker of unease crossed Spock's stoic features as he

grasped Kirk's intentions. "Captain, are you attempting to—"

"Take a leaf from Captain Una's playbook? Absolutely."

Despite the *Shimizu*'s superior speed and maneuverability, the *Ch'Tang* and its firepower were not going to be easy to escape, especially once they got out into deep space and there were no planets or moons to hide behind. One or two good hits from the battle cruiser and they'd be sunk, unless they pulled out way ahead of their pursuer—the same way Una had.

"Captain, the danger—"

"Just do the math, Spock, before it's too late."

A second blast from the Klingons sent the *Shimizu* into a roll. Sparks erupted from a burned-out capacitor. Gritting his teeth, Kirk stabilized the courier's flight and struggled to keep it straight on track for the sun. They zipped past Libros I at maximum impulse, putting the system's planets behind them. Kirk warmed up the warp engine.

"Split-second timing is required," Spock said. "I suggest you turn the helm over to me . . . despite your earlier comments about my piloting."

Kirk transferred helm control to the copilot's seat. "I take it all back, Spock. I can't imagine anyone else I'd rather have at the helm right now."

"I will endeavor not to disappoint."

The sun—a main-sequence star similar to Earth's—took over the view before them, squeezing out the empty space. Kirk could have sworn that he could feel its heat even across space and through the *Shimizu*'s protective hull and deflectors. The cockpit felt uncomfortably hot and stuffy; the environmental systems labored audibly to compensate for the shrinking distance between the small spacecraft and the star. Sweat gleamed on his face, but whether that was from heat or stress was anyone's guess.

"*Are you mad, Starfleet?*" Guras challenged, hailing them once more. "*Turn back before you incinerate yourself!*"

"Not exactly my plan," Kirk said. "But it will do in a pinch."

The Klingons could not be allowed to gain possession of the Key. One way or another, he was going to keep them from getting their hands on it. Cremation was preferable to surrender.

"Spock?" he asked.

The Vulcan's gaze was fixed on the ship's chronometer. "Going to warp in three . . . two . . . one."

An abrupt increase in acceleration, by several orders of magnitude, shoved Kirk back into his seat. Sunlight flooded the cockpit, overloading the brightness filters, as Spock took the *Shimizu* into an insanely tight orbit around the sun, defying the star's powerful gravitational pull and placing a terrible strain on the courier's compromised shields and structural integrity. Vibrations rattled the cockpit and its passengers, causing Kirk to bounce erratically in his seat. The intense solar heat made the cockpit feel first like a sauna, then like an oven. The ship lurched violently toward the sun, tossing Kirk to port. Painful g-forces tugged on his face and body. His arms and legs felt as heavy as neutronium. It was a struggle just to breathe.

"Heat shields . . . buckling," Spock managed to

utter in vibrato. The tremor in his voice indicated that even his formidable Vulcan stamina was being taxed. "Approaching . . . breakaway . . . point . . ."

The ship's hull and engines screamed in torment as the *Shimizu* fought to break free of the star's nigh-irresistible pull. Kirk clenched his jaw to keep from screaming too. The blood rushed from his head. Darkness encroached on his vision, despite the overwhelming sunlight, and he realized he was blacking out.

Hold it together, Spock, he thought. *Hold us together.*

The universe went away.

———

Blinking, Kirk climbed out of a bad dream to find himself slumped in his seat aboard the *Shimizu*. His head throbbed, his mouth was dry, and he felt as though he'd consumed one bottle too many of *tranya*. Dizziness made the cramped cockpit seem to swim before his blurry eyes. A slingshot maneuver could do that to you.

"Spock?"

"Present and conscious, Captain, if feeling distinctly the worse for wear."

Kirk was relieved to see his friend awake and alert in the copilot's seat. He wondered if Spock had been rendered unconscious as well, or if the Vulcan's superior stamina had kept him from blacking out entirely. Kirk sat up straight and squinted at the front viewscreen. Nothing but empty space stretched before them.

"Where are we?"

"Approximately three-point-eight hours from the border of the disputed territory," Spock replied, looking even greener around the gills than usual. "It is uncertain, however, as to whether we or this ship will endure that long."

Kirk didn't like the sound of that. "Explain."

"The strain exerted on the *Shimizu* during the slingshot maneuver, on top of the damage previously inflicted by the Klingons' attacks, has fatally compromised the ship's systems. Life-support is failing, as is the artificial gravity. Long-range sensors and subspace radio are inoperative. Shields are down and the warp engine is overheating at an accelerating rate. A catastrophic failure is imminent, unless we severely reduce our rate of speed, but even that would only delay the inevitable . . . and reduce our odds of reaching neutral space before we completely lose all life-support."

"Oh, is that all?" Kirk said wryly. Now that Spock had mentioned it, Kirk noticed that the air in the cockpit already tasted stale, while the temperature had him sweating feverishly. A steady decline in gravity accounted for his lightheadedness. "What about the Klingons? Are they still in pursuit?"

"Undoubtedly, but the breakaway factor served to give us a substantial lead on the *Ch'Tang*, albeit at considerable cost to our own vessel. Maintaining that lead, however, also argues against reducing our speed, despite the terminal strain on our warp engine."

Kirk absorbed the litany of bad news.

"You paint a vivid picture, Mister Spock. Give me the numbers. How much time do we have?"

"Estimate total life-support failure in four-point-two hours."

"And how long to the border again?"

"Roughly four hours, assuming the engine does not explode before then."

"Not much of a margin for error there." Kirk let out a long sigh. He couldn't help wishing that Scotty was along to babysit the struggling engine, although he knew that there was nothing the redoubtable engineer could do that Spock wasn't also capable of. They could just use a miracle or two at the moment.

"Understood, Mister Spock. Increase speed."

"Are you certain, Captain? The engine—"

"It's a gamble we'll have to take. We're losing life-support, we have no shields, and we're being chased by some very determined Klingons. Speed is our only hope."

"I cannot dispute your logic," Spock said. "Increasing speed to warp eight."

The internal lights flickered worryingly as the moribund ship accelerated. Warning lights and gauges, which were already flashing anxiously, kicked it up a notch or else burned out altogether. A hiccup in the gravity caused Kirk's gorge to rise. The smell of burning circuits contaminated the already less-than-pristine air. Kirk silently apologized to Una for the abuse they were putting her ship through, but figured that was probably the least of her concerns at the moment, wherever she was.

May she be faring better than we are.

He and Spock kept conversation to a minimum to conserve air, but their tense race for the border hardly passed in silence. Frequent alarms and alerts, growing increasingly insistent, strove to remind the men of what they already knew too well: the *Shimizu* was on its last legs. Laboring systems groaned and rattled and creaked in protest, even as they began to break down completely. Gravity went the way of the shields, making Kirk feel like some primitive astronaut from centuries past. Loose items, such as a discarded rations wrapper, a stray microtape, and a data slate, began to drift aimlessly around the cabin until they could be secured. Kirk snatched a floating stylus out of the air and stowed it in a weapons locker below the flight controls to get it out of their faces. Safety straps alone kept Kirk from drifting off his seat. Hours passed both too fast and too slowly.

"Life-support down to ten percent," Spock reported after a time. "And falling."

Kirk appreciated the precision, but his own body was telling him the same thing and much more emphatically. The sweltering heat and thinness of the air reminded him of his last visit to Vulcan; he could have used one of McCoy's restorative tri-ox injections. He was breathing hard, but to less and less effect as smoky, unscrubbed air brought dwindling amounts of oxygen to the cabin. Perspiration dripped down Kirk's face. Spock was better adapted to such circumstances, but even Vulcans needed to breathe; he was running out of air and time too.

"How much longer?" Kirk asked, gasping.

"Approximately six minutes," Spock said. "Not that we are guaranteed succor once we pass the boundary, only a possible end to pursuit."

And even that's questionable, Kirk thought. Would the Klingons stop at the border if there was still a chance of capturing the dying courier ship? Kirk wanted to think that Captain Guras and his compatriots would think twice before pursuing a Starfleet vessel into neutral territory, what with the Organian peace talks on the horizon, but counting on a Klingon to choose discretion over belligerence was never a safe bet. Granted, at this rate, he and Spock were likely to be corpses by the time the *Ch'Tang* or any other Klingon warship caught up with them, but there was still the little matter of the Key.

A violent shudder jolted the ship. Flames erupted at the rear of the courier, filling the vessel with thick black smoke that rapidly infiltrated the cockpit. "*Warning! Warp engine at critical,*" a computerized voice shrieked before breaking apart into static. "*Evacuat—zzzzzz.*"

Kirk placed a hand over his face to avoid inhaling the smoke. He raised his voice over the crackling flames behind him.

"Spock?"

"The engine is melting down. Matter-antimatter containment failing. Estimate one minute to catastrophic breach."

At which point, Kirk knew, the *Shimizu* would explode like a photon torpedo, leaving nothing behind but superheated plasma dispersing into the vacuum.

Perhaps it's better this way, he thought. *At least the Klingons won't get the Key.*

A light flashed on the control panel, almost lost amidst the smoke and alarms.

"Captain," Spock said hoarsely, "we are being hailed."

"The Klingons?" Kirk asked. "Already?"

"Negative, Captain. I believe it is the *Enterprise.*"

Spock activated the comm receiver. "Spock to *Enterprise*, request emergency beam-out."

Through the smoky haze, Kirk spied his ship in the distance. Just on the other side of the border?

"*Aye, Mister Spock,*" Scotty replied. Random bursts of static punctuated the transmission, distorting the chief engineer's familiar accent. "*That's what we've been waiting for.*"

Kirk didn't know whether to scold Scotty or commend him for sticking around on the fringes of the disputed territory. He checked to make sure the Key was still tucked into his belt. They were going to need that if they were ever going to rescue Una and any others lost in that alien universe. Crackling flames, spreading toward the cockpit, made him wonder if they had reached Scotty a few moments too late. He felt the scorching heat of the blaze at his back. He choked on the suffocating black smoke, gasping for oxygen that wasn't there anymore.

"Five seconds to warp containment failure," Spock announced. "Four, three, two—"

A tingling sensation washed over Kirk with seconds to spare. He and Spock vacated the ship in a dazzle of golden sparks.

The *Shimizu's* smoke-filled cockpit was instantly replaced by the cool and calm of the *Enterprise's* transporter room. Gravity and fresh air made Kirk feel immediately at home, as did the sight of Doctor McCoy and Yeoman Bates waiting for him with Lieutenant Kyle over by the transporter controls.

A shock wave caused the transporter platform to

briefly list beneath Kirk's boots. He tensed, anticipating more trouble, but the tremor passed quickly and without lasting effect.

The Shimizu, he realized, *exiting in a blaze of a glory— after holding together just long enough to get us safely home.*

He liked to think that Captain Una would be proud of her valiant little ship.

"So," McCoy said impatiently, while simultaneously scanning them with a medical tricorder, "*now* are you going to tell me what this was all about?"

Kirk coughed the smoke from his lungs, and filled them with fresh air, before answering. "Soon, Bones, soon."

"Are you all right, Captain?" Bates asked, as solicitous as ever. "Can I help you with anything?"

He checked again to make sure the Key was securely tucked into his belt and concealed beneath his sweaty gold command tunic. "No, thank you, Yeoman. I'm fine."

Spock stepped down from the transporter platform. "Which would not have been the case, for either of us, had the transport been a few moments later. My gratitude, Lieutenant Kyle."

"Thank you, sir," Kyle said. "Just doing my duty."

"We've been tracking the *Shimizu* ever since it showed up on our long-range sensors," Bates explained. "Commander Scott refused to give up on you. None of us did."

McCoy belatedly noticed that someone was missing. "Where is Captain Una?"

"That," Kirk replied, sighing, "is a long story."

Twenty-two

"There we go," Kirk said. "Back where it belongs."

He returned the Key to the hidden compartment in his quarters, which no longer felt quite as secure as it once had, despite Spock's repairs to the breached vault, which had been discreetly executed during the crew's postponed shore leave on Chippewa Prime. The decorative trapezoidal panel slid back into place, concealing the compartment and its singular contents from view once more. The Key was safely under lock and key.

"For now," Spock observed. "It will be necessary to remove it from hiding again if and when we return to Usilde in hopes of retrieving Captain Una—and any surviving castaways—from the other universe."

"Another universe," McCoy murmured. "I still have trouble wrapping my head around that, despite that unsettling business on the other side of the looking glass a while back." He regarded Spock with a critical eye. "For the record, I still think you looked better with a beard."

"That is your opinion, Doctor," Spock said. "You'll forgive me if I regard that as less than definitive."

Bowing to the inevitable, Kirk had finally let McCoy in on the secret, which, in retrospect, he probably should have done before. *If I can't trust Bones . . .*

"So what are you telling Starfleet about this?" the doctor asked.

"Good question," Kirk said. "At present, just that Captain Una returned to Usilde on a private mission to search for some old shipmates who had gone missing in action years ago and that she chose to remain behind to continue the search. I also felt obliged to mention the abandoned Jatohr citadel now that it's fallen into the hands of the Klingons, but the Key is still our secret for the time being, although I confess to having second thoughts about that." He contemplated the panel masking the Key's hideaway. "Maybe there's been too many secrets for too long."

"I don't know," McCoy said. "From what you've told me, perhaps April was right to keep that Key under wraps. This poor universe is dangerous enough without some horrific new technology added to the mix."

"Careful, Doctor," Spock chided him, "or you may be mistaken for a Luddite."

"Damn straight I am, at least when it comes to alien super-weapons from another reality!"

Kirk could see where McCoy was coming from. Starfleet was still coping with the revelation that the Romulans had developed a working cloaking device. The Key had the potential to dramatically shift the balance of power in the galaxy if it fell into the wrong hands—or even the right ones.

"Well, we kept it away from the Klingons," Kirk said. "That's something."

"Indeed," Spock agreed, "although the Klingons' discovery of the Jatohr citadel presents significant challenges when it comes to returning to Usilde in the near future.

I cannot imagine that the Klingons will soon abandon a find of such magnitude."

"Nor can I," Kirk said, "but we'll have to find a way to get back to that control room. I fully intend to keep my promise to Una, if it's at all possible."

"That's a big *if*, Jim," McCoy said, "if you don't mind me saying so."

"You're not wrong, Bones, although I wish I could say otherwise." Kirk turned away from the hidden vault and headed for the exit. "Clearly, I've got a lot to think about."

In the meantime, the bridge awaited him. No doubt Yeoman Bates had a fresh batch of reports and requisitions for him to sign off on.

———

The woman who called herself Lisa Bates waited until she was certain that Kirk's quarters were empty before quietly letting herself into the suite. One of the many perks of being the captain's yeoman was ready access to his quarters, which came in handy sometimes.

Particularly if you were a spy.

Major Sadira of the Tal Shiar, the elite Romulan intelligence service, was fully human, but her loyalty belonged to the Romulan Star Empire, who had gone to great lengths to create the false identity of "Lisa Bates." In truth, she was descended from human prisoners captured during the first Earth-Romulan war and had been raised since birth to serve the praetor to the best of her abilities. Starfleet may have only recently gotten a good look at natural-born Romulans, and become aware of their shameful Vulcan roots, but her adopted people had been spying on the humans and Vulcans since long before the founding of the Federation, and she was hardly the only Tal Shiar operative under deep cover in Starfleet and elsewhere.

As she quietly made her way across Kirk's quarters, she reflected, not for the first time, on how serving as the captain's yeoman was the ideal posting for a spy. She saw all the paperwork requiring Kirk's signature, was expected to take notes during crucial meetings and exploratory missions, and routinely came and went from his quarters, all while flying under most everyone's sensors. To use a human idiom, which she had assiduously absorbed into her repertoire, she was the proverbial fly on the wall, inconspicuously observing almost everything that went on aboard the ship, including a number of matters she was not supposed to know about.

Like the existence of the Transfer Key.

The bugs she had discreetly planted in Kirk's quarters had paid off handsomely. She had been waiting patiently for an opportunity to acquire the device ever since Captain Una had first purloined it. Unlike that rogue captain, however, she did not have to employ anything as crude as a phaser to break into the hidden compartment. Careful examination of the covert surveillance footage captured by her spy-cams had yielded the combination to the locking mechanism hidden behind the trapezoidal panel.

Thank you, Mister Spock, she thought, *for so helpfully demonstrating the new combination to the captain.*

She smiled slyly as she removed the Key from the

vault. Knowing Spock, it was highly likely that a silent alarm was now informing him and Kirk that the secret compartment had been accessed, but she had no intention of lingering long enough to get caught red-handed. It would take some time for Kirk and Spock to figure out who was responsible for this latest theft, and she planned to be long gone by then.

Holding on tightly to the Key, she took out the disguised communicator hidden in her beehive hairdo and set it to a certain top-secret frequency.

"Major Sadira to *Velibor*," she said in Romulan. "The prize has been obtained. Request immediate retrieval."

"*We read you, Major*," a voice replied. "*Stand by*."

Using the communicator aboard the *Enterprise* was a calculated risk. In general, she preferred to conduct any such communications via more indirect channels and from more secure locations—such as, say, while on shore leave. The *Enterprise*'s recent layover at Chippewa Prime had, in fact, provided her with an ideal opportunity to make all necessary arrangements for this very operation.

It was a shame that stealing the Key necessitated blowing her cover, but she judged the one-of-a-kind alien weapon to be worth it. An opportunity like this was why she had been planted on the *Enterprise* in the first place.

Plus, she was getting damn sick of fetching Kirk coffee.

———

Kirk couldn't believe his eyes when the silent alarm blinked upon his armrest.

Again?

This time he did not hesitate to react immediately. He punched his chair's comm switch. "Security to the captain's quarters, on the double!"

He sprang from his chair. "Mister Sulu, you have the bridge. Spock, you're with me."

"I expected as much, Captain," the first officer said, already relinquishing the science station to join Kirk.

They were halfway to the turbolift when Uhura called out.

"Captain! I'm detecting an unauthorized transmission coming from somewhere inside the ship."

Kirk paused in his tracks. "Can you pinpoint the exact location?"

"In just a moment, sir." Uhura isolated the signal, then looked at Kirk with a confused expression. "The transmission, it's coming from . . . your quarters, sir."

The Key, Kirk realized. *Someone's after the Key . . .*

He started again for the turbolift, only to be halted by an urgent cry from Chekov.

"Captain! Ship uncloaking ten degrees to starboard."

"What?"

Kirk whirled around in time to see the blackness of space shimmer like a mirage upon the main viewer before revealing the presence of a Romulan bird-of-prey within firing range of the *Enterprise.* He gaped in shock at the enemy warship, which took its name from the intimidating raptor painted upon its hull. A ship just like this one had attacked several Federation outposts only a year ago—and had nearly destroyed the *Enterprise.*

"Raise shields!" he ordered, hurrying back to his chair. "Full power."

Chekov responded quickly. "Raising shields."

Spock hastily returned to his station as well. He peered into his scope. "Captain, readings indicate that something—or someone—was beamed off the *Enterprise* in the instant before we raised our shields."

Kirk had to be impressed by the split-second timing, even as he feared he knew where the unknown party had been transported from. "Let me guess. Somebody beamed from my quarters onto the ship."

"Attempting to verify that now," Spock said, "but the odds are your supposition is correct."

So we know where and how, Kirk thought, *but who . . . ?*

"Captain, the Romulan vessel is hailing us," Uhura said.

Kirk stared grimly at the bird-of-prey. "Put them through."

"Aye, sir."

Kirk expected the saturnine countenance of a Romulan commander to appear upon the screen, so he was taken aback when Lisa Bates, of all people, smirked at him from across space. Startled gasps from Uhura and others greeted the shocking visual. Even Spock looked momentarily taken aback.

"*Hello, Captain,*" Bates said, with a sardonic tone Kirk had never heard from her before. "*Consider this my resignation.*"

Kirk still couldn't process this. "Bates?"

"*That's Major Sadira, if you please. I'm afraid the ever-attentive Yeoman Bates was something of a convenient fiction.*" She plucked at the fabric of her red Starfleet

Acknowledgments

I remember exactly how this project began for me. I was attending Shore Leave, one of my favorite fan-run *Star Trek* conventions, when I ran into Dave Mack, who was signing his latest novel at a dealer's table. Dave quietly mentioned that he and a few other Trek authors were thinking of collaborating on a big, multi-volume saga in celebration of *Star Trek*'s upcoming fiftieth anniversary, and was I interested in getting in on the action?

"Definitely," I replied. "Count me in."

Many e-mails later, and after conferring with the good folks at Pocket Books and CBS, we hammered out an outline for what eventually became known as the *Legacies* trilogy. But that was just the beginning of the collaboration. As each of us got under way writing our respective volumes, we stayed in constant touch: throwing ideas and suggestions and new twists and details back and forth to each other in hopes of making *Legacies* everything we hoped it would be. In short, we had a blast.

So, many thanks to my esteemed and imaginative collaborators, Dave Mack, Dayton Ward, and Kevin Dilmore, without whom this book would literally have not have been written, and particularly to Dave for inviting me to take part in the first place.

But we weren't in this alone. Thanks are also due to

our expert editors, Ed Schlesinger and Margaret Clark, for guiding us through the process, and to my agent, Russ Galen, for handling my end of the contract. I also want to thank Diane Carey for fleshing out Captain Robert April's crew in her own work, which I shamelessly cribbed from in this book.

Finally, and as always, I relied heavily on the support and encouragement of my girlfriend, Karen, as well as our two four-legged assistants: Sophie and Lyla.

Here's hoping we can have just as much fun on *Trek*'s sixtieth anniversary!

About the Author

Greg Cox is the *New York Times* bestselling author of numerous *Star Trek* novels and stories, including *Miasma, Child of Two Worlds, Foul Deeds Will Rise, No Time Like the Past, The Weight of Worlds, The Rings of Time, To Reign in Hell, The Eugenics Wars* (*Volumes One* and *Two*), *The Q Continuum, Assignment: Eternity,* and *The Black Shore*. He has also written the official movie novelizations of *Godzilla, Man of Steel, The Dark Knight Rises, Ghost Rider, Daredevil, Death Defying Acts,* and the first three *Underworld* movies, as well as books and stories based on such popular series as *Alias, Buffy the Vampire Slayer, CSI: Crime Scene Investigation, Farscape, The 4400, Leverage, Riese: Kingdom Falling, Roswell, Terminator, Warehouse 13, The X-Files,* and *Xena: Warrior Princess*.

He has received three Scribe Awards from the International Association of Media Tie-In Writers and lives in Oxford, Pennsylvania.

Visit him at: www.gregcox-author.com

STAR TREK: LEGACIES

WILL CONTINUE IN

BOOK 2:
BEST DEFENSE

by David Mack

Turn the page for an exciting excerpt . . .

Una limped alone in a land without shadow. Two merciless suns, high overhead, scorched the white salt flats. Had it been hours or days since she had crossed the dimensional barrier to this forsaken place? Time felt slow and elastic. The glaring orbs of day seemed never to move.

Perhaps this world is tidally locked to its parent stars.

It was a rational explanation for the endless noontime, yet it fell short of explaining what truly felt askew to Captain Una about this bizarre alien universe. Plodding toward a distant sprawl of hills backed by rugged mountains, she was plagued by the sensation of running while standing still, as if in a dream. Far ahead, haze-shrouded hilltops bobbed with her uneven steps and lurched in time with her wounded gait, as salt crystals crunched beneath the soles of her dusty, Starfleet standard-issue boots.

Both halves of her uniform—its black trousers and green command tunic—were ripped and frayed in several spots. It was all damage incurred on the planet Usilde in her home universe, during her harried escape through traps wrought from brambles, nettles, and thorns. To reach the citadel created by extradimensional invaders known as the Jatohr, Una had been forced to defy the taboos of the indigenous Usildar, who both feared and despised the alien fortress, which had appeared without warning years earlier in one of their rain forest's larger lakes. What Una knew and the Usildar did not was that the alien stronghold was also the key to traveling between this blighted dimension and the one she called home—

which meant it was also her only hope of rescuing the other members of an ill-fated *Enterprise* landing party, who had been exiled here eighteen years earlier while she had been forced to bear helpless witness.

I am no longer helpless. And I will bring my shipmates home.

She swept a lock of her raven hair from her eyes, noted the delicate sheen of perspiration on the back of her pale hand. Peering ahead, she found no tracks to follow, no road to guide her journey. Her training nagged at her. It demanded she proceed based on careful observation and rational deduction, but there were no facts here to parse. Only level sands and blank emptiness, stretching away to a faded horizon. And yet, Una knew she was moving in the right direction. It wasn't that her Illyrian mental discipline gave her any special insight into this *universum incognita*; it was something more basic and less rational. It was instinct. A hunch. A feeling.

Doubts haunted her. She slowed her pace and looked back. As desolate as she found the landscape ahead of her, it was a feast for the senses compared to the vast yawn of nothing at her back. Nothing interrupted the marble-white void of the sky or the featureless expanse of the desert stretched out forever beneath it. Waves of heat radiation shimmered in an unbroken curtain, giving the boundary between earth and air the sheen of liquid metal. But nothing else moved here. Nothing living flew in the air; nothing walked, crawled, or slithered across the parched soil. There was no wind to stir so much as a mote of bleached dust from the ground.

The hills looked just as barren, and the mountains

behind them were forbidding. But for all their threat of hardships, they also promised shelter and a break from the monotony. And so Una pressed on toward them, confident her shipmates would have made the same choices eighteen years earlier. *Martinez would not have let himself or the others perish in the open desert,* she assured herself. *He would have sought shelter, water, and resources—all of which are more likely to be found in the mountains than on this sun-blasted plain.*

Una wondered if she would recognize her old shipmates after so long apart—or they, her. The last time Martinez and the others had seen Una, she had been an eager young lieutenant, a helm officer aboard the *Enterprise* under Captain Robert April. Back then, they had perpetuated her Academy nickname "Number One" because of her history of taking top honors in nearly every academic and athletic endeavor with which Starfleet could challenge her. Rather than chafe at the sobriquet, she had appropriated it, after a fashion: because her native Illyrian moniker was all but unpronounceable by most humanoid species, she had chosen to serve under the name "Una" since her earliest days at Starfleet Academy. In later years, after she had climbed the *Enterprise*'s ladder of rank to serve as executive officer under the command of Captain Christopher Pike, it had been a welcome coincidence that Pike had proved partial to addressing his XO as "Number One," a holdover from ancient Terran naval traditions dating back to that world's age of sail.

Perhaps the only former crewmate of hers who could pronounce her true name was Commander Spock. She had long admired his penchant for favoring his cool, logical Vulcan heritage over his more emotional human ancestry. In his youth, of course, he had exhibited a disturbing tendency to betray his heightened emotions by raising his voice on the bridge—an unseemly habit Una had helped him overcome, in the interest of honing his sense of decorum as a Starfleet officer. Where many of their peers might have bristled at Una's catechism, Spock had taken her counsel to heart with a near-total absence of self-consciousness.

Spock and I have always understood each other better than most people do. But his devotion to logic blinds him to the power of hope.

If not for the compassionate understanding of Spock's captain, James T. Kirk, the current commanding officer of the *Enterprise*, Una's mission might already have ended in failure. She had taken a grave risk in stealing the Transfer Key—a device of not only alien but extradimensional origin—from its longtime hiding place in the captain's quarters of the *Enterprise*. Having recently perused Kirk's report of a similar device he encountered in an alternate universe, and Spock's report of how a transporter malfunction had opened a pathway to that universe—first by accident, then a second time by design—she had gleaned new insights concerning the alien gadget she and Captain April had seized on Usilde in 2249. With that resource at her command, Una had planned to power up the now-abandoned Jatohr facility on Usilde and open the doorway between her universe and this one, to which her shipmates had so long ago been cruelly exiled by the Jatohr. To make that opportunity a reality, she had risked ending her career in a court-martial and jeopardized the imminent Federation-Klingon peace talks to return with the Transfer Key to Usilde—an action that had served only to attract the Klingons' attention to the primitive planet and the advanced alien technology it harbored.

Regardless, Una had hoped there would be time to save her friends and escape with the Transfer Key. To her dismay, the other five members of her Usilde landing party, as well as four officers "blinked" off the bridge of the *Enterprise*, were nowhere to be found when, at last, the gateway between universes was opened once more. And so she had made a fateful decision: she struck a bargain with Kirk and Spock. They would keep the Transfer Key safe from the Klingons and return to Usilde in sixty days to reopen the door between universes. Which meant Una had that long, and not a day more, to find her lost shipmates and return with them to her arrival point in the desert—which she had marked with an X, scorched into the salt with the phaser she had borrowed from Kirk—for their long overdue homecoming.

It was an outrageous proposition. A mission doomed to fail.

Una didn't care. She had beaten impossible odds before.

She would either bring her shipmates home . . . or die here with them.